Praise for the Alex Verus novels

"Harry Dresden would li... be a little nervous around h... with a uniquely powerful, ... good remind me why I got ... first place."

—Jim Butcher, #1 ... the Dresden Files

"Benedict Jacka writes a deft thrill ride of an urban fantasy—a stay-up-all-night read."
—Patricia Briggs, #1 *New York Times* bestselling author of *Fire Touched*

"Jacka puts other urban fantasists to shame . . . A stellar blend of thoughtful philosophy and explosive action populated by a stereotype-defying diverse cast."
—*Publishers Weekly* (starred review)

"A fast-paced, high-stakes adventure . . . The real power of Jacka's series comes from the very human journeys and revelations to be found for each character in the course of this story."
—*RT Book Reviews*

"Tons of fun and lots of excitement . . . [Benedict Jacka] writes well, often with the ability to bring places to life as much as his characters, especially the city of London."
—SF Site

"[An] action-packed story with witty dialogue . . . A wonderfully witty and smart hero who's actually pretty awesome in a fight."
—All Things Urban Fantasy

"Benedict Jacka is a master storyteller . . . A brilliant urban fantasy that is so professionally polished and paced that you barely remember to come up for air."
—Fantasy-Faction

"Everything I love about an urban fantasy: action, magic, an interesting new world, and a character that I really liked."
—Under the Covers Book Blog

Ace Books by Benedict Jacka

FATED
CURSED
TAKEN
CHOSEN
HIDDEN
VEILED
BURNED

burned

BENEDICT JACKA

ACE BOOKS, NEW YORK

An imprint of Penguin Random House LLC
375 Hudson Street, New York, New York 10014

BURNED

An Ace Book / published by arrangement with the author

ISBN: 978-0-425-27576-4

PUBLISHING HISTORY
Ace mass-market edition / April 2016

PRINTED IN THE UNITED STATES OF AMERICA

10 9 8 7 6 5 4 3 2 1

Cover photograph: The Shard London © Roy Bishop / Arcangel;
flame © Potapov Alexander / Shutterstock.
Cover design by Judith Lagerman.
Interior text design by Laura K. Corless.

Penguin
Random
House

burned

chapter 1

The call came just before seven.

It was a Saturday evening in December. I'd closed late; it was the last weekend before Christmas, and the shop had been packed all day. It was past six when I finally shooed out the last customers, shut and locked the door, and turned off the lights before heading upstairs. Hermes had sneaked in again and was lying curled up on my armchair, the white tip of his bushy tail tucked in around his nose. I dropped onto the sofa with a yawn and started going through my e-mails.

My eyelids were drifting closed when the communicator chimed. I'd been so drowsy I'd barely even seen it coming. Hermes opened one amber eye and watched as I pulled myself to my feet, took out the blue-purple disc from my drawer, and activated it. A miniature holographic figure in blue light materialised on top of the disc. "Hey, Talisid," I said, setting the disc down on my desk. "What's up?"

"Are you alone?"

"Yes, why—?"

"There's no good way to tell you this," Talisid said.

"Levistus has sentenced you to death. You're to be executed in one week."

Hermes lifted his head. He shifted position slightly as he did so, black forepaws stretching straight out, white neck and chest exposed as he looked at me and the image of Talisid. With his colouring, he looked exactly like a larger-than-average English red fox. Blink foxes don't have any visible traits that set them apart from mundane foxes; only the look in the eyes gave any hint that—

"Alex?" Talisid said. "Did you hear me?"

I'd been staring at Hermes. I'd heard Talisid's words, but they weren't registering. "Yeah," I said. I found myself looking at the fur on Hermes's back and tail, watching the hairs move and shift. "What?"

"I can't talk long," Talisid said. "There was a closed Council session. The resolution goes into effect one week from today at six P.M. Once it does, you'll be an outlaw. Your property can be seized and any mage or Council representative of the British Isles can take hostile action against you with no legal repercussions."

"This Saturday?"

"Yes. There's more. The resolution also applies to your dependents. That means all three of the rest of your team. Luna Mancuso, Anne Walker, Variam Singh. Their names are listed with yours."

I stared at Talisid.

Talisid looked behind him at something out of view. "I have to go. I'll call in an hour or two and we'll decide what to do. There may be some way around this."

". . . Okay."

"We'll speak soon." Talisid's image winked out.

I found myself alone in the room with Hermes. I walked away from the desk and dropped back onto the sofa in the same spot I'd been sitting in. It was still warm. The call had taken less than sixty seconds.

I felt stunned, disconnected. None of this seemed real. Earlier in the year, I'd become a Keeper auxiliary, and in the months since, I'd spent more and more time working with them, taking on new cases almost every week. I'd thought that things had been going better with the Council, not worse. Now—this. I tried to think, work out how this could have happened so fast, but my thoughts kept slipping away. I reached for my phone and touched the number of a contact. It rang five times before it was picked up. "Hey, Alex."

"Luna," I said. "We've got a problem." I gave her the news in a few short sentences.

Once I'd finished, there was a pause. "Oh, shit," Luna said at last.

"Yes."

"Have we got a plan?"

"Not over the phone."

"Okay. What should I do?"

"Get Anne," I said. "Get Vari."

"Got it." Luna hung up.

I set the phone down and looked at it. The flat was quiet; the only noise was the sound of the city outside. An airplane was passing by far above, the sound drifting down through the Camden streets.

Luna had asked if I had a plan. I didn't.

There was a thump as Hermes jumped to the floor. I turned to see him trot across the carpet to where my hand was dangling off the edge of the sofa. He sniffed my fingers and looked up at me, amber eyes alert and questioning.

"It's okay," I said, forcing a smile. "We'll figure something out."

Hermes sat back on his hind legs. I looked over him towards the window and to the night sky visible beyond.

ıııııııı

When Luna sets her mind to something, she doesn't hang around. The gang started arriving within the hour.

Variam showed up first. I felt the signature of the gate spell from the storeroom on the ground floor, followed by the sound of Variam bounding up the stairs two at a time. He came striding through the door, wide awake and quick. "Luna told me," he said. "It's true? Levistus?"

I nodded.

"How?"

"Let's wait until everyone's here."

Variam nodded, probably assuming that I was doing it that way because it was more efficient. "Were you at a ceremony?" I asked.

"Sort of," Variam said. He was wearing his black turban and the dark red formal robes that Arachne had made for him last year. They were the dark red of glowing coals, the colour chosen to set off his brown skin. It was hard to be sure, but the robes looked less baggy on him than they had been. Variam's small, but ever since starting his apprenticeship with Landis he'd been putting on muscle. "Was a drinks thing."

"Landis okay with you leaving?"

"Yeah, but he's going to want an explanation when I get back."

I was spared from having to reply to that by the signature of another gate spell. We both looked towards the door as Luna walked in. "Anne's on her way," she said.

"How long?"

"I think she had someone with her," Luna said. She was wearing a pale close-fitting top and dark leggings, and her hair was up in a ponytail, slightly matted with sweat; she must have come from the gym without stopping to change. "But she got the message."

"You were out duelling?" Variam asked.

"Some of us don't get to go to fancy parties."

"Excuse me?" Variam said, obviously annoyed. "I *asked* if you wanted to come."

"Yeah, how did you think that was going to play out, again?"

"Well, sorry for trying to—"

"Jesus!" I said. "You two are literally under sentence of death and you're *still* doing this? Really?"

Luna and Variam shut up, looking away. We waited in silence.

Anne arrived just before eight. She climbed the stairs more slowly than Luna and Variam had, and she paused in the doorway, looking between me and Luna and Variam. "I'm sorry I'm late," she said in her soft voice.

"It's fine," I said. "Take a seat."

"Ah . . ." Anne hesitated. "There's something I should probably tell you first."

"What is it?"

"I asked someone else to come," Anne said. She didn't look comfortable. "I hope that's okay."

"What?" Variam said. "Who?"

"He's downstairs," Anne said. "Outside the shop." She looked at me, obviously waiting for my response.

I looked ahead through the futures, picking out the one in which I rose and left the room. I followed my future self downstairs and through the shop, watching as he opened the door and looked out into the street to see—

I snapped back to the present and watched the future vanish. I stared at Anne. "Him?"

"He was there when I got the call," Anne said defensively.

And what the hell was he doing at your place? I didn't ask. Luna looked at Anne. "Who are you guys talking about?

"You know how things ended last time," I told Anne. "Why is he even here?"

"Probably because of me," Anne said. She looked straight at me. "I know you two have had problems, but we need the help."

I looked away. Variam looked between the two of us. "Okay, are you two going to spit out the name anytime soon? Because this is getting old."

"Fine." I got to my feet and walked downstairs, following the path that my future self had taken a minute ago.

The shop floor was dark and I switched on the light, the glow bathing the room. Yellow-white light glimmered back at me, refracted through crystal balls and glinting off the steel of the knives and ritual daggers laid out on the far table. I unlocked the shop door and opened it. Cold air rushed in, dry and near freezing and carrying the scent of winter.

The boy—young man, really—was standing out on the pavement, his breath making white puffs in the air. He wore a thick coat and his black hair was peeking out from under a woollen cap. No glasses this time; he'd apparently lost them since I'd last seen him. We looked at each other.

"Sonder," I said.

"Hi," Sonder said.

There was a pause. "It's kind of cold," Sonder said. "Can I come in?"

I thought about it for just long enough to make it clear that I was thinking about it, then stepped aside. Sonder entered and I shut the door behind him. The sounds of the street faded and we were alone in the shop.

"Okay," I said, turning to Sonder. "Why are you here?"

"Anne—"

"I know what Anne told you. Are you here to help Anne, or the rest of us?"

Sonder hesitated. I saw the futures shift between possible answers, then die away, and I knew I wasn't going to get a reply. "The guy behind this is Levistus," I said. "You understand what you're risking, getting involved with us?"

Sonder frowned slightly. "I'm not an idiot."

I sighed slightly. "Come on up." No one else was coming. I just wished I knew whether adding Sonder would make things better or worse.

ı ı ı ı ı ı ı ı ı

Variam and Luna didn't react when I led Sonder into the living room—Anne had obviously broken the news to them while I'd been downstairs. Neither Luna nor Variam looked one hundred percent enthusiastic—Variam had never liked Sonder all that much, and while Luna and Sonder had been sort-of-friends in the early months of Luna's apprenticeship, they'd never been close. With hindsight, that friendship had probably been more on Sonder's part than on Luna's. Luna's early contacts in magical society had been few and far between, and to begin with having a mage her age who actually treated her well had probably been a nice change, but as she'd started to get to know people on her own initiative she'd drifted away. Sonder had wanted to stay friends—actually, more than friends—and Luna had given him a fairly definite rejection. I still didn't know how well Sonder had taken that.

Sonder was looking around the living room. "This brings back memories."

"Thanks for coming," Anne said.

"Like I promised," Sonder said. "You guys still play Settlers?"

"We've had a bit less time to spare for that stuff lately," I said.

"You going to take a seat?" Variam asked.

"Oh, sure." Sonder took a step forward, taking a final glance around as he did, and paused. "Uh, what's with the fox?"

Hermes was sitting by the doorpost to my bedroom, ears pricked up and tail curled around his forepaws. He'd sat watching as everyone else arrived, and now he returned Sonder's gaze blandly. "Why don't you ask him?" I said.

Sonder gave me a puzzled look.

"His name's Hermes and he lives here," I said. "Look, we're a little pushed for time. Is it okay if we save the recaps for later?"

"Oh. Okay."

A chime came from the desk. Luna twisted around. "Talisid?"

I nodded and went over to pick up the communicator focus. Sonder took a seat a little way away from the others as I walked back, set the disc down on the coffee table in the middle of everyone, and activated it.

Blue light flickered, materialising into the figure of Talisid. He scanned left and right, looking at everyone's faces, pausing very briefly at the sight of Sonder before turning back to the others. The only one he didn't register was Hermes, outside the radius of the focus's visual field. "You're all here. Good."

"Can you talk freely?" I asked.

"Yes."

"Then," I said, "let's hear it from the beginning."

"The Council met this afternoon," Talisid said. "It was a closed session of the Senior Council only. There were two items on the agenda, and the proposal for your execution was one of them. Levistus was the author. The vote was three to one."

The Light Council is the decision-making body of the Light mages of Britain. It has thirteen members: six nonvoting, known as the Junior Council, and seven voting, known as the Senior Council. Beneath them is a sprawling organisation and bureaucracy (of which Talisid's a member), but it's those seven members of the Senior Council who call the shots.

The knowledge that the Senior Council had authorised this sent a chill through me. Within Britain, the Senior Council have nearly absolute power. There are few laws that restrict them, and there's no higher authority to appeal to. If they wanted me dead . . .

"What charge?" Sonder asked.

"Conspiracy and sedition against the Light Council."

"*What* conspiracy?" Luna said.

"The resolution doesn't specify."

"They have to show some kind of evidence," Variam said. "Don't they?"

"No, they don't," I said. "Keepers do, because they answer to the Senior Council. The Senior Council doesn't answer to anyone." I looked at Sonder to see if he'd disagree. He didn't.

"That's all it takes?" Luna said, incredulous. "Three votes?"

"There were only four present."

"How is this even possible?" I said. I managed to keep my voice steady, but it wasn't easy. "It's the middle of December. The Council's supposed to be in recess."

"Which is undoubtedly the reason this is happening now," Talisid said. "Levistus called an emergency session at exactly the time at which those Senior Council members most likely to oppose him were out of the country. By contrast, his two closest supporters were both attending. Four is enough for a quorum."

"Okay," I said. "So if they've passed the resolution, why aren't Keepers kicking my door down right now?"

"They can't," Sonder said.

Everyone turned to look at Sonder. "They didn't have full attendance," Sonder explained. "The Council can pass resolutions with a quorum of four, but not emergency resolutions."

"Sonder's correct," Talisid said. "Any resolution passed with less than full Senior Council attendance has a one-week delay before it goes into effect. It's a safety measure designed to prevent quorum abuses."

"A *safety* measure?" Luna said. "So what, we get a week to live instead?"

"How is this even possible?" Variam said. "The Council can't just pass death sentences like that. There has to be a trial or something."

"I think we just had it," I said.

"This is bullshit," Variam said. "I was there for Cerulean's trial in the spring. It took them two months to even schedule it, and he wasn't even there!"

"Cerulean was a Keeper," Sonder said. "Well, is a Keeper . . . I mean they haven't actually formally expelled him, and . . . anyway. They can't pass sentence on a Light mage without a trial, but . . ."

"But I'm not a Light mage," I finished. "What's the exact definition of a Light mage as far as this goes?"

"You have to either be recognised by the Council, or you have to have an official Council position," Sonder said. "Like being a Keeper."

"You're kind of a Keeper," Luna said.

"I'm a Keeper *auxiliary*," I said. "I'm guessing that doesn't count."

"I'm afraid it doesn't," Talisid said.

"Okay," I said. "So that's me. What about Luna, Variam, and Anne? Why are they caught in this?"

"The resolution applies to you and to your dependents,"

Talisid said. "That has a very specific meaning in Council law. A dependent is anyone for whom you've taken sole responsibility. Luna falls into that category due to being your apprentice. Anne and Variam also, since you sponsored them for the apprentice program."

"But I *didn't* sponsor them for the apprentice program! I just—"

"I know," Talisid said. "Unfortunately, it seems you did so well enough that the Council was convinced."

I felt an ugly sinking sensation in the pit of my stomach. When I'd first met Anne and Variam, they'd been in the Light apprentice program, sponsored by the rakshasa Jagadev. After Jagadev kicked them out, I'd invited Anne and Variam to live with me, and generally tried to give the impression to the mages who ran the apprentice program that I'd taken over their sponsorship. It had worked—even though they technically weren't allowed to be there anymore, no one had challenged me over it. I'd kept them in the apprentice program.

And by doing so, I might just have killed them.

"Can't we challenge that?" Sonder said. "If they were never officially sponsored . . ."

"It would be difficult," Talisid said. "They were de facto sponsorship members for long enough to be officially recognised."

"But they were never actually signed in, right?" Sonder said. "If we made the Council admit that they never officially went through the ceremony—"

"Then it would just be me and Alex getting executed instead?" Luna asked.

"That wasn't what I meant," Sonder said hurriedly. "I just, um . . ."

"Really?" Luna said. Her voice was icy. "Then what *did* you mean?"

"I'm afraid it's a moot point," Talisid said before Sonder could reply. "Any legal challenge would take far too long. Much more than a week."

"Okay," I said. "Important question. You said Anne, Luna, and Vari's names are on this resolution. Are they listed as *being* my dependents, or are they listed *independently* of whether they're my dependents?"

Talisid's image reached for a piece of paper. "The first," Talisid said after a moment's pause. "The exact wording is 'and his dependents, to whit.'"

"Then if they weren't my dependents, they wouldn't be covered by the resolution. Yes?"

Talisid looked troubled. "Yes. However, I'd feel happier if you were working against the resolution itself."

"What are you getting at?" Variam asked me.

"Contingency plans. Okay, Talisid. How do we get out of this?"

"The resolution was passed by the Senior Council," Talisid said. "It can be overturned by the Senior Council."

"How?"

"The purpose of the week's delay is to allow for opposing votes," Talisid said. "If an absent Council member sends in his vote during that time, the vote is treated as if it had been made at the meeting itself."

"And the vote was three to one," I said. "So if the three Senior Council who weren't there vote against it . . . ?"

"It would only take two. Council resolutions require a majority vote."

"Okay," I said. "What are the options?"

"The four members of the Senior Council present were Levistus, Alma, Sal Sarque, and Bahamus," Talisid said. "That leaves three yet to vote. Spire, Druss the Red, and Undaaris. Druss should be the easiest to convince; if Levistus wants to destroy you, Druss will probably vote the other way for no other reason than to oppose him."

"And the other two?"

"Unclear. Both are swing voters not aligned with either Levistus or Druss."

"So we'll have to convince them?"

"Most likely."

"Can you arrange a meeting?"

"Wait," Sonder said. "They're Senior Council. You can't just walk up and—"

"No guarantees, but yes, probably," Talisid said. "In this context, a refusal will simply be a fast way of saying no."

Sonder turned to stare. "How soon?" I asked.

"Both are out of the country, but they're scheduled to return before Monday. I should have something for you by tomorrow."

"Is there anything else we can do?"

"At present, no," Talisid said. "Ah, one other thing. While we are pursuing the political angle, I would counsel against taking any . . . extreme . . . measures in an attempt to resolve the problem independently. It would complicate any potential solution."

"We'll keep that in mind."

"Until tomorrow, then." Talisid paused, looking around the circle. "For now, just hold on. I promise I'll do everything I can."

I nodded. Talisid's image winked out and the communicator went dark.

"Everything he can," Variam muttered. "Believe that when I see it."

"He's not going to screw us, is he?" Luna asked.

"Wait, what?" Sonder said. "Why would he screw you?"

"I know we've had our disagreements with Talisid," I said. "But he's never actually betrayed us or lied to us."

"That we know about," Luna pointed out.

"If he really wanted to screw us over, he wouldn't have made this call at all," I said. "He could have just waited. It's not like I have many other friends on the Council to give me the news."

"Getting the news early doesn't help much if we can't do anything about it," Variam said.

"He's given us time."

"Yeah, but is it actually going to help?" Luna asked. "This whole getting votes thing—is it going to work?"

"Sonder?" I said. "You're the expert on Council politics."

"I'm not really an expert. I wasn't even back in the country until . . ."

"You know more than the rest of us," I said. "Does what he said match up with what you know?"

"I guess," Sonder said reluctantly. Sonder is on the political track for the Light mages, and he's become one of the Council's rising stars. He'd spent last autumn and winter in Washington, making contacts with the North American Council, and now he had some sort of position with the Keeper bureaucracy. "I mean, yes, Druss and Levistus are enemies, everyone knows that. It's the whole Isolationist-Director thing. Spire's supposed to mostly represent independents. Undaaris kind of goes all over the place."

"So they're swing votes, like he said."

"Pretty much."

"But we only need one of them?" Luna said.

"Not exactly," I said. "You heard what Talisid said. Any of those three can send in their votes after the meeting. He didn't say which way. If one of them votes *for* Levistus's proposal . . ."

"Then we're screwed," Variam said. He looked grim. "What are the odds like?"

"We need two out of three to vote in our favour," I said. "Three very powerful, very important mages who probably have a lot of things they'd rather be doing than helping us. And if *any* of them votes against us, then it's over. And I'm pretty sure Levistus has got a lot more ways of buying votes than we do."

Silence fell. I didn't look around or raise my head. I knew what I had to do, but I didn't want to say it.

"Okay," Sonder said. "Well, I guess we should consider the obvious."

"Which is?" Luna asked.

"Talking to Levistus," Sonder said.

We all turned to stare at him.

"Look, he obviously wants something. Couldn't we find out what it is?"

"Uh," Luna said. "I think Levistus just made it pretty clear what he wants."

"No, all he did was pass a proposal," Sonder said. "Look, Council mages do this all the time. It's a negotiating tactic. It's just meant to force you to go to the table and work out a compromise."

"Sonder," I said. "Do you know why Levistus is doing this?"

"Well . . . I assume it's something to do with what happened back three years ago, right? With the fateweaver and Belthas . . ."

"No," I said. "It's about what happened *this* year. With White Rose."

"But Levistus wasn't involved with White Rose," Sonder said.

We all looked at Sonder.

Sonder looked around. "Was he?"

"I had a meeting with Levistus during the White Rose affair," I said. "Just before the indictment against Vihaela was issued. You were in Washington at the time. Levistus gave me a choice. Either I backed off White Rose, stopped going after them, or he'd destroy me. That was how he put it. And not just me, but all of my allies and friends as well. That's what this is about. And the fateweaver, and Belthas too, but mostly it's White Rose. Levistus tried to make me follow his orders. I said no. People like him, they don't forget something like that. He's been storing it up, waiting. Now the bill's come due."

"Translation: he wants us all dead," Luna said.

"Okay, maybe we can do some kind of legal challenge," Sonder said. "I could go to the Conclave and—"

"You've got to be fucking kidding," Variam said. "You think they're going to overturn a Council resolution? In a *week*?"

"It's not impossible . . ."

"Conclave is in recess until the new year," Variam said. "And even if it wasn't, they don't have the authority."

"There've been cases where they've vetoed a Council decision," Sonder said.

"Like how many times? Twice in the past fifty years?"

"There's another way," Anne said quietly.

Luna, Variam, and Sonder all turned to Anne in surprise. Anne's so silent in these discussions that it's easy to forget that she's even there. "How?" Luna asked.

Anne nodded at me. "That was what you were getting at with that question about dependents. Wasn't it?"

The others looked at me questioningly. "The resolution applies to my dependents." I didn't want to speak, but I forced myself to. "If you weren't my dependents, it wouldn't apply."

"You mean before the end of the week?" Variam said.

"It's tight, but it's possible."

"Wait a second," Luna broke in. "That'd help us. It wouldn't help you."

Variam frowned. "Yeah. I mean, that wouldn't stop . . ."

I looked back at Variam silently.

I saw Variam's expression change as he got it. "Oh, no. No way. You are not trying to do this self-sacrificing shit."

"I'm with Vari," Luna said. "We are *not* just giving up on you."

"It might be a good idea," Sonder said. "I mean, if—"

Variam pointed at Sonder. "Shut the fuck up!"

"I just think we should look at the alternatives."

Luna opened her mouth, and I could tell she was about to lose it. "Stop it," I said, putting steel into my voice. "We don't have time for this. Not now."

Luna's eyes flashed, but she obeyed. "I'm not sacrificing anything," I said. "I'm going to work with Talisid to try to get this resolution blocked. But no matter what I do, there is a good chance it's not going to work. If that happens, I want to have a backup plan. I'm not exposing any more of you to this than I have to."

"I don't like it," Variam said with a frown.

"I don't care." I looked around the circle. "So, new issue. How can we get the three of you out of being my dependents by the deadline?"

There was a moment's silence. "Well . . ." Sonder said. "They could apprentice to another mage."

"I'm *already* apprenticed to another mage, you dumb-arse," Variam said.

"You know how long Council approval takes," I said. "Especially at this time of year. I don't think we could get an apprenticeship approved in time, and even if we did, it wouldn't change things. If they're including Vari on the list, then it's as good as saying that being someone else's apprentice doesn't stop me from being his sponsor."

"Wait!" Sonder said. "That's it!"

"What?" Luna said. From her expression she still wasn't in a good mood.

"We can't get an apprenticeship through in time, but we *can* change a sponsor." Sonder looked excited. "Someone I know did it last year. I remember because it was just before I left for Washington. All you need is for one mage to testify that they're taking responsibility for the sponsorship, and for two other mages to stand as witnesses."

"But how long would it take to go through?" I said. "If it's another . . ."

Sonder was shaking his head. "It doesn't need Council approval. All you have to do is get it notarised by a representative from the apprentice program."

"Vari?" I said. "Does that sound right?"

"Beats me," Variam said. "I know you can change it, but I dunno how."

"It's legal," Sonder said. "I promise."

I looked around. "Okay. So if we do this, who should we be asking?"

"Landis," Luna said instantly.

I looked at Variam. "Would he be willing?"

Variam thought a second, then nodded. "Yeah. Getting him to take on Luna and Anne's going to take some convincing, but he'll do it. He's not going to leave them out in the cold."

Landis is Variam's master, and a Council Keeper. I remembered back when Variam wouldn't have trusted a Keeper as far as he could throw him. For Variam to say something like that about Landis meant a lot. "Landis would be sponsoring me for the program?" Anne asked. "But I'm not even a member anymore."

"Doesn't matter," Sonder said. "You don't have to be attending classes. You just have to *not* be sponsored by Alex."

"Okay," I said. "Sounds good. That just leaves one problem." My eyes rested on Luna.

"It'll work," Sonder said. "I've seen . . ." He saw where I was looking and trailed off. ". . . Oh."

"Oh?" Variam said. "Oh, what?"

"What Sonder's describing will work for you and Anne," I said. "Not for Luna."

"But Landis could . . ." Variam stopped.

"Yeah," I said. "Even if Landis takes over her sponsorship, she'll still be my apprentice. Which means she'll still be on the hit list."

"Well . . ." Sonder said. "You could get the apprenticeship dissolved."

I felt a brief flash of anger. *And that's what you've been wanting, isn't it?* It had been the subject of one of the last conversations I'd had with Sonder, the previous year. He'd wanted Luna away from me, from my influence . . .

I saw Anne's eyes turn to me and forced the feelings down. This wasn't the time. "I don't *want* to stop being Alex's apprentice," Luna said. "Not like this."

"But if it's the only way . . ."

"It doesn't matter," I said. "You know how slow Council courts are. By the time we'd brought a petition for dissolution, had it received, set a hearing, gone to the hearing, had the hearing resolved, and had Luna entered into the records as an independent apprentice, we'd be dead five times over."

"What if you ran?" Anne said.

"You mean out of the country?" Luna asked.

"That could work," Variam said. "Just pick someplace where they have crappy relations with the British Council so the Keepers can't get an extradition."

"And while you're gone, Alex could go through the courts with the dissolution," Sonder said. "Then you could come back afterwards."

"Sonder, if Luna has to run, it'll be because the resolution's gone through and is also applying to *me*," I said. "I'm not going to be in much of a position for court proceedings."

"Oh."

"I guess that could work," Luna said slowly, "but . . ."

"Better exiled than dead," Variam said.

"But then what?" Luna said. "It's not as though it's going to expire, is it?"

"No," I said. "It won't. If you do this—if *any* of us do this—we'll be exiled until the Council decides to repeal the resolution. Which probably means forever. We'll never be able to come back to our old lives."

"I don't want to do that," Luna said. "Not if there's any other way."

"What other way?" Variam said. "Because if this vote thing falls through, which seems pretty likely, then the Keepers are going to be showing up right at your door. And don't think you can hide and wait for it to blow over. Catching people is what the Keepers do."

"I don't like the idea of running away," Luna said.

"There might not be a choice!"

"Maybe there is."

We all looked at Luna. "What are you talking about?" Variam said.

"The problem is that I'm Alex's apprentice, right?" Luna said. "What if we changed that?"

"How would—?" I began, then stopped.

Variam got it a second later. "Taking your journeyman tests?"

"It'd work, wouldn't it?" Luna asked. "The resolution says Alex's dependents. Well, if I'm a journeyman mage, then I can't be *anyone's* dependent."

"It would work . . ." I said slowly, "but . . ."

"No, it wouldn't," Variam said. "Have you seen the waiting lists for those tests? They're months long."

"Actually, they're not," Luna said.

"Okay," I said to Luna. "You've obviously got something in mind. Let's hear it."

"Here's the thing," Luna said. "I know your plan's always been for me to take those tests someday, but I was worried that the Council would do something to block it. Claim I was an adept and wasn't allowed, or something like that. So I went and looked up the laws. Turns out, *any* apprentice has got the right to demand to be tested as a journeyman. There are only three conditions." Luna held up her fingers, ticking them off one by one. "First, you have to be officially recognised by the Council as an apprentice. Done that. Second, you can't be wanted for any crimes or breaches of the Concord. Done that too. Third, you have to have been sponsored for the apprentice program and you have to have been attending classes for at least fifteen months. I've put in more than twice that long." Luna lowered her hand and looked around. "No requirement for Council approval. Doesn't even say that you have to be a mage. It just says you have to be a recognised apprentice. I checked. And there's a time limit. When you put in the request, you can demand for the tests to take place within a time window. The minimum you can ask for is five days." Luna raised her eyebrows. "It's within the deadline."

"Okay, that might be what the law *technically* says," Sonder said. "But no one actually does it."

"No rule says you can't."

"It doesn't matter," Sonder said. "You couldn't get the trial agreements done."

"No rule saying you need those, either."

"You two arc losing us," I said. Both Variam and Anne were looking puzzled. "What are you getting at?"

"Those waiting lists Vari was talking about?" Luna said. "They're not for the tests. They're for the meetings with the mages setting the trials. The reason it takes so long is that they need to agree on what each trial's allowed to contain. If you skip that part, you can jump the queue."

"Yeah, except that there wouldn't be any restrictions on what you got," Sonder said.

Luna shrugged. "Not like we'd be able to get much out of them if we negotiated it anyway."

"That's crazy," Sonder said. "They could send *anything* at you! They could kill you!"

"Meh," Luna said. "They pretty much never kill apprentices in those tests anymore. Last one was more than ten years ago and that was only because he had a heart condition."

"Wait," Anne said. "That's supposed to be good news?"

"Is it really that much more dangerous than the stuff we do anyway?" Luna asked.

"All right." I held up a hand. "Let me think a second."

The four of them quieted, looking at me. "Luna," I said after a moment. "You've got a lesson with Chalice tomorrow morning, right?"

Luna nodded.

"Then I'll come along with you. If she thinks you're ready, then we'll go ahead with your plan."

"I don't think this is a good idea," Sonder said.

"Then please see if you can find anything better," I said. "For Luna, and for all of us. We don't exactly have a lot of options here. You know a lot more mages who are experts on Council law than I do. If you can dig up anything that'd help us, we'd be very grateful."

Sonder didn't look happy, but he didn't argue. "Vari," I said. "I'm guessing Landis'll be going home after the party. Can you meet him there? Break the sponsorship transfer plan to him?"

"Yeah," Variam said. He looked at Anne. "You'd better come too. He's going to want to talk to you."

"Then that's enough for tonight," I said. I was tired and having trouble concentrating. All of a sudden, I wanted to be on my own. "Let's get some sleep."

The others didn't move. "What about you?" Luna asked.

"I'm going to be fighting the political angle with Talisid."

"With us," Variam said.

I sighed. "Yes, with you. Now come on. You've got things you should be doing."

All four were reluctant, but I eventually got them moving, chivvying them out of the living room and down towards the storeroom and the small patch at the centre that had been cleared and box-warded for gates. Sonder was the most eager. Anne was the most reluctant; she lingered at the door and I think she would have stayed if Variam hadn't been pressuring her to go. Luna went without protest, but she kept an eye on me, and I knew that she'd be expecting me tomorrow. It felt like a long time before the last gate closed and I was left alone in the storeroom.

chapter 2

I trailed back upstairs into the living room and dropped onto the sofa. All of a sudden, the energy that had kept me going through the discussion was gone.

Like all diviners, I'm a thinker. When I get a problem, my first instinct is to unpack it, holding it up and turning it around to look at it from different angles. Sometimes I see the answer instantly, but other times it needs more work, and that's when I go to other people for advice. All the time I'm talking it over with them, only half of my mind is on the discussion. The other half is picking away at the problem, examining it in the light of their suggestions, waiting for the flash of insight that signals a solution. Sometimes it's a half solution, sometimes it's a full solution, but it's rarely wrong. When I get that feeling, I know I'm on the right track.

But sometimes I don't get that feeling at all.

Luna's, Variam's, Talisid's, and Sonder's suggestions had been logical, and the courses of action we'd settled on made sense. I thought it could work. But I didn't *know* it would work. And without that, I was feeling a lingering unease that wouldn't go away. My limbs were cold, and I shivered.

The weather outside was freezing, and even here in my room the heat didn't seem to be winning.

Something cool nudged my hand. I looked up to see Hermes next to me, standing on the carpet. "I don't know," I told him. "It might work. Maybe . . ."

Hermes gave me a questioning look.

"No," I said. "I'm not sure." I shook my head and got to my feet. I felt off balance, and over the years, I've learned that when that happens, there's one person I should be talking to. "I'm going to Arachne's. Want to come?"

Hermes blinked once.

I got my coat, then walked to the desk and took out my gate stone for Arachne's lair. Despite the name, it wasn't a stone but a piece of wood, old and weathered and carved with runes. I wasn't expecting any trouble, but all the same, I looked into the futures in which I gated to Arachne's lair. Down to the storeroom, through the portal, and—

Ow. What the hell?

I looked again. Pain, violence. As I focused, the futures shifted. Combat, more violence . . . I pulled back, resetting myself, starting a path-walk, and this time I was paying full attention. What would happen if I used this gate stone, stepped out into Arachne's ravine, and stood there?

I'd get the crap beaten out of me, that was what. "Okay, change of plans," I told Hermes. "We've got some trouble waiting outside Arachne's lair." I moved my future self around, trying to find out more about the attackers. Human, that was obvious. Two . . . no, three. "Team of three. First two are either adepts or sensitives, I think. Third one . . ." I tried a future in which I shone a torch in that direction, getting a clear look before I was clubbed to the ground. "Wait a minute. I know that guy." White, early twenties, close-shaven brown hair. I'd never seen him, but I recognised the face all the same. Maybe a photo . . . ?

I snapped my fingers. "Got it. Wolf."

Hermes cocked his head at me.

"Yeah, you wouldn't know him. It's not his real name: he's an ex–Light apprentice, James something. Water magic, got kicked out of the apprentice program then declared himself to be a full mage. No one listened and the Keepers have pulled him in a few times for petty stuff. That was how I saw his file." I frowned. "I wonder what he's trying to do . . ."

Hermes waited.

"Wow," I said. "They're using clubs. You know, I don't think they're trying to kill me at all. I think they just want to give me a good old-fashioned beating." I raised my eyebrows. "Old school."

Hermes tilted his head, then back again.

"Because they want to send a message, I'm guessing." I frowned as I tried to look through the futures in which my future self got beaten to a pulp, then shook my head. "Well, whatever it is, these guys are amateur hour."

Hermes opened his mouth to show his teeth.

"Yeah," I said. Hermes can't talk, but he and I understand each other pretty well. I'd have some help for this one. I put down the gate stone and headed for my room. "Let's gear up."

I took my armour out of the wardrobe and pulled it on. My armour is a suit of dark mesh with raised plates covering stationary areas, matte black and flexible. It looks serious, and it is. The reactive mesh isn't impenetrable, but it's very tough and it responds to attacks, changing its shape to deflect a blow. The plates have grown and thickened over the years, adjusting to the shape of my body. I added my standard collection of items to my belt and pockets and then descended one floor.

My safe room is locked, warded with multiple effects, and lined with steel. I went through the locks and pulled open the metal door, then stepped inside. Hermes stayed out in the hallway, and I didn't blame him. While the Arcana Emporium's supposed to be a magic shop, the magical items I have on sale on the ground floor are strictly small potatoes. Weak wands and orbs that require a mage to wield them and don't do anything all that spectacular even then; ambient focuses that can work on their own by drawing in local energy but have only the most limited of effects; old accoutrements that have been used enough times to have accumulated a little resonance. But for every twenty or thirty items I get that are weak or faded, I pick up one that's genuinely dangerous. My safe room is where I keep them.

The imbued items were on the left wall. A crocodile-hilted sword stood out, gleaming dully in the light, as did a small white-and-blue lacquered tube. I didn't go near either of them. Instead I went to a tall cabinet in the far corner and opened it. Inside was a small but formidable arsenal. I tapped one finger to my lips and studied the choices.

Mounted in pride of place at the centre of the collection was a Heckler & Koch MP7. It's a nasty, compact little firearm the size of a submachine gun. I'd taken it off a guy called Garrick a few years ago—he hadn't come back to reclaim it, and in exchange I hadn't gone after him for trying to shoot me through the head with a sniper rifle, which seemed to me like a fair trade. Using it, I could probably kill all three men outside Arachne's lair in about ten seconds.

"Overkill," I decided, and glanced briefly at the pair of handguns on the shelf underneath. One was my old 1911; another was a smaller-caliber automatic that I'd acquired earlier this year at the expense of some guy whose name I'd never learned. They were less suited to extended combat than the MP7, but they'd get the job done.

"Overkill." I took down a sword from its mountings and half-drew it from its sheath. Metal hissed against leather, and I turned the blade, watching it glint in the light. The sword was a *jian*, a little over two feet long. I'm familiar with most blades, but I generally prefer smaller ones. It smelt of oil . . . and blood? I shook my head. *Imagination.* The blade was clean. "Overkill," I said again, resheathed the blade, and hung it back up. The next item I took up was a can of pepper spray. The stuff's illegal in the U.K., but it's not hard to get if you know where to look. The pepper spray went back, to be replaced by a quarterstaff. It was a dull grey in colour; to an observer, it would look like steel. I held this one for a little longer before deciding. The heft felt good, and I spun it once, hearing the metal *whoosh* through the still air. "Still overkill," I said at last. The staff went back in the cabinet and I closed the doors, walked out of the safe room, and locked the door behind me, feeling the wards reset as I did. Hermes had watched the entire process with curiosity. As I turned to go downstairs, he trotted to follow.

Down in the storeroom, I went through two more items before finding what I was looking for: a cylindrical length of wood about seven eighths of an inch in diameter and a little under three feet in length. The Japanese would call it a *hanbo*; native English speakers might call it a dowel, baton, or cudgel, but more likely they'd just call it a stick. I spun it in one hand and nodded. Now just one more thing on the defence side . . .

Ah. I went out of the room, unlocked the back door, and stepped out into the freezing air. The dustbins out in the back alley were black plastic. I picked the lid off one of them and held it in my left hand, testing its heft. Thick plastic, but still light. "Perfect," I said, and went back inside.

A glance at the futures confirmed that my ambushers weren't going anywhere. I went back upstairs and did a leisurely warm-up. Neck rotations, arm circles, then several different leg stretches. I paid particular attention to the hamstring muscle at the back of the thigh; it's easy to get a strain there if you don't warm up properly. Once I was done I went back downstairs, picked up the stick and the dustbin lid, and checked to see if my ambushers were in a good position. There wasn't any way to nail it down precisely, but the futures in which I opened the gate right now were a little less favourable than I liked, so I waited around, running through a few practice strikes and blocks. Most of my shop and flat is warded from gates; the spot I was standing in was the single small volume in which the wards on the shop were shaped so as to allow space magic to function unhindered. After five minutes, I felt the futures shift and checked. About an eighty percent chance that they were going to be in an L formation rather than a surround. *Good as it's going to get.* "Ready?" I asked Hermes.

Hermes blinked once.

I tucked the stick under my arm, took out the gate stone, and began channelling. Using a focus item is easy for most mages—all you need is the item and a bit of applied knowledge. It's harder for me, but I'm very familiar with the location I was gating to and I wasn't in any hurry. After a couple of minutes the air before me darkened and formed an oval. Through the portal, stars twinkled through the shadows of bare branches. I was looking out onto the darkness of Hampstead Heath.

Hermes disappeared, teleporting through the gate and away into the night. I stepped through, taking the stick out from under my arm and letting the gate vanish behind me. As it did, I stabbed right.

The man to my side had just started his forward rush, his arm raised. He was a force adept, and the spell he was using would have made the club in his hand come down with crushing force, enough to break my arm if I stood to meet it. He couldn't, however, see in the dark. The tip of my stick hit just beneath his breastbone, sinking deep as the momentum of his rush drove him onto it. He lost his breath in a gasp as he went down.

I twisted left, raising the dustbin lid as I did to catch a blow as it landed on the hard plastic, the shock going up my arm. *Second man.* I couldn't see what he looked like, but I'd spent time watching the futures in which he attacked. This one's adept ability was perception-based. He moved in the pitch darkness of the ravine as though it were broad daylight, swinging his club like a baseball bat, and I gave ground. The dustbin lid rang under the rain of blows. Blue light flashed to my right and I sidestepped, feeling a spell whip past, letting the adept come between me and the threat. He did, and as he stepped in, I reversed course, moving in to meet him, shield high and weapon low. His club glanced off the lid; mine found his ankle. There was the distinctive *crack* of wood on bone and the adept yelled, hopping, tumbling to the ground. I stepped in, dropping my stick, ducking low; another spell flashed overhead as I drew my stun focus from my pocket and stabbed the adept with it as he tried to scramble to his feet. Life magic passed into him in a green flicker, and I came to my feet in the same motion.

In the pale blue light illuminating the ravine, I could see that both adepts were down. The first was struggling and gasping; the second was still. The light was coming from the third man and the staff of glowing blue energy in his hands. It would have looked impressive if he hadn't been staring with his mouth open. My preparations—planning, weapon selection, warm-up, waiting for the right moment to gate, and gating—had taken a bit under half an hour. The fight had lasted around five seconds. Pretty typical for a diviner.

I walked back towards the first adept as he struggled to breathe, picking up my stick as I did, and hit him with one carefully measured blow. There was a *thud* and he dropped. I turned to the mage and raised my eyebrows. "You coming?"

Wolf—James—stared at me.

"You coming?" I said again. James was about thirty feet away. "Or do I have to go to you?"

"Go to—!" James seemed to bolster himself. "You know who I am?"

"Yes, your name's James Redman and you're probably one of the weakest elemental mages in Britain."

"My name's *Wolf*!"

I sighed. "Sure it is."

"You come near me and I'll fuck you up!"

I just looked at him.

"What, you want a piece of me?" James hefted the glowing staff. "Bring it, bitch! And that's—that's a dustbin lid? You're coming after me with a fucking *dustbin lid*?" James gave a slightly hysterical laugh. "You know who I am? You think you can take me? You—"

James kept talking and I tuned him out. Most of the time, when people posture, you don't really need to listen to the words. The content is always more or less the same—they're tough, you should be scared of them, yadda yadda yadda. The real communication is done with body language and tone of voice. I already knew that James wasn't going to take a shot at me, not in any time frame that mattered. Instead I looked into the futures where I tried talking to him, seeing what information I could pick out. How about if I tried guessing who'd sent him . . . ?

Well, it's not Levistus. Not that that was really a surprise: Levistus would have sent a much higher grade of assassin. Not Morden, for similar reasons. Not Onyx, not Deleo, not Cinder, not Crystal, not Lyle, not Barrayar, not Avis, not Ordith, not Sagash, not Darren, not . . . *Okay, I have way too many enemies to do this one at a time.* I pulled back my focus and looked to see if any name I could come up with would work. Didn't seem like it. *Someone new? Probably not all that high on the power scale, if this is the best they can send . . .*

"—well? You hearing me, bitch?"

"Stop calling me 'bitch,'" I said absently. "A bitch is a female dog. I like dogs."

James stared at me. "I'll call you what I want, *bitch*."

"Whatever. Look, James—"

"My name's *Wolf*."

"James. I've got things to do. You got hired to send me a message, right? Let's hear it."

James gave me a disbelieving look.

"Last chance to do this the easy way."

"Oh yeah?" James spread his arms wide. The staff flickered in one hand. It looked like a standard elemental weapon, designed to apply kinetic energy, possibly with some on-hit effect. "Let's do this! Come on!"

I sighed. "Hermes?" I said out loud to the sky. "Any time you're ready."

Hermes blinked into view behind James and sank his teeth into the back of James's ankle. James screamed, staggering. He tried to twist around to see what had bitten him but Hermes hung on, letting James's momentum drag him around. James flailed awkwardly one-handed with the staff, trying to beat Hermes away, before managing to get a grip with both hands and swinging back as hard as he could.

The moment before the staff landed, Hermes blinked out of existence, teleporting away. The swing hit only air and James staggered sideways.

"Hey," I said from behind him.

James spun. I let him get most of the way around before introducing my stick to his head. He hit the ground and I continued to apply the stick to various points on his body until he stopped trying to cast spells. By that point, the light from the water staff James had been using was gone, along with the staff itself (concentration-based spells and beatings don't mix), so I took out my pocket torch and clicked it on, shining it downwards. "Ready to talk?"

"Oh, fuck," James moaned. He was lying on the ground in a fetal position. "It hurts."

"Who sent you?"

"I don't know! I just—"

I struck down, deliberately making the blow slow enough to see coming. James caught a glimpse through the light and raised an arm to protect his head. The stick landed on his right hand with a snapping *crack*. James screamed.

"Okay, James," I said once he'd quieted down enough to hear me. "This game is called 'How many of your bones do I have to break before you answer my questions?' Right now the counter is on 'one.' In another twenty seconds, I'll be advancing it to 'two.'"

"All right! Jesus, it was Symmaris, okay? It was Symmaris!"

"And what did Symmaris tell you to do?"

"Just to—just to rough you up a bit, okay? Nothing serious, we weren't going to hurt you or anything."

"Uh-huh. And what were you supposed to tell me afterwards?"

"To stay away from Drakh."

I paused. "What?"

"From Drakh. For the job. You know?"

"What job?"

"I don't fucking know. They—"

I lifted the stick.

"No! Jesus, I'm telling you the truth, I swear! There was some thing, some, some job you were supposed to be doing, working with Drakh, I don't know, something important, and Symmaris, she wanted to warn you to back off, right? That was all she told us. That was it!"

I stared down at James, searching through the futures. It sounded flimsy, but as I explored different interrogation options, I realised to my surprise that he was actually telling the truth. I shook my head. "You really came to the wrong neighbourhood."

"Look, please, just let me go. I didn't know. I'll tell Symmaris whatever you like, I swear—"

"I don't work for Drakh," I said.

James paused. "Huh?"

"I don't work for Richard Drakh," I said again. "Your boss got the wrong guy. If you'd done your homework and asked around instead of coming here, you and your boys could be back at home having a pint right now." I gestured back towards the two adepts. The one I'd hit with the stun focus was stirring and moaning. The other had rolled over onto his side and was throwing up. "Get your mates and gate. If you pull anything like this on me a second time, you won't be around for a third. Understand?"

James nodded quickly. "Yeah. Okay."

"Get lost."

James stumbled to his feet and hurried over to the two adepts. I watched patiently as he started opening a gate. "James?" I said when he was a minute into the spell.

I saw the muscles in James's back tense. The blue light around his hand flickered and he nearly dropped the spell. Slowly he turned, shoulders hunched, the whites of his eyes showing.

I flicked the beam of the torch down to where the two adepts had fallen. "They dropped their clubs."

James stared at me, then down at the shadowy outlines of the clubs where they lay on the ground.

"Pick them up, please," I said. "I'm not cleaning up after you."

Slowly James obeyed, holding the wooden cudgels awkwardly in his injured hand, then went back to opening the gate. By the time he was done both adepts were on their feet, one supporting the other. The three of them shot scared looks at me as they shuffled through the gate and out of sight. I watched it close behind them. The blue light faded and I was alone in the darkness.

"Idiots," I said into the night. I checked to make sure no one else was coming, then walked to the edge of the ravine. Hermes blinked into position behind me, trotting at my heels. I pressed two fingers to one of the roots beneath the oak tree, waited for the signature of the open connection, and spoke. "Arachne? It's Alex. We need to talk."

।।।।।।।।

Usually Arachne's lair is one of the few places I can relax. Its wards and defences are extensive, and I know that Arachne's been steadily improving them over the last few years. It's not just paranoia: magical creatures like Arachne have no protection under the Concord, and if any mages decide to pick a fight with her, no one on the Council is going to do anything about it. Arachne's only defences are those she creates herself, and though she never talks about it, I know she takes it seriously. Sitting here in the cavern, I was almost certainly safer than I was in my own shop.

Except that for the first time in years, being here wasn't making me feel safe. Sure, I could hide here—for a while. But not forever.

"That's the story," I said. I was sitting on one of the sofas, next to some bolts of red and blue silk. Hermes had hopped up onto another sofa and was watching with ears pricked.

"I see," Arachne said. Arachne is a spider the size of an SUV, black-haired with highlights of cobalt blue; she's probably my oldest friend and one of the very few people I really trust. She'd been working on a dress when I'd arrived, but as soon as I'd started to give her the news she'd put it down and moved in close. Now she was resting in such a position that her front legs were only a couple of feet away, near enough that I could smell the herbal scent of her body. She'd been listening for twenty minutes, speaking only to ask for clarification. "Do you know anything further about your three attackers?"

"Honestly?" I said. "Right now I don't much care. They're small fry. I've got bigger problems."

"Small problems that aren't dealt with can become larger problems," Arachne said. "Besides, I suspect the two may be related."

I shrugged.

"It concerns me that they knew to stage an ambush here," Arachne said.

"Yeah, they knew where to find me," I said. "But if I don't deal with this Council proposal, then it won't *matter* that they knew where to find me, because inside of a week I won't be here, or anywhere else in the country, or maybe not even alive. I do not have much room to manoeuvre here!"

Arachne looked at me patiently. "There's no need to be snappish."

I sighed, passing a hand in front of my face. "I'm sorry. I'm just off balance." I looked up at Arachne. "Any good ideas? Because I could really use some."

"Moving Variam and Anne to Landis's sponsorship is an obvious decision," Arachne said. "Pushing Luna through her journeyman tests is more risky, but seems to be the best of the possible alternatives. Though you'll need help from Chalice."

"We're meeting her tomorrow morning. I still hadn't completely made up my mind on whether to trust her." I shrugged again. "Guess now I've got no choice."

"But that still leaves the question of your sentence," Arachne said. She studied me, eight eyes unblinking. "You understand why this is happening."

"Yeah. It's the bill coming due for pissing off Levistus."

"No," Arachne said. "Levistus is the short-term manifestation of a long-term problem. If it hadn't been Levistus, it would have been someone else."

"What long-term problem?"

"Your independence," Arachne said. "Over the past few years, you have been offered numerous chances to side with those more powerful than yourself. Levistus tried to recruit you, as did Morden. Richard offered you your old place at his side. Talisid wanted you to become his spy. You turned them all down. Instead you have opted to remain separate and apart, beholden to no one."

"You know why we did that," I said. "I know our group's not powerful, not compared to the real players. We can't do much to change things. But at least we don't have to make things worse."

"And that would be viable, were you only involved in small things," Arachne said. "But Levistus's plans are not small things. Richard's return is not a small thing. There are storms coming, and you will be caught in them."

"Then what are my options?"

"Align yourself with one of the greater powers," Arachne said. "Or *become* a greater power. Or die." She paused. "I'm sorry, Alex. I wish I had better news."

I sat in silence. "What if there's another way?" I said at last. "Find something to trade to one of the Council mages. Play them off against one another. I've done it before."

"Perhaps," Arachne said. "For a little while. But understand that to take this road—to make your own choices—is to walk the most difficult path. There will be sacrifices."

I felt a chill go through me. It wasn't physical cold— Arachne's cave is warm. "Will I have you with me?"

"I do not know how long I can stay," Arachne said. "But as long as I can help you, I will."

I reached out and rested a hand on one of Arachne's forelegs. Arachne reached up with her other foreleg to stroke my hair, her movements gentle. I closed my eyes and let myself relax, taking comfort in her presence. We stayed like that for a long time, silent in the lair.

chapter 3

Sunday morning dawned bright and clear. The sun was shining down out of a cold blue sky, and puffy white clouds drifted high above. There were six days until my execution order went through.

Luna and I sat at a back table in one of the cafés along Upper Street in Islington. Despite the time of day, there was a good scattering of people. Islington is an odd, mixed sort of place; from walking the streets you'd get the feeling that it's middle-class and rich, yet if you look at the numbers, it's got one of the highest poverty rates in the country. The other people in the café didn't seem to have much to worry about; they looked like affluent young urban professionals, chatting and laughing over their morning coffees. But maybe there was more to them than met the eye. Just like us.

"Do you guys usually have your lessons in here?" I asked Luna. I didn't need to keep my voice down; Luna had picked us a table against the far wall, a good distance from the other customers.

"Sort of," Luna said. "We switch around."

"I still can't believe that you have magic lessons in a

café," I said. It wasn't news; I'd kept close tabs on Chalice and Luna during the early stages of their relationship, and I still went out of my way to check in with Luna after lessons even now. But it felt weird all the same.

"It's not as though our magic's visible."

"What if something weird happens?"

"Doesn't seem to."

I sighed. "Must be nice being so lucky that you don't have to worry about consequences."

Movement in the futures caught my eye and I looked up. Chalice was about to walk in. "How much have you told her?" I asked Luna.

"Just that there was a problem and that you'd be coming," Luna said. "I figured we shouldn't really be discussing it over the phone."

"Good."

Chalice came walking through the door, saw us, and turned in our direction. She blended in with the morning crowd: a professional-looking Indian woman dressed neatly in dark winter clothes. "Hello, Luna," she said with a smile as she reached our table. She pulled out a chair and sat down. "Verus, it's been a while."

"I know," I said with a nod. "Everything work out with Yarris?"

"Yes," Chalice said. "Thank you for your help with that."

Chalice is a new addition to my and Luna's social circle. Earlier in the year, after months of searching for a reputable Light or independent chance mage to act as Luna's teacher, I'd finally given in to Luna's requests to try something riskier. Chalice was a Dark mage who had approached Luna on her own initiative. I hadn't trusted her then and I didn't fully trust her now, but she'd kept up her end of the deal—she'd started teaching Luna twice a week, and the results had been impressive.

But the relationship was a two-way street. In exchange for her lessons, Chalice had asked that I help her out when she needed it. In a funny way, the fact that Chalice had demanded that had actually made me feel better—I wouldn't have trusted her if she'd claimed to be doing it for free. Equivalent exchange, on the other hand . . . that I could believe. The favours she'd been asking had mostly been investigations, digging up information on other mages. Most seemed to relate to Chalice's past in India, but I hadn't yet been able to ferret out what her long-term goals were. Maybe I'd learn something more today.

A waiter approached. Chalice ordered masala chai, while Luna asked for a pot of red tea. The waiter turned to me; I shook my head and he withdrew. "The tea here is quite good," Chalice said.

"Maybe another time."

Chalice glanced sideways at Luna, then turned back to me. "So I understand there's a problem."

"I'll get to the point," I said. "You've been teaching Luna for nearly a year now."

Chalice nodded.

"Do you think she's ready to take her journeyman tests?"

Chalice considered very briefly. "Yes," she said. "I think so."

I sat back slightly, glancing through the futures in which I interrogated Chalice more closely. I couldn't see any futures in which I reacted to signs of deception. Chalice looked back at me with her dark eyes. As far as I could tell, she was telling the truth. *Well, that's it,* I decided. *We're doing this.*

"I can give you the breakdown," Chalice offered.

I shook my head. "If you say she's ready, she's ready."

Luna was looking between us, eyes bright. "Okay, Luna," I said to Luna. "You win."

"So this is something you've decided to move forward with?" Chalice asked.

"Looks like," I said. "You free to give Luna some coaching?"

"That should be possible," Chalice said. "When are you hoping to schedule the tests for? Next summer?"

"More like the end of this week," Luna said.

Chalice paused. "I'm sorry?"

The waiter reappeared with a tray. Chalice fell quiet as

cups and teapots were offloaded, but I could feel her eyes on me, questioning. The waiter gave us a chirpy "Let me know if there's anything else you need!" and disappeared.

"There's been a bit of a change in schedule," I said once the waiter was out of earshot. "When we said, 'Are you free for coaching?' we meant now. As in, right now."

Chalice gave me a thoughtful look. "Perhaps you should explain."

I filled Chalice in, leaving out the parts that didn't directly relate to me or to Luna. Chalice listened silently, taking an occasional sip from her cup. The scents of the chai and Luna's own tea mixed together, warm and pleasant. "So, like I said," I finished, "time's an issue."

Chalice was silent, and I had the feeling that she was calculating just how dangerous this would be. "Can you help?" Luna asked. "I could really use the practice."

I felt the futures settle as Chalice made her decision. "Yes," Chalice said. "That should be possible." She looked at Luna. "Are you sure about the five-day rule?"

Luna nodded.

"Then we don't have much time." Chalice tapped her nails on the table, then gave a nod. "All right. I'll clear my next few days. I've a prior engagement tonight, but starting tomorrow, we'll train full time."

I saw Luna relax a little. "Thanks."

"Which leaves the question of my payment."

I sighed. *Saw that coming.* "Can I agree to owe you a favour?"

"From the sounds of it, right now, you and Luna are about the worst credit risk possible."

"Thanks," I said. "Look, I'd happily pay you in cash, but you already turned that down. The deal was an alliance. Favour for favour."

"If you're about to be removed from the country or worse, you won't be in much of a position to pay that favour back."

"Fine. What are you angling for?"

Chalice studied me for a few seconds before answering.

"I want to know what your old master is looking for, and what he plans to do with it."

I stared at Chalice. She picked up her cup of chai and took a sip.

"Are you serious?" I said.

Chalice looked at me.

"Why?"

"Call it curiosity."

"Looking for what? And how do you even know about this?"

"There are rumours that Drakh is in the process of assembling a retrieval team," Chalice said. "I don't know what he's attempting to retrieve, and I don't know its purpose. I would like to know both of those things."

"This is absolutely the worst possible time for me to go and investigate something like this."

Chalice shrugged.

"There is no realistic way I'm going to be able to get that done in five days," I said. "Maybe not even fifty days. You're talking about national-level intelligence. If I just try to waltz over there and find this out with no preparation, I'm going to get killed. The cost-benefit doesn't add up."

Chalice tapped her fingers. "You may have a point."

I sat and waited. Chalice looked off into space, frowning slightly. Luna looked between the two of us. "How about this, then?" Chalice said. "If the opportunity arises during the coming week to discover what I want to know, you'll find it out and relay the information to me. Otherwise, you'll owe me a favour."

I looked at Chalice, trying not to let my surprise show. That was a much better deal. "That . . . seems fair."

"It's agreed, then." Chalice drank the last of her tea and straightened. "Luna, I'll meet you tomorrow at Barnet. Early would be best. Nine o'clock?"

Luna nodded. "Okay."

"Well." Chalice turned back to me. "I've got some preparations to make. Keep me up to date if anything develops."

"I will," I said. Chalice rose and left. She went to the counter to pay, then walked out into the street.

"I wonder why she wants to know about that?" Luna said with a frown.

I kept my eyes on where Chalice had disappeared. "Have you ever told Chalice anything about the missions we do for Talisid? About our group?"

"No."

"Anything at all?"

"I do know what 'secret' means. What are you getting at?"

"Out of all the Light and independent mages in Britain, our group probably knows more than anyone else about Richard and what he's up to," I said. "It strikes me as a funny coincidence that Chalice would just happen to approach us."

"Everyone knows you used to be Richard's apprentice," Luna said.

"Yes. But if Chalice has looked—and she has—then she'd also know that I hate the guy."

"You think she knows what we've been doing?"

I frowned. "A better question is, why does she want to know more? Trying to poke into Richard's business is playing with fire. I wonder why she'd take that risk . . . ?"

"You're the one who keeps telling us that Dark mages are always plotting against each other," Luna said.

"Yeah," I said. Inwardly, I was wondering something else. When I'd first met Chalice, she'd implied that the only reason she'd wanted this alliance was for the information I could give her as a diviner. I'd never been absolutely sure that she was telling the whole truth about that. Did she have some agenda of her own when it came to Richard? Maybe *that* had been the real reason she'd approached Luna . . .

"Well," Luna said, "time's ticking. Think it's time to go knock on the Council's front door and tell them I want a journeyman test."

"How do you do it?"

"Formal request delivered by hand to the dean of the

apprentice program," Luna said. She grinned. "I found out where the guy lives. Want to come along?"

"I think it's best if I'm visibly involved with this as little as possible," I said.

That wiped the smile off Luna's face. "Oh," she said. "Right." She paused. "You're going to see those Council members, right?"

"Trust me, I'm really not interested in committing suicide. I'm going to do everything I can to block this thing."

Luna searched my face for a second, then nodded and got up. "Okay. Wish me luck."

"Don't think that's something you're short of."

⁙⁙⁙⁙⁙

Luna headed to Westminster, while I returned home. My shop's closed on Sundays, and I was in no mood to open it anyway. I made some calls.

Getting through to Talisid took a while, and when I finally did, there wasn't much news. He'd put out feelers to Spire and Undaaris and confirmed that both were supposed to be returning to the country by this evening, but neither had responded. He promised to get back to me as soon as they did. I cut the connection, not feeling much better.

Variam had better news. I looked into the futures in which I contacted him and found that he was already in the process of introducing Anne to Landis. It seemed as though it would go better without my interfering, so I decided to leave well enough alone. In the process of finding that out, I also noticed that someone was coming to call. A woman, and a mage . . . a stranger, though. I couldn't sense any immediate danger, but there was no point in being careless. I checked the defences and went downstairs to wait. The bell rang a minute later. I waited twenty seconds, then walked out into the shop and unlocked the front door.

The woman standing outside had European features and long black hair, and was wearing a black fur coat. She looked forty or so, slender, with slight crow's-feet at the corners of her eyes. "Mage Verus?" she said as she saw me.

"That's me," I said. I didn't take my eyes off her. She was standing with her feet together, slightly stiff. She looked nervous.

"I have some important information for you," the woman said.

"Okay."

"We should discuss it in private."

"Okay."

The woman looked down and fumbled in her handbag. Her movements were nervous and jerky. She pulled out a small white card and handed it to me. "Here."

I inspected the card without touching it. It was a business card for a nearby hotel. A room number was written on it in black pen. "What exactly is this?" I asked.

"It's the—"

"The St. Pancras Hotel, yes, it says on the card. Why are you showing it to me?"

"We've scheduled a meeting there for two o'clock."

I stared at the woman.

"Okay?" the woman said. "Do you understand?"

"What exactly is this important information that you need to share?"

"We can't discuss that here," the woman said. "I promise all of your questions will be answered at the meeting."

"Yeah, that's not going to happen."

"But you need to—"

"Lady, I have never seen you before. I have no reason to listen to you and no reason to trust you. If you think I'm going to come to your meeting, you're in for a disappointment."

"But this is important!"

"Then let's hear it."

"I can't—"

"You can't discuss that here," I said with a sigh. This was getting repetitive. "Who are you, again?"

"I'm sorry," the woman said. "I don't feel comfortable identifying myself to you."

I looked at the woman in disbelief, then shook my head and started cycling through futures. People react differently to the sound of their own name than to someone else's. It's theoretically possible to brute-force these kind of problems by doing one syllable at a time, but it's time-consuming and quite frankly it's not worth the effort. It's much faster to try your mental library of every name that might apply to the person first. One reaction jumped out almost immediately, but the name was unfamiliar. But I must have heard it somewhere if I could be saying it . . . where had it been? Oh, right. Last night.

Wait. Really?

"I promise you, it's absolutely essential that we have this discussion," the woman said. "If you—"

"Symmaris," I said.

Symmaris jumped. "How did you—?"

I just looked at her with raised eyebrows. I always find it odd when I get these reactions. People come here because I'm a diviner, and then they're surprised when I know more than they tell me. They never seem to think that divination could also work on them.

"Before you do anything," Symmaris began, "I think you should be aware that I didn't come here alone. And there are other people who know where I am. If I don't return they'll know why."

"Jesus Christ," I said. "What is *wrong* with you?"

"I think that given your reputation, some precautions aren't excessive."

"And I think that after you sent a bunch of thugs to try and break my bones last night, you aren't in any position to be lecturing me about precautions."

"What?"

I raised my eyebrows. "So you didn't send Mr. Wolf after me with a couple of goons?"

"No."

I looked at her.

"Of course I didn't," Symmaris said. "That's ridiculous."

"Right," I said sceptically. I wasn't feeling terribly well disposed towards Symmaris right now. "So now that we've been properly introduced, how about you tell me what this message is."

"I told you, I'm not discussing it out here."

I sighed. "Fine," I said after a moment. "You can come into the shop. Briefly."

Symmaris drew back. "I'm not going into your home with you alone."

"For the love of God. Are you *serious*?"

"You just told me you believe that I'm out to get you," Symmaris said. "Given that, I think I'm being very reasonable not to isolate myself with you."

I stared at Symmaris in disbelief, then shook my head and began to close the door. "Wait!" Symmaris said. "The meeting is going to be at the hotel!"

"I've known you for less than ten minutes and you're already annoying me. I really don't figure on spending the afternoon with you."

"But you have to—!"

I shut the door in Symmaris's face and walked back to the counter.

There was a knocking on the door. "Mage Verus!" The voice was muffled.

I ignored her and checked the compartment below the counter. The 1911 was still there in its hiding place. I glanced through the futures. No immediate danger, but she didn't seem to be going away . . .

Knock knock knock. "Mage Verus!"

"Door's open," I called.

Silence.

"In or out, Symmaris." I dropped down onto the chair behind the counter and leant back. "Your choice."

There was a pause. I waited. Eventually, the door creaked open. Symmaris took a small step inside and looked around the inside of the shop, one hand on the door.

"Close it behind you, will you?" I said.

Symmaris didn't move. "I should remind you that there are people who know exactly where I am."

"Let me get this straight," I said. "You seriously think I'm going to murder you? In broad daylight in the middle of

Camden at eleven thirty on a Sunday morning? If you're this paranoid, why did you even come?"

"I wouldn't have had to, if—"

"Close the door, will you? There's a draft."

Symmaris hesitated, then—with obvious reluctance—closed the door behind her. She turned the handle a few times both before and after she did so, checking to see if it would lock. I rolled my eyes.

Symmaris walked forward. She was wearing an impractical-looking pair of high heels that made her sway slightly as she walked, and as she took each step the tips of the heels clicked on my floor. I stayed sitting in the chair, leaning back against the wall. It was a bad posture for responding to attacks, but I'd already scanned the futures and I was pretty sure that wasn't going to happen. People who are considering violence have a distinctive signature in their futures, and from Symmaris's potential responses, I'd pegged her as the kind who ran away from danger rather than towards it.

Symmaris stopped some distance from the counter.

"I tried calling your shop," she said. "It didn't go through."

"I don't keep the landline plugged in." Any number that Symmaris would likely have found would have been a fake one, but I didn't see any need to inform her of that.

"You could leave a mobile number."

"You're under the mistaken impression that I *want* to be answering phone calls from random strangers."

"The number I found was from the Council list."

"I don't want to be answering phone calls from the Council, either."

"You can't just do that."

"I don't see why not," I said. "People know where my shop is. If they can't be bothered to make the trip to talk to me in person, then it probably wasn't anything very important."

"Well, maybe if you'd been properly listed I wouldn't have had to ask Redman to go talk to you!"

"I notice that even you don't call him 'Wolf,'" I said dryly. "But yes, I'm glad you brought up that subject. Why don't you explain to me why you tried to get those nice young men to 'send me a message' by breaking my bones?"

"I didn't," Symmaris insisted. "Yes, he was supposed to be delivering a message, but he was only supposed to talk to you. I *specifically* told him to talk. And I didn't tell him anything about bringing anyone else."

"Well, congratulations." I leant forward off the wall and clasped my hands in front of me on the desk. "You've got my attention."

Symmaris looked at me, then away. She took a step closer to the shelves at the centre of the shop and started nervously fiddling with the crystal balls. "I know about Drakh's operation," she said.

"Oh God." I looked skywards. "Not you as well."

"I'm not going to ask what he's looking for," Symmaris said quickly. "I don't know anything about that."

"That makes two of us."

"And I'm not saying anything about . . . any decisions you might or might not have made about getting involved in that." Symmaris carefully didn't look at me. She picked up one of the crystal balls, swapping it with its neighbour so that they were lined up in ascending order of size. She paused, then pushed it a tiny fraction back to bring it into line. "I understand it would be very difficult to say no."

"I'm not working for Richard."

"But you can't do it." Symmaris seemed to brace herself and turned back to me. "We can't afford that. We *absolutely* can't afford that. You know how much power Morden's been getting. He hasn't even had his seat for a year and he's more influential than anyone else on the Junior Council. If this keeps going, he's going to have a Senior Council seat himself. Whatever Drakh is doing, it's going to increase the power of the Dark mages even further. It can't go through."

"And what exactly do you expect me to do about it?"

"Don't help Drakh," Symmaris said. "Stay out of this."

"That's pretty much exactly what I'm doing."

"I mean it," Symmaris insisted. "You can't get involved."

"I am not getting involved."

"You don't have to pretend. Obviously, you're in a difficult position, but . . ."

"Oh, good God." I leant back and put my hands over my eyes. "You're not listening to a single word I say, are you?"

Symmaris was silent.

I dropped my hands and looked at her. "What is it going to take to convince you that I'm not working for Richard?"

"Put yourself in Keeper custody," Symmaris said instantly. "Just until all this is over."

I stared at her. "That," I said at last, "is possibly the stupidest suggestion I have ever heard."

"It's the only way. Look, no one is going to believe you're not involved with Drakh."

"Apparently not, if they're all like you."

"It's the best way to prove your good intentions. I mean, if you did that, it would be physically impossible to—"

"I am not putting myself into custody," I said clearly.

"Then leave," Symmaris said. "Go to another country, a shadow realm, something like that. Somewhere completely removed from here until this all dies down."

"I *really* do not have time for this right now."

"It's the only way! If you're not going to let the Keepers take you in, then you need to prove that you're not involved."

"Prove to who?"

"To the Light mages," Symmaris said. "Look, you don't understand. Tensions are very high right now. It's a very dangerous situation. There are some people who think they need to fight. Even if you're not doing anything wrong, they're going to think you are, even if no one tells them to."

"Then maybe you should go back and explain to them that I'm *not* doing anything wrong," I said. "My leaving the country or going into custody is not going to happen. But I'd do either of those things before getting involved in any way with Richard Drakh. Understand?"

Symmaris didn't answer.

"I said, do you understand?"

"Yes," Symmaris said unwillingly.

"Then I would appreciate it very much if you could go

back to your bosses, or your associates, or whoever these 'people' that you're so concerned about are, and tell them what I've just told you. They leave me alone, I'll leave them alone. That's how my relationship with the Council has gone for most of my life, and frankly, I think it's worked pretty well so far. All right?"

Symmaris didn't meet my eyes.

"All right?" I repeated.

"Okay," Symmaris said. "I'll tell them."

"Good. Is there anything else?"

Symmaris shook her head.

"Then if you don't mind, I've got work to do."

"All right," Symmaris said. She walked to the door, glancing over her shoulder. I could tell from her stance that her shoulder blades were tense, and I wondered if she was expecting an attack on the way out. She opened the door, letting a final gust of cold air into the shop, then shut it behind her.

I sat at the counter with a frown, tapping my fingers on the wooden surface. This was the third time inside twenty-four hours that someone had brought up what Richard was doing. And if both Chalice and Symmaris knew, it was a safe bet that soon everyone else would too.

It bothered me that I'd had to learn about this from them. I'd told Luna only a couple of hours ago that our group knew more about Richard than anyone else. It was starting to look as though I'd overestimated. It was true that we hadn't run any active operations for a few weeks. Maybe something had changed . . .

No. There should have been signs. I got up and headed upstairs, then once I was back in my room I started going through my papers. Most of the notes we had on Richard were political. Details of his alliances with Dark mages, rumours on his alliance with Morden. But there had been something . . .

There. Tucked away inside a red folder were three sheets of paper, cracked and dirty. I pulled them out and skimmed them; the writing was in Arabic, but there was a translation paper-clipped to the back. We'd brought the sheets back from Syria at the beginning of the year. The rubbings on the paper were inscriptions from some kind of storage box. Richard had taken the box, and whatever had been inside. It hadn't been the only time, either; we'd learned a couple of months later that he'd made another trip to a location just a few hundred miles away in Turkey.

We'd spent some time trying to figure out just what Richard had been after. It had been an odd anomaly: nearly everything else Richard had been doing seemed to relate to gaining political power in Britain. Why would he be suddenly interested in old Middle Eastern artefacts? There was nothing strange about him paying attention to these kinds of archaeological projects—a lot of mages do that, you never know when something useful is going to turn up—but Richard's activities seemed weirdly specific. It was as though he was looking for something, and that worried me. The box in question had apparently dated back to a Byzantine magical tradition called the Heraclians who'd been heavily associated with magical creatures, but we hadn't been able to learn why Richard would care.

I shook my head and replaced the folder, then shut the drawer. This wasn't my priority right now. I needed to survive this death sentence; once that was done, then maybe I could worry about Richard. What I *should* be worrying about was the fact that a significant number of Light mages apparently believed that I was helping Richard. The attack last night might not be the only one.

I wondered if Symmaris would be able to convince them I was telling the truth. Somehow, I doubted it. She didn't strike me as an especially reliable ally.

⁙⁙⁙⁙⁙⁙

It wasn't until after sunset that Variam rang. "Hey, Alex." He sounded tired. "It's done."

"You put it through?"

"Just got back to Edinburgh. Been a long day."

"How did it go?"

"Well, we found the dean," Variam said. "He, uh, wasn't

expecting visitors. We had to do some convincing, but it worked out. We put in the petition for Landis to take over as sponsors for me and Anne. Landis knows the dean from way back and he smoothed it over. He promised it'd be done by the end of the week."

"That had better be in calendar-speak, not politician-speak. Because if Friday rolls around and they say, 'Oh, sorry, something's come up, we'll have it done by Monday' . . ."

"Yeah, we're on it," Variam said. "We were talking about—" There was a commotion in the background and Variam addressed someone away from the phone. "I said I'd tell him!"

"Vari?"

"I think Luna wants to talk to you," Variam said. "Talk soon, all right?"

"Okay."

There were sounds of movement, followed by a clunk, then Luna's voice. "Alex?"

"Hey, Luna," I said. "Please tell me you didn't aggravate anyone important."

"Well, it wasn't like we had a choice. The guy wouldn't let us in, and . . ."

I sighed. "Did you get a date for your test?"

"Yeah. My journeyman test is this Friday at ten."

I let myself relax a little. "Good."

"Listen, I kind of need to go," Luna said. "There's some social thing that Landis is going to. There are mages who do stuff with the program committees, and Variam said . . . well, anyway. You'll stop by to check in with Chalice, right?"

"I will."

"Okay. Oh, wait, just a sec."

There was another rustle. I waited a few seconds, then I heard Anne's soft voice. "Hello?"

"Hey, you," I said. "Did they treat you okay?"

"It wasn't too bad," Anne said. "At least they listened."

"Going to the party?"

"I don't think that'd be a good idea."

"You don't have to let them shut you out all the time," I said. "I know the Light mages don't trust you, but . . ."

"Isn't the idea for Vari and Luna to make a good impression?" Anne said. "I don't think having me around would help."

I sighed. She was probably right. Anne is one of the few mages I know that the Council trusts even less than me. "What about you?" Anne asked.

"What? Oh. Still waiting on Talisid. I need to be there if he calls."

Anne hesitated. "I could come over."

"Eh," I said. "It's okay. You look after yourself."

"Will you be okay on your own? Luna told me about last night . . ."

"I'm used to it. Safe trip back."

"You stay safe, too."

⁞ ⁞ ⁞ ⁞ ⁞

With Anne's, Variam's, and Luna's problems settled for the moment, I was at a loose end. I still needed to prepare some escape routes just in case worst came to worst, but looking into the future in which I sat at home and did nothing, I could tell that the chances of Talisid calling were a possibility but not a certainty. Which was pretty much the worst possible result from an informational point of view. If Talisid wasn't going to get in touch, I could leave the house and spend the evening shopping for gate stones. If he *was* going to get in touch, I could narrow down the time he'd do it and get other stuff done before and after. But with the futures uncertain, I just had to sit around and wait. It's like that annoying situation where you're getting a package delivered, but you don't know when, and you can't leave the house in case the guy shows up while you're out. Or at least it would be, if postal delivery companies were in the habit of sending you mail telling you how long you've got to live. With nothing else to do, I waited.

I've never liked waiting. It would probably surprise most people—from an outside perspective, waiting is something I do a lot. But there's a difference between waiting for something you're in control of, and waiting for something you're not. There was absolutely nothing I could do to influence Talisid's actions or the decisions of the people he spoke to. If he rang me up and told me that it was a no-go, that the votes weren't getting changed, then that was it. I had no illusions that I could stand up to the Keepers if they seriously decided to hunt me down. I'd have to flee the country or die.

I found myself wishing that I'd taken Anne up on her offer. It was selfish—there wouldn't have been anything for her to do except sit around, and she probably had more important things to do with her time. Still, it would make me feel better.

I looked into the future yet again to see if I could catch some snatches of conversation from the possibilities where Talisid called me, and couldn't see any. Someone else was going to show up before I could wait long enough for there to be a realistic chance of Talisid calling. I looked towards the door and waited until I heard a rustle of movement. "I know you're there, Hermes."

A black nose poked around the edge of the door, followed by a vulpine muzzle. Hermes walked into the room with a leisurely sort of air. "You know, one of these days I'm going to have to figure out how you keep getting in," I said. "If you're blinking to the spot in the storeroom, how are you getting through a locked door?"

Hermes gave me a quizzical look.

"It's not that I mind you showing up. Though you might be safer giving me a wider berth for a while."

Hermes sat back on his hind legs.

I shook my head. "Why *do* you stick around? I know we feed you, but it's not like you need it. And you help out with things like last night. It's not as though you owe me anything. I do appreciate it, but . . . why?"

Hermes tilted his head, then got up, walked to the kitchen, and looked back.

I looked at Hermes curiously. "You want me to follow?"

He blinked at me.

I followed Hermes through the kitchen and to the door leading out to the balcony. Hermes sat and looked up at the handle. I got my coat, then opened the door and stepped out into the winter night.

Hermes blinked out of existence, vanishing from sight. From the flicker of space magic above, I knew he'd teleported onto the top of the building. I climbed up the ladder to find him sitting on the edge of the roof, looking out over the city. I walked up next to the fox and followed his gaze.

I love the view from the top of my flat. The streets around my part of Camden are densely packed enough that standing this high, you can barely see any ground. Instead you see rooftops: peaked roofs, tiled roofs, and the flat rectangles of the apartment blocks, their ventilators puffing smoke into the cold sky. All around, a forest of aerials and chimneys rise up, built ten or twenty or fifty years ago by nameless craftsmen and abandoned to the air. Ever since I was young, rooftops always felt like a secret world to me, parallel to the city and yet apart from it, forgotten by all but a few. When I'd been deciding whether to take over this shop, whether to move in, I think it was this view that convinced me. It wasn't until after I'd climbed up to this spot that I did it.

I realised suddenly that I loved it here. Not just this place, but everything it represented: my shop, the city, the people around it. At some point, the shop and the flat above it had become something more than the place where I lived. It had become my home, and I'd stayed here and weathered all the storms that had come to pass. Standing up on the roof, I could see the section that had been replaced two years before, when the Nightstalkers had blasted through with an explosive charge. I'd survived, and fought, and won, and had the roof rebuilt and reinforced with steel. But none of that would protect me from the Council if they turned against me.

Could I bear to just run away? Uproot myself, flee to another country, leave behind everyone and everything I cared for? All of a sudden I wasn't so sure. Catch a wild animal, take it to a new climate and environment and let it go, and most of the time it doesn't survive.

I didn't want to leave. But would I have a choice?

I stayed up there in the darkness, growing colder and

colder, watching the lights of the city flicker and change and listening to the cars and trains rumble by. Finally when I began to shiver I turned and went back down. Hermes followed me. Once he was back inside my flat, he jumped up onto the armchair, curled up, and went to sleep.

I stayed up waiting for Talisid until the last possible futures of him calling that night had thinned away to nothing. At last, I went to bed. I slept poorly, and started awake several times, searching the futures for danger, but the night was silent and empty.

chapter 4

Morning. Five days until my sentence went through.

The chime of the communicator pulled me out of a confusing dream, and I stumbled to my feet and pulled on my trousers, still half asleep. I splashed water on my face, dragged a comb through my hair, and took a few seconds to run through the most probable paths the conversation could go. It was going to be good news and bad. Once I was as alert as I was going to get, I activated the focus.

Talisid's image materialised on the coffee table. "Verus," Talisid said. "Are you in London?"

"Haven't fled the country yet, if that's what you're asking."

"There's good news and bad," Talisid said. "Good news first. Druss the Red has voted against Levistus's proposal."

"Your work?"

"I'd like to take credit, but no."

"I guess I'll send him a thank-you note if I live out the week. What's the bad news?"

"Spire has declined to meet with you. Officially, he's retiring to his family residence over the Christmas season and is unavailable for comment. Unofficially, I've been led to understand that he is staying neutral. He won't support you, but neither will he vote against you."

"Three to two. So it all comes down to the last vote."

"To Undaaris, yes."

"Has he replied?" I said. I knew what Talisid was going to say, but conversations go a lot smoother when you don't preempt the other guy.

"Undaaris has agreed to meet with you," Talisid said. "I believe he spent a good part of yesterday making up his mind. He hasn't made any commitments, but I would consider his agreement to meet a positive sign."

"So I'm going to have to convince him to vote in my favour," I said. "And whatever I tell him, it's going to have to be more convincing than whatever arguments Levistus has made already."

"Or might make in the future, yes."

"Any suggestions for what I could trade him?"

"How familiar are you with Senior Council politics?"

"Not very."

"Out of the seven members of the Senior Council, Bahamus and Sal Sarque are affiliated with the Guardians," Talisid said. "Levistus and Alma are strongly associated with the Directors. Traditionally, those two pairs have tended to disagree, but Levistus has recently taken a strong stance opposing further Dark encroachment. In doing so, he's won over Sarque. Bahamus and Sarque are divided on this issue, and Druss opposes Levistus in almost all areas, but still, that gives Levistus a reasonably consistent voting advantage of three to two. Spire and Undaaris are the swing votes. Spire leans neutral and independent. Undaaris is a Centrist."

"I thought Levistus had the support of the Centrists."

"Up to a point," Talisid said. "Many of the Centrists are coming round to the Unity Bloc's way of thinking. They're generally opposed to hostile action against Dark mages, and they've been disagreeing with Levistus and Sarque's more aggressive stance. Undaaris isn't going to want to upset his own faction."

"If he was that keen on not upsetting them, wouldn't he have voted against the proposal already?"

"A year ago, he probably would have, but over the past few months Undaaris has been accused of being overly soft on Dark mages and their violations of the Concord. The Crusaders are pressuring him to show strength."

I should probably point out here that if you're finding this confusing, it's not just you. Council politics are complicated as hell—Light mages grow up with it, but I'm not a Light mage. One of the big issues that divides the Council is the question of how they should treat Dark mages. The Unity Bloc are the closest you can get to a "pro-Dark" faction. The Centrists mostly just want to maintain the status quo, though they can be swayed. The Guardians are opposed to Dark mages, but they do so reactively; they try to protect anyone who might get hurt by Dark mages, but they don't advocate attacks unless provoked. Talisid is a member of the Guardian faction, and while we've had our disagreements, I've found his beliefs fairly compatible with mine.

But the mention of the Crusaders worried me. The Crusaders are the most aggressively anti-Dark of all the Light factions, and the most militant. They also have a zero-tolerance policy when it comes to rogues; as far as they're concerned, once a Dark mage, always a Dark mage. In the past, I'd mostly been off their radar—too small-time for them to care about—but the Crusaders had been utterly furious about Morden being raised to the Junior Council, and there had been reports since Morden's appointment of Crusader attacks on Dark mages and suspected Dark sympathisers. I was pretty sure that given the choice, they'd be quite happy to see me dead.

"Which brings us to you," Talisid said. "Just recently, there have been rumours concerning your old master. I don't know if you've heard, but—"

"But he has something planned. Yes, I've heard. In fact, it seems to be all anybody wants to talk to me about. How does this help?"

"From what I've heard, the Council are preparing a

response," Talisid said. "If you can give Undaaris something that he could bring to the Guardians to prove his credentials, it would favourably dispose him towards you."

"What do you mean, prove his credentials?"

"I mean Undaaris wants to get in the Guardians' good books. You scratch his back, he'll scratch yours."

"You mean he *might* scratch mine. Isn't that a pretty thin thread?"

"These are Senior Council members," Talisid said. "I'm afraid that making yourself agreeable is your best chance."

"Being agreeable isn't really one of my specialities."

"No, but you've demonstrated some talent for negotiation. I suggest you use it." Talisid shrugged. "That's all I have."

It wasn't as though I had much choice. "When's the meeting?"

"Ten o'clock. They're delivering you a gate stone."

"Guess I'll go get dressed."

"Good luck. I'll be in touch if I learn more."

Talisid hung up. I looked around and sighed. *Well, at least I'm awake.*

ı ı ı ı ı ı ı ı ı

I spent a while deciding what to wear. People in the Council tend to wear suits for day-to-day work, and mage robes for formal ceremonies. Normally I dress much more casually, and given the choice I'd have preferred to go into the meeting in a shirt and jeans, but it would have sent the wrong message—I was trying to look like a law-abiding member of magical society. In the end I pulled my solitary business suit out from the back of the wardrobe, took it out of its plastic covering, then put it on without much enthusiasm. Once I was done I took a look at myself in the mirror. Dark blue suit hanging off an angular figure, spiky and slightly too-long hair mostly combed back over a pair of dark watchful eyes. I studied the image for a while, trying to figure out how I'd appear to an outside observer. I didn't think I looked much like a Dark mage, but I definitely didn't look like a Light one, either. I waited until 9:50, then used the gate stone.

। । । । । । । ।

Being a diviner has its ups and downs, but at least you don't get caught off guard very often.

The gate took me into a small wood-panelled room, with chandelier lights and pictures mounted on the walls. The air was warmer than my flat. It wasn't flashy, but there was a definite sense that it belonged to someone important. From prior research, I'd learned that Undaaris's primary residence was in Westminster. A quick check through the futures confirmed that that was where I was now.

Someone cleared their throat behind me. "Hello, Alex."

"Lyle," I said, turning. "Long time."

The man standing behind me was the same age as me, though a little shorter. His features were a touch softer and less healthy than I remembered—he hadn't put on weight, but he didn't look as though he'd been getting much exercise. He wore a grey suit that looked noticeably more expensive than mine. "It has been, hasn't it?" Lyle said.

Lyle and I had been friends once, back when we were both apprentices—me to Richard, Lyle to a Light mage. When my apprenticeship blew up, we'd dropped out of contact. Lyle had built himself a career in the political world, while I'd lived as an independent mage, out on my own.

My choice of friends hadn't been very good in those days. I suppose Lyle had never been actually evil, which put him a step ahead of most of the mages I'd met during my time with Richard, but while Lyle had been entertaining, he'd never been particularly trustworthy. When I'd really needed him, he'd hung me out to dry.

All of this flashed through my head in less than a second. "So you're working for Undaaris now?" I asked. I tried to make my voice pleasant. "Or is this a onetime thing?"

"No, I've been acting as Undaaris's secretary. Though it's more like being his second, really. Scheduling and appointments and all that sort of stuff."

"To a Senior Councillor, huh? Going up in the world."

Lyle laughed. "Well, I'll go tell Undaaris you've arrived.

If you could just wait here." He disappeared through the door, leaving me alone in the room. I wondered if that conversation had sounded as forced to him as it had to me.

Thinking about that made me remember the last member of the Light Council that Lyle had been working for, namely Levistus. Lyle had been the one to introduce me to Levistus, thus indirectly starting off the whole chain of events leading to the death sentence I was fighting right now. I wondered whether Lyle remembered it the same way.

Traditionally Council members like to keep applicants hanging around for a while, the better to emphasise how valuable their time is. I suspected that this would be an exception to the rule and that Undaaris would want me in and out as quickly as possible. I was right: Lyle reappeared in only a few minutes and ushered me out into a hallway, up a set of stairs, and through a door. It led into a comfortable-looking study, and standing behind the desk, waiting to greet me, was Undaaris.

Undaaris was white-haired and slim. From my research I knew that he was over sixty, but he didn't look it: he was straight-backed and handsome, and but for his hair could have passed for forty at the most. Life magic treatments; probably the only reason he hadn't had his hair recoloured too had been to make an impression. He was a water mage, though like most Council politicians, there were rumours that he had some mind abilities as well. It wasn't the first time I'd seen Undaaris, but it was the first time I'd been up close.

"Ah, Mage Verus!" Undaaris came bustling around the desk to shake my hand. "Glad you could make it."

"Councillor," I said. I'm not very good at acting respectful, but I did my best. "Thank you for agreeing to see me."

"Not at all, not at all. Can I offer you something to drink? Tea, coffee?"

"I appreciate the offer, but I'm a little preoccupied at the moment."

"Of course, of course." Undaaris glanced at Lyle, who murmured something and disappeared out the door, closing it behind him and leaving the two of us alone.

The last time I'd been alone in a room with a Council member it hadn't gone well. I fought off the impulse to check Undaaris's defences by looking into the futures in which I attacked him—I needed to focus. "Well then," Undaaris said. He sat down behind his desk. "I understand there was something you wanted to discuss?"

"Yes." I sat in one of the armchairs. "It's to do with last Saturday's resolution."

"Yes, well," Undaaris said. "You do understand that any information pertaining to closed Council meetings is strictly confidential."

"I'm aware of that," I said. "However, given the subject of this particular resolution, it doesn't seem like a very good idea for me to wait until it's made official."

"It's still a little irregular . . ."

I looked at Undaaris with raised eyebrows.

Undaaris coughed. "But given the circumstances, I suppose it's understandable."

"I'm under a death sentence." I kept my voice level. "Regularity isn't my foremost concern."

Undaaris looked uncomfortable. "I can't confirm or deny anything along those lines."

"And I assume you can't confirm or deny that the current state of the votes is three to two, either."

"I thought it was three to one?"

"Druss."

"Oh, yes. He would, wouldn't he?"

I waited.

"Well, in that case—hypothetically—you should only need one more vote, yes?" Undaaris said. "Have you considered Spire? He's rather sympathetic to independent mages such as yourself."

"Spire's abstaining."

"And you know that for sure?" I didn't answer and Undaaris sighed. "You seem better informed than I am. These leaks are becoming quite troublesome. I know they're the way we do business, but it would be nice if closed meetings could actually stay secret."

So I could be sentenced without knowing anything about it? "So, aside from Spire, the only one yet to vote is you."

"Ah." Undaaris looked uncomfortable again. "Yes."

"Can you help me?" I asked.

"I'd very much like to, of course . . ."

"I'm not coming to you lightly," I said. "There isn't anyone else left."

Undaaris sighed. "I wish Levistus hadn't done this. I'd known he had his issues, but that resolution came as a complete surprise. And the timing . . ."

"I don't think the timing was an accident."

"No, perhaps not." Undaaris looked straight at me and clasped his hands on the desk. "This is placing me in a very difficult position."

I tried to look understanding.

"Levistus and Alma have been pressuring me over the Birkstead position. And Drakh's name has been coming up over and over again in the last few months. It's become a very sensitive issue. If I vote against this, then when it comes out, it's going to be spun as being soft on Dark mages again."

I had to bite back my response. *I'm so sorry my imminent death is making things inconvenient for you.* Instead I took a measured breath, then spoke once I was calm. "Voting against it could also be seen as a more measured response. Avoiding escalation."

"There is that." Undaaris sighed and tapped his fingers on the desk, then looked up. "Perhaps there might be a solution."

Undaaris was acting as though he'd had a new idea. I didn't believe it—the futures hadn't changed. He'd had this in mind since the beginning. "What did you have in mind?"

"The Keepers are planning an operation," Undaaris said. "I don't know the exact details—operational security is quite tight—but from what I've heard, it involves your old master in some way. I imagine they'd be very grateful for your assistance."

"Assuming they trusted me enough to let me come."

"Well, you're a Keeper auxiliary, aren't you?"

"True. How would this benefit you?"

"Well, it would be a show of good faith, wouldn't it? If you took part and the operation was a success, then they could hardly keep maintaining that you were a danger to the Council. You'd have shown that you'd left your old master entirely behind."

"I'd like to think I've done that already, but I take your point. And I assume you'd like me to make it known that you're the reason I'm joining?"

"Well, yes, that would help."

"And in exchange, you'd feel yourself able to vote against Levistus?"

"It's not quite as simple as that."

"It's pretty simple to me." I was managing to keep my voice calm, but it was difficult. "There's not much point in me helping the Keepers if I get executed at the end of the week. I agree to take on this job, and in exchange, you vote against the proposal. Deal?"

"If the mission is a *success*," Undaaris said. "If it turns out to be a failure, then, well . . ."

"Then they'll assume that it's because I betrayed them," I said. *Lovely. Well, it's not as though they can execute me twice.* "Fine. Then if the mission's a success, you'll vote against the proposal."

Undaaris sighed. "You drive a hard bargain, don't you?" He straightened. "All right."

I studied Undaaris. He looked back at me with an honest expression. "I guess we've got an agreement, then," I said.

"Indeed." Undaaris rose to shake my hand. "Best of luck."

⁀ ⁀ ⁀ ⁀ ⁀ ⁀ ⁀ ⁀ ⁀

Lyle was waiting in the hallway. "Did it go well?" he asked. "About how I was expecting," I said. "Do you know the details?"

"Well, just the basics," Lyle said. He moved to lead me towards the room where I'd arrived, and I followed. "Ah . . . did you take the assignment?"

"Didn't really have much choice." I hadn't bothered to

get the details. The Keepers would know more, and it wasn't as though there was anything he was realistically going to say that could make me turn him down. "How long's this been on for?"

"It's a bit of a rush job, really. We suddenly started hearing about it while we were still in America. They've been pressuring us for support."

"Did they ask for someone like me?"

"Er." Lyle opened the door to the waiting room. "Actually, that was my suggestion."

I looked at Lyle in surprise.

"Well, Talisid called. He'd been hoping to set up a meeting, but I wasn't sure if Undaaris was available, and we got to talking, and, well, it seemed like a possible solution. I hope."

I walked inside. "I see."

"You're not upset, are you?"

I leant back onto the table and shrugged. "Given your motives, it would seem a little ungrateful."

Lyle seemed about to go, then paused. "Is everything all right?"

"Lyle, I'm under a death sentence. I'm not going to be 'all right' until that's fixed."

"Oh. Yes."

I gave Lyle a nod. He started to turn away, then hesitated. "You know . . . when I introduced you to Levistus, it really wasn't . . . I was just trying to help."

I blinked. "Seriously?"

"Well . . . I mean, yes, the Council needed a diviner. And I'd been asked to find one, but . . . You seemed to think I was out to get you. I really wasn't. You'd been out on your own for so long, that was all. I mean, you're an excellent diviner, you always were, but you were spending all your time in that little shop, and it was such a waste. I really didn't expect it to turn out like this."

I stared at Lyle. He shifted uncomfortably. Probably he thought I was angry, but the truth was, I was just puzzled. I honestly didn't know what to say.

"I suppose what I'm trying to say is that I hope this goes better," Lyle said. "You know. Just to make up for things."

"Yeah." I paused. "Thanks."

Lyle nodded. "Well, then. I'll have them call you, shall I?" He closed the door behind him.

I stared after Lyle for a moment, then took out my gate stone to make the journey back.

Back home, the first thing I did was to get out my communicator and check that Lyle had been telling the truth. I didn't want to call Talisid over something so minor, so I looked into the futures where I did. It's hard to read details from future conversations—too much application of free will—but if you focus only on asking simple questions, and if the person you're talking to is sufficiently well disposed towards you to *answer* a simple question, then you can get reasonably reliable results. Somewhat to my surprise, I found that Talisid confirmed it. It really had been Lyle's idea.

It was a minor thing, really, but it still made me pause. When you're under pressure, it's easy to fall into thinking that everyone who's making your life difficult is a bad guy. The idea that all of this crap with Levistus might have started because Lyle was originally trying to do me a *favour* . . . well, it made things feel like less of a conspiracy and more like something else. Black comedy, maybe.

Of course, given how well his good intentions had worked out last time, it wasn't actually much of a reassurance that he might also have good intentions *this* time. I might have a plan of action, but I was very much aware of how many weak links it had. First, I had to be accepted for this mission. Then I had to not only make sure it was successful, but also make sure that I was seen to have made a sufficiently positive contribution. And even if I did all that, there was no guarantee that Undaaris would follow through on his end of the deal. He'd been fairly open about his reasons, but he was still a politician and I didn't have any good reason to trust the guy. A lot of steps; a lot of chances for things to go wrong.

But it wasn't as though I had much choice. I needed to get this resolution blocked, and Undaaris's offer was the only realistic chance I had.

I sighed, put the whole thing out of my mind, and looked into the future to see what would happen if I called Luna. Unsurprisingly, she was busy training with Chalice. I wanted to check in on her, but I figured she didn't really need any distractions. Instead I called Landis.

Landis picked up immediately. His image didn't appear above the disc; the ones Keepers get are audio-only. "Oh, hello, Verus." Landis sounded far too cheerful, but then he usually does. "I imagine you're looking for an update on Vari and his friend, hmm?"

"Actually, no," I said. "I heard there was some Keeper operation in the works. Wondered if you were free for a chat."

"You're getting yourself involved in that? Would have thought you had other things on your mind."

"Yeah, there's kind of a connection. I'll tell you about it in person."

"Well, ours not to reason why. Drop by and I'll put the kettle on."

                    ⋯⋯⋯⋯⋯

Landis lives in Edinburgh, in a tall stone house down a side alley. I found the right door and knocked; no answer. I tried the bell; it didn't work. After a brief glance through the futures I tried the handle. It opened into a dark hallway. I closed the door behind me and climbed the stairs.

Landis, unsurprisingly, was up in his workshop. I've visited his home a few times now and it seems to be his preferred room—Landis's hobby is magical items, particularly ones that explode or set things on fire, and he seems happiest when he's surrounded by his tools and toys. Right now he was in the corner, a tall man with sandy-brown hair, long arms and legs bent over something mounted on a workbench that was glowing with an orange-red light. "Verus!" Landis called without looking in my direction. "Have a seat, there's a good chap. I'll be just a tick."

I checked to see what would happen if I did, and caught an unlikely future of being scalded by a blast of steam. I walked over to the side wall and examined the source of the disturbance; it was roughly spherical, with steam hissing from a small chimney, and was radiating fire magic from the apparatus underneath. The metal sphere was hot enough to burn the skin off my hands. I had no idea what it was, but the nice thing about being a diviner is that you don't need to. I studied the futures for a second, then reached down and twisted a small axle sticking out from the base. The futures of the thing exploding vanished.

"There we go!" Landis straightened up and came across on bounding steps to shake my hand. "Delighted to see you again, Verus. Wish it were under better circumstances, but mere anarchy loosed upon the world and all that, eh? What are you up to with that?"

"Just making adjustments," I said. "Did you know this thing was about to burst open?"

"Really?" Landis bent down to study the apparatus from about six inches away, peering in with one eye closed, then slapped his forehead. "Goodness, you're quite right! Put the thing on when I heard you were coming and completely forgot. Vari usually does it but I've been deserted, sad to say. Younger generation and their flightiness."

"What does it do?" I asked curiously.

Landis blinked at me. "Makes tea, of course." He gave the container at the top a twist to make it come away, then began pouring out the contents into a pair of mugs, holding the metal sphere bare-handed. I wondered briefly how hot that sphere was, and decided it was probably over a hundred degrees. "Do you take milk or sugar? Can't remember for the life of me."

"Neither, thanks."

"Good man! Never trust a fellow who puts milk in his tea. Bad enough if they use the regular kind, but do you know some of them use the skimmed sort? Don't know what the world's coming to." Landis flopped down into one of the armchairs. "Right, then!"

I sat opposite, holding the mug carefully by the handle. "So, this job."

"Ah-ah!" Landis wagged a finger at me. "I've a bone to pick with you first. What's this I'm hearing about you and the Crusaders?"

"The what now?"

"I'm talking about your little tiff with a Mr. James Redman on the Heath a couple of nights ago. Or did it slip your mind?"

"You know about that?" I shook my head. "News travels fast."

"My dear boy, I was at Newbury last night and it was quite the topic of conversation. The detractors of the Crusader faction found it absolutely hilarious. Apparently you beat up all three of them with a dustbin lid?"

"No, I beat them up with a stick. The dustbin lid was for defence. They were Crusaders?"

"Not strictly speaking. Redman's for rent to the highest, and it wouldn't be very high. However"—Landis waved his finger—"the important part is that they were *perceived* to be with the Crusaders."

"Yeah, well, they can perceive whatever they like."

Landis frowned. "My dear boy, I'm not certain you're taking this seriously."

"They sent a dropout and a couple of tagalongs to whack me over the head with clubs," I said. "Quite honestly, no, I'm not taking them very seriously. I've had enemies who are considerably more threatening. Got one to worry about right now, in fact."

Landis looked at me with raised eyebrows.

"What?"

"Hmm."

"What do you mean, hmm?"

"How much do you know about the Crusader faction?"

"I pretty much stay away from them."

"Do they strike you as competent?"

"Not really," I said. "They seem to hate Dark mages and

aren't too picky about who makes the list. I get the feeling they aren't the sharpest knives in the drawer."

Landis sighed. "My dear chap."

"Okay, if there's something you want to say, let's hear it."

"This idea that the Crusaders are some separate group really is quite a misconception," Landis said. "They're simply the more militant wing of the Guardians. Now, I'll grant you that the more extreme ones are not exactly the keenest cutting implements in the storage facility, but when there's a threat that they perceive as serious, then the more capable ones are going to sit up and take notice. And when they do, watch out."

I shrugged. "I already had one come around to visit yesterday. Was more of a nuisance than a threat."

"Who?"

"Called herself Symmaris."

"Long black hair, jumpy type?"

"That's the one."

Landis nodded. "You're in trouble. Watch yourself."

"I'm pretty sure she was more scared of me."

"Verus, my lad, you're in the Council world now. You need to stop thinking like a Dark mage, bash-bash, who's-stronger, slice-'em-in-half. Of course Symmaris is scared of you—frightened little rabbit of a woman. Space mage who specialises in gates, nothing exceptional. But the people she talks to"—Landis raised a finger—"now *that* you should be concerning yourself with. It's not what you can do, it's who you know."

"Yeah, well, since I don't know all that many people, I'm not really sure how that's going to help. Can we focus on the stuff I can actually affect?"

Landis raised an eyebrow.

I sighed and passed a hand in front of my eyes. First Arachne, now Landis. "Sorry. Look, I'm under kind of a lot of stress at the moment. It's not that I don't get what you're saying, I just don't have enough attention to spare. How's the thing with Anne and Vari?"

"Well as can be expected, really," Landis said, accepting

the change of subject. "I had a powwow with Nigel; he's the fellow in charge of admissions. Promised he should be able to get Vari's name through."

"That's something, at least." My tea had cooled enough to drink and I took a sip. "Thanks for doing this. I really do appreciate it."

Landis waved a hand. "Not at all! I've always felt I owe you rather a debt for all the times you've helped Vari, don't you know. Become very fond of the lad. Was actually meaning to have a chat with him about his own journeyman tests one of these days, before all this blew up. Now that your apprentice is doing hers, I imagine that'll give Vari a kick up the behind to do it as well. He seems rather interested in her."

"Yeah, I've noticed." I straightened. "All right. What can you tell me about this mission?"

"Well then." Landis set down his cup and leant back with his hands behind his head. "As I understand it, this all came to light just a few days ago. You know the Council's increasingly concerned about Drakh, of course. Well, somehow or other, they became convinced that the bugger was trying to get hold of old weapons to bring down the Council with."

My memory flashed back to the notes in my desk. *A weapon?* "What kind?"

"Dashed if I know. Doubt they do either, to be frank. In any case, they're quite set on the idea that Drakh wants this one particular relic. Unfortunately for him, it's sealed up in a bubble with no access key, so that was the end of the matter, or so they thought. Except that now it turns out rumours of its sealed status were greatly exaggerated."

This was sounding like a familiar story. "Let me guess," I said. "They want a diviner to help them get inside."

"Actually, that's the interesting part," Landis said. "Apparently there's a particular time window where it opens and closes. Bigwigs just found out a couple of days back, and now they're scrambling to have a strike force ready to go. Seem convinced that Drakh is going to have his own team working to get inside as well."

"Do you think they're right?"

Landis shrugged. "Well, it's a Council intelligence report, so *caveat emptor* and all that. Still, better safe than sorry, eh? If it turns out he isn't after the thing, you can toodle along, help them out, and wander back home."

"Yeah, somehow I doubt it'll be quite that easy. Who's in charge, the Order of the Shield or the Order of the Star?"

"You'd think it'd be us, wouldn't you? But the Order of the Star wanted it for themselves. Jurisdiction, et cetera, et cetera. They'll be calling us in as and when."

The Order of the Star are the Keepers who are supposed to deal with cases directly involving other mages. They're the largest of the orders, but they're still not all that big and I'd met most of them over the past year. "Is Caldera involved?"

"Who do you think's been telling me everything?" Landis gave me a nod. "Expect I'll be seeing you at Keeper HQ. Watch your back till then."

chapter 5

gated back to London. There was a message on my phone from Caldera telling me to report to Keeper HQ tomorrow morning. From the way she phrased it, I had the feeling it wasn't going to be a short trip.

I walked from my storeroom to the front of the shop and dropped into the chair behind the counter. What Landis had told me was bothering me, especially on top of Arachne's warnings from the night before last, and more and more I was feeling as though I was out of my depth. The uncomfortable truth is that in a lot of ways I'm more of a Dark mage than a Light one. I understand threats and the use of force. But things like networking and politics . . . those aren't things I know how to do, not well. I can get by, but I always seem to make enemies.

Arachne had told me that the way I was living was untenable. Staying independent, trying to live apart from the power blocs. There were reasons I'd made the choices I had, and at the time they'd seemed good, but the simple truth was that if I'd acted more like Sonder, gone along with the Council and not rocked the boat, then none of this would be happening.

Levistus wouldn't be after me, and Symmaris wouldn't have come knocking on my door yesterday. I wanted to blame the Light mages, but was it really because of them? Or was it because they saw something in me that really *was* there? Maybe the reason the Council kept treating me like a Dark mage was that, at some level, they were right.

What I was sure of was that right now things were falling apart. I couldn't keep this up, not for long. Even if I survived Levistus's current plot, what was to stop him from simply doing it again? Levistus's power was in his status and his political position, and I had absolutely no way to fight back against that. I had to win every single time; he only had to win once.

A knocking sound brought me out of my reverie. I looked up to see someone tapping on the glass. A woman, with a child by her side and a man behind her. The woman was looking at me; she'd obviously spotted me through the window. She mouthed something.

I looked back curiously. I couldn't figure out what she was saying. She mouthed again, and pointed at the door.

I got up, crossed the shop floor, and opened the door into the cold winter air. "Oh, thank you so much," the woman said in an American accent. "Are you open?"

"Not exactly . . ."

"I'm so sorry, it's just we saw those little figurines on the shelf and they just look *amazing*. We're flying back tomorrow and they'd just make the perfect Christmas present. Could we just come inside? We'll be five minutes, I promise."

I looked between the woman, man, and child, scanning through the futures. No magic. They were normals. A completely ordinary family.

"Please?" the woman asked with a hopeful smile.

I opened my mouth to say no and hesitated. *An ordinary family . . .* "Sure," I said. "Come on in."

⁙⁙⁙⁙⁙

The five minutes turned into fifteen. By the time the woman had made her purchases and finished her thank-yous and left, more customers had followed her in. And by the time those ones were gone, more had come to replace them.

I should probably have shooed them out. I had work to do—researching Symmaris, laying escape plans, trying to figure out ways to defeat a Council resolution. For some reason, though, I didn't want to. I didn't understand Light politics, and I didn't understand the Crusaders or the Council or how I should be dealing with things right now. But this I understood. Dealing with ordinary people, selling them things and answering their sometimes-relevant, mostly silly questions. At another time it might have annoyed me, but right now, this was something I needed. It felt like a stable point in a world that was spinning out of my control.

The customers kept coming, young and old, families and locals and tourists. A handful had some idea what they were talking about, but they were fewer than usual. It was only three days to Christmas, and most of the people were looking for novelties and stocking fillers. Outside, the sun set and the sky faded from blue to grey to black. The streetlights came on one by one, lighting up the buildings in fluorescent orange. Five o'clock passed, then five thirty. I walked to the door and flipped the sign from *OPEN* to *CLOSED*, then stood by the exit, turning away new customers, waiting for the ones still inside to make their purchases and leave. The numbers dwindled; six, then three, then two.

At last only one person was left: a girl, maybe fourteen or fifteen. She was standing by the magic item section, just on this side of the rope, and was staring at something on the shelves. "Hey, there," I said. "We're closing up for the night."

"Oh," the girl said. "Okay." She didn't move.

I recognised the way she was standing and the shape of her futures. She'd been hanging back so that she could get me alone. It happens often enough that I'm used to it; lots of people are afraid that if they talk about magic where they can be overheard, they'll be seen as crazy. They're usually right. "Something I can help you with?"

"Is it . . ." The girl hesitated. "Is it true you sell focus items?"

"Just like it says on the sign," I said. *Focus* is an obscure enough term that I can put it up on the front of my shop without getting hassled.

The girl reached across the rope to touch something on the magic item shelves. "Is that what this is?"

I crossed the shop floor to see what she was looking at. Her fingers were resting on a twisted wand of rowan wood, maybe eight inches long. "Good eye."

"What does it do?"

I raised my eyebrows. "Depends who's using it."

The girl gave me an uncertain look. She was small, five feet at most, with light brown skin and curly black hair. The futures shifted and I could tell she was trying to figure out what to say. "Is it true what they say about you?"

"Some of the things. You'll have to be more specific."

She hesitated. "Does your magic actually work?"

I blinked at her. "You're new at this, aren't you?"

The girl looked embarrassed. "Look," I said. "Why don't you show me what you can do? I might be able to help."

Futures flickered, there and gone. In most, the girl said something and did nothing. But in a few—just a few—she chose to trust me, and in those futures I saw her standing before me, concentrating, a tiny pearl of blue light hovering in the palm of her hand. It was only a glimpse, and then it was gone, the futures vanishing as she turned down the other path. But it was enough.

"Sorry." She cast her eyes down, took a step towards the door. "I've got to go."

"Water magic, huh?" I said. "How many times have you been able to call up that blue light?"

The girl had been halfway to the door; now she froze. She turned and stared at me, eyes wide.

I checked the futures. "Five?"

The girl jumped. "Relax," I said. "I'm not reading your mind."

"How did . . . ?" She swallowed. She didn't finish the sentence, but I could tell she was afraid.

I shook my head. "You really *are* new. No one's taught you, have they? You have no idea what's going on."

The girl didn't answer. She didn't need to. "Okay," I said. I walked away from her, back behind the counter, and sat down. "Go lock the door—there's a switch below the handle. Then grab that chair and bring it over."

The girl hesitated, and I watched to see what she'd do. It wasn't the first time I'd been in this sort of situation, and I'd found through trial and error that the best approach is to ask the kid in question to do these things themselves. Partly it's to reassure them that they can get away if they want to, but a lot of it is forcing them to make the decision: trust me, or not? The futures shifted, then settled. She did as I asked, then sat down in the spare chair in front of the counter, hands clasped in front of her.

"Okay," I began. "Let's start at the beginning. You can think of magical talent as a pyramid. The bottom of the pyramid, and the largest section, are the normals. After that you have sensitives, then adepts, then mages . . ."

＊ ＊ ＊ ＊ ＊ ＊ ＊ ＊ ＊

We talked for nearly two hours. I told her about the basics of how magic worked, exercises to develop it further, what she could expect as she grew into her power, whether she'd turn into an adept or a mage, and how to tell the difference. Then I gave her a brief rundown on magical society: the Concord, Light mages and Dark, and how they worked. Most of all, I told her how important it was not to draw the wrong kind of attention. Novices are vulnerable, and the younger they are, the more danger they're in if they're noticed.

At last I noticed that the girl's eyes were drooping. She was still trying to pay attention, but she was exhausted. She'd probably keyed herself up for this conversation, working herself up to a state of nervous tension, and now the aftereffects were kicking in. "That's enough for now," I said. "You know the basics. Enough to keep you alive, as long as you don't do anything stupid."

The girl nodded and I could sense her relief. "What should I do now?"

I tore a note from the pad on the desk and started writing on it. "This is the name and number of a mage I know who lives here in London." I pushed the note over. "Keep practising for a few weeks, and then when you're more confident, give her a call. She might be able to find you a teacher and she might not, but either way, she won't do anything you don't want her to. She takes confidentiality seriously."

The girl took the paper. "You'd better get home," I told her.

The girl nodded and stood up. She got to the door, unlocked it, paused, then turned back to me. "Why are you doing this?"

"Doing what?"

"You said Dark mages are out for themselves," the girl said. "And Light mages just care about following the rules."

"Pretty much."

"Then why are you helping?"

I shrugged. "Somebody has to."

The girl gave me an odd look, as though she was trying to figure out what I meant. "Okay," she said. "Bye." She paused. "Thanks."

"You're welcome." The girl opened the door and disappeared out into the street.

I watched her go through the futures, then stirred and rose to my feet. I locked the door, pulled down the shutters, and cleaned the counter. Only as I took a last look around before switching off the lights did I realise that the uneasy feeling I'd had before was gone.

How many people like that girl had come into my shop over the years? Hundreds, maybe thousands. All looking for something, help or advice or direction. Sure, most of the customers who visit my shop don't get anything out of it but a funny story and a souvenir, but for the young adepts and mages, it's not funny. It's deadly serious, and what they learn can make all the difference in the world.

I spend a lot of time and energy protecting myself against people who are trying to hurt me. When you do that, it's easy to focus on it more than you really ought to. And amongst other mages, it's mostly the destructive things I've done that I'm remembered for: the Dark mage I studied under, the people I've killed in combat. That's what I'm associated with, and that was why I was being targeted now.

But maybe at the end of the day, the most important things I'd done with my life wouldn't end up being the battles, or the escapes, or the times I've survived against the odds. It'd end up being little things like the meeting with that girl. She'd never told me her name, and there was a good chance I'd never see her again, but the couple of hours I'd just spent had made a difference.

Maybe that wasn't such a terrible legacy to leave behind.

I switched off the lights and went to check in on Luna.

ı ı ı ı ı ı ı ı ı

I took a bus to Islington and walked the rest of the way to the gym, shivering slightly in the cold. Most of the building was dark but I could see light from a couple of top-floor windows. The front door was locked and I had to circle around and enter from the side.

Inside, the building was badly lit and cold. There was no heating, and in the faint light filtering in from the street, I could see my breath in the air. Looking through the futures, I could sense people above, and I started climbing the stairs. As I ascended, I began to hear sounds: stamping feet and the *whoosh* of heated air. It sounded like a fight, but I knew it wasn't combat. The stairs ended in a landing and a hallway, with several open doors. Light was spilling through one of them, and as I approached I saw Chalice silhouetted through the doorway, leaning against the wall. She glanced in my direction, then turned back to the source of the noise. From within the room I felt a surge of fire magic, followed a second later by a rush of movement. I crossed to the doorway and looked inside.

The gym was tall, with high windows looking out onto the night sky. The floor was clear, and standing at the centre were Luna and Variam. Luna was wearing her exercise clothes, and

Variam was wearing the black warded cloth he uses for fights. Both were in fighting stances, and they seemed to be so focused on each other that they hadn't noticed my arrival. I kept quiet, watching.

Luna stepped sideways, circling. She had her whip out, and in my magesight I could see the lash curling away behind her, a line of silver-grey mist, twisting with her movements. Variam didn't move, but his eyes tracked her. I could sense Luna building for an attack; she was about to strike . . . *now*.

The whip lashed out. The strand was thinner than it was at full strength, but still dangerous; Luna's curse is unpredictable, and even a small dose of that silver mist can be deadly Variam threw out a hand, and a shield of flame flashed into existence, burning the whip away. Variam struck back, heat bursts exploding in Luna's path. Just like Luna's whip, they were invisible to normal eyesight, but they each took a half second to form. Luna broke into a run, swerving from side to side; heat bursts flashed to her left and right, barely missing. Luna's whip had already re-formed, and as another of Variam's spells struck in front of her Luna skidded to a halt and sent the whip slashing back out. This time, Variam had to bring up his fire shield directly in front of him, interrupting his attacks, and Luna took the opportunity to strike again. Magic flashed back and forth, quick and deadly, orange-red meeting silver-grey, destroying each other when they collided. It was hard to see who had the advantage. Variam was faster, but he had to devote much of his strength to blocking the whip strikes, while his spells kept missing.

I glanced at Chalice. She was observing the battle, apparently absorbed in the exchange. As I watched, she seemed to come to a decision and bent down to reach into her bag. The object she retrieved was a metal cylinder, painted a dark green. A ring and a lever protruded from the top. It almost looked like a—

Chalice pulled the ring out of the cylinder. "Grenade!" she called, and lobbed it underarm at Luna.

I moved instinctively, but Luna was already spinning, her palm coming up. The grenade bounced on the wooden floor, and silver mist surged from Luna's hand and into the metal. The grenade bounced again, skittered over the floor. Luna stood her ground, the mist of her curse pouring into the thing. The grenade came to a stop only ten feet from her, and—

Phut. There was a fizzling noise, then nothing.

I looked into the futures and saw no explosion. A dud. Luna looked up at Chalice with a satisfied expression.

"At least you got it this time," Variam said, wandering up. He'd stopped his attack as soon as the grenade had been thrown. "Hey, Alex."

"Hey," I said. "'This time'?"

"That wasn't my fault," Luna said. "I wasn't ready."

I looked at Chalice with raised eyebrows.

"I thought you were in a hurry," Chalice said. For someone who'd just been tossing live grenades around, she looked remarkably unconcerned. She turned back to Luna. "Better, but you're still forcing it. Your magic knows where to go. Trust it."

"Yeah, okay." Luna looked at me. "So? What do you think?"

"Pretty good," I said. I meant it. Variam might be technically an apprentice, but he's as capable as any Light mage of his age that I've met, if not better. He might have been holding back a little, but even so, the fact that Luna could go toe to toe with him was impressive. I didn't think those heat bursts would have been fatal, but they would have really hurt. "You're not using azimuth shields?"

"Won't be any in the test," Luna said.

"You're taking this seriously, aren't you?"

"Like she said, we're in a hurry." Luna walked to the bench and towelled off her face. Now that I looked, I could see that her clothing was damp with sweat. "Let's go again."

"Don't you want to give it a break?" Variam said.

Luna flashed him a smile. "Chicken?"

Variam scowled and walked out onto the floor. Luna

tossed the towel back onto the bench and went to join him, unsheathing her whip as she did. The two of them faced off again.

"What do you think her chances are?" I said quietly to Chalice. We were standing next to each other against the wall, out of earshot of Luna and Vari.

"Combat-wise, she's excellent," Chalice replied. Like me, she kept her voice down, and she didn't take her eyes off Luna. "As good as any Light chance apprentice or better."

"Your work?"

"I've shown her some new applications, but all of the work has been hers. She practises hard."

"I've seen," I said. Out on the floor, Luna and Variam clashed again. They were more cautious this time, probing. "I note you don't compare her to *Dark* chance apprentices."

Chalice glanced at me with a slight smile. "Well, that wouldn't exactly be fair."

I rolled my eyes.

"In any case," Chalice said, "I don't think she has anything to worry about as regards combat trials. Light mages usually underestimate how effective chance mages can be. I suspect she'll mop up anything they send at her."

"What about noncombat?"

"You saw what she did with the flashbang," Chalice said. "That's one area we've been working on. She's become quite good at hexing objects. Not as good as she is with living things, but most machines and other devices won't last too long."

I wondered exactly what "working on" meant in that context, and decided not to ask. If we survived all this, I'd bring it up with Luna later. "Okay, that's her strengths. What about weaknesses?"

"Touch," Chalice said. Out on the gym floor, Luna feinted at Variam, then struck. The whip almost made it past Variam's shield, and Variam had to jump away. "We've made progress. Given the timescale, good progress. But it's still dangerous for Luna to lay hands on anyone else. She can do it, but not consistently." Chalice looked at me. "Luna's been in the apprentice program for over two years, correct?"

"Over three."

"And she competes openly in tournaments."

I nodded.

"Then I assume her abilities are well known by now," Chalice said. "The Light mages are aware of what she can do. And what she can't."

I sighed. "Yeah." It was one of the reasons I'd been reluctant to introduce Luna into magical society. Her curse is a powerful protection, but it's a lot less effective against an opponent who knows about it. "We've done our best to stay quiet and I did a little disinformation, but I think at this point we have to assume that it's public knowledge. Anyone in Light society who wants to find out, can find out."

"Then there's a good chance that the mages setting her test will know that too," Chalice said. "It's possible that they'll miss it, given the short time span . . . but I doubt it. If they want to target her weak points, that's where she's vulnerable."

"Is that what you think they'll do?"

Chalice shrugged. "It's hard to know how Light mages think."

"But if *you* were testing her, forcing her to confront her weaknesses," I said quietly, "that's what you'd do. Isn't it?"

Chalice nodded.

"Anything we can do?"

"I'll give her all the practice I can, and I'll make sure she's warned. Beyond that?" Chalice shrugged again. "It's up to her."

I gave Chalice a sideways look. Dark mages have a survival-of-the-fittest attitude when it comes to training apprentices, and their usual approach is to chuck the apprentice in at the deep end and see if they learn how to swim. If they do, great. If not . . . well, that's their problem. I wondered exactly how much of a Dark mage Chalice was.

"Have there been any developments on the other matter we discussed?" Chalice said.

"Your payment?" I said. "As a matter of fact, yes. It looks

like I might be in position to get a very close look at whatever it is that Richard's after within the next few days. So it seems as though you might get exactly what you want." I raised my eyebrows. "Funny coincidence, don't you think?"

Chalice smiled slightly. "Lucky me."

"Yeah," I said. "Lucky you. Why exactly do you want to know what Richard's up to?"

"We all have our reasons."

"'We all have our reasons' is a valid explanation for deciding what colour scarf to buy. It is not a valid explanation for wanting inside information on one of the most dangerous and secretive Dark mages in Britain."

"Actually, I'd say it is."

I looked at Chalice for a second. "When you came to me earlier this year, the deal you offered was an alliance," I said. "That goes both ways. If you want my help, I want to know what you're going to be using this information for."

Chalice was silent, and I didn't speak, watching the futures shift. Out on the floor, Luna and Variam had dropped out of their fighting stances and were having a discussion about something or other. "All right," Chalice said at last.

"All right?"

"Find out what Richard is looking for. Find out what it does. Then I'll tell you exactly why I want to know. And you can decide whether our aims are compatible." Chalice looked at me, her dark eyes giving nothing away. "Reasonable?"

I looked back at her for a moment, then nodded. "All right."

. . . .

I stayed at the gym until late, taking turns with Variam to partner for Luna. The more we practised, the more I came to agree with Chalice's assessment: there were few Light apprentices who could match Luna when it came to combat skill. I couldn't realistically see any Light mage setting Luna a combat challenge that she couldn't ace.

Touch, though . . . well, part of the reason Luna has such

a knack for battle magic is that it's what her curse is good at. Her curse is great at protecting her, and it's great at hurting others. It's *not* hurting others that's the problem. I'd always known that this was going to be the biggest thing Luna would struggle with, but I'd hoped to give her more time with Chalice before her tests. Luna was better at controlling her curse—she'd even reached the point where she could touch someone briefly, as long as she maintained concentration. (Variam had stood in as the test subject for that, which in my opinion showed a really impressive level of trust.) But would it be enough?

It was almost midnight when we finally ended for the day. Luna was dead on her feet, and I wasn't much better. It had been a long day. Variam took Luna home, and I gated back to my flat, pulled off my clothes, and dropped into bed. The bedroom was cold, and I shivered for a few minutes before the sheets warmed up and I fell asleep.

ı ı ı ı ı ı ı ı ı

I drifted through dreams, some comfortable, most not. I was hiding in my room, curled up quiet and still, and someone was nearby. They were looking for me, and they were going to come inside, but I stayed as quiet as I could, hoping that they'd go away, even when I knew they were going to find me.

I didn't notice at first when my room began to change and brighten. Only when the light crept out to fill the room did I open my eyes. The whole far wall was bare to the outside, leading out onto a balcony; gauzy white curtains were the only barrier, stirring gently in the wind. The air blew against my face, warm and dry. I rose to my feet and walked outside.

The light was bright, dazzling, and I had to shield my eyes to look around. I was standing on the balcony of a tall building made of yellowish stone. Below was an open plaza, and all around was a deserted city, empty doors and windows looking back at me from buildings made of stone and brick. Trees grew amidst the streets, their tops showing from between the rooftops, green and vibrant. The city didn't feel inhabited, not exactly, but it didn't feel empty, either. Leaves stirred in the wind, and birds circled against the sky, far above. I could hear sounds of life, if I stood and listened; distant murmurs, maybe of traffic, maybe of people. Not here, not coming closer, but not far, either, as though I could find them if I only knew where to look.

I turned around to see that the room behind me was gone. I was standing on an open, square balcony, chest-high railings surrounding it, the stones cracked and weathered. At the centre, resting in a square of packed earth, was a thick tree growing upwards into the sky. In the shade beneath the tree was a white stone bench.

"You can come out," I said to the balcony.

A girl stepped out from behind the tree. She was small, with short red hair. Back when she'd been alive, she'd always been full of life and movement, but she was standing still now, hands on her hips, staring at me. We looked at each other for a moment.

"You don't look happy," I said at last.

"You haven't done what you promised," Shireen said.

I walked forward, coming under the tree. It was still warm even in the shade. I sat down on the stone bench, not meeting Shireen's gaze. "Things have been . . . difficult."

Shireen didn't sit down. "You know what you need to do," she said. "You told me you'd do it."

"That was before Richard came back. Things are different now."

"No, they're not."

I sighed. "I guess to you they aren't."

Like me, Shireen and Rachel had been Richard's apprentices, back when we'd all been teenagers still growing into our powers. It had worked out badly for me, but worse for them. Rachel had Harvested Shireen, taking Shireen's power into herself and killing Shireen in the process. It had also driven Rachel insane. When I saw Rachel next, she called herself Deleo, and there was very little left in her of the girl I'd once known.

Yet somehow, Shireen's shade didn't want revenge. She wanted me to help Rachel, and she'd made me promise to redeem her. On one level, I guess it said something good about Shireen that she could still want something like that. If I were murdered, I'm pretty sure I wouldn't be so forgiving. On the other hand, I had absolutely no idea how to do what Shireen wanted. And that was a problem, because Shireen wasn't going away . . . and neither was Rachel.

"Rachel is still there," Shireen said. "Nothing's changed."

"I *know*." I looked up at Shireen. "But that doesn't mean I can fix it. What am I supposed to do, ask her nicely?"

"You're the diviner," Shireen said. The past times I'd met her here, she'd smiled a lot, but she wasn't smiling now. "Think of something."

"Rachel hates me," I said. "You said it yourself. I don't think she'd have listened to me even before. And now Richard's back, and he has ten times the influence over her that I do."

"You were apprentices together," Shireen said. "That counts for more than you think."

"Doesn't make her hate me any less. Actually, I'm pretty sure it makes her hate me *more*."

"But she pays attention to you."

"She pays a lot more attention to you." I twisted around to look at Shireen. "Aren't you a lot better suited to this than I am? You used to be best friends, you've got some major guilt leverage going on—oh, and there's the little detail that you're in her head and she can't kill you to shut you up. Wouldn't it make more sense for this job to go to the one who Rachel *can't* disintegrate when she gets sick of talking to them?"

"I can't."

"I know you can talk to her. I've seen her."

"I . . . slip." Shireen gazed over my shoulder, into the distance. "I lose time. I don't know why. Sometimes I blink, and it's been hours. Days, even. It happens more often when Cinder's there. I think something about him . . . he keeps me away. The other, too." Shireen focused on me. "But when you're there, it's easier. I can talk more easily to Rachel, too. It's the connection you have. I think it makes it harder for her to forget."

"Okay," I said. "Any chance I could just hang around somewhere nearby and let you do the talking?"

"She won't listen," Shireen said. "I've tried. I'm too close. All I know is what she knows, what she sees. I haven't got anything else to offer. You do."

"And when Richard tells her to kill me for trying?"

"Richard doesn't want to kill you."

That I had to admit was true. Either he just didn't care, or he had something else in mind, which was something I really didn't want to think about. "Yeah, well, he's still pulling the strings."

"Fine." Shireen sighed. "I didn't want to have to persuade you this way, but I guess there's nothing for it. When I said I wanted you to change Rachel's path, I wasn't just hoping. I know it's possible."

"How?"

"The same way I knew to give you that bit of advice about the fateweaver."

"You went to a dragon?" I said curiously. "Do they exist here?"

"Yes. And before you ask, yes, the same one. It told me that there'll come a time when Rachel will have to make a choice. Either she stands with Richard, or she rejects him. If she turns against him, the way you did, then she'll be free of him forever. It'll hurt Richard badly, take away his strongest weapon. But if she chooses to stay with him, to follow Richard until the end . . . then that's it. Richard wins. And in that future, you die."

I felt a chill. I don't know much about dragons—not many people do—but if they're not actually omniscient, they're the closest thing you're going to get to it short of meeting God. The last prophecy Shireen had told me had been from a dragon, and it had been very, very accurate. "What do you mean, Richard wins? How?"

Shireen shook her head.

"That's it?" I said. "It all comes down to Rachel rejecting Richard?"

"As far as I know."

"Then if it's true—and I hope it isn't—we're screwed. She went all in when she murdered you, and she's had ten years to double down on that. What am I *possibly* going to say to her that's going to convince her to turn back now?"

Shireen shrugged. "I guess you'd better think of something."

"Thanks."

We sat in silence for a little while. Birdsong drifted down from above, and a warm breeze blew across the balcony. Elsewhere is a dangerous place, but I find it more comfortable than I once did. Shireen once told me that it grew easier to navigate this place the more often you came. "There's something else I need you to do," Shireen said. "Something I need you to find out about."

"Sure," I said resignedly. "Why not?"

"I need you to see what you can learn about creatures that grant wishes."

I blinked. "What kind?"

"Any kind."

I puzzled over it for a second. "Why do you want to know about that?"

"It's just an idea," Shireen said. "If I'm wrong, it won't matter. If I'm right . . ." She hesitated. "Let's hope I'm not right. Oh, and one other thing—I don't think you'll find out anything useful from the Light mages. I've got the feeling this is something old."

"Light mages have histories."

"I'm not sure this would be in them."

"You're being cryptic, aren't you?"

"Kinda. There's a reason. Tell you later." Shireen got to her feet. "You'd better go. Short-term problems and all that."

I stood. "What do you mean?"

"You remember those adept kids who were after you?"

"The Nightstalkers?" I said. It had been the same time

I'd been shown what had really happened to Shireen. "Kind of hard to forget."

"That sort of thing." Shireen walked away around the tree, waving over her shoulder. "Later!"

I watched her go, frowning. *What do you mean, short-term problems?* The last time she'd said that, it had meant . . .

Suddenly I wanted to get out of Elsewhere, right now. I focused on calling myself back to my body, willing the empty city to disappear. Wake up, wake up, wake up *wake up wake up wake*—

chapter 6

My eyes snapped open. Above me was my bedroom ceiling, dark except for the faint blurry glow of the streetlights below the window. The house was silent and still . . . but my precognition was shouting that I was in danger. I looked into the future to see what would happen if I stayed where I was.

In just under one minute, someone was going to sneak into my room and shoot me through the head.

My mind kicked into high gear, and all of a sudden everything seemed to be going very slowly, the seconds ticking by one by one. I held quite still, my future self flashing through the possibilities, scouting and searching. Two men in the house . . . no, three. Magic, but not an overwhelming amount of it. They were carrying handguns with silencers.

I thought fast, assigning priorities. First, call for help; second, get a weapon; third, fight. I grabbed my phone from the side table, clicked it to mute, and typed in a code. The ringing icon appeared on the screen and I placed it back down on the table, then I rolled out from under the covers and landed catlike on all fours before rising to my feet.

When Anne, Variam, Luna, and I had begun our surveillance of Richard last year, we'd spent some time discussing
contingencies. Out of all the possible threats, one we kept
coming back to had been the night raid, with enemies infil-
trating our homes while we were alone and helpless. It had
happened before: the Nightstalkers had tried to blow up my
flat while I was sleeping in it two years ago, and Anne had
been attacked in a similar way not long afterwards.

Although we hadn't been able to come up with a really
reliable countertactic, one thing we'd laid in place had been
a panic signal. The code I'd just typed in would ring Anne's,
Luna's, and Variam's phones, and would make them keep
ringing until they shut them off. All four of us had gate stones
to each other's houses. It was just a matter of time until they
showed up.

Hopefully.

I pulled on my trousers, stalking out into the living room,
bare feet silent on the carpet. As I did, I looked into the futures
in which I went downstairs. *Not good.* The men below were
less than thirty seconds away, and they were already climbing
the stairs. Coolly I looked through the futures in which I
searched the room, looking for a weapon. I wanted something
lethal: no concern for overkill this time. The silencers on their
guns had established that, even if I hadn't seen what they were
planning to do with them. Unfortunately, I had no guns up
here— they were down in the safe room. Should have kept
one within reach . . . Too late now. I considered various magical items and dismissed them as too specialised. There was
a dagger resting at the back of my desk; I slid it from its
sheath, walked to the door, then pressed myself against the
wall next to the door frame.

I still couldn't see the three men, but from the futures in
which I opened the door, I knew they were out on the landing.
I held myself quite still, tracking their movement through the
futures. The room was dark and silent. Only the faintest whisper of traffic sounded from outside; from my glance at the
phone I knew it was three A.M. and Camden was as quiet as
it would ever be. I waited.

There was a creak from outside: a footstep on the landing. I didn't move. In the dim light, I could just make out movement as the handle began to turn. I watched silently as it rotated through ninety degrees, then stopped. Slowly, the door began to open, swinging out towards me. I tightened my grip on the hilt of the knife. I could sense the lead man just on the other side of the door, less than three feet away, his gun up and aimed at the bedroom entrance. Couldn't risk waiting for them to pass and taking the rear man. I'd have to knife the first and use him as a shield. Only seconds now until he'd enter. I tensed, ready to spring—

The futures splintered, changed. I heard the whisper-crackle of a radio. A pause, then—"He's awake!" The voice was sharp. "Back up, back up!"

Hurried footsteps sounded, withdrawing down the stairs. "Where?" someone called.

"Shoot the walls. Shoot!"

People overestimate how much a silencer muffles the sound of a gunshot. The noise as the guns opened up was an echoing metallic *bang bang bang*, like a set of extremely loud staplers. The internal wall between the staircase and my living room wasn't reinforced, and the bullets went right through, sending bits of paint and plaster scattering to the carpet.

I'd already jumped back from the door. My precognition had given me enough warning to get out of the line of fire, and I crouched behind the sofa as the bullets whizzed overhead. The men were shooting from the stairs and landing below, and the upward angle meant the shots were going into the ceiling. The shooting seemed to go on for a long time, but it could only have been ten or twenty seconds before the banging stopped and silence fell.

I stayed dead still. My living room was a mess, holes in the walls and bits of plaster covering the floor. Looking into the futures in which I moved forward, I eavesdropped. The men below were whispering to each other.

"... get him?"

"Dunno. Ask . . ."

"... can't hear . . ."

I didn't move, sorting calmly through the possibilities. They'd been aware that I was awake and waiting. However, they hadn't seemed to realise that fact until the last second. It had sounded as though they'd only received the message over the radio. Putting that together, the most probable conclusion I could come to was that there was a mage nearby, watching my house from outside with deathsight or lifesight or something similar. I've got wards against space magic, but the detection spells used by mages from the living family are very hard to block. If that was the case, the three men below probably weren't mages themselves, just adepts or sensitives. That also made sense. When you're scouting a hostile building, you send your pawns in first.

The men were still whispering. It sounded as though they were trying to figure out if I was dead. Working on the assumption that they were being fed information over a radio link, I'd have a small delay between making any movement and the information being passed along. That could be useful.

". . . says he's still there," one of the men whispered.

"They sure?"

". . . get a closer . . ."

". . . crazy?"

More radio chatter. "You heard . . ." one of the men whispered. "Dave, you're on point."

". . . that," the other man whispered back. "Cover me."

I felt the exact moment the pin was pulled from the grenade. All of a sudden the futures were all converging to the same point: in exactly five seconds, there was going to be a shrapnel explosion somewhere in my flat. The only question was where. I heard movement from below as the man rose to make his throw, and I broke cover, darting to the open doorway.

There are a lot of different philosophical and legal positions on the use of force—when it's justified, how much is justified, that sort of thing. People will often say that violence is only justified if it's in self-defence, but that's kind of vague. Probably the most common position I see people advocate is the "minimum force" one—the idea is that in any given situation, you're justified in using whatever the minimum amount of physical force is to protect yourself, but no more than that.

While I can see the logic behind that kind of thinking, it's never something I've entirely agreed with. I'll follow the minimum-force approach in some situations, but as a choice rather than as a rule, and it's not my most instinctive reaction. Instead, my philosophy tends to be that you're justified in using an amount of force that is equivalent to the amount directed at you. So, as a general rule, I tend to think that it's okay to roughly match the level of aggression and/or violent intent of whoever attacks you. That was why, when James Redman and those two adepts had come after me, I hadn't killed them, but I hadn't let them off with a warning, either. They'd tried to hit me with sticks, so I'd responded by hitting them with sticks. Equivalence.

Which is a long-winded way of saying that, while I *could* have acted differently in the short space of time after the pin was pulled on that grenade, having thought about it with the benefit of hindsight, I probably would have done the same thing.

As the grenade came flying through the open doorway, I stretched out my right hand and caught it, then with a flick of my wrist sent it flying back down the stairs at the same angle it had come from. Then I got back behind the sofa.

There was a brief, horrible scream, cut off abruptly.

I waited for the echoes of the boom to die away, then lifted my head and called down to the landing. "Next."

There was a moment's silence, then another volley of gunfire. More plaster went puffing into the air, accompanied by chips of wood and shredded paper. Some of the bullets must have gone through my bookshelf. I hoped they hadn't hit any of my favourites. The books weren't first editions or anything, but some of them had sentimental value.

I crouched quietly and waited for the shooting to stop. I already knew that as long as I stayed here, there were no futures in which I'd be hit. I tried to count the bullets and had got to seventeen or so by the time the shots cut off.

Silence fell again. My ears were ringing slightly from the gunshots, and I couldn't hear anything else over it. I waited and explored the futures in which I looked out down the stairs.

"Wc know you're up there!" one of the men shouted from below.

I didn't answer. I was uncomfortably aware of how vulnerable I was. I was barefoot, dressed only in a T-shirt and trousers, and my sole weapon was a knife. The three men—two, now—had handguns. If they just rushed me, I didn't like my chances. I'd get one, but there was a good chance the other would kill me. Maybe I could stall them. I couldn't see through the short-term combats to check, but I knew help had to be on its way.

Luckily, the men below didn't seem keen on a suicide charge. Not many people are, even when it's the best chance of success. Instead, looking into the futures, I could see they were about to . . . *Really? They didn't learn from the first time?* Well, I wasn't complaining. I moved up to the doorway again.

They did things differently this time. The guy with the grenade let it cook for two seconds after pulling the pin, and the other guy covered the doorway with his gun. Probably would have worked against anyone with normal reflexes. But one of the early tricks I learned with divination was how to apply it to thrown items. I can pick up an object and hit a target first time, every time, with only a second or so to aim—all I have to do is pick out the future in which I get the shot right. It takes a little work to synchronise the divination with your muscle memory, but once you do, it's not hard to adapt it to other uses. Such as throwing stuff back.

I brought my palm around in an open-handed slap as the grenade came flying in, and batted it back down the stairs. There was the bang of a shot, but I already knew it was going to miss. I dropped flat instantly and felt the floor vibrate in the *BOOM!* of the explosion from below. I shook my head, trying to clear the ringing in my ears.

"—you!" the man below was yelling. "Fuck you! You piece of shit!"

I didn't answer. The men below were angry and scared, which was good. They were also alive, which was bad. I could sense a force shield—that was probably how they'd survived the two explosions. The guy hit in the first blast must have been caught by surprise.

Impasse. I couldn't attack; they'd shoot me down as I tried to close the distance. But I couldn't go back and don my armour, either, or else I'd open up the possibility of them rushing me. They could reach the top of the stairs in seconds, and once they were through the choke point of the doorway, my chances of survival would drop fast.

The plus side was that I'd clearly scared them. I couldn't hear what they were saying anymore—they were whispering softly enough that I couldn't make out the words—but the futures in which they tried to force their way up the stairs were few and far between. Unless I did something to make them feel as though they had an opening, they weren't going to try anything just yet. I looked into the future in which I just waited them out, and—

Yes. That was what I'd been hoping for.

From below, I felt a flicker of gate magic. *Not much time.* I hurried to the desk and grabbed a one-shot spell, then moved back to the door. I could still hear the whisper of their voices, and from the futures in which I showed myself, I knew they had their guns trained on the doorway. They were focused on me, but they'd still notice anyone coming up from behind them. Time to change that. "Hey," I called down the stairs. "Catch." Then I flicked the item in my hand around the edge of the door frame.

Force magic flared as the adept below strengthened his shield, but it hadn't been an attack. The small glass marble I'd thrown hit the stairs and shattered, and mist rushed out, clogging the stairwell with fog. I heard a shout, muffled through the vapour, and the *bang* of a shot—too late. I sat back and waited.

"Where is he?" one of the men called.

"Shut up, listen!"

Silence fell. I knew that both of the men had their guns

trained upward, waiting for me to appear out of the fog so that they could shoot. It was a pretty good plan—even with the concealment, once I got close enough, they'd have a decent chance of hitting me as I came down the stairs.

Unfortunately for them, what they should have been watching for was somebody coming *up* the stairs.

There was a thumping, slithering noise, exactly the sound a body would make falling down a wooden stairway. There was a startled yell, followed by the *bang* of a shot. I felt a surge of magic, and green light flashed through the fog. Another thump. Silence.

A soft voice called up from within the fog. "Alex?"

"Are there any more?" I called back.

Quiet footsteps sounded and Anne materialised out of the mist. She was wearing an old, worn child's T-shirt, with a thin jacket and a pair of tracksuit bottoms, both looking as if they'd been thrown on in a hurry. But her eyes were alert, and she was wide awake. "There's no one else," Anne said. "Did they—?"

I gave Anne a quick hug, then pushed her back, scanning her. I couldn't see any blood on her. "Are you okay? That shot didn't hit?"

Anne shook her head. "No. What's happening?"

"Hell if I know." I moved quickly back to the bedroom, threw on a sweater, and started putting my armour on over it. Anne stayed in the living room without having to be told, looking from side to side. "Looks like whoever I pissed off is getting serious."

"Levistus?"

"Doubt it." I pulled on my socks and started tying my shoes. "Some adepts tried to work me over after you guys left Saturday night. I think they're escalating. Can you see anyone?"

From where we were standing, there wasn't much to see except the walls and a limited angle from the windows, but Anne doesn't need to see someone to know where they are. Anne is a life mage, and she can sense the presence of any living creature within a hundred feet or so. Given a little time, she can also tell you their sex, height, weight, general state of health, medical history, and what they had for breakfast that morning, and if she can lay a hand on them, she can start affecting things more directly. That was how she'd dropped those two men on the landing—once she got within touch range the only question was whether she chose to leave them dead or just unconscious. (They were unconscious, of course. I hadn't asked and I hadn't needed to. Anne's magic is very good at killing people, but she doesn't do it unless she has no other option.)

"No one on the street," Anne said after a second's pause. She was frowning. "The alley is empty as well. Shouldn't there be more?"

"Yeah." I came back into the living room and started scooping up items from the table to stuff into my pockets. "Buildings around?"

"Lots of people," Anne said, glancing at the wall. I once asked Anne what people looked like to her eyes and she described them as living webs of woven green light. To her, the walls and buildings probably looked translucent, the glows of the people behind them shining out through the darkness. "Up on the first and second floors, mostly. But they look asleep."

I thought for a second. "Check the buildings behind and the other side of the street. Look for a person awake and standing up, maybe up on the second floor or the rooftop. Anywhere they'd get an elevated view. But no matter what you see, stay still and don't say anything until I ask. Okay?"

Anne nodded. It would be a pretty bizarre request to anyone who didn't know how divination magic works, but this wasn't the first time Anne and I had been through situations like this and we knew each other's quirks. With Anne's futures steady and nondisruptive, I was free to look ahead to see what would happen if we held still and waited.

The futures unfolded: quiet for one minute, then two. This had been an assassination, not a warning, and I could see two directions in which this could go once whoever had sent those men figured out that they'd failed. Option one would be for them to play it safe, cut their losses and withdraw. Option two was to double down. I really hoped that they'd go for option one—

The futures ahead bloomed into fire. "Shit."

Anne didn't look up. "I'm guessing that's not good news."

"We're about to have company," I said. I strode to the cupboard and started rooting through it. I don't keep many items outside my safe room, but I have a few on hand for emergencies. I pulled out an old, gnarled stick and tossed it to Anne. She caught it and looked at me, puzzled. "Air magic focus," I said. "It's meant for extinguishing fires. Pulls the oxygen out of a small sphere as long as you concentrate. Command word is *luthia*, range is about thirty feet. You've got more power to fuel it than I do." I headed for the stairs down.

Anne followed. "What fires?"

"The ones we're about to have." The mist from the condenser had dissipated and the landing between the first and second floors was filled with bodies, two alive and one dead. It was the first clear look I'd had at the three men who'd come to kill me. They were dressed in black and wore ski masks. "They're trying to burn us out."

"How?"

"Fire sprites." I touched the metal door to my safe room and said a word under my breath. There was no visual sign, but in my mage's sight I saw the wards around the room glow, then subside. I'd just locked the room down, reinforcing it against any attack. I really didn't want anyone getting in there.

"What are—? Wait." Anne stopped, looking upwards, frowning slightly. "There."

"There?"

"Up in that building," Anne said, nodding up and towards the wall. "Across the street and two down. There's a man up in the second-floor flat. He wasn't doing anything before, but another guy just appeared out of nowhere. I think it was a gate."

I hesitated, precious seconds ticking past. If I went now, I might be able to get there before the fire sprites attacked, but . . . "No time." I hurried downstairs. "Keep an eye on them and tell me what they do."

Down on the shop floor, I swept the desk clear and then shoved the chair away, clearing space above the runic circle carved into the floor. "What are fire sprites?" Anne asked.

"Mini fire elementals." I tore open a packet of dust and sprinkled it over the circle, making sure to get both of the rings. "Mages store them in embryo form, then feed them concentrated fire magic to start them growing. Really high energy requirements. Once they mature, they go hunting for stuff to burn, and they'll keep burning until they run out of fuel."

"Are they alive?"

"Your magic'll affect them, yeah. Though touching them'll hurt." I glanced up. "Need to do a summon. Try and get some water. Buckets, bottles, whatever. And get the fire extinguisher."

Anne nodded and disappeared into the back of the shop. I grabbed a dull crystal from the drawer out of a selection of similar-looking stones, held it up above the circle, then started chanting.

There was a spike in the futures: gate magic. *Shit*. I was going to have less time than I thought. I kept chanting, calculating futures as I did. Thirty seconds until the summon was done. Ten seconds until the gate would open. This was going to be messy. Well, I was committed now.

Outside, in the street, white light bloomed. I felt the signature of space magic as a gate formed, small and circular, hanging in midair on the other side of the road, well out of range of my shop's gate wards. The face of the gate was an opaque white glow: the gate was masked. I kept chanting, not looking away.

Something came fluttering through the gate, landing awkwardly on the pavement. It looked like a very small dragon sculpted from solid flame, with two wings and a long neck and tail. It raised its head towards my shop, two beady eyes looking out of a lizardlike head, then braced itself and jumped off the kerb, heading for the window.

Fire sprites look cute and pretty, if you don't know what they do. Problem was, I knew exactly what this one was here to do. Second problem: it wasn't alone. Another fire sprite came flying out of the gate behind the first one. Then a second. Then a third, and a fourth, and a fifth.

The first sprite hit the window and bounced, flapping frantically. Others hit a few seconds later. Behind them, I could see that they were still coming through the portal, one after another. Claws scrabbled at the glass as more and more arrived, landing on the window like giant flapping fiery moths. The front window to my shop is bulletproof, magicproof, and fireproof . . . or at least I thought it was. As I looked at the futures, I amended that last descriptor to "fire-*resistant*." Turns out that pretty much everything burns if you heat it up enough. It took the sprites less than thirty seconds to melt their way through.

Luckily, that was long enough. I finished my chant with a shout of "*ettul a nahame!*" and threw the crystal down to shatter at the centre of the circle.

Summoning is a form of ritual magic, which is essentially a longer, more complicated version of focus magic: it's how you produce more elaborate effects that don't fall within your magic type (or anyone's magic type). Rituals are much slower than normal spells, don't have anywhere near the same flexibility, and usually require various rare ingredients that are obnoxiously difficult to get.

But when they work, they *really* work.

The shards of the crystal came alight, sapphire energy swirling upwards from the broken fragments to take form. A humanoid figure materialised by the counter, vaguely feminine in shape and sculpted from blue light with yellow-gold accents forming patterns on the chest, arms, and head. It turned its blank eyeless face towards me, waiting.

I pointed at the fire sprites. "Eat them."

The creature swivelled to face the fire sprites. The first was just in the process of melting its way through the bottom left corner of my window. The blue-and-gold figure leant forward slightly, as though bracing itself.

I heard footsteps behind me, coming to an abrupt halt. "I've got—" Anne began, then stopped. "What *is* that?"

"Spell drinker," I called without looking back at her. "It's on our side. Don't kill it!"

"If you say so." Anne's voice was dubious. She took a step forward, coming up to my side just as the glass in the corner of the window frame liquefied and began to drip away, and the fire sprite that had melted the hole came squeezing through.

I've made more than a few enemies over the course of my life, and during the past five years, several have seen fit to come and pay me a house call. My shop and flat are well supplied with weapons, but against heavy-grade opposition, weapons aren't always enough, as I was reminded a few years ago when a construct smashed its way through my front window and tried to strangle everyone on the premises, myself included. Once that affair had been dealt with, I went out looking for a defence system that was easy to maintain but also had enough punch to stop a significant magical attack on the level of the one I'd just faced. I'd considered an elemental, as well as several variants of magical sentry, but in the end I'd decided to go for a spell drinker.

Spell drinkers are magical creatures, and they're sapient, if not particularly smart. They can be summoned as an elemental can, but behave quite differently. Elementals take a fair bit of energy to summon, but once they're there, they're there. The only thing limiting their effective duration is how compatible the environment is with the element in question. Spell drinkers work very differently. They burn through their energy reserves fast, but they can replenish those reserves off pretty much any source of magical energy they can get close to—that means active spells, charged and imbued items, constructs, magical creatures, and even mages if they're not careful. They're not the safest creatures to summon, but as long as there's a source of magical energy around that's stronger than you, you're usually okay. Just point them at the magical thing you want to get rid of, and get out of the way.

As the fire sprite entered the shop, the spell drinker came bounding forward, moving with a weird loping grace. It reached out its hand to touch the fire sprite, and as its fingers brushed the fire, the sprite was sucked into the spell drinker's hand. It was like watching a cloud of liquid go down a plughole. One moment the fire sprite was there, spreading its wings, then it was gone.

Another chunk of glass melted and folded, this time at the top of the window, and another fire sprite tried to get inside. The spell drinker's fingers caught it from underneath and it was sucked into nothingness. The third sprite vanished even faster than the first two.

"It's pretty powerful," Anne said quietly.

"Yeah," I said. "Just one problem." I pointed out through the glass and out into the street. "They're still coming."

The fire sprites hadn't stopped streaming through the gate. The street was full of them, scrambling over cars and flapping over the centre of the road. As I watched, a fourth and a fifth fire sprite tried to force their way through the holes in the window and died, but there were at least fifteen more of the things and I didn't think the spell drinker could stop them all. Already the window was more holes than glass; molten streaks were running down the sill and to the floor, and the temperature was rising.

As I watched, the window frame at the bottom left corner caught fire in the heat. *"Luthia!"* Anne called, levelling the wand. The flame winked out. Another sprite had its life extinguished as it came flapping through the growing hole at the centre.

"Anne," I said, my voice tense. "These things are alive, right?"

"Luthia!" Anne called, and another patch of flames vanished. "Yes."

"How much is it going to hurt if you life-drain them?"

"I'd rather not find out."

"I think that's about to stop being an option."

Anne looked in the direction in which I was pointing and let out her breath in a hiss. The door was starting to glow with heat, and flames were licking around the frame and keyhole. Oddly, despite all the attacks I've had to deal with over the years, my front door had never been damaged, meaning that I'd never replaced it, and as a result it was still made of wood. As we watched, the door flash-ignited, flames leaping out. Anne levelled her focus and called out the command word. A small circle of fire winked out, but the instant the spell ended, the area ignited again.

"Not going to work," I said. "Too hot."

"Luthia," Anne said. *"Luthia. Luthia."* She paused. "Crap."

I turned and grabbed the CO_2 extinguisher from behind the counter, then yanked off the tag and lifted it up. It only took me a few seconds, but by the time I'd turned around again the door was ablaze. Pieces of wood were red-hot and glowing, embers crumbling off to scatter to the floor. Orange-red claws reached through, scrabbling. The spell drinker was still busy with the fire sprites coming through the window. Each time one of the tiny elementals came through, it died, but there were always more.

Anne wiped out a patch of fire that had started to spread along the window. "How long until the fire brigade get here?"

"Not soon enough, and it won't make any difference." I could see glimpses of the sprites through the widening holes in the door.

"Luthia!" Anne lowered the focus, then straightened up and took a deep breath. "Okay." She tossed the focus back at me without looking and I caught it. "Time to do this the hard way."

The door groaned and fell inwards, the bottom half breaking away and falling in with a *thump*, ablaze in flames. Fire sprites came through, one, two, three. One landed on the herb rack and ignited it in a *whoof*. The other two arrowed straight at us.

Anne was waiting. She stood with hands by her sides, fingers extended and spread. As the first sprite dived at her, her hand flashed up to touch it.

The reason that life mages are feared isn't because of their lifesight. A life mage who can lay hands upon another living creature can control their biology, to heal or repair . . . or to kill. Green light flashed, something moving from the sprite into Anne almost too fast to see, then Anne was whipping her hand back and the fire sprite was falling lifeless, sprawling on the floor to dissolve into shapeless flame. The second one had aimed for me. I picked the future in which it missed and ducked aside, feeling the rush of heat in my hair as the thing swept past and hit the counter, its claws carving black streaks on the wood. Anne caught it before it could take off again, her hand curling around its neck and snapping back. The fire sprite shimmered and died, leaving flames licking at my desk. I sprayed them with CO_2 until they went out.

I looked at Anne. "You okay?"

Anne lifted her hand, examining it. The palm and fingers were an angry red, but as I watched, leaf-green light glowed around her arm and the red burns began to recede. New skin grew to replace the burned patches, and in only seconds Anne's hand was unmarked. "I'm fine," Anne said. She turned away without meeting my eyes. "Let's kill the rest."

I gave Anne a troubled look. ". . . Yeah."

The battle at the window was still going, the spell drinker holding the line against a seemingly endless stream of fire sprites. The sprites threw themselves through the holes, fearless and quick, but they couldn't hurt the spell drinker: every time the blue-and-gold figure touched one of them, light rippled through its body and it moved with greater vigour. The small amount of damage the heat was doing was being outweighed by the extra vitality it was draining from the elementals. The sprites were too simple-minded to coordinate their attacks—they just went for one of the two existing holes in the glass, scrambled through, and became food.

Anne strode towards the fire sprite on the herb rack. It looked up, opened its mouth to hiss at her, and died, its body dissolving into flame as Anne passed by without breaking stride. The herb rack was on fire, filling the air with the scent of burning verbena and lavender, and I moved up behind Anne to douse it with the extinguisher, white gas rushing over the flames and snuffing them out. Anne killed a fourth fire sprite near the door and stood ready, hands by her sides, waiting for the next target.

We're winning this. Anne was blocking the door and the spell drinker was blocking the window. The sprites weren't intelligent enough to figure out a way through. We just needed to hold the line—

A horrible vision flashed through my precognition. I looked ahead for just one instant, then shouted at Anne. "Anne! Back to me, run, NOW!"

Anne didn't hesitate. She darted back, crossing the shop floor to my side. I caught her and pulled her down behind the counter.

Fire magic surged, and the shop flashed red with a roar. A wash of heat and scorching air rolled over my head.

I stood to see that the entire front of the shop was a sea of flame. The window, the door, and everything within ten feet of the front wall was ablaze. It was moving too fast; natural fire spreads slowly, but this one moved like a living thing, tendrils running out along the floor. The first rack of shelves smouldered and ignited, the flames growing in seconds from licking tongues to an inferno. I could feel the magic pouring down into the street from above, some kind of spell I didn't recognise. I'd seen basic fire-starting before, but nothing like this. Anne caught up the focus and levelled it, shouting *"Luthia!"* A small patch of fire flickered for half a second, one or two tendrils going out, then it jumped forward again, reclaiming the part of the shelves Anne had just extinguished. Already the fire had spread to the entire front half of the shop.

I caught Anne's arm and pulled her back. "It's no good!" I shouted over the roar of the flames. "Run!"

Anne didn't argue. The fire sprites were dancing in the inferno, revelling in the heat; the spell drinker was still up and moving, but more slowly. As I watched, it caught one more sprite and extinguished it, then another wave of heat stung my eyes and made me blink away. Two or three more sprites came flying out of the blaze. They were moving faster now; the fire seemed to be energising them. I snapped out a command word and a wall of force flared up along the line of the counter, cutting off the magic item section and the space behind the counter from the rest of the shop. The sprites slammed into the wall and went tumbling to the floor.

"Alex!" Anne shouted from behind me; she'd made it back into the corridor. I took one last look over the shop floor and saw that it was hopeless. The fire had engulfed the shelves and was creeping closer to the counter. A haze of smoke was in the air, stinging my eyes and throat, and only the forcewall was stopping it from growing even worse. I backed into the corridor and pushed the door shut behind me. I had one last glimpse of the spell drinker, still fighting the sprites amidst the roaring flames, then the door slammed and we were left in darkness.

Spots swam before my eyes as my vision adjusted to the gloom of the stairs. Even with the door closed, I could still smell smoke, and I could still feel the heat. The forcewall wouldn't hold back the fire for long. "Come on," I said, pulling Anne by one hand. Anne's night vision is good, but she can't outright ignore darkness the way I can. "Up."

Anne let me lead her up the stairs. The roar and crackle of flames died away as we ascended. "Have you got anything that can put that out?" Anne asked.

"In a manner of speaking," I said. "Can you find the mage who's maintaining that spell?"

"I think it's the two men on the second floor there." I felt Anne twist as she pointed. "They're looking down at the shop. I can't tell if it's them, but—"

"Good enough. Cover me."

We'd made it back up to the landing where the assassins had been stopped. The ones Anne had knocked out were still knocked out; the one dead from the grenade was still dead. I crouched down in the darkness, searching quickly through their belongings. I found a pistol and a spare clip of ammo, but what I really wanted were some more grenades. The two unconscious men didn't have any. I switched to the dead one.

"Alex?" Anne said. "The spell drinker's hurt."

"Fire sprites?" I asked. I was glad the light wasn't on.

Grenades don't kill in quite as horrible a way as some weapons, but the effects they leave still aren't pretty, and I didn't need the distraction. The clothes under my fingers were pockmarked with sticky holes.

"Seven . . . make that six."

"Tell me if they move up." My fingers closed on cool metal, egg-shaped with an irregular shell. *That's one.* I flicked quickly through the futures in which I kept searching, but all my fingers found was blood. *It'll have to do.*

I headed up, opened the door at the back of the kitchen, and stepped out onto the balcony. Cool air flooded into my lungs, a relief after the heat of the flames, but I could still smell smoke, even out here: the fire was spreading. I spoke to Anne, keeping my voice quiet. "Follow me up to the roof, but stay low. Keep the building between you and the men in that building opposite. Watch them and tell me if they move. Okay?"

Anne nodded. The cold, deadly manner she'd shown downstairs had vanished, and in the faint lights of the city she looked normal again. I couldn't help feeling relieved; Anne's other side might be good in a fight, but seeing it makes me uneasy. I climbed up the ladder, crouched at the back of the roof, and started searching through futures.

The first priority was target confirmation. I looked to see what would happen if I walked up to the front of the roof and stood there in plain view. *Ouch.* Okay, the people in that second-floor flat were definitely bad guys. As an aside, I noted that the fire on the ground floor was strong enough to light up the entire street. I had no idea of how to put it out . . . no, no time for that. Human threats first. I lifted the grenade and began tracing arcs.

Like I said, I'm very good with thrown weapons. Coordinating the divination results with your muscle movements takes practice, but any diviner can do it if they're willing to put in the effort. It works with guns too, but back when I was learning the trick, thrown items were what I had, so thrown items were what I got good at. This was an unusually tricky shot; not only was I doing it at long range and in the dark, but there was a roof in the way. Almost impossible for a normal human. Ten seconds' work for me. *Too high. Still too high. Too low. Frame hit. That's the angle. How much delay? One second . . . no, a bit longer. Pulling the pin changes the trajectory. Recalculate . . . there.* I pulled the pin from the grenade, let the lever spring free, waited one and a half seconds, then threw it into the darkness. One heartbeat. Two heartbeats—

There was the distant sound of shattering glass as the grenade went through the window, followed half a second later by the explosion. The detonation was much quieter at this distance: less of a bang, more of a hollow *pboom. That's for burning down my shop, you bastard.*

"Anne?" I said.

"He's hurt," Anne said. Her eyes were distant as she looked down towards the other building. "Badly. He's crawling away."

"What about the other one?"

"He's gone." Anne frowned. "I can't see where he—wait." Anne turned, looking left over the rooftops. "He's there! I think—"

"Move!" I grabbed Anne's hand and ran away from the direction she'd been looking, pulling her stumbling behind me.

There was a flash from behind us, and the chimneys and aerials around us were lit up in dull red light as fire magic bloomed with a *whoompf.* Hot air washed over our backs. I knew the light of the fireball had painted us as targets, and when the second one came I was ready. I jumped the small parapet linking one roof to another, then yanked Anne to the right. Something that looked like a glowing red spark shot past, hitting the ventilators of the apartment block ahead and exploding with another *whoompf* and a flash of flame.

Before the mage behind us could throw a third fireball, I'd put a chimney stack between us and him. I kept moving, using the ventilators and chimneys as cover, then circled around. The plaster of the roof was scorched and warm, but the ventilators were metal and the chimneys were brick and there was nothing to burn. I reached the chimneys at the back and peered around the edge.

Flames were licking up from the edges of my house. From the fact that I could see them, I knew that the fire had spread all the way up to my flat, and I knew that the building was gone. Even if the fire brigade arrived in the next minute—which they wouldn't—there was no way to save it. No time to mourn. Right now I needed to survive.

"Do we run?" Anne whispered. She'd stayed with me as I'd moved.

"I'd like to—" I stopped abruptly as I felt gate magic behind us. I looked into the futures in which we fled back over the rooftops. "Shit."

"We could try the railway line . . ."

"More gunmen behind us." I looked back towards my house. "And that guy in front. Great."

A man had appeared on top of my roof, or what would have looked like a man if it hadn't been wreathed in flame. The shape walked forward, ignoring the smoke and licking fire, and paused at the parapet, scanning the rooftops ahead. I saw futures in which we were spotted and pulled back, relying on my divination to track his movements.

"He's the one from before," Anne whispered.

"I know," I said in a low voice. "Fire mage." Spells have a distinctive signature, and the fireballs and flame shield carried the same fingerprint as the spell that had created the blaze in my shop. "Any chance he's hurt?"

"No."

"Figures."

"How did he get across so fast?" Anne whispered.

It was a good question. A gate spell would have done it, but gates are typically slower than that. I looked into the futures in which we moved. *Not good.* The men behind were positioned four rooftops down, behind cover, and they were waiting for us. If we went the other way, we'd be clearly visible to the fire mage's heat vision. As long as we stayed in the cover of the chimneys, we could stay hidden, but as soon as we left . . .

"They're waiting for us," Anne said quietly.

"I know." I thought quickly. The fire brigade had to have been called by now, and once they were here it might create enough confusion for us to slip away. What was worrying me was how these people were getting onto the roof so fast. I looked ahead, and—"Shit!"

Gate magic bloomed again, and a portal opened on the roof above my flat. More men came through, hurrying to get out of the smoke. From a glimpse into the futures they were carrying guns too.

"More mages?" Anne said in dismay.

"No," I said, biting off my words. "Gunmen." I knew what was happening now. "They've got a gate specialist. She's moving these guys in."

"She?"

"Symmaris, unless I miss my guess." *Damn it.* I knew who these men were working for now, but it wouldn't do me any good. I should have paid more attention to Landis.

"Alex," Anne whispered. "They're coming closer."

I checked the futures and confirmed it. *Shit, shit, shit.* Mage ahead, gunmen on both sides, and the building was on fire. If we made a break for it they'd just gate ahead of us. I looked into the futures in which I tried to snipe the men in front. No good—the fire mage would see us too easily. The ones behind? Not the left, we'd get spotted . . . right might work. "Stay down," I whispered. "I'm going to try and slow down the ones behind."

"All right."

I moved back, being very careful to keep the ventilators between myself and the fire mage. Fire mages can see heat; if he got a clear line of sight, I'd stand out in the darkness like a torch. Once I reached the farthest chimney, I crouched and checked the gun I'd taken from the assassins. One bullet in the chamber, two more in the clip, and I had a full clip spare. The suppressor wouldn't do much to muffle the gunshot, but it would hide the flash in the darkness. That would be useful. I held still and waited.

Ten seconds, twenty. Futures flickered: if I moved forward I'd run the risk of getting shot. *Lean right? Other way.* I rose slightly, braced my elbow against the chimney, then leant carefully up and left, sighting the long barrel towards the chimney stack twenty feet away. The streetlights all around us cast a fuzzy neon glow, reflecting off the low clouds above to create a faint ambient radiance, just enough to pick out the outline of the chimneys and parapet. I felt the futures shift; there was a man behind those chimneys, waiting for me to make a move. If I showed, he'd fire. I held perfectly still.

A dark shape moved from behind the chimney stack. I waited exactly long enough to get a clear shot, then fired twice.

The pistol jerked in my hands with its double *bang*, and the figure ahead staggered and dropped. I ducked back as a gun opened up with a *rat-tat-tat-tat-tat-tat*. Bullets chewed into brickwork and went whizzing overhead. I scrambled away, then went running back, keeping my head down.

Anne was still where I'd left her. "Got one," I whispered, crouching next to her.

"He's dying," Anne said. There was a faraway look in her eyes as she looked back towards where I'd shot the man, then she took a deep breath and shook her head. "The three at the front are moving up."

I ejected the empty clip and loaded the spare. It was the last: ten rounds, plus one in the chamber. I wished I'd had time to grab more weapons. *Time to improvise.* "Can you— shit. Back!"

Anne moved without my having to grab her this time. We just made it to the ventilators before the chimney we'd been hiding behind exploded in flame. It wasn't a fireball; the flame kept burning and spreading, even though there was no fuel.

There was the stuttering of gunfire, and bullets whined overhead. Anne ducked down, and I swore silently. *Bastard's trying to burn us out.* Well, why not? It had worked for him before. One gunman ahead, two more and the fire mage behind. But if we could break past the single man, we might be able to make it to the railway . . .

Only chance we've got. I dug out a pair of gold discs from my pocket. "Anne," I said quietly. The flames were still spreading towards us; we had maybe twenty seconds. "When I say go, run forward and right. Draw the fire of the guy ahead. I'll put up a forcewall."

Anne looked up at me for a second, then nodded. I tossed the discs ahead and to the right, lobbing them over the chimney. The sound of them landing on the roof was muffled by the roar of the flames. I took a glance back; the fire was less than twenty feet away and the heat was scorching my skin. "Go!"

Anne darted up and forward, leaving herself clearly exposed to the man ahead. I called out the command word just as I saw the muzzle flash in the darkness. The wall sprang up, invisible and impenetrable, angled to block the man's line of fire. Anne was a slim shadow in the darkness, running out of cover towards the back of the roof, then coming to a skidding halt at the edge.

I was already moving, going left, sprinting the twenty feet to the next stack of chimneys. I rounded the edge to see the man who'd been shooting at Anne, a black-clad shape lit by the glow of the flames. I was standing almost within arm's reach, and yet he was too fixed on his target to notice. His rifle clicked dry and he crouched down, fumbling for a new magazine.

I aimed my pistol at the side of the man's head and fired. He dropped without a sound. "Anne!" I shouted.

Anne reversed course, running back around the forcewall, silhouetted against the blazing fire behind. I could still hear gunfire over the roar of the flames, and as she cleared the edge she stumbled. "Anne!" I shouted again.

Anne caught herself and kept running, making it to my chimney. "Are you—?" I started to say.

"I'm fine." Anne's voice was harsh. "Come on."

I didn't argue. We ran down the rooftops. I could hear sirens in the distance. A little farther and we'd be—

Fire, pain, death. I grabbed Anne's arm, jerking her back and making her gasp. A red spark shot down from above, landing ahead of us and erupting in a blast of flame.

I spun around to see what looked like a fiery angel soaring behind us in the night sky. The fire mage was gliding on wings of orange flame, hanging over the blaze on the apartment roof behind us; he was just at the top of his arc and starting to descend. I lifted my gun and fired, but I didn't have time to aim and the mage sent another fireball arrowing down at me. I dived, but it's hard to dodge area spells and this time I didn't quite make it. Searing pain flashed in my leg and arm and I went tumbling to land behind another parapet wall.

From the other side of the wall I heard the *thud* as the fire mage landed on the roof. He was maybe thirty feet away. My arm and leg were screaming at me, but it was my left side that had taken the burn and I'd kept hold of the gun. The wall was a couple of feet high and blocked my line of sight, but I could get a fix on him with my divination. Fire shields are great for melee, but they don't stop bullets. All I needed to do was get off a shot—

Burning death jumped out at me. In every future in which I rose to shoot, I died, the flesh searing off my bones. The fire mage was waiting, and the instant I came into view he'd see my body heat and incinerate me. I searched for an angle I could rise from. Couldn't throw—*shit!* I needed a distraction—

There was a low hiss to my right.

I looked. Anne was lying flat behind the same wall, maybe ten feet to my side. She was looking straight at me, and her eyes were steady. She pointed at herself, then up and over the wall.

I stared at her for a second, then my eyes went wide. *No!* I shook my head, suddenly panicked, wanting to talk but afraid of being heard. *Don't—*

Anne took a deep breath, then bounded to her feet and jumped over the wall.

I felt the stutter of a spell as the futures flickered. The

fire mage had been focused on me; he hadn't been prepared for Anne to charge. The futures in which I'd be incinerated vanished and I came up to one knee, levelling my gun.

Anne was running straight towards the fire mage, still wreathed in his flame shield. She was moving fast. The distance from the parapet wall to the fire mage was thirty feet, and Anne was already less than a second away from reaching him.

She wasn't fast enough.

A red spark flashed out and Anne disappeared in a bloom of flame, just as my gun sighted on the mage. I aimed for the centre of the fiery shape and opened fire, shooting as fast as I could, *bang bang bang.* I saw the figure stagger, then death flashed in my futures. Another fireball, and I couldn't move fast enough to dodge it. I dropped flat and curled into a ball, trying to take the blast on my back armour.

Fire magic surged. I heard a *whoompf*, horribly loud and far too close. Searing heat washed over me . . .

. . . and nothing.

I held quite still. I didn't dare move; I was afraid to find out how badly I'd been burned. All of a sudden, the rooftop was quiet.

I looked into the futures in which I stayed where I was. I could still hear the sirens from below, and I looked into the extended futures, not quite able to believe it. Still nothing. I opened my eyes and looked around. Behind me and to the right, a patch of rooftop was glowing with heat, fragments of paint turned to glowing embers. The spell had missed, and I stared at it, fascinated at just how close I'd come to dying. If that had burst above—

Anne!

I pulled myself up to look around. From where we'd come, the roof of the apartment was still burning, but the blaze was dying away. There was no sign of the fire mage. But on the roof just ahead, a dark figure was lying still.

My heart lurched. Forgetting about the fire mage, I ran forward. As I reached Anne, I smelt a too-familiar scent, thick and sweet and putrid. It's the smell of burnt flesh, and once you know what it is you never forget it. Full of dread, I reached down to touch Anne's body. *Oh God, please don't be dead, please don't—*

Anne jerked, and I pulled away. She rolled over onto her back, and the sight of her made me flinch. Her clothes were black and irregular, and so was the skin of her hands and face. It was too dark for me to see clearly, but I knew it was bad. But she could heal herself, if I could just get her somewhere . . .

Gate. I'd grabbed my emergency gear from my table, and one of the items was a gate stone to Anne's flat. "Anne," I said quietly. "I'm going to gate us to your flat. So you can heal. Okay?"

There was no reaction for a second, then Anne's hand found mine and she squeezed. Her skin felt wrong, cracked and wet. I didn't let myself think about why. I kept hold of her, while with my other hand I dug through my pocket for the small piece of carved wood. "I'm gating," I said, forcing my voice to keep steady. "Just hold on."

Anne squeezed my hand again.

I held the gate stone and concentrated, sending power flowing into the item. I've got very little talent for gate magic, but I'm good with focuses, and over the past year one of the things I've spent my time on has been practising with gate stones. It paid off now. Light bloomed and an oval-shaped portal appeared in midair above the rooftop. "I'm going to lift you," I said to Anne. I knew this was going to be agonising for her. "Hang on."

Anne gave my hand another squeeze, then let go. I slid one arm under her shoulders, slid the hand with the gate stone under her knees, then heaved her up. I felt Anne's muscles go rigid, but she didn't make a sound. The gate was holding steady and I took one last look back over my shoulder.

The fire on the apartment roof had died away and I could see clearly back to my shop. Flames were leaping into the sky from where the roof of my flat was. There was no sign of the fire mage or the other gunmen. Maybe they'd jumped off the roof, or gated out, or maybe they'd died and their bodies were somewhere in the darkness; I didn't know, and right now I didn't care. I could see the edge of a fire engine below, and jets of water were spraying up towards my flat, but just from a glance I knew there was no way they could save the building. My shop and flat were gone.

Holding Anne in my arms, I stepped through the gate and let it close behind me.

chapter 7

The gate closed behind me, leaving us in darkness. Anne and I were alone.

I crossed the carpet and kicked open the door to Anne's bedroom, scanning the futures for danger. The inside of Anne's flat was warm, and the night outside was quiet and still. We were in Honor Oak, south of the river, and the fire and our enemies were far away. I entered the bedroom, letting my divination guide me, then set Anne down as gently as I could on the bed at the centre. I could hear her breath in the silence, raspy and quick. Carefully I took my arms away from under her, then walked to the door, flicked on the light, and turned around.

Even though I'd been braced for the sight, my first reaction to Anne's injuries was to close my eyes. I took a breath, then forced them open again. Anne's skin was mottled with a mix of colours—white, red, tan, and coal—and the front of her clothes had burned away to reveal cherry-red burns across her stomach and breasts, spreading up to her neck and face. The burned skin looked moist and weepy, and already angry-looking blisters were forming. Although her body looked bad, her left arm was worse. The skin there wasn't red, but black, cracked and charred, and across the forearm it had peeled away entirely, revealing red muscle and white bone. I moved closer and the smell hit my nostrils again, putrid and rich. Bile rose in my throat and I swallowed, fighting back nausea.

Anne opened her lips and spoke, keeping her eyes closed. "If you're—" She stopped, took a breath, and tried again. Her voice was raspy. "If you're going to throw up, don't do it on me."

I took a breath and regained control. "Sorry." I started to say *Are you all right?* and stopped myself. "What can I do to help?"

Anne's breath rasped. "Water."

I hurried to the kitchen and filled a glass, letting my mind focus on the mundane task. Big glass . . . she wouldn't be able to drink from the edge. Needed a straw. I went through the drawers. Anne's kitchen is small and tidy. I found a packet of drinking straws and tore it open before hurrying back.

Anne hadn't moved, but I could sense magic working inside her body, complex spells layered on top of one another. She didn't open her eyes as I leant in and fed the straw through her cracked lips. Anne's face wasn't as badly hurt as the rest of her body, but it still wasn't pretty. Red streaks ran up her cheek and past her eye, and a patch of her hair had been scorched away, the scent of burnt hair mixing with burnt flesh. Anne drank slowly and steadily until she'd emptied the glass. I set it down on the bedside table.

Anne licked her lips and spoke again. She still didn't open her eyes, but already her voice was stronger. "Are we safe?"

"I don't think they tracked us," I said. "How bad is it?"

"Third-degree burns," Anne said. The rasp in her voice had gone. "Fourth on the arm. I'll manage."

"Do you need anything?"

"Time." Anne was quiet. "What happened to the shop?"

"Screw the shop," I said. "Do whatever it takes to make sure you're better. Okay?"

"Okay." Anne paused. "Alex? There's . . . one thing."

"Name it."

"I can repair this. Most of it." Anne drew in a breath. "But . . . it would help if I had more."

I knew what Anne was asking. Healing magic takes energy. Major healing takes a lot of energy. One way for Anne to do that is to take the energy from her own body, but she can also take it from others. That had been what she'd done to the fire sprites, draining their life force and using it to repair her own injuries. But Anne has limited capacity: she can't "store up" energy beyond a certain point. Repairing this would take more than she had to spend.

I touched Anne's unburned right hand. "Take what you need."

"Thank you," Anne said quietly, then paused. "You should sit down."

"Oh." The last time Anne had done this to me, I'd gone out like a light. "Right." There was a small armchair back in the living room. I went back, carried it into the bedroom, then set it down next to the bed. "Okay," I said, sitting and taking Anne's hand in both of mine. "Do it."

The last time Anne had life-drained me, it had been like having the energy and strength pulled from every part of my body at once. It had been horrible, and as I took Anne's hand my muscles were tense, my mind dreading going through the same experience again.

But this time was different. I saw the spell take shape, reaching out to touch me, but there wasn't the same draining sensation. Instead it was more of a drift, a flow. I felt myself growing tired, my eyes becoming heavy, but it was the sleepiness of being curled up in a warm bed. I fell into a drowsy state, the world floating away.

As I rested, I saw something strange. Out of the grey mist a glowing form took shape; it felt as though I was seeing it with my eyes, and yet I wasn't. It was a human body, luminous, its skin and flesh formed from glowing green light. As I looked closer I saw that the light wasn't solid, but woven, tendrils and vines laced into a tight-knit whole. Parts were reddened and blackened, the vines warped and fraying at their ends, but as I watched I saw that they were regrowing, new shoots stretching out from the damaged ends to interweave with the others. It was both slow and incredibly intricate, like watching someone repair a ripped tapestry with a needle and thread, one strand at a time. There was something fascinating about the deftness of the work. There were no missteps, no mistakes, every new thread of glowing green weaving into the greater pattern. I kept watching until the image faded away and I drifted off to sleep.

At some point during the night I came half awake to see that Anne was leaning over my chair, her face close to mine. Her body was glowing with soft green light, and she was whispering to me. I tried to make out the words, but they blurred together and Anne turned into Arachne and I was curled up on one of the armchairs in Arachne's cave, surrounded by bolts of silk. Arachne was somewhere in the back, working away on some creation of hers, and I turned over and went to sleep.

‖‖‖‖‖‖‖

I woke up slowly and gradually. I could hear voices around me, and the light seemed brighter. From outside, a bird was singing. It was morning.

". . . you're okay?" It was a girl's voice, and it took me a moment to realise that it was Luna. "I mean, you don't look as though . . ."

"I'm fine." It was Anne, and she was speaking from right in front of me. I could feel her hand on mine. "The dangerous time was last night."

"Are you sure?"

"I've had worse, you know."

"I still wish I'd been there." Luna paused. "What about Alex?"

"Well, he's awake. Why don't you ask him?"

I opened my eyes. Morning sunlight was streaming through the window, illuminating the pale green walls of Anne's room. Variam was sitting by the desk, bent forward with his elbows on his knees, and Luna was hovering nearby.

She still looked worried, but she perked up as she met my gaze. "You're okay?"

"Kind of tired." I yawned. I felt sleepy, and my limbs were heavy, but I wasn't hurt. Actually, I felt very comfortable, which was weird given that I'd just slept in my armour. Must have been Anne's work. "When did you guys get here?"

"Not long. I was talking to Anne and—crap, kitchen! I forgot!" Luna turned and ran out into the living room. "I'll be back!" she called over her shoulder.

I looked at Anne. "What was that about?"

"Oh, Luna was offering to make some food," Anne said with a smile. She was lying on her bed, covered with a blanket, and she looked better—actually, *much* better. I couldn't see her left arm or her body, but the skin on her face was smooth and unmarked. Only the clumps burned out of her hair betrayed how recently she'd been hurt. It made her look like a sea urchin with pattern baldness, but her eyes were peaceful. "I was hungry, and she said she'd take care of it."

Variam shifted position on his chair and glanced down. I realised that Anne was still holding my hand. Anne seemed to realise it at the same instant, and let go. "How are you feeling?"

"Good. A lot better than last time."

"I was trying not to take so much this time," Anne said. "More like sharing."

"Well, whatever you did, it worked."

Anne smiled. "Oh." She carefully reached out with her right arm to pick something off the table, then dropped it into my hand. "Here."

I looked at it curiously. It was a spent bullet, slightly deformed. "Where did . . . ?"

"From that last run around the forcewall," Anne said. "I took it out last night. They can do tests on bullets to figure out where they came from, can't they?"

"You were shot as *well*? Why didn't you tell me?"

"I didn't want you to worry."

I gave Anne a disbelieving look, then shook my head and turned to Variam. "Any news?"

Variam snorted. "From us? No. Who did this?"

"They didn't exactly announce themselves, but if I had to guess, I'd say Light mages," I said. "Whatever's going on, some people really don't want me involved."

Luna came bustling in with a tray. "Here." She set it down on Anne's bed. "Uh, it might have got a bit burnt."

The tray held muesli, toast, fruit, bacon, and eggs. The muesli and fruit looked fine, the toast and bacon were blackish, and I had no idea what had happened to the eggs. I played it safe and took an apple. "Hey!" Luna said. "That's for Anne."

"It's all right," Anne said. "He needs it too." She pushed herself further up against the headboard, then reached for the bowl with her right hand. She didn't seem to be in pain, but I noticed she kept her left arm beneath the covers and out of Luna's and Variam's sight.

"So what happened last night?" I asked.

Both Luna and Variam looked away. "We screwed up," Luna said. Her voice was strained, unhappy.

"You had your phones off?"

Luna nodded. "And before you say it, I know we weren't supposed to. You told me back when we set this up, keep it on all the time. I just forgot."

Crappy reason to get yourself killed. I looked at Luna for a second. She didn't meet my eyes, and I decided not to push it. "I guess it could have been worse."

"It nearly *was* worse!" Luna said. "You both nearly died!"

"Yeah, well, it might have been better this way," I said. "If you'd gated in while the ground floor was on fire . . ."

"But I'm not her," Variam said. He was quieter than usual. Vari and Anne have a complicated relationship and in a lot of ways they don't actually have much in common, but Vari's deeply loyal to his friends. Failing to protect Anne must have stung his pride.

I shook my head. "What's done is done. I'm guessing you were busy training or something."

Luna hesitated. "Yeah."

Something was nagging at the back of my mind. There was something I was supposed to be doing. "What time is it?"

"Ten thirty."

Suddenly I remembered. *Caldera*. "Crap." I stood up, feeling my armour adjust to my movements, and nearly fell over. My head was spinning.

"Alex!" Anne caught my arm, steadying me. Her grip was surprisingly strong. "Careful."

"Have you got a phone I can borrow?"

"You can use mine."

Anne had an old-model iPhone in a black case. I took it and dialled the call-block prefix followed by a number, then put the phone to my ear and let it ring. My legs were still a little shaky and I walked out through the living room and into Anne's kitchen. Pans were on the stove, there was a tinge of smoke in the air, and there was something in the sink that looked like a failed prototype. You can always tell when Luna's been using the kitchen.

There was a click as the number picked up. "Caldera."

"It's Alex."

"Alex?" Caldera's voice sharpened. "Where the hell are you?"

"Long story." There was a knock at Anne's door. I heard Luna say something, then there were footsteps as someone went to answer it. I checked quickly for danger and found nothing. "There was a bit of a holdup."

"No shit you had a holdup. I told you the briefing was this morning at nine. I've left three messages already. What were you doing, getting a lie-in?"

"You're in front of your computer, right?"

"Yes. Why?"

"Log in to the Met Police database and check their incident reports for my street in Camden Town. I think this'll go faster if you see for yourself."

There was a pause, and I could faintly hear the click of keys. Voices sounded from Anne's bedroom. I could tell the instant Caldera pulled up the report. "What the *hell*?"

"I had a spot of trouble."

"You're okay?"

"Yeah." I didn't mention Anne. Caldera's basically one of the good guys and I've come to trust her, but she and

Anne don't get on. "I'm guessing there's a bit of activity there."

"Yeah, you could say that." I heard keys click and Caldera's voice rose half an octave. "*Five bodies?* Alex, what the *hell*?"

"I woke up with a bunch of guys about to shoot me in the head," I said testily. "I was kind of working from limited options."

"I want to know everything that happened. Get your arse over here right now."

"I need to do one thing first," I said. "I've got a bunch of items still on site. Some are the kind that you guys don't want the normals getting hold of, if you know what I mean. Can you clear me for access?"

"So you can do what?"

"Take stuff away," I said. "Look, I have a lot of personal belongings still there. I don't want them all going into police impound. Please?"

Keys clicked in the background. "This says the place is gutted. I don't think there's going to be much left."

"The protected stuff will be."

There was a pause. "All right," Caldera said after a moment. "But you are coming in straight afterwards. No sidetracks. And you're not leaving until you've put in a full report. Clear?"

"Okay. Are they looking for me?"

"There's no arrest warrant, but they've made the connection with the explosion two years back. Make sure you steer clear of MI5 until Rain's had a chance to talk to the liaisons."

"I will." I paused. "Caldera? Thanks."

"Just get here in one piece, all right? I don't want to spend my afternoon picking you off the pavement."

"I'll be there in a couple of hours."

⎜⎜⎜⎜⎜⎜⎜⎜

I returned to the bedroom to discover that the new visitor was Sonder. He and Variam were facing each other, with Luna and Anne watching from the sides. As I entered, Luna and Sonder turned to me.

I looked between everyone. "Something wrong?"

There was a slightly longer pause than there should have been. "No," Luna said. "We're fine."

I looked at Anne questioningly. "Everything's okay," Anne said in her soft voice. "Sonder, do you want to sit down?"

"Uh," Sonder said. "Sure." Variam scowled.

I set Anne's phone back on the table. "I need to go back to my shop."

"I'll come with you," Luna said.

"You're due for your lesson with Chalice."

"It can wait—"

"No, it can't," I said. "It's Tuesday morning and your test is on Friday. Nothing you could do at the shop is more important than you passing that test."

Luna made a face but didn't argue. "I'm staying with Anne," Variam said.

Which would leave Variam and Sonder glaring at each other over Anne's bedside. Well, with Anne there, I didn't think Variam was going to do anything stupid. "Okay," I said. "Luna, let me know how things go. I'll check in later."

|||||||||

I own a small farmhouse deep in the country in Wales, at the end of an isolated valley. Over the years I've turned it into a bolt-hole, with a stock of food and emergency equipment. Which was just as well, because right now my equipment list consisted of my armour, the magic items I'd managed to grab last night, and not much else. Luckily my wallet had been in the pocket of my trousers, along with my most important gate stones, but my phone and everything else that had been on my bedside table were in all likelihood a smouldering wreck.

I gated to the house in Wales, changed out of my armour, took a shower in near-freezing water that left me shivering (the heating doesn't work that well), then got a new set of clothes. As I did, I found myself thinking about how long I had left. Four days until my sentence went through. The stress of last night's attack had driven it out of my head, but now I could feel time pressing again.

The gate stone to my back room in London wasn't working, which was disappointing but not really a surprise. Gate stones only take you to one location, and the exact layout of that location is attuned to them when they're created. If the location changes too much, they stop working. I'd been using this gate stone for years, but I wouldn't be using it anymore. I activated one of my few remaining gate stones to travel to a park in Camden, then walked to my house.

You know that whatever's happened to your home is bad when you see the signs before you even turn down your street. A yellow-and-blue-checked police car was blocking off the end of my road, with a bored-looking police officer standing in front of a line of tape. I'd had some vague ideas of sneaking in, but one look at that made me change my mind. I'd brought along a prepaid phone from my emergency kit, and I used it to call Caldera. After a brief delay Caldera told me to wait where I was.

A few minutes later a man appeared from behind the tape, ducked under it, scanned the street until he spotted me, then ambled over in my direction. "Morning," he said. "Who might you be then?"

I took a look at the man. He was in his twenties, with a London accent, and was wearing a *POLICE* vest with lots of useful-looking gadgets clipped onto it. From a glance through the futures I knew he was who I was waiting for. "My name's Verus."

The officer nodded. "All right."

"And how about you?"

"I'm from SASU."

"I thought you guys were called SCD-14 or something."

"We got reorganised again."

For the most part, the police and security services of the United Kingdom are run by normals and for normals, with as little involvement with the magical world as possible. This means that when the two worlds overlap, neither side is particularly well equipped to interact with the other. On these occasions someone has to clean up the mess, and in the London Metropolitan Police, that someone is SCD-14, or SASU, or whatever they're called at the moment, and their job is to liaise with Light Keepers to keep things orderly. From my perspective, dealing with SASU is a mixed blessing. On the plus side, they're a lot less likely to panic and call in the armed police to have you shot. On the other hand, they're considerably harder to fool than normal police, and they have a habit of doing things like not telling you their name.

"Fair enough," I said. "Can I ask what your orders are?"

"Officially, I'm supposed to escort you onto the site so that you can retrieve some personal belongings," the man said.

"And unofficially?"

"Make sure you don't cause any trouble," the man said. "Are you going to?"

"No."

The man nodded. "Come on then." We ducked under the *POLICE DO NOT CROSS* tape and walked down my street.

My shop was at the centre of a collection of police and other emergency vehicles, along with a crowd of people in police vests and high-vis jackets, most of whom seemed to be standing around waiting. The shop itself was a blackened, burned-out husk. It was still standing, but I got the impression that it wasn't by much.

"Are MI5 here yet?" I asked the officer.

"They're stuck in traffic," the officer said. "Did you want to talk to them?"

"Not particularly."

"Suits me."

The inside of the shop was worse than the outside. The shop floor was cinders and ash, charred metal skeletons of shelves peeking out from the debris. I took a glance towards what had been the magic item section and saw that it was gone. The forcewall had probably shielded it for a while, but once the wall had dropped, that section must have taken the full brunt of the fire and now there was nothing left but black husks. There had been over a hundred magic items in there.

Granted, none had been particularly valuable, but they'd been familiar to me and I'd developed an odd sort of affection for them. All gone now. "How many rooms are intact?" I asked the officer.

"Just the one above," the officer said. "Firemen were saying it was reinforced. Only reason the whole place didn't collapse."

I nodded. "That's where we're going."

The stairs up to the first floor had collapsed, and someone had put a ladder in place to get up to the first-floor landing. I climbed it and stepped off carefully over what was left of the banisters. The landing creaked but held.

"Hey!" someone called down from above. I looked up to see a man in full-cover plastic gear on the landing above. "You'd better not come walking over my corpses!"

"We're staying here," my companion called as he climbed up behind me.

"Good," the man in the mask called down. "Haven't finished picking out the teeth yet." He turned back to the subject of his attention and I got a sickly whiff of burned flesh. I turned away before I got too close a look at what he was doing. I'm not squeamish, but I've got my limits.

The door to my safe room was blackened but didn't seem damaged. "Have they had a go at it with a battering ram yet?" I asked.

"Didn't have clearance," the SASU officer said. "This thing safe?"

"Mostly." It wasn't, but it would be once I deactivated the wards. I touched the key points and murmured the deactivation commands under my breath, keeping an eye on the defences in my magesight. The wards had taken a beating but weren't malfunctioning, which was a relief; the last thing I wanted was for them to blow up some random PC who got too close to the door. Once I was sure it was safe I turned the handle and gave the door a shove. The heat had warped the metal and I had to thump it with my shoulder a couple of times before it gave way.

The contents of the safe room were the only part of my

house that still looked the same. The heat obviously hadn't lasted long enough to ignite the contents. "Got a torch?" I asked the policeman.

The policeman pulled out a small Mag-Lite and clicked it on, shining it around the safe room. The white circle of the beam flicked from one item to another. "You sure you want to stick around for this?" I asked the policeman.

The policeman shrugged.

"Suit yourself." I pulled on a pair of leather gloves, then pulled out a black sports bag from where it had been lying underneath the bench. The first item I went for was my mist cloak, hanging on a hook against the far wall. Once it was stowed in the bag I felt a little better. My mist cloak's not entirely safe, but it's saved my life enough times that I feel a lot more comfortable having it to hand.

"What's that thing?" the policeman asked.

I glanced around to see that the officer was shining the torch on the scabbarded sword hanging on the wall. The circle of light picked out the crocodile carved into the hilt, and he was staring at it.

"Bloodsword," I said. *Interesting.* The officer had to be a sensitive, if not an adept. That sword isn't the most powerful imbued item I own, but it's got the strongest aura, and I doubted he'd picked it out by coincidence. "Don't touch it."

The officer examined it from a careful distance. "What does it do?"

"Cuts through just about anything, and gives its wielder enhanced strength and speed. It also sends pretty much anyone who picks it up on a murderous rampage."

"What do you use it for?"

"I don't," I said. "Frankly, I can't think of many situations where turning into a psychopathic berserker would really improve things very much."

"So why are you keeping hold of it?"

"So no one else can use it," I said. I didn't mention the other powers it had. That sword is a very nasty piece of work, and I haven't yet figured out any good solution as to what to do with the thing. Carefully, I took hold of it by the scabbard and lifted it off the hooks. For a moment I could hear a song somewhere at the back of my mind, wordless and voiceless, urging me to stop and listen. I blocked the impulse off and dropped the sword into the bag. The music in the back of my head lingered briefly, then faded.

I added the green egg and the locked darts, putting each in a separate pocket of the sports bag, then started scooping up the lower-priority stuff. Once I was done clearing the tables I opened the weapons cabinet and took the MP7 off its hooks.

"Have you got a licence for that?" my companion asked.

"If you're going to ask me questions about everything here," I said, "this is going to take a while." I added the other handguns, followed by the ammo, the *jian*, and most of the rest of the weapons. The officer stayed silent.

Once I was done I turned back to the tables. They'd been stripped nearly bare, apart from one item lying alone at the centre: a white and blue tube of lacquered wood, carved with flowers. I stared at it, exploring the futures in which I picked it up. Nothing. I rechecked—again nothing. I didn't move forward. My magic might tell me that the thing was safe, but I still didn't want to touch it.

"Is there a problem?" the officer asked.

"I hope not." The thing in that tube had taken its last victim only a few months ago. Maybe it was still fed.

"What is it?"

"You're better off not knowing," I said. "Trust me." I took a deep breath and picked the tube up. Nothing happened and I slid it into one of the side compartments in the bag. I didn't like keeping it so close to the other items, but I liked the idea of having it in my pocket even less.

There were things still left in the safe room, but my bag was full and I had everything I really needed. I brushed past the officer, came out onto the landing, and paused.

The remains of my shop and flat were all around me, the walls burnt black and smelling of smoke and charcoal. From outside I could hear the policemen chatting, and above the doctor was still working away on those bodies. The building didn't feel like a shop. It felt like a crime scene—a *wrecked* crime scene. Nothing was familiar and I didn't feel as though I belonged here.

There was no way to fix this. The building might still be standing, but it was gutted. Anyone wanting to replace the shop would have to wait for the police investigation to be over, then demolish all the parts of the old building that were left, then clear the ground and set new foundations, *then* build a new shop from the ground up.

I'd owned this shop for seven years. It had been a hobby at first, then a vocation, then my home, but it had always been part of my life. Now it was gone.

"Is there a problem?" the officer asked from behind me.

"Yeah," I said. "Just not one I can fix." I slung the bag over my back and started climbing down the ladder.

॥॥॥॥॥॥

We made it out of the police cordon without incident. Once we were at the point at which the officer had met me, he stopped. "All right. Off you go."

I gave him a nod. "Thanks for the help."

"Sure," the officer said. "Make sure I don't have to do it again."

I paused, looking at the man. The tone of voice had been neutral . . . a little too neutral. "You don't like me very much, do you?" I asked.

"Not really."

"I didn't start this."

"There were five dead bodies around that site," the man said. "Two on the roof and three on the stairwell. All killed by fire or gunshot wounds. You going to tell me you didn't have anything to do with it?"

I was silent.

"We like things quiet, here at the Met," the officer said. "Orderly. Every time you people get involved it gets a lot less orderly. Our lives would be easier if you all went away."

"You think that I wanted this?" I said. "You think I *wanted* my house shot up and burned down?"

The officer shrugged.

"You're all heart," I said.

"Don't know who started it," the officer said. "Not really our business. But do us a favour and take your fighting somewhere else."

I looked back at the officer in silence, then walked away.

chapter 8

I dropped my gear back at the safe house in Wales, then checked in with Anne, who told me that she was fine, that Variam was with her, and that Sonder had gone in to Keeper HQ. The two hours I'd promised Caldera were up, and I didn't want to waste any more time. I gated back to London and hurried to join Sonder.

The headquarters of the Keepers of the Order of the Star and the Order of the Shield is in Westminster, an old Victorian building with carvings on the outside and ugly brown walls on the inside. I never used to have much to do with the place, but since I became an auxiliary member of the Order of the Star last winter I've been in and out pretty often. It might have been my imagination, but as I walked down the hallway, I had the sense that the place felt busier than usual. The noise from the offices was louder and there were more people in the halls. No one gave me any second glances—apparently news of my death sentence hadn't had time to spread. The Keepers work for the Council, but they tend to be too busy with their cases to be very well informed about what's going on within the higher ranks. I found Caldera's office, knocked, and entered at the "Come in!"

Caldera's office looks pretty much like that of any other cop, papers and clutter scattered across a pair of coffee-stained desks. Caldera used to share the place with another Keeper named Haken, but their relationship took a nose-dive around the same time I became an auxiliary, and Caldera hasn't gotten another partner since. In the absence of anyone telling me not to, I'd taken to using the second desk myself. Right now the office was occupied by three people. One was Sonder, sitting in my spot; he gave me a glance, then looked back at the man sitting in the spare chair.

Caldera was sitting behind her desk, a beefy woman in her thirties with thick powerful arms. "You're late," she told me as I walked in.

From the tone of voice and her conversation earlier, I gathered that not only had Caldera not heard about my situation with Levistus, but Sonder hadn't told her either. "Busy morning," I said.

"At least you're here," Caldera said. "Pull up a seat."

"So the briefing on the op was this morning, right?" I said, sitting down.

"Yeah, about that," Caldera said. She nodded at the man sitting in front of the desk. "Captain?"

"There's been a change of plans," the man said. His name was Rain, a tall, fit-looking man with dark skin and close-shaven black hair. Rain is Caldera's immediate superior in the Order of the Star, which in practical terms makes him our boss. I'm not close to Rain, but over the past year I'd come to like him; he's got a no-bullshit manner which I find refreshing. "How much do you know about the situation?"

"There's another relic weapon sealed up in a bubble," I said. "Drakh wants it and so does the Council, the bubble's going to open at some point in the next few days, and you're the one who's got the job of pulling it out when it does."

Rain glanced at Caldera.

Caldera shrugged. "I didn't tell him."

"You're pretty well informed about something that's supposed to be a secret," Rain said. "I suppose I shouldn't be surprised. All of what you say's correct. The time in question is tomorrow evening. The operation is going to commence at four P.M. Be here in the morning."

I nodded.

"However, that's not why I've called you here," Rain said. "As you know, Drakh wants that weapon. Our most recent intelligence indicates that he is intending to dedicate significant forces towards retrieving it. Initial estimates put the numbers of his recovery team at ten to fifteen Dark mages."

I raised my eyebrows. It wasn't really a surprise, but I figured I should act the part.

Sonder looked startled. "That's got to be a mistake."

"Actually, that was the low-end guess," Rain said.

"But Dark mages never work together in those numbers," Sonder said. "The most we see in a cabal is four or five."

"I'm just passing on what I'm told," Rain said. "Apparently the intelligence analysts have finally started taking Drakh seriously."

"I thought they weren't even sure he was still alive?"

"Seems they've changed their mind about that too." Rain looked at me. "For obvious reasons, the Council don't want to kick off with a Dark cabal that big. I've been asked to explore the possibility of a negotiated settlement."

"Okay," I said. I was getting the nasty feeling I knew where this was going.

"We've made overtures through neutral parties to mages we believe to be members of Drakh's cabal," Rain said. "They've agreed to a meeting this evening in the Barbican. Both parties are allowed to bring no more than two members." Rain looked between me and Sonder. "I want to send you."

"What?" Sonder said. "Why?"

"Because we're not Keepers," I said. I didn't take my eyes off Rain. "If word gets out that the Council are negotiating with a Dark mage, it'll hurt their image. They're supposed to be the ones in charge, not Drakh. If they have to get his agreement, instead of just dictating to him . . ."

"That's about the size of it," Rain agreed. "Apparently the Council think that sending Keepers to negotiate with Drakh's agents would send the wrong message."

"So having us go gives what? Plausible deniability?"

"Pretty much."

"It's not going to work," I said. "We're still Keeper auxiliaries. Dark mages won't make any distinction between us and full Keepers. They'll see it as just as much of a sign of weakness as if you'd gone yourself. Actually, they'll probably see it as *more* of a sign of weakness than if you'd gone yourself."

"Yeah, well, these are the orders I've got," Rain said. "You can send an official protest, but I wouldn't waste your time. However, since neither of you are full Keepers, I can't order you. This is volunteer only."

Sonder and I looked at each other. Sonder didn't look all that happy, and I couldn't blame him. This had all the earmarks of an operation run by Council bureaucracy. "Why us?" Sonder asked. "Why not pick a mind or charm mage or something?"

"The choice was left to my discretion," Rain said. "I'm choosing you."

"Why?" I said.

"Because Dark mages don't trust Light mages," Rain said. "And when they're dealing with people they don't trust, they've got a habit of shooting first and asking questions later. The only Light mages they do trust, even the tiniest bit, are ones they have a personal connection with. Which brings us to you."

My heart sank. *Oh, great.*

Sonder looked confused. "Personal— ?"

"The two mages we're going to be negotiating with are called Cinder and Deleo." Rain looked between us. "I understand you know them."

"I don't—" Sonder began, and then stopped.

A few years ago, Sonder and I got involved in a messy little business involving a Light mage named Belthas. Belthas had been after a new technique for draining the life and magic from the dwindling number of magical creatures in our world, and I got between him and what he wanted. Belthas lost the argument in a very final way, which (given that he'd been one of Levistus's closer allies) had almost certainly been a major contributing factor to the situation I was in right now. For complicated reasons, that same battle had also led to me and Sonder working with Cinder to rescue Deleo, aka my ex-fellow-apprentice Rachel.

All this had been back in Sonder's rebellious phase, before he decided to throw in his lot with the Council. From the expression on his face, it was obvious he wasn't comfortable being reminded. From the expression on Rain's face, it was obvious that he knew about our past history, or at least who it involved. The fact that he wasn't pressuring us implied that he wasn't trying to use it as leverage, but pleading ignorance wasn't going to work.

"We don't have time for you to chew it over, Sonder," Rain said. "If you say no, I'll need to find someone else, and fast. Are you in or out?"

Sonder took a few seconds to answer, and I could see from the switching futures that he was making up his mind. "In," he said at last.

Rain looked at me. "Verus?"

Much as I hated the prospect of coming face to face with Rachel, I really didn't have much of a choice. I needed to make a good impression if I wanted that vote from Undaaris, and Rain would be the one submitting the report. "I can't say I'm exactly thrilled to be dealing with those two, but you're right, they probably will react better to us than other auxiliaries. Not that that's saying much." I shrugged. "Actually, I kind of appreciate that you trust me enough to give me the job."

"You haven't given me any reason not to," Rain said. "Keep it that way and we'll be fine. I understand there was some trouble this morning?"

"Someone tried to assassinate me and burned down my house."

"Are you still in danger?"

"Probably," I said. "If you could spare Caldera, it'd help."

Rain glanced at Caldera.

"I'm going to be babysitting them anyway, right?" Caldera said with a shrug. "When do you want us back?"

"The meeting with Cinder and Deleo is at eight," Rain said. "Be here for the briefing at six." He looked between us. "Anything else?"

I shook my head. Sonder did the same.

"Then I'll let you get to it. Good luck." Rain stood and walked out.

Caldera turned to me. "All right, what the hell have you got yourself into this time?"

"I wish I knew. I've only got half of it."

"Then tell me that half."

"Over the past few days I've been hassled by mages and adepts with ties to the Crusader faction," I said. "I don't know who's sending them, but they know about Rain's operation, and for some reason they're convinced I'm working for Richard."

"Who were the attackers?"

I shook my head. "The only one I got a close look at was the fire mage, and he had a flame shield. The best lead I've got is a mage called Symmaris. She called the day before and warned me off. When I told her to get lost, this happened."

Caldera frowned. "So what, they think you're trying to retrieve the relic, but you're on Richard's team?"

"Yes," I said in frustration. "And it doesn't make any bloody sense. Even if I *was* working for Richard, I'd probably be the least powerful mage he had. Why go after me?"

"Have you got any proof that it was really Light mages?" Sonder asked.

"No. And before you ask, I don't have any proof that it was Symmaris either, except for the fact that someone on the other team was using gates really damn well."

"Anyone else you've pissed off recently?" Caldera asked.

I hesitated. If I was going to bring up the topic of my death sentence, this would be the time to do it. It was tempting to come clean. Over the past year I'd come to trust Caldera, and she's a good person to have in your corner.

But in this case, I wasn't at all sure she *would* be in my corner. Caldera might be one of the good guys, but she follows Council law, and according to Council law, right now, I was an enemy. Once that resolution was passed, as a Light Keeper, Caldera would be duty-bound to bring me in. And I knew Caldera. She'd do her job, no matter what.

But I didn't want to lie to her either. "There's something else," I said. "I just can't tell you what it is."

Caldera frowned. "Alex, if this relates to what's going on—"

"It's not that I don't want to, I literally *can't*," I said. "It's covered by Council secrecy." Which was true. "All I can tell you is that it's the reason I'm on this job in the first place. I'm guessing you already noticed I didn't get called in the usual way."

"Had been going to ask you about that, yeah." Caldera looked at me, but I already knew that she wouldn't push it further. "Does it relate to last night's attack?"

"Not directly, as far as I know." Which was also true. I was pretty sure that it was Symmaris and her friends who'd been behind the assassination attempt, even if I couldn't prove it.

There was an awkward silence. "All right," Caldera said at last, and got to her feet. "Let's go see if we can find these new friends of yours."

⁙⁙⁙⁙⁙

On my suggestion, our first stop was the room in the building opposite my shop, where the fire mage had launched his initial attack. It was still in the cordon, and I didn't particularly want to deal with the police again, so Sonder and I waited nearby while Caldera talked her way in. Once she was alone in the room, she opened up a gate and the two of us stepped through.

"Your work, I'm guessing," Caldera said as she closed the gate behind us.

"They started it," I said. Grenades make quite a mess. The walls had been shredded by shrapnel, and feathers from the ruined bedding were everywhere.

"Sonder?" Caldera said. "What are you getting?"

"Give me a sec," Sonder said, frowning as he stared into space. Sonder is a time mage, and his speciality is timesight, the ability to look back through past events in your current location. Most time mages can do it, but Sonder's particularly good at it. For obvious reasons it's a highly in-demand skill among Keepers, which is one of the reasons Sonder's become quite successful in his career.

I nodded down at the feathers. "Any bloodstains?"

"The cops got a few," Caldera said. "They'll be in the lab for analysis."

"Any chance we could get them?"

"Not for at least twenty-four hours."

"Eh," I said. There are some powerful tracking spells you can pull off if you have a piece of the target's body, but that was too long. "They'll have used an annuller by then."

Sonder stirred. "Anything?" Caldera asked.

"Just glimpses," Sonder said. "They were using a shroud. And a radio, giving directions, I think. One of them gated out, the explosion went off and wounded the other, he called for help, then he gated away too."

"Any ID on the mages?"

Sonder shook his head. "Shadow masks."

"Guess we can't expect them to be stupid all the time." Caldera held up her hand, and brown light gathered around it as she started working on another gate. "You guys head back before those guys start wondering why I'm talking to myself. I'll meet you at the park."

Caldera's gate led us back to the park we'd arrived from. It was the same one I'd used earlier in the day: a small secluded circle of greenery fenced in by high buildings, with tree cover heavy enough to hide a gate spell, even in winter. I stepped down onto the hard earth and waited as Sonder came through behind me. The gate winked out, leaving us alone.

"When are you going to tell her?" Sonder asked.

I sighed. "Hopefully never."

Sonder frowned. "That's not—"

"If everything goes to plan, the resolution won't pass," I said. "It fails and goes into the archives in a file marked

'Secret.' If things *don't* go to plan, then Caldera's going to be the least of my worries. Either way, I don't see how telling her about something that is illegal for us to know is going to help very much, given that the first thing she'd be obliged to do would be to prosecute us for breaking Council secrecy."

"What if it turns out it *was* Levistus who sent those men?" Sonder asked.

"It wasn't Levistus."

"How do you—?"

"Because Levistus has me under a death sentence." I tried not to let my impatience show. Sonder is intelligent, but he's no strategist. "There is absolutely no reason for him to work this hard to get me killed when as far as he knows he only has to wait a few days and the Keepers will do it for him."

"Caldera is going to find out sooner or later."

"Yeah, she is," I said. "So if you're so keen on making sure she's informed, why haven't you told her already?"

"Me? Why?"

"Why not?" I said. "If you care that much."

Sonder was silent.

I looked at Sonder. The winter sky was overcast, and the light filtering through the clouds made him look older than he was, but to my eyes he still looked young. "You know, Sonder," I said, "one of these days, you're going to have to figure out whose side you're on."

Sonder gave me a sideways look. "What do you mean?"

"I mean that if you keep sitting on the fence, then sooner or later someone is going to come along and push you off."

"I just work for the Council," Sonder said. "I don't want to take sides."

"Yeah, well, 'the Council' isn't one side," I said. "Why do you think they have so much trouble dealing with mages like Richard? If they had their act together they'd be telling him to back the hell off. But they can't, because they spend too much time fighting amongst each other and going after people like me." I shrugged. "They're going to fall apart at this rate. When you've got people like Levistus running the show, it doesn't matter that you've got people like Caldera lower down."

The crunch of footsteps announced Caldera's arrival, and we both turned to look. "Well, looks like your hunch was right," Caldera said to me as she walked up. "The three bodies in the stairwell were too badly burned to ID, but the cops have managed to finger one of the ones they found on the roof. He was a low-level thug with ties to some of the more radical Crusader groups. Good bet the others are the same."

"Have you got any leads on Symmaris?"

"We've got her address in Kew. What are you planning to do with it?"

"Go over there and shake her down a bit."

"We haven't got enough for an arrest."

"I know."

Caldera gave me a curious look. "What are you hoping for? Rattling the tree to see what falls out?"

"It's worth a shot, but I've got something else in mind."

"Do you still need me?" Sonder asked.

"Yes," I said. "I'll explain along the way."

ııııııı

Kew Gardens is to the southwest of London what Hampstead is to the north: pretty, clean air, lots of trees and flowers, and incredibly expensive. Symmaris's house was on a corner and looked bigger and more spacious than the norm, set slightly back from the street but still not all that excessive by mage standards. There was a front garden with a hedge.

"Okay," I said. The three of us were at the end of the road, out of sight. The street was empty, with the vaguely deserted feel that the middle-class parts of London always seem to have during the daytime. "Caldera, you've got enough links to Symmaris to justify a visit, right?"

"Sure."

"So here's the plan. The three of us go in and you and I question her. I figure that just seeing me there is going to scare her. Important thing is that we make sure that we do it in whichever room she uses for day-to-day activities."

"Okay . . ."

"Now, I don't know if we'll get anything," I said. "If we do, that's a bonus, but it's optional. The idea is to rattle her. We get her scared, then we leave."

Caldera looked slightly puzzled. "How does that help?"

"The impression I've got of Symmaris is that she's not exactly brave. And she's nowhere near the top of the food chain; she's working on someone else's orders. If we scare her enough, there's a good chance that the first thing she'll do is go call her boss. Right?"

"I guess."

"So once we're out of the house, we wait. I'll use my divination and look through the futures in which we go back. Once I've got a fix, we go back for another talk. You say that there's something you forgot to ask." I turned to Sonder. "That's where you come in. While Caldera and I are talking to her, you use your timesight and look back at what's happened in the room. With a bit of luck you should be able to make out the details of her conversation. You can figure out who her boss is, and maybe get something incriminating."

"The room's going to be warded," Sonder said.

"Against scrying, sure. Maybe not against timesight."

"It'll be both," Sonder said. "I mean, time and space magic overlap anyway, it's not exactly hard. I don't think I've ever seen a Light mage's house that doesn't have timesight wards."

"Okay, that makes it harder, but your timesight's pretty good. It's exponentially easier to see through a temporal shroud the closer that period is to the present, right?"

"Technically it's not an exponential relationship. It's more like—"

"You get the idea."

Sonder thought for a second. "As long as the wards aren't stronger than average, and as long as it's within ten or fifteen minutes, I should be able to get a clear read. Any longer than that and I might start losing fragments. Also, I'll need to know where to look."

I nodded. "So we need some way to make sure that when she has that conversation, it's at a location we can reach."

Caldera was looking unimpressed. "You don't know that she *is* going to have that conversation. And even if she does, her boss isn't likely to say anything incriminating over the phone. If he's smart, he won't even be using a phone."

"But there's a good chance she'll let something slip."

"She might not," Sonder said. "I mean, if she's that scared, she might just run away or something."

"Yeah, let's just keep it simple," Caldera said. "Take a look at her garden for me."

I blinked. "Say again?"

"That front garden," Caldera said. "Use your divination and tell me what it looks like."

I gave Caldera a puzzled look, then examined the futures in which I walked down the road and pushed open the gate. "Okay, so . . . it's a garden. Decent-sized hedge, some shrubs, and there are creepers growing on trellises. And there's a fountain. What am I looking for?"

"How neat does it look?"

"Pretty neat, I guess."

"How about the house? Same way?"

"Yeah." I looked at Caldera curiously. "Why?"

"All right, let's go," Caldera said. She started walking down the road.

I looked at Sonder, who shrugged. We followed Caldera.

Symmaris's garden *was* nice. It would have been prettier if it weren't midwinter, but even so, the wisteria climbing through the trellis looked well tended, and the grass was perfectly smooth. Caldera marched straight up the path to the front door and rang the bell.

There was a long silence, then the intercom clicked. "Hello?"

"Mage Symmaris?" Caldera asked.

"Who is this?"

"I'm Keeper Caldera of the Order of the Star. We'd like to ask you a few questions."

There was a pause. "What about?"

"Open the door, please."

The intercom was silent for a moment as Symmaris hesitated again. "This isn't a very good time . . ."

"Mage Symmaris, we're here on a Council investigation," Caldera said. "There are two ways this can go. Either you come out and talk to us, or you get a new door."

My eyebrows climbed at that. While Caldera had been talking I'd been studying the wards on the house, and they were heavy duty: the standard gate protections, as well as the shrouds that Sonder had been referring to, but there were reinforcement and attack wards as well. If Caldera tried to smash the door down I did not want to be in the blast radius. "Uh, Caldera?" I murmured. "I don't think—"

Caldera held up a finger to silence me. "Well?" she said into the intercom.

"Wait! Wait!"

"You going to let us in?"

"Give me a second!"

Caldera looked back at me. "She coming?"

I looked into the futures. "Yeah. About two minutes."

We stood on the cold doorstep. Two minutes and twenty seconds later, there was the scrape of metal as a viewing slot opened in the door. "Can I—I mean, I want you to show me your signet."

Caldera complied, holding up the leather wallet that concealed her symbol of office. There was a pause. "All right," Symmaris said hesitantly.

"Open the door, please," Caldera said again.

To my surprise, Symmaris obeyed. The door swung open to reveal a neatly decorated hall with a mirror, hanging rugs, and dainty-looking ornaments lined up on shelves. Symmaris was several steps back from the door, and as she saw me her eyes went wide. I'd deliberately stayed off to the side and out of the field of vision of the door slot and the hidden camera I'd spotted at the top of the porch. "You!" Symmaris said.

"Hello, Mage Symmaris," Caldera said. "How are you doing today?"

Symmaris pointed at me. "What's he doing here?"

"Mage Verus is a Keeper auxiliary," Caldera said. "He's also not the one asking the questions. Are you aware that there was an incident involving a breach of the Concord last night?"

Symmaris seemed to be standing only a few feet away, within easy reach, but appearances were deceptive. There were wards ready to go; at least one was a force effect and . . . yes. If I lunged for her she'd say a command word and throw up a barrier blocking the entry hall. "What?" Symmaris said.

"An incident involving a breach of the Concord," Caldera said. "Know anything about it?"

"I—no. I don't know what you're talking about."

Not the best piece of deception I've seen. Even if I hadn't already been sure that Symmaris had been involved, the look on her face would have been enough to confirm it. "Were you in Camden Town last night, or involved in any way with mages operating there?" Caldera asked.

"No," Symmaris said. "Of course not."

"Mind telling me your whereabouts between two A.M. and four A.M. this morning?"

"What? Why?"

Caldera nodded. "Get your coat."

Symmaris stared at her. "What?"

"We're going down to the station."

"What?"

"We're going down to the station," Caldera repeated. "We'd like to ask you a few questions."

"But—" Symmaris looked scared. "I don't—"

"As I said, there was a breach of the Concord last night," Caldera said. "And now there are dead bodies to clear up. We take this sort of thing seriously."

"But what's that got to do with me?"

"Because the attack was made on Mage Verus's place of residence," Caldera said. "The same location you visited two days ago and demanded that he . . ." Caldera turned to me. "What was it again?"

"Demanded that I leave the country," I said. "And implied that something unpleasant might happen if I didn't."

Symmaris was looking increasingly panicked. "That wasn't what I said!"

"Oh," I added. "And that was after she admitted to being the one who sent those adepts who tried to beat me up the night before."

Caldera looked at Symmaris with raised eyebrows.

"It wasn't me! He's lying!"

"You can explain it down at the station," Caldera said. Behind us, Sonder was watching curiously.

"No!" Symmaris said. She pointed at me. "I'm not going with him! He wants to kill me!"

"Then if it wasn't you, who was it?" Caldera said. All of a sudden her voice was hard. "You didn't do it? Then tell me who did."

Symmaris hesitated. "I . . ."

Caldera shook her head in disgust. "Get your coat."

"No, wait! I can't!"

"I'm not asking."

"I can't go down to Keeper headquarters!"

"Then give me something," Caldera said. "Because if I don't have someone else to pull in, it's going to be you."

"All right, all right!" Symmaris held up her hands. "Off the record, okay?"

"I don't care about the record. I just want answers."

"All right." Symmaris took a deep breath. "It was Maradok. He came to me and said that I needed to convince Verus to stay away from Drakh."

"And then what?" Caldera said. "You helped him gate in? Maybe some of his friends?"

"No! I didn't do anything like that. I mean I talked to Redman, and I went to meet with Verus, but that was it. All I did was call Maradok and pass on the message. If he—if anything happened after that, it was nothing to do with me."

I stared at Symmaris. Her eyes shifted away, and I was quite sure that she was lying. *Bullshit it's nothing to do with you.* Someone had been making those gates—someone who'd been familiar with the area around my shop—and I didn't buy for a second that the Crusaders had somehow found *another* gate expert to bring in on the plan.

"So why does Maradok want Verus gone?" Caldera said.

"Because he's working with Drakh!"

"And you know this because . . . ?"

"Because he's going to be the one who does it." Symmaris pointed at me. "The relic that the Council's looking for? Verus is the one who's going to give it to Drakh!"

"And how are you so sure?"

Symmaris threw up her hands. "I don't know! You think Maradok tells me this stuff? Maybe he got it from a diviner or something. *I* don't care."

"Okay, I am getting sick of this," I said. "I haven't been working for Richard for—"

Caldera raised her hand, and I cut myself off with an effort. It was bad enough that Symmaris had had a hand in burning my house down, but trying to claim that it was justified . . .

"Who was involved in the attack last night?" Caldera said.

"I don't know," Symmaris said. But her eyes shifted again.

"What did Maradok say when you last spoke to him?"

"I haven't heard from him. He doesn't talk to me."

"Then why—?"

"Look, I've told you everything I know," Symmaris broke in. "If you want to ask questions, go to Maradok, not me. He's the one who has a problem with Verus. It's nothing to do with me. I can't—I'm not going with you. Good-bye!"

"Caldera!" I snapped.

Caldera's much quicker than her bulk would suggest. She jumped back just as Symmaris made a gesture with her hand and the door slammed shut in our faces with a *bang* of metal on metal. Caldera steadied herself and looked at the closed door. It would have missed, but not by much. From within Symmaris's house I heard the hurried patter of feet, then silence. The three of us were alone.

"Well," Sonder said. "Okay, then."

"She going to answer if we try again?" Caldera asked me.

I checked for a few seconds, exploring the possibilities thoroughly. "No. I think she's gating." I looked at Caldera. "I can probably find a way through those wards."

"No." Caldera shook her head. "We're done." She turned and walked away.

I caught up with Caldera as she reached the gate, Sonder hurrying after me. "We're cashing out already?"

"Can't bring her in," Caldera said. She turned out onto the pavement and we followed. "She'd walk in a few hours, and there'd be hell to pay."

"Wait," Sonder said. "You just told her you were going to bring her in for questioning?"

Caldera gave Sonder a patient look.

"You were bluffing?" Sonder asked.

"There is no way in hell Rain would authorise bringing her in on this evidence," Caldera said. "Not with this thing with Drakh on our plates. He'd tear my head off if I actually arrested her."

"Funny," I said dryly. "I'm pretty sure we've pulled adepts in for questioning with less than this."

"Says the guy who wanted to do a ludicrously complicated plan involving timesighting an imaginary conversation."

"All right," I admitted. "Your plan was better. How did you know to play it like that?"

"You told me she was the jumpy type," Caldera said. "You saw how neat and tidy that house looked? People like that, best way to scare them is to threaten to take them out of their comfort zone."

It wasn't something I would have thought of, but this is why Caldera's good at her job. I guess we're all limited by our frames of thinking. I'm a diviner first and foremost, so when I come up against a problem, divination's what I fall back on. But for all the Council's weaknesses, a Keeper badge carries weight. To Light mages, the thought of coming under that kind of investigation is scary. Caldera understands how to use that much better than I do.

"Who's Maradok?" I asked.

"He," Caldera said, "is a problem."

I looked at Sonder.

"He's with the Guardians," Sonder said. He looked worried. "Well, he's supposed to have Crusader sympathies, but . . . He's with Council intelligence. And he reports directly to Sal Sarque."

"To—oh, shit." Sal Sarque was one of the three votes cast against me on the Senior Council. And according to Talisid, he was Levistus's ally. This was just getting worse and worse.

"There's more," Caldera said. She didn't look happy. "Maradok's been detailed to the Keepers for tomorrow's operation. He's one of the mages involved in planning it."

We were approaching the end of the road. I stopped, forcing Caldera and Sonder to pause and look at me. "Are you serious?"

"Just heard from Rain this morning."

"The guy who wants me dead is in charge of *planning the mission I'm going on*?"

"He doesn't have operational command," Caldera said. "He's just the liaison."

I put a hand over my eyes. "You have got to be fucking kidding me."

"It's time we got back for the briefing," Caldera said. "We'll report to Rain once we're there."

chapter 9

I t was later that evening.

Rain pattered on the glass roof above our heads and left moving streaks on the panels to the side. It was one of those winter showers where the drops are only a few degrees above freezing, on the edge of becoming sleet or snow, and they'd been falling steadily for the past two hours. We were standing on a landing between two escalators, about ten feet above street level. Steel-and-glass skyscrapers rose up around us, brightly coloured ventilators poking up near their bases, and the paving stones were slick and wet. At the foot of the escalator, on the other side of the road, an office building rose on concrete stilts, lines of windows glowing white-and-yellow in the night.

"Anything?" Rain asked. The weather didn't seem to bother him, which given his name probably shouldn't have been all that much of a surprise.

I shook my head. "Not yet."

"It's freezing," Sonder said. He was wearing an anorak, but it wasn't stopping him from shivering.

I felt the same way but kept it to myself. The bottom of the escalator was open to the air and the icy breeze that blew up from the wet concrete was biting right through my coat. I'm happy being a diviner most of the time, but if there's one thing that makes you envious of elemental mages, it's standing in the cold.

We were on the edge of the Barbican, just on the other side of London Wall. London is an old city, but the Barbican is one of the few places where old has been entirely driven out by new, a dense rabbit warren of stone and concrete and stacked square apartments, grey and brown and cold. The architectural style is called "brutalist," and if you've ever seen the place you'll understand why. The Barbican is home to a girls' school, an arts centre, various different residential towers and blocks of flats, and (at least for tonight) the Dark mages Cinder and Deleo, who were going to be joining us for a nice peaceful chat.

At least, that was the plan.

"Have you decided what to do about Maradok?" I asked Rain.

"How do you mean?"

"Caldera said she told you what we got from Symmaris," I said. "I figured you've been deciding how to deal with it." I looked at Rain. "Made up your mind?"

Rain was silent.

"I'm guessing that's a yes."

"You know Maradok's involved in the Drakh operation."

"Yeah, and he's a Light mage with the ear of one of the Senior Council," I said. "Look, you don't need to sugarcoat it, all right? There's no way you're going to prosecute him."

"Right now, no," Rain said. "Not while we're in the middle of this."

I looked away. Down on London Wall, through the rain-streaked glass, the traffic rolled by.

"But after this is over—assuming that you haven't worked out some other arrangement—then yes."

I looked at Rain in surprise.

"Don't get your hopes up," Rain said. "There's pretty much zero chance of an indictment. But I can ask some awkward questions. Enough to stop them trying it again."

It was more than I'd expected. "Thanks."

"You're part of my team, and you do good work," Rain said. He nodded at me and Sonder. "I'm going to check in with Caldera and the other backup. Report in as soon as you get something." He turned and walked away down the escalator.

I looked after Rain. "Huh."

"He seems to like you," Sonder said.

I gave Sonder a glance. "Is that a problem?"

"No."

I raised my eyebrows and looked away. Out on the road, a bus rumbled past, city lights reflecting off its red sides.

"You haven't said anything about Symmaris," Sonder said eventually.

"I think I just did."

"I mean what she told us."

"About what?"

"About you getting that relic for Drakh."

I rolled my eyes. "Not you as well."

"I'm serious."

"Sonder, ever since I entered mage society, I've had to deal with Light mages assuming the worst of me. First they assumed that because I was Richard's apprentice, I must be a murdering psycho. After I left him, they *still* assumed that I was a murdering psycho. Now they think that I'm going to go *back* to Richard to become a murdering psycho. This isn't anything new."

"But they're acting like they know it's going to happen."

"No, we've got one report *saying* that they know it's going to happen. Which, by the way, comes from a proven liar."

"It seems like they believe it."

"It doesn't matter what they believe. If someone tells me they believe I'm going to take up Morris dancing, I'm not going to go out and buy a set of bells and a subscription to *Morris Dancer Monthly*."

"It's not the same thing."

"It *is* the same thing. I'm not going to turn into a murdering psycho, I'm not going to take up Morris dancing, and I'm sure as hell never going back to working for Richard. What I do is *my* choice. Not theirs."

"Then why are they so sure?" Sonder said. "What if they did get it from a prophecy? Or a divination?"

"Divinations can be misinterpreted. And the only prophecies that are that accurate come from dragons, and the Council doesn't deal with dragons."

"But what if they *are* right?"

"Okay, Sonder," I said. "You know what? Let's play your game. Let's say they are. What are you going to do? Sell me out to the Council?"

"That's not what I meant . . ."

"Then you'd take matters into your own hands? Kill me yourself?"

"What? No!"

"Then let's say Levistus's proposal gets voted through," I said. "All of a sudden my status with the Council is kill-on-sight. Are you going to help me, or turn me in?"

Sonder was silent. "I don't want to pick either way," he said at last.

"You're not going to have a choice. If you have information about where I am, then you either keep it to yourself—in which case you're betraying your oath to the Council—or you sell me out. There's no in-between. For someone like you, on the inside of the Council, then it's all shifting allegiances and politics. But for someone like me? I've got people I can trust, and people I can't. Which are you?"

Sonder met my eyes for an instant, then his gaze flicked away. He looked down at the floor. "I don't know."

The communicator in my ear chimed. "Verus?" Caldera's voice said.

I turned away. "Receiving."

"Coatl just picked up a gate. Expect company."

"Understood," I said. The communicator cut off and I looked at Sonder. "We're up."

Sonder nodded. I had the feeling he was relieved to have

an excuse to end the conversation. We took the escalator and walked over the bridge into the Barbican.

ııııııı

The inside of the Barbican is railings and brown stone, long walkways separating hulking mounds of brick and concrete. The sounds of traffic faded as we moved deeper into the maze, until it was only a murmur in the distance. The path we were following ran straight, then opened up into a giant empty space, looking down upon a long artificial lake. Blocks of flats and an arts centre were placed on the other side, their white-yellow lights reflecting off the dark water. One or two figures moved on the plaza, but not many. Despite the lack of people, it didn't feel empty. It felt as though we were being watched.

"Wish Rain had brought some snipers," I muttered.

"The Council wouldn't have authorised it," Sonder said. He was still shivering; the wind was blowing off the water and it was bitterly cold.

We set out across the walkway. Freezing rain fell from above, stinging my face until the walkway led us back under cover, bringing us to a four-way crossroads. More walkways led off in all four directions, shadowed paths illuminated by patches of electric light. To one side, its top almost brushing the pipes mounted on the ceiling, was a twisted golden sculpture with two gigantic heads.

Sonder looked around. "Is this the place?"

"Looks like." I checked to see what would happen if we waited. Nothing.

"Are they coming?" Sonder asked when I didn't break the silence.

"No," I said. The nearer of the two heads on the statue leered at me. Its face was shining gold metal, sculpted into something like a theatre mask, one half of the mouth curved in a smile. The eyes were frozen in different directions; one stared straight at me, the other rolled upwards as if having a stroke. I put it out of my mind and reached out, searching for Rachel and Cinder.

"Maybe they're not coming," Sonder said after a pause.

"No such luck. Wait." I checked quickly to verify. "Got them."

"Where?"

"Down that walkway." I looked again at the futures in which we walked down there, this time examining the layout. "Mm."

"What's wrong?"

"They're here already." I pointed at the walkway straight ahead of us. "We follow that, it'll lead us into a corridor. Cinder and Deleo will be at the middle. Trouble is, it's enclosed."

"So no one's going to be able to see us," Sonder said. He looked worried. "Are there other ways out?"

"Side doors, but it'll take a few seconds to get there." I chewed my lip. "What worries me is that Caldera and Coatl's teams aren't going to have any kind of line of sight. If everything goes to shit, they won't reach us for a good thirty seconds."

Sonder was silent. He might not be in the same league as Luna or Variam, but he's had enough combat experience to know exactly how deadly a thirty-second delay can be. If Cinder and Rachel got the drop on us, that would be far longer than they'd need. "How much advance warning will you have?"

"Less than I'd like. Deleo's too unpredictable. How fast can you put up a stasis?"

"Maybe three seconds. Two if I'm lucky."

I looked at him.

"That's not going to be quick enough, is it?" Sonder said.

"Not even close."

"Use a slow instead?"

"Use a slow instead. I'll throw out a one-shot to block the corridor with a forcewall, and then we run. You ready?"

"As I'll ever be." Sonder took a breath. "Let's do it."

We set off down the walkway. It opened up briefly, giving us a view out onto an outside street, and then the walls and ceiling closed in again. We walked past windows close enough to touch and automatic doors that opened at our presence, carrying the scent of carpets and air conditioners. Soon we came out into a long, wide corridor that curved slightly to the left, enough to block off the view of the other end but still leaving long sight lines. Cylindrical pillars ran from the floor to the low ceiling, and yellow-white lights shone down from only a few feet above. As we kept walking, a man and a woman came into view, standing side by side at the corridor's midpoint.

The man was standing to the left, arms hanging loose by his sides, and his name was Cinder. Cinder has the build of a weight lifter, with thick arms and wide hands; most people would peg him as a thug, but he's smarter than he looks, not to mention a lot faster. He's a powerful fire mage, but I wasn't half as worried about him as I was about the woman on the right.

As usual, Rachel was wearing a mask. This one was a black domino, covering only her eyes and leaving bare the lines of her face. I've met Rachel a few times over the past years, and I've started to think that that mask is some sort of tell. When Rachel wears it, she's more fully Deleo; quicker to anger, more violent, less sane. When her face is uncovered, she's different, closer to the girl I once knew. Without her mask she seems to remember her old self more clearly, but I think that actually makes her hate me more. I'm not sure which is worse.

The last time I'd spoken to Rachel was two years ago. The conversation ended when someone else made the mistake of calling Rachel by her old name, at which point Rachel had disintegrated her. Briefly I wondered just what the hell Shireen was expecting me to do here, then I put the thought out of my mind. I reached a point about thirty feet away from Cinder and Rachel, and stopped. Sonder came to a halt a little behind me.

"You know," I said to Cinder, when neither of the Dark mages spoke, "these meetings would go a lot faster if you guys would keep to schedule."

"Changed our minds," Cinder said. He glanced at Sonder. "Wondering if you'd show up."

"The deal was two people," Sonder said. He couldn't fully hide his nerves, but at least his voice didn't shake.

"And the mages on the way in?"

"Let's cut the bullshit, all right?" I said. "Not like you guys are exactly unprotected." I hadn't spotted their backup, but I knew it would be there.

Cinder shrugged. "Okay. Talk."

I could feel Rachel staring at me. It was creepy, but I couldn't sense any threat of violence . . . yet. "The Council are a little concerned about Richard's plans to go treasure hunting."

"That's sad."

"I think they're going to get more than sad. If Richard goes for it he'll be breaking the Concord."

"Last I checked, that relic wasn't in Britain," Cinder said. "Not really Council business."

I silently cursed Rain and his operational security. This was the sort of thing it would have been useful to know *before* going into the meeting. "If you get into a fight with the Council team, it's going to become their business real fast."

Cinder shrugged again.

"The first clause of the Concord gives the Light Council national authority," Sonder said. "Under the Arrancar ruling, the relic is Council property unless specified otherwise. You can't just go and take it."

"Yeah, well, it ain't *under* the Council's authority, is it?" Cinder said.

"That doesn't matter . . ."

I tried to remember the wording of the law Sonder was talking about. The first clause of the Concord establishes the Light Alliance as the governing body of the magical world, then delegates the authority down to the Light Councils of the respective magical nations. So if this thing was in another nation's territory, and Richard's cabal got it, could the British Council grab it off them? *Shit, I have no idea.* I didn't know enough Council law to argue this one.

The sound of footsteps behind us made Sonder and Cinder halt their argument. I turned my head slightly, being careful to keep Rachel in my field of vision. A man dressed in a long coat was coming down the corridor towards us. He was overweight, with greying hair and glasses, and quite obviously had no idea who we were. As he saw the four of us staring at him, he slowed and came to a halt, looking between us. "Er," he said. "Am I interrupting something?"

Cinder met the man's gaze. "Get lost."

"I don't . . ." the man started to object, then trailed off. Cinder kept staring at him, and I could see the wheels slowly turning behind the man's eyes. I wondered if he understood exactly why his instincts were telling him to run. "I'll go the other way," the man said, and backed off.

Cinder watched him go, then shook his head in disgust. "Normals."

"What are you doing here?" Rachel said.

I turned to realise that Rachel was staring at me. "Even I do jobs sometimes," I said.

Rachel threw back her head and laughed. Sonder shifted uneasily. "A job?" Rachel said. "You don't do jobs."

"I'm doing one now."

Rachel's laughter cut off and she stared at me, her eyes meeting mine through her mask. "Which of them brought you?"

"What?"

Rachel's voice sharpened. "Don't play stupid. Was it him, or her?"

"I . . ." I tried to look into the futures to figure out which was the right answer. If I picked the wrong one, it was going to send Rachel into a rage. Except that as far as I could tell, *both* answers were wrong. Or could be wrong, I couldn't figure out which, her moods were shifting so quickly—

"Tell me!"

"Her," I said. *She has to mean Shireen, right?* "It was her."

Rachel stared at me for a second, then her face twisted in sudden fury. "Liar!"

Oh shit. All of a sudden the futures were filled with violence, approaching fast. Rachel stalked towards me and I backed away, keeping my fists closed. "Wait," I said urgently.

Suddenly Rachel stopped, turning to stare to her left, at an empty patch of corridor. "No," she said. "I won't."

Sonder and I exchanged nervous glances. Rachel seemed to have forgotten about us, and the futures of violence had vanished as quickly as they had appeared . . . but they could come back. I tightened my grip on the discs held in my hands, feeling the edges of the one-shot digging into my palms.

"Why should I?" Rachel demanded. "It's his fault!"

"Del," Cinder said in his rumbling voice.

Rachel made an impatient gesture towards Cinder without turning to look. "How do you know?"

"Deleo," I said carefully. The last thing I wanted to do was draw her attention, but . . . "Are you talking to Shireen?"

Rachel turned to stare at me, her expression suggesting I'd just said something so stupid that it didn't deserve an answer. "Do you know *anything*?"

"Less and less, it's feeling like. Look, is there—?"

"Why does he want you?" Rachel said abruptly.

"Who?"

"I'm Chosen," Rachel said. She was staring at me. "Not you."

"Um," I said. The futures danced and flickered, shifting lightning-quick to match Rachel's thoughts. "Yes. You're the Chosen."

"Then why does he want you?" Rachel took another step towards me, and involuntarily I stepped backwards to maintain distance. Rachel didn't seem to notice. "I waited for him."

I had no idea what to say. The same spark of fear that always comes when I talk to Rachel was dancing under my thoughts. Normally in conversations I can see enough of the threads to guide their direction, choose the response that will get the reaction I want. That doesn't work on Rachel, and it's the biggest reason she scares me. I don't like losing control. "You don't have to wait any longer," I said. "You're free to do what you want."

Rachel laughed. There was something disturbing to the sound, and I felt Sonder shift again. "Is that what you think?" Rachel asked. She looked almost pitying. "None of us are."

"Okay," Cinder said. "Think we're done here." He took a step towards Rachel.

Rachel ignored him. It was as though she'd forgotten Sonder and Cinder even existed. "I thought it would be funny," she said. "You always thought you were so clever, didn't you? I wanted to see when you finally figured it out. But it's not enough. Seeing your face makes me sick. You don't deserve to come back."

"Okay, I think we're getting off topic," I said. Danger was dancing in the futures, and I held my arms tense, ready to throw. "I'm going to assume negotiations are over."

"Del," Cinder said. "Come on." His eyes flicked towards me with a warning look.

"I don't think—" Sonder began.

"I'm not letting you come back," Rachel said.

"I'm not coming back," I said.

"You're right." Rachel's lips curved in a smile. "You're not."

"Sonder!" I shouted, and jumped left.

Suddenly everything was happening at once. A green ray flashed from Rachel's hand, lancing through the air where I'd been standing as I flung two gold discs left and right; Sonder threw out his arm and Rachel's movements slowed, her limbs drifting through the air as though she were wading in deep water; the gold discs hit the floor at the edges of the corridor and I snapped the command word and a wall of force flared up, cutting us off from Cinder and Rachel at the same time that Cinder's own wall of fire roared into life between us, blocking our view. The second disintegration ray hit the force-wall but I was already running, dashing away down the corridor with Sonder a few steps behind, the roar of the flames in our ears. Behind I felt the forcewall break and a third disintegrate spell slashed out—too late. We were away.

We kept running until we were back at the statues. I ducked down at the crossing, using the low wall of the walkway as cover as I scanned for pursuit. Sonder ran past and ducked down beside me. "See them?" Sonder panted.

"No." If we stayed put the result would be . . . nothing. I

looked further ahead, ignoring the chiming of my communicator. Still nothing. "They're not chasing."

"I can put up a stasis," Sonder said, breathing hard. He stood, narrowing his eyes and focusing, and after a moment's pause the corridor that we'd just left shimmered and was replaced with what looked like a curved mirror running from wall to wall.

"Receiving," I snapped. My communicator shut up. "Whoever's pinging me, stop it."

Rain's voice sounded in my ear. "What happened?"

"Deleo had one of her little moments, that's what." My voice was shaking and I forced it back under control. "And we're fine, thanks for asking."

"Hold your position and wait for rendezvous."

"Understood." I cut the connection.

We stayed like that for a few minutes while Sonder maintained his spell. Some random woman with a handbag and a fur coat passed us by. She asked me why there was a shiny mirror blocking the corridor. I told her it was a work of abstract art and that we'd been posted to supervise. She gave me a weird look and left. Once she was gone I told Sonder to drop the stasis field. Cinder and Deleo weren't coming.

Rain and Caldera came running up a few minutes later. "Anything?" I asked.

"They had a gate ready to go down one of those side entrances," Caldera said. She looked pissed off. "By the time we got there they were gone."

"What was it?" Rain said. "A setup?"

"No," I said. I'd managed to calm myself down. "It was Deleo being nuts."

Sonder nodded. "It was going okay to start with. Cinder was talking, but then . . ."

Rain held up a hand to signal for Sonder to wait, then looked into space; I knew he was listening to something from his earpiece. "Okay," he said, then turned back to us. "Cleanup crew's on their way. Get back to HQ for debriefing. Caldera, make sure they get there."

....

The debriefing took approximately ten times as long as the meeting. The best that can be said of it was that it gave us both plenty of time to recover.

"No," I said yet again. I was sitting with Sonder in one of the interrogation rooms, facing Rain and some Council bureaucrat who'd introduced himself as Charles. "Cinder was not trying to kill us. Deleo was."

"How can you be so sure?" Charles said. He was slightly overweight and wore a business suit with a gold tiepin.

"Because we aren't suffering from third-degree burns." I was trying to keep my patience, but it was getting difficult. I'd disliked Charles at first sight, and his tendency to ask stupid questions hadn't improved my opinion. "Cinder is not incompetent. Hell, for all I know, he was trying to protect us."

"Why would he want to protect you?"

"Because he was the one actually trying to negotiate. Deleo was the one who started shooting."

"Ah, yes." Charles picked up a piece of paper from the notes in front of him and adjusted his glasses, studying it. "You claimed that the Dark mage Deleo was the one who initiated hostilities, correct?"

"Correct."

"What did you say or do to trigger her attack?"

"Because she didn't like my face," I said. "Or she was in a bad mood and wanted someone to take it out on. Or she just hates me on general principles. God knows that's logical enough for Deleo. Even if I were a mind mage and could read her thoughts, I guarantee it wouldn't make any sense to you."

"I'll be the judge of that," Charles said. "However, on that subject . . ." He looked at Sonder. "Do you have anything to add to Mage Verus's account?"

"No," Sonder said. I wondered if I sounded as tired as he did. "It happened as he said."

Charles nodded. "Very well. I am required to inform you that an independent time mage will be called in to verify your accounts. I must also inform you that until such verification can be completed, the two of you are forbidden from revisiting the site of the incident."

Sonder stared at Charles. "Why would I *want* to?"

"He wants to make sure you don't mess with the temporal record," I said wearily. "In case you're trying to cover something up."

Sonder gave Charles a disbelieving look.

"It's standard procedure in cases of violent incidents."

"Of course it is," I said.

"Councilman," Rain said. "If you have no further questions, can we release Sonder and Verus? I'm going to need their services tomorrow."

Charles nodded. "I think we have all we need for the present. Please be advised that you'll be required to make yourself available for further questioning at any time over the next two weeks."

Yeah, I thought. *I'll make that my number one priority.* "Sure."

"Thank you for your cooperation." Charles stacked his notes, rose to his feet, and nodded to Rain. "Keeper." He left the room.

"Asshole," I said once the door was closed.

Rain didn't quite smile. "Go home," he said. "Get some rest."

I knew Rain was right; the aftershock from the adrenaline rush had faded away, leaving me tired and bad-tempered. Still, there was one thing I wanted to get straight with him. "For future reference, when I'm supposed to be negotiating, it'd help if I actually knew the details of what I was talking about."

"I know," Rain said. "Operational security. But tomorrow, the full team is being briefed and I promise you'll be in on it. Fair?"

I nodded.

Sonder looked troubled. "Do we really not have Concord authority?"

"Legal grey area," Rain said. "The mission planners say yes. But they're also very keen that the details don't leak."

"In other words, they aren't all that sure everyone else is going to agree with them," I said.

"That's about the size of it." Rain got to his feet. "I'll see you tomorrow for the briefing."

Sonder and I left the interrogation area together. Once we were in the gate room, Sonder turned to me. "Deleo thinks you're going back to Richard."

I sighed. "Apparently everyone does except me."

"But you're not going to," Sonder said. "Are you?"

I looked up in surprise. "You finally believe me?"

"I never thought you were lying."

"About everything, or just that?" Sonder started to answer and I waved him off. "Forget it. Let's call it bygones."

Sonder took out a gate stone, then paused and looked back at me. "Were you okay with tonight?"

I shrugged. "We're both alive."

"I meant working with me."

"I never had a problem working with you," I said. "It was you not trusting me that was the issue."

"I know, but . . ." Sonder hesitated. "We make a good team, right?"

I looked at Sonder for a second, then gave him a smile. "I guess we do."

Sonder smiled back, then looked awkwardly away. "Um. See you tomorrow."

ı ı ı ı ı ı ı ı ı

I checked in with Anne to find that her burns had healed and she was walking around. Variam was there too; he'd been guarding her all day. Luna was still training with Chalice and wasn't expected back until the early hours of the morning. Anne tried to convince me to stay the night, but I turned her down. Given what had happened last night, I really wasn't comfortable sleeping over and putting her and Vari in danger too. Instead I took a gate stone to Arachne's lair.

Gating is one of the fastest ways to travel, but even so, by the time I reached the Heath, I was tired and drained. All I wanted to do was find a dark place, sit down, and do nothing, and if the night hadn't been so freezing I think I would have. It took a long time for Arachne to answer the signal and open the gate, and when she did I trudged down the tunnel past the glowing lights, my head down.

"Hello, Alex," Arachne said as I walked in. "What's wrong?"

I dropped onto one of the sofas with a sigh. "Really shitty day."

I told Arachne about the assassination attempt and the destruction of my shop, our abortive investigation, and the meeting with Cinder and Rachel. "I'm used to bad days, but I think this is the worst I can remember," I said once I was done. "I just lost my home, my shop, and about half my possessions. I've had more people than I can count try to kill me, and the only reason they didn't manage it is that Anne took a fireball to the face."

"But she's alive," Arachne said. "And so are you. Possessions aren't important, Alex. It's people that matter, not things."

"Yeah, well, I don't seem to be doing that well when it comes to dealing with people, either. We found out who sent those guys, and there's nothing we can do about it. Rain says he'll try, and maybe he will, but I'm not kidding myself. There's no way the Keepers are going to prosecute someone that close to the Light Council, not for attacking someone like me." I twisted around to look up at Arachne. "You know the worst part? Nothing's getting any better. We tried investigating the Crusaders, and it was a dead end. We went to meet Cinder and Rachel, and that was a dead end too. It feels like everything's getting worse and worse."

"I did warn you."

I had no answer to that.

"There's one detail I think you may not have fully paid attention to." Arachne had moved closer until she was looming over me, her front legs on either side of my body and her eight eyes and fangs close to my head. It probably would have given most people nightmares, but I actually found it kind of comforting. Don't know what that says about me. "Symmaris took her orders from Maradok, who in turn takes his orders from the Senior Council member Sal Sarque. Yes?"

I nodded. "And Maradok's involved in this operation tomorrow."

"And Sal Sarque was one of the two other Senior Council mages who voted in support of Levistus's proposal for your execution," Arachne said. "However, it appears he did so for quite different reasons. When it comes to the question of how to deal with you, Levistus and the Crusaders appear to be at cross purposes."

I looked up at that. "How do you mean?"

"That assassination attempt represented a major expenditure of resources," Arachne said. "Whoever that fire mage was, he was clearly one of their heavy hitters. You're right that the Keepers are unlikely to prosecute them, but even so, launching such a blatant attack will have consequences for the Crusaders. Assassinating an independent mage such as yourself would already have hurt their reputation. A failed assassination is the worst of both worlds."

"I guess." I hadn't thought about it that way. "Where are you going with this?"

"If the Crusaders only wanted you dead, the most logical course of action would have been to simply wait out the week. Instead they took a significant risk in attempting to eliminate you. That indicates that their goal is different to that of Levistus. Levistus wants you dead, but it seems that the Crusaders were quite serious in that message they delivered via Symmaris. Their priority is to keep you away from that relic."

"You think Symmaris was telling the truth?" I said with a frown. "They really *do* believe that I'm going to get it for Richard?"

"All the evidence points that way," Arachne said. "I suggest you talk to this Maradok. Find out what he wants."

"Joy." But it made sense. "Yeah. I think I will."

We sat for a little while in silence. "You know, I don't think it was just the attack that really got to me," I said. "It was the thing with Rachel and Shireen."

"With Shireen?"

"Oh yeah, I didn't get the chance to tell you, did I?" There was too much to keep track of. Had that conversation with Shireen really only been last night? I told Arachne the story. "I don't know what I'm supposed to do," I finished. "Rachel can't even talk to me for ten minutes without trying to kill me, and Shireen wants me to be her counsellor? And now she's saying that if I don't then something worse is going to happen."

Arachne was quiet. "You know more about dragons than I do," I said. "Draconic prophecies . . . are they ever wrong?"

"No."

"But isn't there any room—"

"No."

I looked away. "Great."

"Listen carefully, Alex," Arachne said. "Dragons—true dragons—do not exist in time in the way ordinary creatures do. A draconic prophecy is not a prophecy, in that they do not look into the future. They perceive all points in time coterminously."

"So . . . they see it in the present?"

"Present, past, and future have little meaning to them. But if they see something, then in *your* future, it will happen."

"But I can change my future. I *know* I have free will, I see it every time I use my divination."

"And dragons can see your exercise of free will. Including the choices you will make."

I frowned. "That doesn't make any sense."

"Only within your system of logic." I started to answer, and Arachne raised a foreleg to interrupt me. "Don't argue this one, Alex; you'll just become frustrated. It's not something humans have the capacity to fully understand."

I still couldn't make sense of it, but Arachne was right; arguing would only be frustrating. In any case, thinking of Shireen had reminded me of that last request of hers. "Do you know anything about creatures that can grant wishes?"

"That's an odd question. Why do you ask?"

"Shireen wanted to know," I said. "I don't know why. But she also seemed to think it was something old. And something that wouldn't be in the Light histories."

"Why not?"

"She didn't say."

"Hmm." Arachne settled onto her back legs.

I watched curiously as Arachne crouched in silence. Normally Arachne seems to have all the answers; it's rare I ask her something that makes her stop and think. "Can you think of anything?" I said at last.

"I once knew the names of every magical creature that walked the earth," Arachne said. "Of those that could grant favours or boons, I can still remember three score without trouble. But something hidden from the Light histories . . . that points to something old indeed. To the jinn."

"As in genies?"

"Genies, djinn, shayatin. They have many names. To the best of my knowledge, they are the only creatures in this world with access to true wish magic. Or were."

"Are they gone?"

"Not gone. Changed."

"Changed how?" I said curiously. "And why wouldn't they be in the Light histories?"

"The answer to that is a long tale, and a dark one," Arachne said. "The important part is this: if you care for your friend, tell her to stay away from the jinn and everything to do with them."

I thought for a second. "The jinn are supposed to have come from the Middle East, aren't they? That item that Richard got hold of earlier this year was from Syria. And just tonight Cinder let slip that wherever this relic is, it's outside the U.K." I looked at Arachne. "Do you think that's what Richard's after? A jinn that's bound or locked away? And the Council want it too?"

"If they do, they are fools," Arachne said. "The jinn have no reason to love mages. None at all. If either the Council or Richard gained the services of a jinn, it would bring them nothing but ruin. If that truly is what those mages are after, then you would be best off having as little to do with that relic as possible. Don't open it, don't touch it, don't try to use it. Keep as far away as you can, and once you've fulfilled your obligations to the Council, run."

I looked up at Arachne. Her eight eyes stared down at me, and I could tell she was deadly serious. Slowly, I nodded. "All right."

"For your sake, I hope they're looking for something else."

I looked back towards the tunnel. It was late, and I needed sleep. "Guess I'll find out tomorrow."

chapter 10

It was the next day. A night's sleep had restored my energy and will; I wasn't quite at full strength, but I was good enough. A little over three days left.

"Are there any Keepers *not* going on this mission?" I asked Caldera quietly. The two of us were walking down a corridor in the heart of the Westminster headquarters. Others were moving in the same direction, both ahead of us and behind, and most of the offices we'd passed along the way were empty. It felt as though everyone in the building was headed for the same spot.

"All leave's been cancelled," Caldera said. Ahead of us, a Keeper paused to hold a door open; Caldera nodded her thanks as we caught up to him. "The ones who aren't attached to the units are on standby in case something else goes wrong."

Up ahead, I could hear the murmur of voices—a lot of voices. It sounded as though we were approaching a crowd. "Have you ever been on this big an operation before?"

"In Britain."

"How about outside Britain?"

"This'll be a first."

The corridor we were in opened up into a large room shaped like an amphitheatre. The walls were painted white, with equipment hanging from the ceiling, and at the centre was a wide circular table made out of translucent crystal. Rows of seats formed a semicircle around the table, with a raised mezzanine floor above the seats; there looked to be seating for close to a hundred, and already the room was more than half full, with more people filing in every minute. Keepers were everywhere, in battle gear and mage robes and in civilian clothing; they were talking quietly in pairs and small groups, their voices filling the air with a steady buzz. The far side of the room was occupied with computer equipment, and people who looked like technicians were holding discussions over tablets and displays. Magical auras were everywhere, overloading my mage's sight with the signatures of hundreds of active spells, elemental and living and universal magics all mixed together to the point where I had trouble telling them apart.

I came to a halt in the entryway, dizzy from all the input. There was too much to take in. "Come on," Caldera said over her shoulder. "Let's find a seat."

I caught up with her, nearly tripping as I looked around. "Stop staring," Caldera said. "You look like a tourist."

A voice called out to us from our left. "Hey, you ugly lot. Who let you in?"

We both turned to see a fat, bearded mage with South American looks grinning at us. "Oh, bloody hell," Caldera said. "Didn't know they were desperate enough to bring you along."

"Love you too, Caldy." Coatl looked at me. "Yo, Verus. You still letting her drag you around?"

I grinned back at him. "Could be worse. I could get assigned to you."

Coatl is from Brazil, a Keeper who arrived on an exchange program a while back and liked Britain enough to stay. He's a mind mage, which isn't one of the types I usually get on with (old prejudices), but I'd first met Coatl earlier this year and to my surprise had come to like him. He's highly irreverent and insults people a lot, but he's honest and if he does use his magic to listen in on my thoughts, he does it subtly enough that I haven't noticed.

As Coatl led us through the crowd, I spotted other mages I recognised. Slate was sitting on one of the front benches, talking to his partner Trask; farther to the back was another Keeper I knew called Lizbeth. Over on the far side was Landis, leaning nonchalantly against the wall, and Rain was standing next to the central table, having some kind of discussion with a pair of men in formal mage robes. And up on the mezzanine floor was . . . I blinked. "Coatl," I said, tapping his shoulder and nodding upwards. "Is that who I think it is?"

Coatl glanced up. "That's the one."

Caldera followed our looks. "The old guy in blue?"

"His name's Alaundo," I said. I'd never seen him before, but I recognised him from pictures, a white-haired man in robes leaning on a twisted staff.

"Oh, him?" Caldera said. "I see his name on the intel forecasts. Didn't know he ever came in."

"He doesn't," Coatl said, dropping down onto a bench and putting his feet up. "Wonder what the Council promised him to make him show up?"

"They're pulling out all the stops, aren't they?" I said. Master Alaundo is the foremost diviner for the Council, and probably the most famous diviner in Britain. He was supposed to spend most of the year on his private estate on the Isle of Man, only leaving for very special occasions. I had to admit, I was impressed. Alaundo is a living legend in divination circles.

I was about to turn back when something caught my attention. The man Alaundo was talking to had hair the same shade of white, but he was thinner and more sprightly. He had his back to me, but as he shifted position I caught a glimpse of his face. I hadn't seen him for years, but I recognised him instantly; it was my old teacher, Helikaon. I'd studied with him for a while after leaving Richard. *How many diviners are the Council bringing in on this thing?*

"Hey, Alex," Caldera said. "You hear that?"

I turned back to Coatl. "Sorry, what?"

"Cinder and Deleo had a couple of men running backup for them last night," Coatl said. "They put up a barrier and chucked tear gas to make us back off. Force and space magic. Caldera thought you'd know who they were."

"Was the force user tall and skinny with black hair?"

"Wearing a mask, didn't get a good look at him. But tall, yeah. Powerful, too."

I nodded. "Onyx. Morden's Chosen, just like Deleo is Richard's. He's bad news; keep your distance if you can. But I don't know anything about a space user on their team."

"He seemed pretty young from what I saw." Coatl shrugged. "Oh well. You'll probably meet him soon enough."

"Yeah, that makes me feel better."

A double chime sounded, echoing softly through the room. Looking around, I saw that the mages still standing were finding their seats. I sat next to Caldera as the people in the room turned to look towards the centre. A man in mage robes stepped up to the central table and the sounds of conversation fell to a murmur.

"Good afternoon, Keepers," the man said. He looked to be in his fifties, with close-cut brown hair and a square face. I'd never spoken to him, but Caldera had pointed him out in the past; this was Nimbus, an air mage and the Director of Operations for the Order of the Star. "I'm sure you've all been speculating about today's operation. Before we start, I'd like to extend our thanks to the Council members who've been assisting us in our preparations, and to the members of the Order of the Shield who'll be providing operational support on the ground."

Nimbus didn't seem to be making any effort to raise his voice, but it echoed loudly; some spell or other. A few stragglers were still filtering in through the doors, spreading out around the room to find seats or standing against the walls. Looking around, I could see that the Keepers were paying attention. I've seen Keeper briefings get pretty rowdy, but it didn't look as though there would be any back talk this time.

"As some of you may know, over the past year, the Dark mage Richard Drakh has been expanding his power base in

Britain," Nimbus said. "At present he holds influence over a large but loosely organised cabal of Dark mages. Our current assessments indicate that Drakh maintains this control due to his possession of several powerful Precursor relics. We have learned that Drakh is currently attempting to acquire another artefact, this one more powerful than those he already owns. He will attempt to retrieve this relic tonight."

A figure standing behind Nimbus had caught my eye. He had receding straw-coloured hair and was dressed in mage robes in muted colours. "Caldera," I murmured. "Guy behind Nimbus, third on the right. Is that who I think it is?"

Caldera didn't look at me. "Don't do anything stupid."

"But is it—?"

"Maradok, yeah. *Don't* do anything stupid."

Nimbus was speaking. ". . . of the utmost importance." He looked towards Maradok. "Councilman Maradok."

Maradok stepped forward. "The relic in question is held within a bubble realm." He had an upper-class English accent, and spoke in a matter-of-fact tone of voice. I wondered if he'd sounded the same way when ordering my assassination. "The bubble realm can only be accessed from one precise geographical location. The location in question is within the city of Aleppo in Syria."

A murmur went up from around the audience. Glancing around, I saw looks of surprise, but not as many as I might have expected; some of the audience had probably heard about this in advance. Bubble realms are small pocket realities, fully disconnected from our world; they're rarer than shadow realms and usually older, not to mention potentially a lot more dangerous. In the centre of the room, the table lit up and a translucent map of Syria appeared in the air above the projector, its borders marked in black and the neighbouring countries in white. A red circular dot was located in the northwest of the country.

"As you may be aware, Syria is in the midst of an extended civil war," Maradok said. "Control of the country is divided between government forces, rebels, and Islamic State militia." As Maradok spoke, sections of the map turned pink, green, and grey respectively. "Aleppo is one of the battlegrounds and currently contains elements from all three forces, in addition to civilians and neutral parties." The map zoomed in and the red dot expanded into a city layout. The colours signifying ownership were still there, but they were blotchy and irregular, mixed up with each other. One spot in the bottom right was marked with a glowing red star. The areas around it were a mixture of grey and green.

"Since learning of Drakh's plans, the Light Council of Britain has been in contact with the Light Council of Syria," Maradok went on. "The Syrian Council have agreed to permit our operations within the designated time window. They have further agreed to provide gate staging points for our use, as well as operational intelligence on the military situation. However, they have warned us that the area in question is not currently under government control. They have also warned us that local Dark mages, as well as Dark mages affiliated with Islamic State, may be attempting to access the relic."

"Sounds like a great place," I muttered to Caldera.

"Shh."

"The bubble realm is believed to be a storage facility," Maradok said. "Although our intelligence suggests that it has no stationary wards or bound guardians, the realm nevertheless has a strong defence mechanism. It is protected by a time lock that only permits access under certain highly specific astrological conditions. Those conditions will be satisfied tonight, and when they are, the gate to the bubble realm will open for a period of slightly under three hours. Once this time has elapsed, the gate will close. Once this happens, our current predictions suggest that the astronomical alignment required for another entry will not reoccur until next autumn at the earliest. Our intelligence also suggests that gate access from inside the bubble realm will be highly problematic. Anyone still inside the realm when it closes will most likely be trapped for a minimum of nine months."

Out of the corner of my eye, I saw Keepers glancing at each other. Maradok paused for a moment, then went on. "The relic in question is believed to be held within an archaic model of Minkowski box." The map of Syria disappeared, to be replaced by a three-dimensional image of a grey elongated rectangular container with an overlapping lid. As Maradok looked up, the box rotated, giving everyone a good view. "According to our current information, the box contains a bound magical creature, held in stasis. The creature is believed to be highly powerful and extremely destructive. Should you attain possession of the box, do not open it under any circumstances. Return it to a representative of the Council at the earliest possible opportunity."

"Bloody hell," Coatl said to me under his breath. "This thing Pandora's box, or what?"

"Yeah," I said. I'd heard of Minkowski boxes, but didn't know much about them. "I don't remember that story having a happy ending."

"*Shh,*" Caldera said.

Maradok nodded to his side. "Captain Rain."

Rain stepped forward and the map of Aleppo reappeared, this time zoomed in. "We have scouted the area around the bubble realm's access point," he said. "Once on the ground, we will split into two teams. The containing force, led by Captain Elandis, will establish a perimeter around the building containing the access point. Meanwhile, the strike team, led by myself, will enter the bubble realm and retrieve the relic." He looked around. "Any questions?"

Someone near the front raised their hand. "Yes?" Rain asked.

"What's the layout of the bubble realm?" a Keeper I didn't know asked.

"We don't know," Rain said. "We'll have to find out once we get inside."

Another keeper I recognised from Red's spoke up. "What kind of backup do we have?"

"Keepers from the Order of the Shield will be detailed to your units on an individual basis."

"What about reserves?"

"From the information we've been given, gate and teleportation magic within the bubble realm will not work reliably," Rain said. "That means no mobile reserve. We'll have what we bring in."

There was a pause. "Any other questions?" Rain said.

Another Keeper spoke up from out of my line of sight. "What happens if the time's running out and we still haven't found the relic?"

"Then we pull out," Rain said. "The primary objective is to prevent Drakh from acquiring the relic. Retrieving it ourselves is a secondary priority. If we can't get to it, but Drakh can't either, that's good enough for us."

The Keepers seemed to like that, judging from the reactions. I glanced at the Director of Operations, Nimbus. His expression was neutral, and I wondered whether his priorities were the same as Rain's.

"Is that it?" Rain said when no one else spoke up. "Then report to your squad leaders for your assignments. Lead elements gate out in two hours." He looked around. "Good luck."

The room broke out in conversation, the Keepers discussing what they'd just heard. I looked at Caldera. "You think it's going to work?"

"With this much?" Caldera said. "It bloody well should, unless your old master brings an army." She shrugged. "Guess the Council's finally taking him seriously."

"Mm," I said. I wasn't sure if that was good or bad.

"Sounds like I'm outside," Coatl said. "You going in with Rain?"

Down at ground level, I saw that Maradok was making his way to the exit. "I think I need to have a chat," I said to Caldera and Coatl. "Back in a sec." I rose and headed down through the crowd.

I caught up with Maradok before he made it out of the room. "Councilman?" I said. "Excuse me?"

Maradok turned. Up close, he looked older than he had at a distance, with a long face and receding hair the colour of dirty straw. He could have been a civil servant, except for his eyes—they were blue, with a certain detached quality to them. He didn't show any sign of surprise at seeing me. "Ah. Mage Verus, is it?"

"That's right. Mind if we have a word?"

"I don't see why not," Maradok said. "Let's find some-where a little quieter."

⋅ ⋅ ⋅ ⋅ ⋅ ⋅ ⋅ ⋅ ⋅ ⋅

"So how can I help you?" Maradok asked.

We were in a side room off one of the corridors. The door was closed, but I could still hear voices from the Keepers in the auditorium. Far enough away to be private, but still close enough to discourage any kind of violence—not that that was very likely in the middle of Keeper HQ, but I've learned to be careful about these things. Maradok didn't seem terribly con-cerned one way or the other, but I had the feeling that he'd taken the location into account too.

The Light Council doesn't have an official intelligence service. In theory it's something the Keepers are supposed to handle, along with all of their other duties. In practice the only Keepers who do any real intelligence work are the Order of the Cloak, and since they specialise in dealing with normals, it's easy for most mages to forget that they even exist. When it comes to dealing with other mages, Keepers act solely as police, under strict Council control.

But just because the Council's intelligence services aren't official, that doesn't mean they don't exist. According to rumour, each of the major Council factions has its own pri-vate intelligence network, and those networks handle every-thing from surveillance to information brokering to outright assassinations. I'm pretty sure that Talisid's involved with one of those networks, even if he's never told me exactly how. If Caldera was right, Maradok was of the same breed. You'd think that since they were both with Council intelligence, then Maradok ought to be on my side. Pity things don't work that way.

In any case, I'd had some time to think about how to approach Maradok, and I'd decided to take the direct approach. "Could you stop trying to kill me, please?"

Maradok looked at me.

"This is the part where you're supposed to say that you have no idea what I'm talking about," I said. "Then you ask where I've been getting these crazy notions, and when I explain, you tell me that you know nothing at all about the events I'm referring to. Given that we're both busy men, how about we save ourselves some time and skip to the part where we tell each other what we really want?"

Maradok regarded me with those calm eyes of his. I could sense him making up his mind, and the patterns the future made were unusual ones. Normally when someone's making a decision, I see the possibilities shift and flicker. Maradok's potential futures didn't flicker; they jumped from one fully formed set of actions to another, with a brief pause for consideration between each. After a moment, the actions settled. "That seems reasonable."

"Good." I paused. "Are you going to stop trying to kill me?"

"That rather depends on you."

"Depends on what?"

"On whether you continue participating in this operation."

"I don't exactly have much of a choice."

"Then I'm afraid your odds of survival are not high."

"Would you mind explaining exactly what your issue is?"

"We really have no personal quarrel with you," Maradok said. His manner was polite and courteous, rather like a bank manager explaining why he's not going to increase your overdraft. "Personally, I would be quite happy to see you enjoying a long and healthy life in some peaceful location. Unfortunately, this does not seem to be an option."

"You think I'm working for Richard Drakh," I said flatly.

"Actually, no."

I blinked. "You believe me?"

"About your claim to have separated yourself from him? Yes, on the balance of probabilities, I would be inclined to believe it."

"Then if you know I'm not helping Richard," I said, "why are we having this conversation?"

"Well, therein lies the problem," Maradok said. "Not *working* for your old master and not *helping* your old master are different things."

"Why would I want to help him?"

"That's a very interesting question."

"To which the answer is that I'm not going to."

"Unfortunately, the divinations disagree."

"What divinations?"

"I'm sure it won't surprise you to know that we've had our eye on Drakh for some time." Maradok leant back onto a desk, half-sitting on the edge. "In doing so, one of the resources we made use of was of course divination. Our long-term divinations consider it reasonably likely that within the next few years, Richard Drakh's personal power will grow to the extent that it rivals the Light Council. This process involves you."

I looked up sharply. "How?"

"I'm afraid I'm not at liberty to disclose any details. I will, however, give you one relevant piece of information. You, Drakh, and the relic are connected. In some way, you are instrumental to his gaining the power of the creature trapped inside."

I stood very still. "How?"

"I'm not at liberty to say. The important part, from your point of view, is that you are a necessary component. Without you, Drakh doesn't get what he wants."

"So if I'm dead, Drakh's weakened," I said flatly. "Is that about the size of it?"

"That's about the size of it."

"This is insane," I said. "You launched an assassination attempt that got multiple people killed because of a divination?"

Maradok raised an eyebrow. "As a diviner, I would have thought you'd be more sympathetic."

"That's not how divination works. Looking an hour into the future, sure. Maybe a day. But months or years? That's nothing but a wild guess."

"You seem to be very confident."

"I have quite extensive experience with divination in life-or-death situations. You can't make those kinds of long-term predictions with any kind of accuracy. If your diviner told you that he could, he's a con man."

"That's an interesting assessment," Maradok said. "Would it change your opinion if I told you that the mage responsible for giving this particular divination was Master Alaundo?"

I stopped.

"And yes, I am aware of the difficulties regarding long-term divinations," Maradok continued when I didn't speak. "The potential future in which you enable Drakh to gain access to the creature within this relic is only a possibility. It is, however, a likely possibility. And unfortunately for you, out of the futures in which you do *not* help Drakh in this way, the ones most likely to occur are the ones in which you are no longer alive."

"The only way in which I don't help Richard is if I'm dead," I said quietly. "Is that it?"

"Those appear to be the most probable alternatives."

"What about the less probable ones?"

"There are always uncertainties," Maradok said. "In this case, there is a narrow range of possibilities in which none of the above events come to pass. The probability is low enough that we are disinclined to pursue that as a strategy."

"In other words, you think the safest option is just to kill me and be sure," I said. "Can you suggest some others?"

"The alternative is that you remove yourself from this operation," Maradok said. "I'm sure you can understand that given what we've just discussed, the prospect of you being closely involved in the Council operation to retrieve this relic is . . . troubling. Especially given the presence of Drakh's forces. We would feel very much more secure if you were as far away from this relic as possible."

"I *can't* remove myself from the operation because if I do, the proposal sentencing me to death is going to pass through the Council. Which your boss Sal Sarque voted for. The only reason I'm getting anywhere near this relic is because you're trying to get me killed to stop me getting anywhere near the relic!"

"Life is full of ironies."

I looked at Maradok in disbelief.

"Let me be clear," Maradok said. "We want you as far away from that relic and from your old master as possible. Whether that removal is done via geography or mortality is optional. From your point of view, I would recommend the former."

"Say I do," I said. "Let's say I resign from this operation right now and never go near Syria again for as long as I live. Would Sal Sarque reverse his vote and make sure the proposal doesn't go through?"

"Verus, you have an established history of tricking and outmanoeuvring other mages. I'm afraid that a simple verbal promise that you'd stay away from the relic is not enough."

"Then what would you need?"

Maradok shrugged.

"Do you understand just how little choice you're leaving me?" I said. "If I don't back out of this operation, you're going to try to kill me. But if I do back out of this operation, the proposal will go through on Saturday and then the Keepers *will* kill me. I do not have any other options."

"You have other options," Maradok said. "You leave. Pack up and find yourself a new home. I hear New Zealand is very nice this time of year. Or perhaps Argentina. Maybe travel for a while. I'm sure a diviner as competent as yourself won't go hungry. I can assure you that as long as you remove yourself from the affairs of this country, we will lose all interest in you."

"And Levistus's men?" I said quietly. "Once they have a hunting licence from the Council, you think they won't track me down?"

"If that's your concern, I suggest you contact Levistus to make your own accommodations."

"He won't. He made that very clear."

Maradok shrugged again. His body language clearly communicated that this was not his problem.

"How about a third option?" I said.

"Such as?"

"I'll take part in this operation," I said. "I'll get hold of this relic. And I'll make sure it's delivered personally to you. If I do that, will you believe that this divination's wrong?"

"We do not want you in proximity to this relic," Maradok said. "Regardless of whom you claim to be retrieving it for."

"I don't care. I've had it with people telling me that I'm secretly working for Richard. I'm going to prove you wrong if I have to personally dump this thing in your hands. And when I do, I want a fucking apology from you."

Maradok just looked at me. I turned and walked out.

* * * * * * * * * *

"You told him *what*?" Caldera asked me.

"It was the best I could think of."

The two of us were on standby in one of the transit rooms. There are several of them in Keeper HQ; they're designed to be used for gate spells, and they're protected by complex security systems meant to ensure that only Keepers and other mages with clearance can gate in or out. We'd just spent the past hour in secondary briefings with Rain and other Keepers, and now we were waiting for the go order. This was the first chance I'd had to get Caldera alone.

"Jesus, Alex," Caldera said. "I know I'm not one to talk, but you think you could manage *not* to piss off the brass?"

"What else was I supposed to do?" I said. "Maradok wasn't budging. At least this way if I can get this damn relic there's a chance he'll back off."

"Assuming you don't catch a bullet on the way in." Caldera frowned. "Hate to say it, but have you considered taking his advice?"

"*You're* telling *me* to back off and be cautious?"

"Don't be a smart-arse."

"It's not an option," I said. "I have to do this job. And yes, it's the same reason as before, and no, I'm still not allowed to tell you why. Sorry."

"Mm," Caldera said. She was giving me a considering

look. Caldera is a cop, and like most cops she's good at ferreting out secrets. Sooner or later she was going to learn what was really going on, and I had the feeling that she had a good idea already.

Movement in the futures caught my eye. "There's someone I need to talk to," I said. "Back in a minute."

"One sec," Caldera said. "Have you told Coatl?"

"No."

"You okay with me doing it?"

I thought for a second. I don't trust Coatl as much as I do Caldera, but he'd had plenty of chances to stab me in the back in the past and he hadn't taken them. Besides, I couldn't see how letting him know could make things significantly worse. "All right. Tell him that if he picks up anything to do with another assassination attempt, I'd really appreciate hearing about it."

Caldera nodded and I headed out into the corridor. The person I was looking for was nowhere in sight, but I knew where he was . . . and more to the point, he knew that I knew. I went around the corner, found the right door, let myself in, and closed it behind me.

"Took you long enough," Helikaon said. He was sitting at his ease on one of the chairs, an arm resting along the desk. "So what have you managed to get yourself into this time?"

Helikaon looks about sixty, though I know for a fact that he's more than a quarter of a century older. His dress was simple by the standards of the Keepers: worn trousers and an open-necked shirt that left his arms bare. He looked like an elderly workman if anything, which in some ways isn't that far from the truth. "Let's say that things are a little worse than usual," I said.

Helikaon was the second of my two teachers, and while it was Richard from whom I learnt the fundamentals of magic, it was Helikaon who taught me what it really meant to be a diviner. Helikaon is a master, and he's probably forgotten more about divination than I'll ever learn, not unless I live to at least fifty, which didn't seem terribly likely at the moment. Like Alaundo, Helikaon works on contract for the Council, but unlike Alaundo, he's never shown any interest in acquiring influence or power. I asked him why once, and Helikaon made it clear that he considered the great majority of Council politics to be nothing more than an elaborate waste of time that painted a target on your back. Helikaon is extremely careful about his personal safety.

"First question," Helikaon said. "What the bloody hell are you doing here?"

"So I'm guessing you know about the Council resolution."

"I might live on rocks, but I don't hide under them." Helikaon looked at me with eyebrows raised. "Well?"

"I'm trying to get the resolution overturned."

"You're going a bloody stupid way about it," Helikaon said. "Hanging around with a bunch of Keepers? How long before one of them tries to put a knife in your back?"

"How much did Alaundo tell you?"

"Enough to make it clear you've outstayed your welcome. What was the first thing I taught you about fights?"

"Not to be there when they happened," I said with a sigh. "It's complicated."

"No. It's not." Helikaon pointed at me. "Get out of here. Right now. You can send your apologies later. Don't stop until you've put a few countries between you and everyone else."

"I can't leave, not yet. I've got people that are depending on me."

"This is about that girl, isn't it? Your apprentice?"

"She's scheduled to take her journeyman test on Friday," I said. "The resolution doesn't come due until Saturday. If I still haven't managed to sort anything out by then . . . then maybe I'll be going with your plan."

"And what makes you think you'll be free to leave?" Helikaon said. "What happens if the Keepers decide to pick you up Thursday night and hold you a couple of days for questioning? Forty-eight hours in a cell and oops, isn't that funny, looks like now all of a sudden you're guilty of something else. You think that hasn't occurred to them? You think they're stupid?"

I was silent. "Listen, Alex," Helikaon said. "This operation doesn't matter."

"If it doesn't matter, why are you helping them?"

"You think I'm taking a trip to Syria?" Helikaon snorted. "World travelling's for the youngsters. I'm staying back here with Alaundo. Bit of path-walking and we can tell them what they need to know without ever leaving the building. That's the smart way to do things. And if things go wrong, turns out your old master has brought along a bit too much for the Council to deal with . . . well, that's what the Keepers are paid for. Let 'em deal with it."

"Do the Keepers know that's your attitude?"

"Stop trying to change the subject. I'm not going in on the ground because it doesn't matter who gets this relic. Doesn't matter if the Council gets it, doesn't matter if Drakh gets it. I don't risk my life for them. You shouldn't either."

"I'm not doing it for the Council."

"Doesn't matter who you're doing it for." Helikaon pointed at me. "You remember what I told you, back when you first came to me? When you asked me whose side I was on?"

"You said you weren't on anyone's side," I said. It had been one of my first memories of Helikaon, and it had left an impression. "You said that someone's always going to be in charge, and that it didn't matter if they were Light or Dark, they'd still need diviners."

"Because the only guy who wins in a war is the one selling the bullets." Helikaon shook his head. "I told you back in that business with the fateweaver. Don't get involved. You didn't listen. You've been getting deeper and deeper."

"If you're going to tell me to stop it, that's not really an option right now."

"Too late for that. It's time to cut and run."

"And Luna?" I said. "The others who are in the firing line? What about them?"

"Cut 'em loose."

I looked at Helikaon. He met my gaze without blinking, his eyes flat and hard. "Last call, Alex," Helikaon said. "Warning lights are on and the needle's in the red. Are you going down with the ship, or not?"

I was silent for a little while. I didn't want to risk alienating

Helikaon . . . but at the end of the day, I already knew what the answer was going to be. I'd been walking a different path from him for a long time. "If I have to run, then I'll run," I said at last. "But I'm not abandoning my friends."

Helikaon looked back at me for a long moment, then got to his feet and walked out of the room.

I watched the door close. I could tell from looking into the futures that Helikaon wasn't coming back, and I wondered if he ever would. I had the feeling that the answer might be no.

chapter 11

Most people in the world don't travel much. In a lot of cases it's because they just don't want to. Either they don't have any real interest in seeing other places, or they're too occupied with the life they're living already. But for a lot of people, it's not a case of not wanting to, it's that they can't—either they don't have the time or the money, or there's something actively preventing them from leaving. When you're in that second group, you usually have fantasies about getting to travel and see the world, visiting different cultures and having new experiences. There are people who spend their whole lives dreaming about journeys overseas.

So it's really kind of sad that once you finally do get to spend a lot of time travelling, you tend not to appreciate it very much. Take me, for instance. I've visited more countries of the world than I can easily remember. I've even visited places *not* in this world, from bubble realms to shadow realms to the dreamscapes of Elsewhere. I've stood upon the tops of towers and looked out over castles the size of cities, walked through ancient forests where the trees have passed hundreds of years without hearing a human footstep, seen impossible alien landscapes that could never exist on Earth. Unfortunately, in pretty much every one of those cases, I've generally had more pressing concerns to worry about—either there are people trying to kill me, or people who might want to kill me, or things that aren't people that might want to kill me, or people or things that don't necessarily want to kill me but nevertheless are important enough that it's highly advisable for me to pay attention to them instead of spending my time sightseeing. Usually the place I'm visiting becomes a blur, a few brief images standing out in my memory while I spend my time dealing with various threats and problems. And by the time they're all sorted out, it's time to move on.

A prime example was the location I was at now. Aleppo is one of the oldest inhabited cities in the world and it's famous for its historical heritage. It used to form one end of the ancient Silk Road, and it's been ruled over the centuries by Romans, Byzantines, Mameluks, Ottomans, and just about everyone else who had an empire in the area. Each of them left behind their own architectural legacy, and the Old City is supposed to be fascinating. It would have been nice to wander around and see the sights.

Right now I was not wandering around and seeing the sights, for three reasons. First, it was dark. Second, the city was in the middle of a civil war. And third, I was supposed to be conducting surveillance on the inhabitants of the building across the street. Which was why, instead of enjoying the experiences of travel and new cultures, I was crouched on a dusty rooftop, hiding behind a parapet, shivering in the cold, and trying to make sure that no one on the other side could see me, since from looking into the futures I already knew that they had assault rifles and were following a policy of shooting first and asking questions later.

In case you're wondering, this isn't an especially unusual night for me. Sometimes I really question my life choices.

"You know," I said quietly, my voice just loud enough to carry to where Caldera was lying by my side, "this is a pretty crappy way to spend Christmas Eve."

"Get used to it," Caldera whispered back, not taking her eyes off the building ahead. "You got a count?"

"Can't get close enough," I whispered back. The street was a wide one, and the wind was blowing towards us, so there wasn't much chance of being overheard, but I kept my voice down all the same. "At least twenty." It could be more; any of the futures in which I tried to move closer devolved into shooting, and once that happened my future selves didn't really have the time to get an exact count.

"Whose side are they on?"

"Don't know, don't care." The men in the opposite building could be rebels, or Islamic State, or heavily armed tourists for all I knew. "Whoever they are, they're not friendly."

A chill wind blew across the rooftop. The building we were on looked as though it had been a coffeehouse, once, before the war. Some sort of explosive had demolished the rear half and left it in ruins. Caldera was silent, and I could tell something was bothering her. "What's wrong?" I whispered.

"What are they doing here?" Caldera whispered.

"I know," I whispered. "I don't like it either." Yes, this was a war zone, but it was far too much of a coincidence that these guys had just happened to set up shop in the one building in Aleppo that we had to visit. Especially since they were obviously on the alert.

"You think Drakh's in there?" Caldera whispered.

"I can't sense any magic."

"Me neither, but they could be staying dark." Caldera looked at me. "Drakh and his mages hole up in the basement, use those guys as a screen?"

"Maybe," I said doubtfully. It didn't feel right to me.

Caldera looked up, frowning, then put one hand to her ear. "Received, on our way," she murmured. "Out." She looked at me. "Captain wants us back."

We crept back and down to the first floor. Four men were waiting for us in the ruined remains of a bedroom: Captain Elandis, another Keeper I didn't know, and a pair of Council security men. "Verus," Elandis said. He was tall and thin, with aristocratic looks and a faded scar on one cheek. "Let's hear it."

"Twenty at least, maybe more," I said. "Can't tell which faction they're with, but they're not friendly."

"We've already got a count," Elandis said. "And they're Islamic State, incidentally. What I want to know is defences. Traps, wards, anything that's a risk."

"I can't see any," I said. "Guns, yes, but they don't seem to have any magical protections at all."

"Mines or explosives?"

"Just a few grenades."

Elandis nodded. "Get back to your positions. I want to know if anything changes." We returned to our positions on the rooftop and waited.

Time passed. The rooftop kept getting colder, and I had to rub my arms to keep myself warm, staying behind the parapet to make sure I wasn't seen. Once we heard a distant burst of gunfire from somewhere off to the east, but it soon died away. There was little movement from the rooftop opposite. In the movies, war zones are filled with shouts and dramatic charges, but a real battlefield just looks empty, to the point where if you don't know what to look for, you probably won't notice that it's a battlefield at all. Everyone with any brains is behind cover with their head down. I could just make out the two shapes on the rooftop across from us, but only because I had my divination to help. Occasionally one of them would shift position, the movement almost invisible in the darkness.

"How long to our window?" I whispered.

"T minus thirty-five," Caldera whispered.

"This is wrong," I whispered. "Why aren't we seeing anything?"

"You think Drakh isn't there yet?" Caldera whispered. "Going to gate in last minute?"

"That makes no sense. He *has* to secure the place first."

"So maybe he's there already after all."

Then why aren't there any wards? I didn't like this. We were missing something.

Caldera looked up, listening to something I couldn't hear. "Elandis gave the order," Caldera whispered. "They're going in."

I nodded.

A minute passed, then two. Something flickered on my senses. "Feel that?" Caldera whispered.

"Gate magic," I murmured. A moment later it came again. It was followed by other spells: air and water, and some kind of living magic that was hard to pin down. It was coming from the building opposite. More spells, complex and quick. I couldn't hear anything or see anything, but I knew that something was happening.

The shapes of the two rooftop guards hadn't moved. They were still sitting up on that rooftop, quiet and still. Then as I watched, a cloud of darkness seemed to swallow one of them. I saw the second one turn his head, there was a scrape of movement, then something rolled over him too fast to see and he vanished.

"What the hell was that?" I said quietly. The rooftop was still again, and empty. If I hadn't been watching closely I never would have noticed anything.

"Shh," Caldera said.

Minutes ticked by. There was still no sound, but I could sense magic. Gradually the feeling of the spells being used changed: less like combat magic, more like defence and utility. They weren't fighting anymore—they were digging in.

Caldera cocked her head, listening, then looked at me. "We can go in."

⌁ ⌁ ⌁ ⌁ ⌁ ⌁ ⌁ ⌁ ⌁

We went down the stairs and crossed the street, picking our way between the burnt-out cars. By the time we reached our target building's front door, it was being guarded by two Council security with submachine guns. They let us through without comment.

Inside was a hive of activity. Council security were everywhere, setting up defence posts and clearing lines of fire, while Keepers worked on defensive wards. Scattered around on the floor were bodies, and a Council security man was going around picking up their dropped weapons. There was one just by the door, and I took a look as we passed. He'd been killed by a single bullet to the back of the head. The safety catch on his rifle was still on.

Rain met us by what had once been a shopping counter. "Verus, get down to the basement and start checking at the entry point. Caldera, go with him."

"You don't need me up here?" Caldera asked.

"Securing the area is the perimeter team's job," Rain said. "Getting the relic is ours."

Caldera shrugged and obeyed. We headed for the staircase, and I saw a blue-green flash that made me turn my head. A Keeper was going around the room, cleaning up the bodies. As I watched, he reached the corpse by the door that I'd noticed earlier. He pointed a hand downwards, there was another blue-green flash, and the body puffed into dust. I turned away.

⁙⁙⁙⁙⁙

The basement was dark and cold and hadn't been used in a long time. Broken barrels were lined against the far wall, and a thick layer of dust covered the floor. Someone had thought to come down and set up an electric light with a portable generator, and its hum was the only sound in the gloom.

Two Keepers, Slate and Trask, were waiting for us at the bottom of the stairs. They're from Caldera's order and they're partners, more or less. Slate is stockier and lighter-skinned, while Trask is taller and darker, but both are tough, and look it. I regarded them with mixed feelings. Slate and Trask know their business, but I wasn't looking forward to working with Slate.

Slate gave me his usual scowl upon seeing me. "Over there," he said, jerking his head.

The far wall of the basement was different from the rest. The other walls were crude brick, but this was finely worked stone carved into a frieze of leaves and branches; the bricks and mortar to the left and right were old, but something told me that the wall in front of me was older still. It had stood here for a long, long time before workmen had turned this area into a sublevel of the building above.

I couldn't sense any magic from the wall. It didn't hold any energy or charge, and a quick glance through the futures confirmed that it wouldn't respond to any standard tests. But in a little under half an hour, this would become an active gate into a bubble realm. If the Council's intelligence report was accurate, no password or key was required. Anyone with the ability to channel through focus items could do the job. I looked ahead, trying to confirm whether—

"Well?" Slate said from behind me. "Can you open it or not?"

I shot an annoyed look back at Slate. "Not with you yakking on, I can't."

Slate rolled his eyes. I went back to studying the futures. Again they were disrupted.

I sighed. "Slate."

"What?"

"Can you give me some peace and quiet?"

"Didn't say anything."

"No, but you're *going* to, and it's breaking my concentration."

"That doesn't make any sense," Slate said, aggrieved. "I'm just—"

"Look, just take his word for it," Caldera interrupted. "It'll go a lot faster."

Slate looked bad-tempered but he obeyed, and looking ahead I could tell he'd actually stay quiet this time. I searched through the futures in which I waited out the time and tried to open the gate, exploring the paths.

It was fifteen minutes before zero hour when Rain came downstairs. Caldera spoke to him quietly, and Rain raised his eyebrows but waited. I kept path-walking for a minute longer, then went over. "Well?" Rain asked.

"It's going to work," I said. "Gate'll be accessible right on the dot."

"Any hostiles on the other side?"

"No."

"What's the environment?"

"Dark, cold, empty. Feels deserted. No traps or wards or guardians. It's big, though. We're going to have to search."

"Any sign of Drakh or his cabal?"

"No."

Rain nodded. "Coatl's looking for you upstairs."

। । । । । । । ।

I came up the stairs into noise and commotion. The bodies had been cleaned away, but Council security were hurrying around and I could hear someone giving orders. I could feel more wards being woven, stronger ones this time, and there was a sense of urgency in the air.

Coatl was waiting for me near the stairs. He was wearing a suit of body armour that made him look rather out of place, like an office worker dressed up for a reenactment. "Hoi, Verus," he said. "You've got a problem."

A Keeper came striding past, shouting something about getting snipers on the roof. "You mean all this?" I said.

"No," Coatl said. "There's a Keeper in your squad by the name of Ares. Square face, short hair, balding. Took a call just before going down. Couldn't make out most of it, but it was about you, and it didn't sound friendly."

"The I-don't-like-him sort of unfriendly? Or I'm-going-to-shoot-him-in-the-head?"

"Dunno, but I'd watch your back if I were you."

"Great." I sighed. "Well, I've gone on missions with Keepers planning to murder me before. At least this time I know which one it is."

A squad of three Council security came running past, weapons up and faces grim. They jogged out the door and disappeared into the darkness, another man pulling the door shut behind them. "What's going on?" I asked.

"Eyes in the sky are tracking a group headed right for us," Coatl said. "A hundred at least, and they're armed. Doesn't feel like a coincidence to me."

"Me either. You going to be okay?"

Coatl snorted. "I'll be hiding behind the battle-mages. We'll keep 'em off you."

"Let's hope so." If they couldn't, we'd be trapped. "Good luck."

"You too."

⁅⁅⁅⁅⁅⁅⁅⁅⁅

By the time I made it back down to the basement, it was packed. Keepers and security men were crammed into the room, and I had to squeeze through the crowd. Despite the numbers, they were keeping a respectful distance from the wall. Landis had arrived too, and he gave me a cheery wave and a pat on the shoulder as I passed.

Rain was waiting at the front. "We good?" he asked.

I checked the futures. "Looks in order."

Slate was staring at me, and I could guess why. He wanted to know why Rain was taking my word for it. From flickers in the future I knew other Keepers were wondering the same thing, but none spoke out, maybe because they already knew what the answer would be. Rain had made the decision to trust me, and that was that. Which made me a member of the team . . . at least until Rain changed his mind. If he did, I knew Slate would turn on me without thinking twice, and he wouldn't be the only one.

The room fell silent as the minutes slipped by. I spent the time examining the bubble realm I'd soon be entering. The more I saw of this place, the less I liked it. It might not try to kill us on first entry, but it wasn't friendly. I could hear the murmur of whispered conversations from behind me, but as the last sixty seconds ticked away, even that died down. I knew everyone else was counting. Fifteen seconds. Ten. Five. Four. Three . . .

"Time," someone said from behind me, but I was already moving. I placed my hand on one of the leaves carved into the stone, channelled a thread of magic into it, then stepped back.

For a moment nothing happened, then a split opened in the ancient stone. Slowly and silently, two gates swung back into nothingness. As they did, they seemed to submerge themselves in shadow, as though they were sinking beneath the surface of some black liquid. The opening gates revealed a black veil, smooth and vertical and faintly reflective, and they kept swinging back until they had disappeared behind the darkness. A rectangular opening in the wall looked out at us, black and empty. From beginning to end the process had been absolutely quiet.

The Keeper force looked back at the entrance. There was something eerie about the silence. "Verus?" Rain said. "Is it safe?"

For answer I walked into the darkness. "Wait—" Rain started to say, then the black veil swallowed me. A chill seemed to slide along my skin as I passed through, then I was on the other side.

I came out into darkness. Not the darkness of the cellar, but the kind of total pitch-black where you can't see your hand in front of your face. It was cold but not freezing, and my shoes echoed on hard stone. I pulled a torch from my belt and clicked it on; the beam was weak and feeble, but it pushed back the darkness enough to create a splash of light around my feet. In the glow, I could see that the stone I was standing on was pale and flat. I couldn't see any walls or furniture, or for that matter anything at all. I might have been standing in the middle of nowhere.

Turning around, I found that I could see back into the basement, though the view was shrouded and darkened, like looking through a dirty window. The gate hung unsupported in midair, no sound coming through the veil. There was a figure approaching the gate; it was Rain, and as I watched, he passed through, his boots coming down onto the stone. He looked up, saw me, and walked over. "Next time," he said, "you can just say yes."

"We didn't really have time to sit around while I convinced them it wasn't a trap."

More Keepers were coming through behind Rain, along with Council security. As the mages arrived, light spells began to flicker into existence: white, red, blue, grey. I saw

Caldera come through, an orb of brown light igniting at her palm as she peered around her, with Landis following closely behind. The lights illuminated the place but didn't seem to reach very far. I still couldn't see anything above us or to either side.

"Lumen," Rain called, and a petite woman who'd just stepped through the gate changed direction to walk towards us. She wore white and violet robes that made her stand out against the body armour and fatigues of the security men behind her. "Let's turn the lights on."

Lumen nodded and raised one hand. A sphere of pure white light appeared and began to float upwards. It grew larger and brighter as it did, until it was ten feet high and so bright I had to look away.

"Brighter," Rain said.

"I'm trying."

"We need to see."

"I'm *trying*." Lumen sounded frustrated. "Something's wrong."

I started to look back at the sphere and had to shield my eyes. The amount of white light pouring out of it was so intense that I couldn't even look nearby without being dazzled. But when I turned away, I realised what Lumen meant. At our feet, the light was turning night into day . . . but only where we were standing. By the time the light was thirty feet away, the shadows were starting to return, turning the stone into gloom, and by fifty feet I couldn't see at all.

"We need this place lit up," Rain said. "Use more power."

"That's what I'm trying to tell you," Lumen said. "It's not helping."

"Rain," I said quietly. I kept my voice down but didn't hide the urgency in it. "You might want to keep everyone together."

Rain looked around. A few of the Keepers and Council security had started to drift away, and as they had their lights had faded into the gloom, almost disappearing from sight. "Everyone stay close!" Rain shouted. "Keep in visual range!"

The Keepers who'd been starting to drift away stopped and the group pulled together again. In truth, no one had gone far—pack instinct had kept anyone from wandering off—but even so, it had taken only seconds for us to almost lose contact. Rain turned back to the woman next to him. "Talk to me."

"There's something not right about this place." Lumen kept her voice down too. "The air's clear, there shouldn't be any visual interference, but light isn't propagating the way it should."

"You know physical laws can work differently inside bubbles," I said. It's one of the big ways they differ from shadow realms. A shadow realm is grown as a reflection of a location in our world, but the creator of a bubble realm can shape it into damn near anything, which includes messing with the laws of physics.

"Options?" Rain asked me.

I shrugged. "If Lumen's right and this is light-based, then everyone using visual spells is going to have their effective range cut. Fire mages definitely; probably the water and light mages too. Caldera's tremorsense might still work. My pathwalking definitely does."

Rain nodded. "Then you're at the front with me."

⁞⁞⁞⁞⁞⁞⁞⁞⁞

Our force formed up and headed into the darkness. There were a total of eleven mages under Rain's command: me, Caldera, Landis, Slate, Trask, and half a dozen more that I knew less well. I was the only auxiliary; everyone else was a member of the Order of the Star or the Order of the Shield. Accompanying us were nearly thirty Council security. All carried guns, and some were transporting heavier equipment: demolition gear, maybe, or heavy weapons. It's rare for the Council to send more than one or two Keepers on a mission. Even dedicated combat operations usually don't merit more than six. This was the largest Keeper group I'd ever been a part of.

It was a formidable force, but it didn't make me feel particularly reassured. In theory the Keepers are supposed to work for the Council as a whole, with no loyalty to any one particular faction. In practice, every major Light political faction has sympathisers among the Keepers and the auxiliary corps. If you're lucky, this just means that they'll leak information. If you're not . . . well, I've had Keepers try to kill me before. Given the state of affairs with Maradok and Levistus, I was going to be pretty surprised if the same thing didn't happen again before the day was out.

But I could feel Caldera's presence behind me, with Landis nearby, and that did make me feel better. "Caldera?" I murmured, dropping back. "Keeper to our right. Square face, starting to lose his hair. Know the guy?"

"Who—?"

"Don't look."

Caldera obeyed, waiting until she could sneak a sidelong glance. "Ares?"

"That's the one."

"He's Order of the Shield. Haven't worked with him before."

Landis fell into step on the other side. "I know the chap. What's bothering you?"

"Coatl told me to keep an eye on him." I kept my voice very low. Ares was far enough away that he shouldn't be able to overhear, but there are spells that can boost one's senses. "Apparently he doesn't like me very much."

"Hmm." Landis stroked his jaw.

"Hmm, what?"

"Well, he's got no reason to love Dark mages, I can tell you that," Landis said. "Still, he's no loose cannon. Wouldn't expect him to go tilting at windmills."

"It's not windmills I'm worried about." If the guy was working for Maradok, it wouldn't be hard for him to arrange an "accident" while people were distracted. "What's his magic type?"

"Fire. Good at what he does. If you're that concerned, I'd keep your distance if I were you."

"Should have worn your armour," Caldera said.

I kept quiet in response to that one. *There's a reason I didn't.*

A shape formed out of the darkness ahead: a bridge,

made out of the same pale stone and sloping upwards. To either side of the bridge, the stone stopped abruptly. Behind it was only a void. Rain came to a halt and gestured towards me; I walked forward to catch him up. "What's down there?" Rain asked, pointing into the blackness.

I looked into the future in which I stepped off the edge. It's one of the more difficult tricks to do as a diviner, not because the spell's a particularly complicated one, but because of the mental state you need to be in to make it work. Divination only sees possible futures; to look into the futures in which you do something potentially suicidal, you have to be willing to actually do it. To get it to work you have to use a kind of self-hypnosis, putting yourself into a trance of pure dispassionate curiosity. I saw my future self plunge into the darkness and fall. And fall. And fall. All-enveloping blackness, air rushing as I plummeted down a bottomless pit . . .

My survival instincts shouted *no!* and the future in which I fell off the edge vanished. "Nothing," I said to Rain. "Don't fall off."

The bridge turned out to be less of a bridge and more of a ramp, bringing us steadily upwards before levelling off onto another platform. My divination led us to a second ramp. Behind us, I was vaguely aware of Council security igniting chemical flares, one at the base and top of each ramp and others spaced out at intervals on the flat. They burned with a bright red glow, but even so, the darkness swallowed each one in seconds. It would be easy to get turned around here.

On the third platform I slowed and stopped. "This one's got four ramps leading off," I told Rain. "Two going down, two going up."

"Which way to the relic?"

"I'm going to need to check on my own."

"Do it," Rain said. "I'll get the air and earth mages to check for air movements and tracks. Meet back here in five minutes."

I walked into the darkness. The blackness swallowed me in seconds, the lights from Rain's group becoming a fuzzy grey glow and then disappearing completely. It would scare most people, but I've spent a long time learning how to navigate with my divination, and I can move faster in pitch darkness than most people can in full daylight. I did a circuit around the platform, stopping at each ramp to examine the futures in which I explored off on my own. One was easy to rule out. The other two were harder, but after a while I was fairly sure of our orientation.

I started to turn back, then hesitated. With my divination I knew that if I went straight back at this angle, I'd reach Rain. But a stray future had caught my eye, and I still had a minute or two before the time limit was up . . .

Nothing ventured, nothing gained. I moved left, letting my feet tread softly on the stone. I knew that I was circling around the main body of the group. Peering into the darkness, I saw the first traces of light and heard muffled voices. I looked into the futures in which I drew closer.

". . . any of your business," Caldera was saying.

"I'd say it is," Ares said. "And yours."

"You have a problem with Verus, take it to Rain." Caldera was down on one knee, one hand to the stone. She looked as though she'd been checking for something, but now her head was twisted around to look up at the other Keeper. "It's his job."

"Actually, it's your job." Ares squatted down, looking steadily at Caldera. "Has Verus told you why he's here?"

Caldera shrugged.

Ares gave Caldera a curious look. "So you don't know."

"He's an auxiliary."

"The Council's declared Verus an outlaw. As soon as the resolution becomes public, he's to be executed on sight."

Caldera turned to stare at him.

"It's nothing personal," Ares said. "Just orders."

"I think you're full of it," Caldera said.

"No bullshit. It's real."

"You got a warrant?"

"You know that's not how it works."

Caldera shook her head and looked away.

"We don't have to like what the Council tells us to do," Ares said. "We just have to do it." He rose to his feet. "You don't believe me? Ask him yourself." He walked away into the darkness.

Caldera didn't look after him at first, but once Ares was gone, she got to her feet and stared down at the stone, brow furrowed. A chime sounded in my ear from the communicator, and I knew our five minutes were up. Caldera turned and walked back towards the body of the group, and I followed.

Rain was at the centre of a small group of mages. ". . . eyes in the sky won't do any good," another man was saying to Rain. I knew him vaguely: he was an air mage called Stratus. "Just too dark."

Rain looked at me. "Either of the upward ramps should work," I said. "It looks as though they join up further on."

Rain nodded absently. "That matches. Caldera?"

Caldera looked up, caught off guard. "Huh?"

"Any tracks?"

"Tracks, right." Caldera shook her head. "No."

"Then we go straight," Rain said. "Let's move."

The group started moving again, and I fell back into my position a couple of steps behind Rain. I could feel Caldera's eyes on me.

⁓⁓⁓⁓⁓⁓⁓⁓⁓

We kept walking through the darkness, our lights the only illumination in a black and silent world. There were more junctions, ramps leading up and down from flat platforms, each as featureless as the last. With no maps or landmarks, we had to stop each time and rely on detection spells. I could feel Rain growing restless, and I knew why: almost an hour had passed. In about two hours, the gate would close. Our safety margin was shrinking fast.

My divination was our main guide now, but I could feel Ares's presence towards the back of the group, distracting me. Already my thoughts had started to branch down worrying paths: was he here to make sure the relic was recovered, or to make sure I didn't get out? What was Caldera going to do? And was it just a coincidence that he was a fire mage? The fact that he used fire magic didn't necessarily prove anything—elemental mages are the most common family, and there are more fire mages than any other type by a long way—but I couldn't help but think about that attack on my shop, and that figure wreathed in flame. He'd been a trained battle-mage too. A Keeper from the Order of the Shield would be a pretty good fit . . .

I pushed the thoughts away and went back to our more immediate problem. I'd been putting together a mental map of this place, using the futures in which I explored the side ramps to gain additional information, and a nasty suspicion was starting to nag at me. I sped up slightly, catching up to Rain. "We might have a problem," I said quietly.

Rain glanced at me. A sphere of blue light was hanging in the air over his shoulder, but his skin was so dark that it soaked up the glow, making the whites of his eyes stand out in an eerie way. Ahead of us, two Council security men were on point with torches. "This is not a good time for problems."

"I've been mapping out this place and the pattern is looking like a spiderweb. Lots of paths leading in to a central point."

"And?"

"The design doesn't make much sense for a place with only one entrance," I said. "It makes plenty of sense for multiple entrances."

"You think Drakh's cabal are in here too," Rain said quietly.

"It's been bugging me how easily we got in here," I said. "If Richard wants this relic so badly, why didn't he put a proper guard on the entrance? Those men weren't a match for a Keeper force. Unless they weren't really meant to stop us at all. Just to slow us down and make us think we're winning. Meanwhile Drakh's group slip in from the other side."

"If you're right," Rain said, "what can we do about it?"

"Call a halt," I said. "If I path-walk searching specifically for other mages, without any other interference, I should be able to find them."

Rain was silent.

"It'll give us some advance warning."

"Assuming they're there at all," Rain said. "And assuming that they aren't retrieving the relic already, in which case we need to be faster rather than slower."

". . . Yes."

Rain shook his head. "We can't afford the time. I'll put everyone on alert, but we're cutting it close as is. Stay as close as you can to the front and watch for ambushes."

I made a face but didn't argue. As I moved up to catch up with the point men, I heard Rain starting to give orders.

The farther we went, the faster a pace Rain set. At each junction, he allowed less time to search out a new path, sometimes taking no more than thirty seconds' break before we set off again. I understood why he was doing it, but it was frustrating. Rain was using elemental mage thinking: strike fast and hard, counting on your toughness to shrug off any hits. If I'd been alone, with time to search, I could have found a path through and been sure whether it was safe. But the presence of the Keepers and the Council security was clogging the futures—I couldn't stop and build a proper chain without one of them bumping into me and disrupting it. And the darkness was making it hard enough already. If we ran into an ambush, I wouldn't be able to give much warning.

And just as I was thinking that, it happened.

We'd just reached the top of a ramp when something flashed on my precognition. I stopped dead, got one good look at what was going to happen, and snapped at the two point men just in front of me. "Look out!"

The two of them turned to stare. I wheeled. "Rain! Incoming!"

"Shields!" Rain called instantly, raising his hand as he did. A barrier of blue light, translucent and slightly curved, materialised in front of the two point men, who were already scrambling back. Other mages began to cast shields of their own, and that was the point at which the mages ambushing us figured out that they'd been made and opened up on us.

Fireballs came flashing out of the darkness, dull red beads of light that exploded into bursts of flame upon striking a target. The first two detonated on Rain's shield, then a volley of force missiles came scything in, horizontal and razor-sharp, thrown with enough power to cut a man in half. Water shields are good against fire, not so good against force. The blades broke through, hissing past, and I heard a scream from behind. I was already running, breaking right. I couldn't see what was happening, but I knew that I needed to get out of the line of fire. Already the Keepers and Council security were shooting back, and I could hear the staccato *takatakatakatak* of the submachine guns, combined with the *whoosh* of battle-magic, fire and force and air.

The bubble realm was total chaos. Everything was pitch-black, fire was coming in from different directions, and I had no idea what was happening. I could hear shouts and screams, conflicting orders. People were spreading out in the darkness, trying to find cover or a clear shot, the two sides intermingling. A figure appeared out of the darkness in front of me, backing away, casting a spell; we both saw each other and did a double take as we tried to work out who we were looking at. The man was dressed in black, with a mask, and as I saw it I realised he had to be one of our attackers; I swerved back into the gloom. He didn't shoot after me, probably still unsure of who I was. The battle was darkness and screams and confusion, spells and bullets striking friend and foe. I saw a future in which I was shot and dodged right, saw another in which I was hit by a spell and dodged left, and ran right into someone else.

This one was taller, his shape illuminated in the glow of a light to the side, and he was quicker on the draw. He caught my movement out of the corner of his eye and swung his gun towards me; it was some sort of assault rifle and I ducked out of the line of fire, grabbing the rifle by the hand guard. We struggled briefly, wrestling for the gun; he was wearing a ski mask and as our gazes met I saw blue eyes go wide. He hesitated for the tiniest instant, then drove a kick at me that would have broken a rib. I slid aside, hit him in the face, then got both hands on the rifle and twisted it out of his grasp. He stumbled and fell but turned the fall into a roll; I felt the flash of some kind of magic, and as he came up he was holding a submachine gun. I turned and ran, losing myself in the darkness then throwing myself flat. From behind I heard a sharp *takatakatakatak!* and felt the burst go over my head. The futures cleared; I pulled myself to my feet and kept running. Up ahead was a ramp, sloping upwards, and I took it.

As I jogged up the ramp, the sounds of the shots and yells began to die away. I slowed and stopped, listening, and realised that I'd gone right through the battle and out the other side. The Dark mages were in between me and Rain's Keepers.

I could find somewhere safe to hole up in the darkness and wait for the fighting to be over. On the other hand, my instincts were telling me that that ambush had been designed to stop us, not to kill us. Which isn't to say that Richard was going to be bothered about a few dead bodies, but it wasn't the objective. What he wanted was that relic, and if I kept going, I might be able to interfere.

It only took me a few seconds to make my mind up. I was still playing on Rain and Caldera's team, and I still needed that relic found. Besides, I prefer to take the initiative when I can. It's always better to have the other guy reacting to you.

The next platform had a couple of men on it. They weren't friendly, but I was able to skirt around them to reach another ramp. As I approached the top, though, I began to slow down. Once again there was someone there, but this time it was someone I wasn't going to be able to dodge so easily. I came to a stop just below the lip of the ramp, searching through the futures for ways in which I could get past. *Damn, she's right in the way.* If only she were a little farther out, I might be able to sneak—

"You going to hide there all day, Verus?" a voice called out of the darkness.

I sighed. *So much for sneaking.* I straightened and walked out into the open.

The platforms had been getting smaller, and this one was no more than sixty or seventy feet across. As I walked out over it, a green glow appeared out of the gloom. The glow became a pair of floating orbs of light, each the dark green of holly leaves, and standing between the orbs, her arms folded, was a woman called Vihaela.

Vihaela is dark-skinned and tall, with black hair that curls up at the tips. She's good-looking in an unusual sort of way—striking rather than pretty—and she dresses well, in layered clothes of brown and black. I'd come face to face with Vihaela exactly once before, for only a few minutes, but that had been more than enough for her to make an impression. Being a Dark mage comes with a certain automatic intimidation factor—yes, it's technically possible for one to be weak and unthreatening, but no one really believes that when they're standing in front of you—but however you measure threat levels among the Dark mages of Britain, Vihaela would be right at the top of the list, which would probably have to be written from hearsay given how few mages would voluntarily step into the same room as her. Vihaela has a reputation for being an expert with life and death magic, and an extremely skilled torturer. As for her abilities as a battle-mage, the last time I'd seen her, she'd taken on Caldera and Slate at the same time without breaking a sweat. As if that weren't enough, she was tied to Morden definitely, Richard almost definitely, and all in all was easily among the top five people I least wanted to come face to face with in a dark abandoned place. All of a sudden I wasn't so sure that going forward had been such a smart move.

"That's better," Vihaela said. "Bring any friends?"

"Why?" I asked. I kept my voice steady and my muscles relaxed. I was pretty sure Vihaela could read physiological signs the way Anne could, and I didn't want to show fear. "Feeling lonely?"

"Little bit." Vihaela sounded cheerful. She usually does. It doesn't make her any less creepy: rather the reverse. "Nice gun. Planning to use it?"

I was still holding the assault rifle. I didn't raise it. "I'm kind of on the clock," I said. "Mind if I ask you something?"

"As long as it's interesting."

"I can't help noticing that you're standing right in front of that ramp," I said. "Almost as though you're on guard."

"I'm hoping some of your guys will make it up here eventually," Vihaela said. "Don't see why the guys down there should have all the fun."

"Yeah," I said. "Fun. So would you have any particular objection to me going past?"

"Awww," Vihaela said with a smile. "You're so polite. Much nicer than the Keepers."

"So is that a yes?"

"Try and get by me and I'll turn every drop of fluid in your body into acid."

I wondered briefly if Vihaela could actually do that, and decided I didn't want to find out. I was only wearing one protective item: a fire-hunger stone, designed to ward against against fire- and heat-based spells. Against Vihaela's magic it wouldn't do a thing. "Can I put that down as a maybe?"

Vihaela sighed. "Look, Verus, right now I don't have a reason to hurt you. Be a good boy and run along before that changes."

I started to answer and then paused. At the edge of my hearing I could hear shouts from down below. Something in the futures . . . "You were asking if I'd brought any friends?" I said. "I've got someone I think you should meet."

Footsteps sounded behind me and I stepped to the side. Vihaela looked in the direction of the sound with interest. A moment later Landis came striding out into the light. "Ah, Verus!" Orange-red light glowed around Landis; he smelled of smoke and flame, but he seemed to have come through the battle without a scratch. "Started without us?"

"No, I was waiting for you."

A group of Council security appeared out of the darkness behind Landis. One was obviously wounded, but the others had their guns up, and as they saw Vihaela they sighted on her. "No need for that, chaps," Landis said, waving a hand without turning around.

The Council security hesitated, glancing at each other. "Sir?"

"Let's try to make sure you all get home in one piece, eh? Go secure the ramp and get a signal to Rain."

The Council security looked at Landis, looked at Vihaela, then lowered their guns and backed off into the darkness. "Really?" Vihaela asked. She'd watched the guns being trained on her with mild curiosity. "Not even as a diversion?"

"A little expensive for my tastes," Landis said.

"All the same to me." Vihaela took a couple of steps forward and stretched, interlacing her fingers above her head, then looked at Landis appraisingly. "Landis, right?"

Landis dipped his head. "Delighted to make your acquaintance."

"You *are* polite." Vihaela studied Landis for a second, then smiled. "You know, I was a little sore about never getting to face you in the White Rose raid."

Landis made a open-handed gesture, as if to say *after you*.

Vihaela shifted her stance slightly. It was only a small movement, but suddenly the futures looked very different. Landis took a half step back, his body tilted at forty-five degrees to Vihaela, left hand down, right hand at his waist. The moment seemed to stretch out, both mages perfectly still. I held my breath, not daring to move. I was close, if not quite near enough to be caught in a stray blast, but I was looking at where Vihaela was standing. She'd moved a little forward from the spot she'd been guarding, and already the base of the ramp behind her was starting to disappear into the gloom. *Just a little farther . . .*

Landis moved and suddenly both mages were casting. A fireblast darted out from Landis, Vihaela countered with something too fast to see, spells flurried with a *crack . . .* and then the two of them were standing still once again. Landis's stance had shifted and Vihaela was smiling. "Not bad," she said.

Landis didn't answer.

Green-black light struck from Vihaela's hands, arcing in. Just before it hit, a shield of flame appeared, only a couple of feet in diameter but in exactly the right position to block the attack. Energy cracked and the spell came apart. Vihaela tried again, this time from the other side. Again Landis blocked.

"So you can actually fight," Vihaela said. "What are you doing with the Keepers?"

"Chatty type, aren't you?" Landis said.

"You know, that fire shield won't do a thing against bullets," Vihaela said conversationally. "One shot from those men behind you and you're dead."

"If you think that'll work, why don't you chance your arm?"

Vihaela smiled again. "Where's the fun in that?"

"You know, my dear, I really don't have all day," Landis said. "If you're going to—"

Vihaela struck again, and this time she didn't stop. Green-black energy darted at Landis and I had a fleeting impression of living magic, twisted and deadly, intended to kill or cripple. A shield of fire formed around Landis, leaping out at and destroying the spells as they came in, then the air around Vihaela exploded in a bloom of flame. Vihaela came striding out, her footwork smooth and precise, the dark light of her own shield a shadow around her. She struck back and Landis countered, the spells too quick to follow. I've seen my share of mage duels, but I still couldn't track the movements. Landis and Vihaela were just too fast, their spells too complex. I was lucky that Vihaela was too busy to pay any attention to me; even with my divination, if she attacked me like that, I didn't fancy my chances.

But in the course of the battle, Vihaela had moved, and she wasn't standing in front of the ramp anymore. *Here goes nothing.* I stepped back into the darkness, letting the gloom envelop me . . .

Vihaela sent a last spell at Landis and pivoted away, breaking off. "Don't even think about it, Verus," she called out, not taking her eyes off the Keeper.

"Why don't you go ahead, Alex?" Landis said without looking at me. "We might be here a while."

"I told you what I'd do if you tried to get past me," Vihaela said. Her voice was confident. "I don't need the light to know where you—"

Hidden in the darkness, I pulled my mist cloak from my pack and slung it around my shoulders.

I'd spent a long time debating whether to wear my armour for this trip. In the end the thing that had swayed me had been the chance of betrayal. My armour's good against low- to medium-strength attacks, but depending on it to protect against a high-level battle-mage is kind of the equivalent of crashing your car at a hundred miles an hour and expecting to be okay because you're wearing your seat belt. Anyone from the Keeper force who wanted me dead would be able to study me at their leisure before attacking, and they'd have more than enough time to decide exactly how hard they needed to hit me to be sure of a kill. (Admittedly my armour would have been *great* at stopping glancing hits from spells and stray bullets in that battle down below, but you can't have everything. Imbued items are possessive, and they don't play well with others.)

My mist cloak is a shapeless covering of soft grey cloth. It's unobtrusive and radiates no magic, and it had been easy for me to keep it concealed in my backpack. It doesn't stop attacks, but it makes me almost completely invisible to magical senses like deathsight or lifesight. To Vihaela, it would have seemed as though I'd simply vanished into thin air.

Vihaela cut off midsentence, and for the first time that I'd seen her, she actually looked startled. Landis didn't give her a chance to recover, hitting her with a combination of spells, a fireball and another explosive blast striking at the Dark mage before walls of flame sealed her into a box of searing heat. For a moment Vihaela was on the defensive, all her attention on protecting herself, then she recovered, walking out through the wall of fire and counterattacking Landis while a flick of her wrist sent a field of dark energy to hover at the base of the ramp, blocking it off. I couldn't tell exactly what the spell did but I knew it wouldn't be anything good.

But she was too late. In those few seconds, I'd made it onto the ramp and up and out of range.

I kept running as the sounds of battle faded behind me. I was *really* pushing my luck now—too many people had seen me, and if Landis couldn't keep Vihaela busy I was in serious trouble—but you don't put someone like Vihaela on guard duty unless it's for something important. I knew I had to be close.

And as it turned out, I was.

The ramp levelled off onto another platform, much larger this time. As I looked through the futures in which I explored it, I knew that this was the last one. There was another ramp leading down but no more leading up: we'd been gaining height with each one, and this was the place we'd been ascending to. There was nowhere higher to go.

Sitting in the centre of the circular platform was a stone sarcophagus. It wasn't large, but it still stood out for being the only object or furnishing I'd seen in this entire desolate bubble realm. Half a dozen figures were clustered around it, two of them bent over the sarcophagus and the others on guard. All had their faces concealed by masks or by spells, but it wasn't hard to figure out whose side they were on.

I hesitated. My mist cloak would keep me hidden as long as I stayed in the darkness, but the Dark mages had a pair of bright electric lights throwing a white glow around the sarcophagus, providing illumination for them to work by. *Maybe sit here and wait?* I looked into the future. The Keepers could follow the trail the same way I had . . .

. . . but not in time. The Dark mages would be finished in only a few minutes. Landis and the rest wouldn't make it by then.

Stealth was out. My mist cloak can hide me from magical senses, but not from bright light. Fighting wasn't even worth considering. I didn't want to take on *one* Dark mage, much less six. Maybe it was time to think outside the box. What would happen if I just walked up and talked to them?

Interesting. Depending on how I made the approach, they might or might not be jumpy enough to attack, but I couldn't actually see any future in which they killed me. Maybe Richard had given them orders to avoid fatalities if possible.

The Council wouldn't care very much one way or the other about a few dead security operatives, but killing a Keeper would have repercussions.

Or maybe it's not about repercussions. Maybe it's about me.

I hesitated for an instant, then made up my mind. *Time to live dangerously.* I laid the gun down on the stone, then walked out into the light.

chapter 12

The Dark mages spun to face me. Black energy leapt to the hands of one, fire to the hands of another. I kept still, not making any sudden moves. The good news was that I was pretty sure that Rachel and Onyx weren't here. If they had been, they'd have shot first and asked questions afterwards. "Hi, guys," I said. "How are you doing?"

Several of the Dark mages just stared at me. I think the sheer lunacy of what I'd done had caught them off guard. "Looking to die, Keeper?" one of them said.

"That's not really up to you, is it?"

Two of the mages turned to look at each other. "Burn him?" the fire mage asked.

"I wouldn't," I told him.

"Yeah?" the fire mage said. From the subtleties of the magic playing around his hands, I could tell it wasn't Cinder. *Pity.* "Give me a good reason."

"Because it's not your decision." I turned to one of the figures at the centre of the group and played my best card. "It's Morden's."

The Dark mages stared at me in silence. I looked back

at them without blinking. "This guy nuts?" one of the others asked.

"Fuck it," one of them said. "Just kill him." But he didn't move.

I kept looking at Morden. His face was shrouded in darkness, but I knew it was him. "Well?"

"You're very confident for one caught alone," Morden said. There was an odd buzz to his words, and the pitch was different. The more he spoke, though, the more I could recognise his voice. Spells can only hide so much.

"So, here's what I had in mind," I said. "You guys pack up and leave, and I won't say anything to the Keepers about who you are or what you were doing here. We all go home happy."

One of the Dark mages laughed. "That's an interesting offer," Morden said. "Unfortunately for you, you're in no position to enforce it." He gestured to the two mages by the sarcophagus. "Get back to work. You two, if Verus tries to interfere, incapacitate him. Make it painful but nonfatal, please."

The mage Morden had been talking to looked unimpressed at the "nonfatal" part but obeyed. "I'd go with my plan if I were you," I said.

"Or you'll do what?" one of the Dark mages said.

"Or I'll let you go," I said. "Then once you're gone, I'll give a full report to the Keepers. In particular, I'll explain how you, Morden, were personally involved in attacking Keeper personnel and taking a relic against express Council instructions." I looked at Morden's back. "How much longer do you think you'll keep that Council seat once that happens?"

Morden paused.

"Take your time," I said.

"Verus, you've survived until now by not putting yourself in direct opposition to the mages you deal with," Morden said. "I would advise against changing that."

"Everyone finds something to take a stand for sooner or later."

"You think the Council will take your word for it?" Morden said. "With your reputation?"

"You think they'll care? The Crusaders and the Guardians hate you *way* more than they hate me. Levistus and the rest of his faction will jump on it hands first. I mean, I could let them do a mental probe, but honestly, I doubt they'll even want one. They couldn't care less if I'm telling the truth. They've been looking for an excuse to get rid of you ever since you walked into the Conclave."

Morden stayed silent for a moment. "Interesting," he said at last. He turned to face me, his face shadowed and blank. "You make a compelling case. However, there appears to be one point you have overlooked. To speak to the Council, you have to be alive."

I felt the mood in the group shift. The two mages who'd been working on the sarcophagus looked up. I could sense spells ready to go, primed and eager. "Not quite," I said.

"Why?" Morden said. His voice was soft. "Think fast, Verus."

"Because time mages can use timesight," I said. "Mind mages can use telepathy. Space mages can scry. The Council might be bad at a lot of things, but one thing it's not short on is resources. If you kill me, there are a dozen ways they can find out that it was you, and once they do, you're done. Oh, I'm sure you could get away, but you'll never hold Council office again." I looked at Morden. "Ever since I first met you, this Council seat is what you've been working towards. Now you've got it. Is this relic really more important to you than the ambition you've spent your whole life pursuing?"

"And if it is?" Morden said quietly. "Are you willing to take that risk?"

I shrugged.

Morden stared at me. The bubble realm was dead silent. I couldn't hear the battle from below, or any movement from behind us; we were alone in a tiny circle of light, the only living things in a dead and empty world. The other Dark mages were tense, ready. I knew there was no way I could dodge this many attacks from this short a range. If Morden gave the word, I'd be dead in seconds.

But I couldn't see any futures in which that happened. And

that was why I'd been willing to try this insane plan in the first place. Trying to divine a future through conversations with other free-willed creatures is one of the hardest uses of divination magic, but if you're good—and I'm very good—then you can pick up a sense of what is and isn't possible. And while I'd been hiding in the darkness, I'd noticed something: I couldn't detect any futures in which Morden actually killed me. There'd been plenty where I'd been attacked by the other Dark mages (usually if I'd done something to provoke them), but I'd never seen Morden himself raise a hand against me. In fact, in quite a few futures, he'd been the one keeping me *alive* when another Dark mage had wanted to kill me and be done with it.

For whatever reason, Morden didn't want me dead. Maybe my guess had been right, and he didn't dare take the risk of killing a Keeper auxiliary, not where it could be traced back to him. Maybe he wanted me alive so that he could use me in some future plan. Maybe it was some other reason that I had no way to know about. It's the same story as always with my magic—I know what's going to happen, but I don't know why. But sometimes, you don't need to know why. You just have to be willing to take advantage.

"Withdraw," Morden said.

The fire mage stared at Morden. "Are you—?"

Morden didn't look at him. "Don't make me repeat myself."

The fire mage looked at Morden in disbelief, then stared at me. He wasn't the only one. Even behind the masks, I could feel the enmity in those stares; if I'd been alone, I wouldn't have fancied my chances. But Morden's authority held, and one by one, the Dark mages rose and disappeared back into the darkness, leaving the lights behind them. Morden and I were left alone.

"This won't earn you the Council's gratitude, Verus," Morden said. "Or their loyalty. They'll turn on you soon."

"I guess you'd be the expert on that."

"Just remember what I've said," Morden said. "I'll be

seeing you." He turned and walked away. The blackness swallowed him and I was left alone.

I stood quite still for five seconds, checking to make absolutely sure that he was gone, then let myself sag, the breath coming out of my lungs in a huff. All of a sudden my muscles felt weak. I walked on shaky legs to the sarcophagus and knelt down, bracing myself against the stone. I could feel wards on the thing, half deactivated—the Dark mages had almost broken through before I'd interrupted. I could probably finish the job, given a little time. I fumbled in my pocket for a conductor probe. Most of my attention was still on Morden and his cabal, and I was tracking them through the futures, looking at the possibilities in which I pursued them, making absolutely sure that they were gone. I was focused on the Dark mages in front of me and the wards on the sarcophagus that I was kneeling next to, and it didn't occur to me that the electric lights were still on, illuminating me clearly in the middle of the open platform, and so when the attack came from behind it caught me almost completely by surprise.

My precognition saved me, but only just. Futures of pain and death screamed at me and I threw myself into a backwards roll, heat washing over me as a narrow beam of fire passed overhead. I came to my feet to run and had an instant to see the next spell coming in. I saw all the possible directions in which I could dodge, the futures making a curving shape on the open stone floor. Before the next spell hit, I had just enough time to get to anywhere within about a ten-foot radius.

The spell coming in on me was going to create a blast of flame with *more* than a ten-foot radius.

Divination's good for dodging. It's not always enough.

Searing heat flashed around me and the world went red. I managed to take the worst of the blast on my back and keep running, trying to get out of the light; a third spell missed but I could smell burning hair and cloth and knew that my clothes were on fire. There was pain all through my torso and I rolled on the ground, frantic, trying to put the fire out; my cloak was engulfed in flames and I tore it off and let it fall. Another spell was coming in and I managed to dive away just before it hit, lighting up the darkness in flame.

All of a sudden everything was still. My clothes were smouldering and there was pain down my back and right arm, but I wasn't on fire and for now at least I was hidden by the darkness. At the centre of the platform the electric lights cast their glow, and to the right my cloak was a burning mass, but everything else was black. I didn't move.

Flame shimmered in the darkness, and a man emerged onto the edge of the circle of light. His figure was hidden by a shield of fire, but I knew who it was. "Come on out, Verus," Ares said. His voice echoed weirdly through the flame shield. "Let's make this quick."

Very slowly, I backed away. Pain was still spiking through my body, but it wasn't as bad as it should have been. I could feel a strange sensation at the top of my chest, and carefully and quietly I touched my hand to the top of my shirt. My fire-hunger stone was there, hidden underneath my clothes . . . or at least it had been. As my fingers brushed it, I could feel that it was twisted and warped. The stone had burnt itself out, but it had absorbed enough of that fireball to keep me alive.

Ares kept walking forward. I kept backing away. I was hurt, but I could still run. More importantly, I knew that he didn't know where I was. Fire mages can see heat, but the supernatural darkness was obviously messing with his magical vision as well as his normal eyesight, otherwise he'd have picked me out already. More Keepers had to be on their way. As long as I stayed quiet and didn't let him hear me . . .

Ares walked forward. I couldn't see what he was doing through the fire shield, but he seemed to be looking or listening for something. I kept easing backwards very slowly. As long as I stayed out of sight, he had to guess at which direction I'd gone in. For all he knew, I was moving towards one of the ramps—I couldn't from my current position, not easily, but he didn't know that. Ares walked towards my burning cloak and stopped again. I saw him turn to look in my direction.

Lucky guess? I kept creeping away, letting my feet fall

softly on the stone. Ares was out of sight now, and I had to track him through my divination. I saw him look down, then up, then start walking towards me. I sped up a little. He kept following.

How does he know where I am? I couldn't understand it. He *couldn't* see me, the darkness was—

I felt a sinking feeling in my stomach. *Oh crap.*

Ares wasn't looking up, he was looking down. He was tracking me by the heat of my footsteps.

I thought fast, fighting off panic. The pain was making it hard to concentrate. I could try to shoot him, but I could tell from my magesight that his shield was reinforced with kinetic energy this time—he'd obviously learned his lesson from two nights ago. Without my fire-hunger stone, the next hit would kill me. Run? No, he'd hear the movement and block off my movement with walls of fire. I could feel the edge of the platform behind me, a black void falling away into nothingness. One of the one-shot items I carry with me is a life ring, an air spell that slows your falling speed. I could break the ring and jump off, and I'd drop at a slow, steady rate . . . except that there was nothing to drop *to.* I'd be falling for ever.

Almost out of time. If Ares caught me up by only a few more steps, he'd see me. As if he could tell that, Ares sped up. I had to choose—

The platform shook, trembling as if in a very small, localised earthquake. Brown light bloomed in the distance, fuzzy and vague, and a figure came striding out of the darkness. "Ares," Caldera said. Her voice was flat. "Back off."

I felt the flame shield around Ares wink out, replaced with his own light spell. "What are you talking about?" Ares asked.

"I'm not that fucking stupid, all right?" Caldera said. "Back off from Verus, right the hell now."

I felt the futures flicker as Ares considered lying, then decided against it. "You know," he said, "this would have been a lot easier if you'd stayed out of it."

"Yeah, well, I'm not." Caldera was ready to attack; I could sense it and I knew Ares could too. "What's it going to be?"

"The Council have ordered—"

"Don't care."

"You *work* for the Council."

"Yeah?" Caldera said. "Then if this is all so official, where's your warrant? How come Verus was allowed on the op?" Caldera came to a halt a little way from Ares, her hands by her sides, her gaze locked onto him. "Know what I think? I think you've got someone paying you under the table to bump Verus off. Which makes you guilty of treason. So unless you've got legal authority that you can show me, then you're going to walk away. Or we'll find out whether fire mages can fly."

"Verus isn't on our side," Ares said.

"Still don't care."

Ares shook his head in frustration. "You know what the consequences are going to be for this."

"You haven't got a warrant and you're not the ranking officer," Caldera said. "Means you're not in charge. Simple as that."

Ares studied Caldera. "I suppose to you it is, isn't it?"

"Well? Going to make a fight of it?"

Ares looked at Caldera for a long moment. "No," he said at last. "I won't kill a Keeper. Not an honest one, at any rate." He shrugged. "You win this one, Caldera." He walked away.

Caldera turned to watch Ares go, tracking him as he disappeared into the darkness. Only once he was gone did she turn to me. "Alex? You all right?"

I walked into Caldera's light. I didn't have far to travel; Ares had been very, very close. Caldera's eyes widened as she saw me. "Jesus. You look like shit."

"Thanks," I said wearily. "Help me get to that sarcophagus?"

Caldera moved to my side and let me lean on her as I limped back to where the Dark mages had set up their electric lights. "How badly did he get you?" Caldera asked.

"Burns on my back and arm," I said. "I can run, but I'm not going to be doing much fighting. What happened to Landis and Vihaela?"

"Vihaela's here too?"

"You didn't see her?"

"Too busy tracking you," Caldera admitted. "Hope Landis is okay. That woman's bad news."

We reached the sarcophagus and Caldera helped me down. I pulled out my conductor probe and started working on the wards. "Thanks," I said quietly, without looking at her.

"Don't worry about it."

"I don't have many friends. When someone goes out on a limb for me, I notice."

"Yeah, well, don't get too used to it. If he had had a warrant, I'd still have kicked his arse, but I'd have arrested you right after."

"Could you have done it?"

"Done what?"

"Beaten him."

"Probably not," Caldera admitted. "But he didn't know that."

I worked in silence a little longer. "Sorry for not telling you what was going on," I said at last.

"Just get this frigging relic so we can go home."

ı ı ı ı ı ı ı ı

Traps and other obstacles are only really effective when defended. Rivers, minefields, barbed wire, and similar inconveniences can slow down an armed force, but on their own, they're just a nuisance. Rivers can be forded, minefields can be cleared by engineers, and an apron of barbed wire can be removed by a single person with enough determination and a set of bolt cutters. Add some hostile snipers, though, and all of a sudden those obstacles take a major jump in difficulty. If you have to clear a minefield while someone's shooting at you, then you've got a problem.

The wards on the sarcophagus were elaborate, and moderately powerful. But without any hostile mages trying to blow my head off, getting through them was really just a matter of time. And when some people did show up, they were on our side.

"Verus, Caldera," Rain said. Slate and Trask were with him, along with a scattering of security men. "You all right?"

"In one piece," Caldera said.

"What happened?" Rain looked around. "And where did those lights come from?"

"We had some visitors," I said absently, not looking up from the sarcophagus. "There." I straightened up. "Go ahead and roll it."

Caldera nodded and put her hands to the sarcophagus lid; it was solid stone and probably weighed close to half a ton. Caldera levered it up and slid it aside, dropping it to the floor with a *thud*.

Rain took a step forward and hesitated. "Is it safe?"

"Wards are down," I said.

Cautiously, Rain moved forward. As he came closer to the lights, I saw that the side of his coat was cut and darkened with what looked like blood. It didn't look like he'd received any healing, but then we hadn't brought along any healers; it's Council policy not to deploy life mages on missions. Rain didn't seem to be seriously hurt though, and after only a moment's pause he reached into the sarcophagus to draw out a box. It was small, no more than a foot or so square, and crafted out of some kind of dull metal. I could feel time magic radiating from it. "This it?" Rain asked.

"It's a Minkowski box, or close enough," I said. "Can't promise more than that."

"Time?" Rain said to one of the security men.

"Fifty-five minutes, sir."

"It'll take us nearly that long to make it back," Slate said. "I say we get the fuck out."

Rain looked at Trask. "Are any of the other teams still engaged?"

Trask shook his head. "Nothing on the comms."

"All right," Rain said. "Tell everyone to fall back to the regroup points. Anyone who can't regroup, withdraw on their own. We are *leaving*."

Slate nodded and turned, disappearing into the darkness.

Trask put one hand to his ear and began issuing orders. Caldera looked around to see that I'd moved. "Alex?"

"I'm coming," I said absently. While Rain had been talking I'd moved to the site of my brief, abortive battle with Ares. On the floor was a small pile of ash and charred cloth. I knelt down, running my fingers through the remains.

Caldera walked over to me. "Alex? You okay?"

"More or less," I said. I'd been hoping against hope that my mist cloak might have survived, but as I looked at the remains I knew that there was no way. Imbued items aren't like machines; you can't replace their parts. They're either alive or they're dead. My mist cloak was dead.

I'd been trying to avoid using my mist cloak for some time. I'd made the mistake of relying on it a little too much a couple of years ago, and I'd nearly been lost forever. Ever since then, I'd steered clear of it when possible, going out with my armour instead. But looking at the charred remnants, the first thing I felt was a sense of loss. My mist cloak's saved my life more times than I can count. Even that time two years ago, it had only been trying to protect me, in its single-minded way, and it had protected me one last time now.

"Come on, Alex," Caldera said. "It's just a cloak."

I got to my feet and walked away, Caldera at my side. I didn't look back.

⁞⁞⁞⁞⁞⁞⁞⁞⁞

The journey back was quicker than the journey in, but there was also more of a sense of urgency—we were on a clock, and everyone knew it. The marker lights placed at the top and bottom of each ramp showed us our way back, but between them we were plunged into blackness. I had to take point again, guiding us back from one island of light to the next. Not all the lights were deserted, either; I found men clustering around several of them, in ones and twos and threes, mostly Council security who'd become separated in the fighting and had pulled back to the lights to wait for rescue. They joined up with us as we passed, swelling our numbers.

One of the first people we picked up was Landis, and I felt a little relief as I saw him standing at his ease in the light, fiddling with some contraption he'd been carrying in his pocket. "Landis," I said. "You're okay?"

"Hmm?" Landis glanced up. "Ah, Verus. Where did you get to?"

"Where did I—?" I shook my head. "What happened with Vihaela?"

"Oh, her. Was a bit of a sticky situation there for a while." Landis stuffed the gadget into his pocket and fell into step beside me. "She does know what she's doing, doesn't she?"

"That's one way of putting it. What happened?"

"Well, we were in the middle of our little difference of opinion when she made her apologies and left." Landis looked thoughtful. "Honestly, I have the feeling she was just trying to slow us down."

We kept moving, picking up people as we went. Rain was constantly on the comms, giving orders and coordinating. From time to time someone would call out how long we had until the gate cutoff. Forty minutes, thirty-five, thirty . . .

"Alex," Caldera called from behind me. "Hold up."

I stopped and retraced my steps. Rain was in the middle of a small crowd, illuminated by half a dozen lights, and he was on the communicator to someone. "Can you figure out your position?" he said. "Yes . . . Look for the lights. Can you see the lights?"

"What's going on?" I asked Caldera quietly.

"One of the units got cut off," Caldera said under her breath. "They managed to hold out but they lost their bearings in the fight. They're somewhere near but we don't know where."

Rain listened a little longer, then cut the connection and looked at Slate. "How long have we got?"

"Twenty-seven minutes."

"Verus? How long back to the gate?"

"Only three more ramps," I said. "Five minutes if we run."

"We can search," Slate said.

"We don't have time," another Keeper said.

"Yes, we do!"

"Can't risk everyone for one security team."

"There's long enough—"

"Not if something goes wrong."

"Enough," Rain said. "Slate. Do we have any way of reliably tracking them?"

Slate was silent. "We could try," he said.

Rain stared at Slate, then past him into space. The others fell silent, watching Rain. I felt the futures shift, then settle, and Rain looked back at Slate. "We pull out."

Slate looked at Rain angrily. "You're going to leave them?"

"They knew the risks when they took the job." Slate started to answer and Rain made a negative motion. "Discussion's over. Lumen, Trask, get everyone moving. We're heading out."

I sighed. I was burnt, tired, and aching. I really didn't want to do anything more today. "Rain," I said.

Rain paused, looking back at me with a frown. "We don't have time for—"

"I'll find your guys," I said. "Caldera can guide you the rest of the way. Just leave the door open."

꠵꠵꠵꠵꠵꠵꠵꠵꠵

There were arguments. Caldera objected and so did Rain. I shrugged it off and walked into the darkness.

It was a relief to be on my own again. Divination magic is solitary by nature, and in a lot of ways being alone is a diviner's natural state. It's just so much *easier* to look ahead when you don't have a bunch of other people talking and moving and messing up your carefully-laid-out future paths. Other mages can understand the theory of how divination works, and they can try their best not to disrupt you, but even the best of them can't compete with simply walking off by yourself. So what if I was enveloped in darkness? To my eyes, the mass of noise and chaos following Rain's Keepers stood out like searchlights against the void. It didn't take me long to find the missing Council security—they were hardly any distance away at all. I headed down the nearest ramp on a path that I knew would take me to them.

But despite the time pressure, I didn't hurry as much as I should have done. I was tired—not just physically, but mentally. Yes, I was carrying muscle strains and burns from my fight with Ares, but those were superficial; the problem was something deeper. I'd lost too much, been on the run for too long. I felt rootless, unattached.

I came to a stop at the foot of the ramp. Up ahead were the Council security men I'd come to find. To the left and to the right was only emptiness. I found myself wondering what would happen if I just wandered off, sat down somewhere, and closed my eyes. The gate would shut behind me and I'd be left alone. I wouldn't have to worry about Levistus, or assassinations, or politics. Peace.

Of course, Luna and Anne and Variam would still be out there. Just because I was gone, that wouldn't stop the resolution from being passed.

And then there were those three men. There are more than enough mages who treat other people's lives as expendable. If I left them here, I'd be as bad or worse.

I shook off the lassitude and walked forward to meet up with the men I'd come to find.

⁞⁞⁞⁞⁞⁞⁞⁞

The three Council security were happy to see me, to say the least. One had taken a bullet in the fighting—probably friendly fire from a stray round—and needed help to move. There was a brief argument where the younger of the three men almost-but-not-quite suggested leaving the wounded man behind so that we could escape. I made it clear that we had plenty of time to get him out the normal way, and thankfully the third man (a sergeant who'd managed to keep a level head despite the suffocating darkness) backed me up. The sergeant and I each slung one of the wounded man's arms over our shoulders, and we set off, the younger recruit leading the way, his eyes white as he tried to point his gun and torch in every direction at once.

I'd left Rain's group twenty-four minutes before the gate was due to close. It took me three minutes to find the missing security men, four minutes to get there, and one to get them moving. The journey back to the gate took twelve minutes, pushing ourselves but not so much so as to risk an accident. We made it through with three and a half minutes left. Plenty of time.

⁞⁞⁞⁞⁞⁞⁞⁞

A cold line slid along my skin as we passed through the veil, and then we stepped out into dazzling light. We were back in our world.

Light and noise overwhelmed my senses. I'd spent so long in the darkness and silence that it felt as though a crowd of people were yelling and shining spotlights in my face, and I put my free arm up to shield myself. As my ears and eyes adjusted I realised that the basement was packed with Keepers and Council security, and they *were* yelling. I tried to step back into a defensive stance, but it was hard with the wounded guy's arm around my shoulders, and I braced myself to dodge.

"Hey!"

I turned to see Caldera grinning at me. A medic and another guy took charge of the wounded man, and Caldera clapped me on the shoulder, making me stagger. "You really are something, you know that?" Caldera said.

"What did I do this time?" I said. I had to raise my voice to be heard over the shouting.

"What?"

"What are they yelling at me for?"

Caldera stared at me. "They're cheering."

I blinked. Come to think of it, the voices didn't *sound* angry. Looking around, I saw what I hadn't noticed at first, that the people looking at me were grinning rather than scowling. The mood wasn't angry—it was happy. "Why would they be cheering?"

Caldera gave me a disbelieving look. "Seriously?"

Slate and Trask pushed their way through the crowd towards me. Slate was shaking his head. "Are you fucking serious?" he said. "You actually found them?"

"Well, yeah."

"Why?" Slate said.

I shrugged.

Slate shook his head again. "Frigging diviners." He walked away.

Trask started to follow, paused, and looked at me. "Nice work," he told me before going after Slate.

"What happened to Ares?" I asked Caldera.

"Made an early exit. He's already gated back to London."

"What about the attack? Wasn't there a small army headed right for here?"

"Coatl told me," Caldera said. "Those guys didn't have any magical support. Elandis's unit tore them apart. After half of them went down, the rest turned and ran."

"What about—"

"Alex," Caldera interrupted. "We won, okay? It's over."

The sergeant who'd been helping me carry the wounded man came up to me. "Mage . . . Verus, wasn't it?"

"That's right. Your man okay?"

"He'll live, thanks to you." The sergeant offered me his hand. He was about forty, with a compact build and piercing blue eyes, and he wore a black beret. "Never introduced. Sergeant Little."

I shook the man's hand. "Alex Verus. Glad I could help."

Sergeant Little nodded. "We lost two men today. Without you, it would have been five. I won't forget that, and my men won't either. You ever need help, you call us up."

I wasn't sure what to say. "Thanks."

Little nodded again, and gave a tip of the hat to Caldera. "Keeper."

"Caldera," a voice said from behind us. We turned to see Rain. "We're leaving in ten minutes. Get everyone ready."

"Got it," Caldera said, and left.

Rain gave me a slight smile. "Enjoying being hero of the hour?"

"Honestly, it just feels weird," I said. I still didn't understand why all of a sudden everyone was happy with me. "I didn't do that much."

"You guided us in, grabbed the relic single-handed, and

then went back to rescue a few men when you could have just led us out. Seems like plenty to me."

"I spent half that trip doing basic divination and the other half running away," I admitted. "Doesn't feel that impressive."

Rain shook his head. He doesn't smile much, but he was smiling now. "You want some kind of reward or something? I'm already going to be writing this up in my report, but if you're looking for something special . . ."

A reward from the Council? Now that was a weird thought. "I don't think—" I stopped as an idea occurred to me. "Actually, now you mention it, there is one thing . . ."

ıııııııı

We gated back into Keeper HQ to an enthusiastic reception. Medics and life mages came rushing out to lead the wounded away, on foot or on stretchers. Mostly, though, people were cheering us, or laughing and joking. There's a rush to surviving a combat operation, a kind of euphoria. The Council security squads had taken losses, yet all the same, I had the feeling that this had gone better than they'd expected.

Maradok was waiting for us at the centre of the room. His gaze rested on me for a moment with no visible surprise, and I wondered if Ares had already delivered his report. Then Maradok's eyes fastened on the box in Rain's hands. I walked up to Maradok, a step behind Rain.

"Councilman," Rain said.

"Captain Rain," Maradok said. "Congratulations on your—"

Maradok stopped as Rain turned and passed the box to me. I stepped forward and smiled at Maradok. "Hello, Councilman. I believe I made you a promise."

Maradok looked at me, his blue eyes expressionless.

I took another step forward. Maradok reached for the box but I held on to it. "And if you send any more assassins like Ares after me," I said in a low voice, "then I will mail them back to you one piece at a time."

Maradok's hand stayed on the box. So did mine. "I think

this matter should be considered closed," I said quietly. "Don't you?"

Maradok looked at me. I looked at him. I felt the futures shift, then settle. "Very well," Maradok said.

I let go of the box. Maradok started to turn away. "Oh," I said. "One more thing."

Maradok paused. "And that is?"

"I think you owe me an apology."

Maradok looked at me unemotionally for a few seconds. "Don't push your luck." He turned and walked away.

Rain and I watched him go. "Some history?" Rain asked.

"Actually it's pretty recent," I said. As I watched, Maradok disappeared through the door. I got one last look at the dull metal box before it vanished. I wondered exactly what was in it, and whether it really had been a bound jinn, and decided I didn't care. The Council would lock it up in a storage facility somewhere, and as far as I was concerned, it could stay there. It wasn't my problem anymore.

"Come on," Rain said, patting my arm. "Let's get you to debriefing."

"Joy," I said with a sigh. "Couldn't I deal with some more Dark mages instead?"

Rain snorted, and we turned away, moving to join Caldera and Landis. A few more hours, then I was going home.

chapter 13

Once we were done at Keeper HQ, I went back to Anne's. My burns weren't serious, but they did need attention—I asked Anne if she was still too badly hurt to do any healing, but she was insistent on helping. She was as good as her word, and by the time she was done, I was too tired to want to leave. Luna and Variam arrived shortly afterwards, and of course, all of them wanted to hear the story. It took a long time, especially with the interruptions.

"I can't believe you did that," Luna said once I was finally done. "I wish I'd been there."

"I don't," I said. "I want you alive and in one piece for your journeyman test."

"Is he okay?" Luna asked Anne.

"Hey," I said. "I'm right here."

"You'd just say you were fine."

"He *is* fine," Anne said with a smile. "All he needs is a little rest."

"So what about the arsehole that tried to burn your face off?" Variam said. "What are we going to do about him?"

"Nothing."

"He fried Anne and burned down your house and you're doing *nothing*?"

"Correct," I said. "Because right now, he's not a threat. He was acting on orders. Now that the Council have got their gizmo, Sal Sarque and Maradok haven't got a reason to try any more assassination attempts. Especially given how their last ones turned out."

Variam gave Anne a disbelieving look. "You're actually okay with this?"

"I'm more than okay with it," Anne said in her quiet voice. "I don't care if he burned me. I've had worse."

"But what if he comes after us again?" Luna said. "He already tried to kill you twice."

"With a reason, and with orders," I said. "Ares isn't Deleo. He's not going to try to kill me just for the hell of it. Anyway, what's the alternative? Go to war with Maradok's faction? We've got enough enemies already." I shook my head. "No. I can get a new home, and Anne can heal anything that can be healed. What I can't replace are the three of you. I'm not putting you at risk for some payback."

"I hate letting people like him get away with this shit," Variam said.

"At some point a conflict has to stop," I said. "This is an opportunity for this particular one to stop. I don't want to keep it going unless we have to."

Neither Luna nor Variam looked happy, but they didn't argue. "Okay, more cheerful stuff," I said. "How'd the training go?"

Luna and Variam looked at each other. "Good," Luna said after a slight pause.

"No problems?"

Luna shook her head. "Not really."

"So I guess tomorrow's your last training day before the test," I said. "You going to be practising all the way through?"

"No," Variam said. "Chalice said she'd train Luna up until early afternoon. After that she's supposed to go relax."

"She said I could go do what I want," Luna said. "That's not the same thing."

"She told you to go take a break."

Luna didn't answer. There was an awkward silence. I looked between Luna and Variam.

"Okay," Anne said when nobody spoke. "I need to go and get some food for dinner. Vari, could you come along?"

Vari looked up. "You've seen anyone watching?"

Anne shook her head. "No, but better safe than sorry."

Variam nodded. "I'm ready to go."

Variam waited by the door as Anne put on a cardigan and a coat. Anne was moving comfortably again, and the skin on her hands was smooth and unbroken—as far as I could tell, she was back to perfect health. It was hard to believe that only yesterday she'd been so hideously burnt. The door clicked shut behind the two of them and Luna and I were left alone.

"So did you ask her to get Vari out of the way, or what?" Luna asked.

"You really think Anne needed me to tell her?" I said. "Luna, there are a lot of things you're good at. Hiding your feelings is not one of them."

Luna didn't meet my eyes.

"Okay," I said. "It's been obvious for a while that something's on with you and Vari. I haven't been saying anything, but if there's a problem, it might be a good idea to talk about it."

"There isn't a problem."

I didn't say anything.

"Fine, I'm lying." Luna sighed. "Why does this stuff have to be so complicated?"

"What's wrong?"

"There's nothing wrong," Luna said. "It's like Vari said. Chalice told me to train tomorrow morning, then take the rest of the day off. She says I'll perform better if I relax for the last half day."

"Makes sense. So . . . ?"

"So tomorrow's Christmas Day."

"Okay."

"Vari invited me to his family's place."

"Okay . . ."

"His mother's going to be there. And his cousins."

"So what's the problem?"

Luna slumped back in her chair. "I don't *know*. Vari wanted to know if I could come and we had this stupid fight. He asked if I was busy with anything else and I had to say no, and then he asked why I didn't want to come and I couldn't come up with a reason."

"Hmm," I said. There had been something between Luna and Variam for a while. I'd never pressed her on it, but I'd been wondering if things were ever going to come to a head. "Sounds like there was a reason, just not one you wanted to tell him."

Luna didn't answer.

"You should probably at least be straight about it with yourself."

"It's going to sound stupid."

"Doesn't matter if you sound stupid, so long as you don't do something that *is* stupid."

"All right," Luna said. "It's like . . . Okay. Say I go along. Then what?"

"What do you mean?"

"As in, what's it going to turn into? He's going to be a Keeper some day. He probably could take the tests any time he wanted to. And there's no way in hell I'd ever fit in with his family. I don't fit in with his magical life *or* with his family life. It's just setting myself up for trouble. Isn't it?"

"Which bit are you worried about?" I said. "You think his family is going to have an issue with you not being Sikh?"

"Well, they will, won't they?"

"Don't really know," I said. "I've never met them. But I've seen what Vari's like. It's hard for me to believe he could be as close as he is to Anne and to you if he came from a family with really serious issues that way. Anyway, won't know unless you try."

"It's still horrible timing," Luna said. "That was one of

the reasons I was pissed off with him. We shouldn't be doing this stuff now. I mean, it already slowed us down, we could have been there to help you and Anne on Monday night if we hadn't . . ." She trailed off.

I waited for Luna to carry on but she didn't. I didn't ask exactly what she was referring to—it was their business, and besides, I had a pretty good idea. "Look, don't get me wrong. It really does mean a lot to me that you wanted to be there to help. But you aren't responsible for protecting me every minute of the day."

"But it's not even over! We still don't know if this thing with Levistus is going to work out. And I have to worry about my tests on Friday. This is like, the worst *possible* time to be getting distracted with this stuff."

"Maybe that's *why* he's doing it now."

"That doesn't make sense."

"Think of it this way. If this thing with Levistus and your tests doesn't work out, one or all of us could be dead by next week. In which case this is all the time you're going to get."

"Great," Luna said, rolling her eyes. "I feel so much better."

"We aren't exactly living normal lives," I said. "Regular people get to say things like, 'Oh, I'll finish university and then get a job and then in a few years I'll start thinking about stuff like that.' They don't have to worry about getting assassinated in their sleep. But for us . . . let's just say that I doubt anyone who knows my history is going to be selling me life insurance. And you don't exactly go out of your way to be safe."

Luna shrugged. "I'd rather run the risks."

"So why don't you want to run this one?"

Luna was silent. "I don't know," she said at last.

I looked at Luna. "Do you want my advice?"

"I guess."

"You said you're worried about getting distracted," I said. "Seems to me as though you're *already* distracted. Yes, if you go meet Vari's family and things go badly, then it'll throw you off your game. But going into your journeyman tests with it hanging over your head is probably going to be just as bad. I don't know exactly what the state of play is between you and Vari, but I do know you. You always feel better when you face something head-on than when you put it off."

"Mm."

"One other thing," I said. "These things have their own momentum. If you put them on pause for long enough, it can be hard to get them back. You might be willing to put things off for weeks or months or years, but I don't think Vari would be. He's kind of the type who likes straight answers. And he's got his pride. I don't think he'll put up with being left hanging for ever."

"He's a pain in the arse," Luna muttered.

"He can be," I said with a grin, then looked at Luna seriously. "But you could do a lot worse. And you have, in the past."

"Don't remind me." Luna buried her head in her arms. "Ugh. Why is this stuff so difficult? It was so much easier when all I had to worry about was getting to classes on time."

"You might have to get used to that," I said with a smile. "Once you pass those tests, you'll be a full mage. You won't have me telling you what to do anymore. All the decisions are going to be up to you."

"I'm not sure I *want* to make all the decisions."

"Can't stay an apprentice for ever," I said. "You're going to be a pretty powerful mage someday. When that happens, people are going to be looking to you to lead them."

Luna made a face, and I had to laugh. "Okay," I said. "For now? Just talk to Vari. Let him know what you're worried about, and listen to what he has to say. Then see how things go from there."

"Yeah, okay." Luna paused. "Thanks."

* * *

Anne and Variam came back shortly afterwards, carrying shopping bags. Anne made a late dinner, and we relaxed as we ate. By the time we were done it was midnight and everyone was yawning. Luna and Vari left; I was about to head back to Wales, but somehow or other Anne persuaded me to stay over. I used a sleeping bag and was out like a light within minutes of lying down.

: : : : : : : : :

C hristmas Day dawned bright and clear. Two days left.
Noon found me in Islington outside the gym, where I'd found a place with a view of the front and side entrances. I watched the cars go by, soaked up what I could of the weak sunlight, and walked up and down periodically to try to stop myself from freezing. Eventually I saw Luna appear from the side doors. Variam was with her, and the two of them were talking to each other as they came out onto the street and turned towards the station. Maybe it was my imagination, but Luna's body language looked a little more relaxed than yesterday. I watched them go, smiled slightly, then headed into the gym.

Chalice was on the upper floor, packing away her gear. "Oh, hello, Verus," she said. "I was wondering if you'd show up."

"I did promise. Want some lunch?"

"That'd be lovely."

: : : : : : : : :

W e walked to the same café where Luna and I had spoken to Chalice on Sunday and ordered. Chalice had the sports bag that she'd used to pack away her training gear under the table, and I couldn't help but wonder what the other customers would think about the contents. Knowing Chalice, she could probably arrange it so that no one would happen to look.

"Well, the test's tomorrow," I said once the waiter had gone. "Are you going to go see the results of your handiwork?"

"Tempting, but I'll pass," Chalice said. "I don't think it would do Luna any favours to have a Dark mage as her guest."

"Same could be said for me," I said dryly. "But I think that ship's sailed. Thank you for doing this on such short notice, by the way."

"These inconveniences happen," Chalice said. "Besides, I've become fond of the girl. I'd like to see her succeed."

I glanced at Chalice.

Chalice gave me an amused look. "Dark mages do have feelings, you know."

"Well," I said, "you've held up your part of the deal. Ready to hear what I've learned?"

"That would be nice."

I told Chalice the story. I left out some of the more personal details—I didn't really see the need to give Chalice a rundown on exactly which groups were trying to kill me, and why—but I did tell her what I knew and suspected about that relic. It took a while.

"Do you have any definite proof that the item inside that box held a bound jinn?" Chalice asked when I was done. "Or any other kind of magical creature?"

"No," I said. "It's speculation only. Though it does fit with what else we've learned."

"What about the motive?"

"That's the weak link," I said. "I know you asked about that specifically. Unfortunately, that's exactly what *we* want to know, too, and without that, it's pretty hard to make sense of what he's after."

Chalice stared down at the table, obviously thinking. The waiter had brought our order while I'd been talking, but the cup of tea in front of Chalice was untouched. "Do you think Richard was hoping to make use of that thing?" I asked.

"Yes," Chalice said. "Morden wouldn't have been there if it wasn't critical in some way. The question is how."

"One of the questions. Okay, Chalice, cards on the table. You probably now know as much about that operation as anyone on the Council. I think it's time you told me why you're so interested."

"Fair enough," Chalice said. "How familiar are you with the Dark factions?"

"Calling them factions is a bit of an overstatement," I said. "If you mean the beliefs they subscribe to, then yes, I know the basics."

"Which one was your old master a member of?"

"None, really. Or all of them, depending on how you saw

it. He believed in what you'd call the pure Dark credo. Power over all, no matter where it came from. But he didn't follow anyone else."

Chalice nodded. "There have always been some Dark mages who favour the idea of joining with the Council. You could call them the Dark equivalent of your Unity Bloc. In this country, Morden is their most well-known face, but it's not an idea limited to Britain. There are similar movements in many places."

"They're not 'my' Unity Bloc," I said. "But yes, I'm familiar with some of the groups. Do you lean that way?"

Chalice raised an eyebrow. "You think that because I'm a Dark mage and not a crazed psychopath, that means I must be one of the 'civilised' ones? Wanting to join with the Light mages?"

"Just asking."

"In my experience, most British mages don't really appreciate how much freedom they have," Chalice said. "You live under a set of laws in which Light, Dark, and independent mages are—in theory, at least—equal. Yes, I know that they're very much imperfect, and unevenly enforced. But that doesn't change the fact that you have far more independence here than would be possible in most other countries. Take that shop of yours. One mage, unaffiliated with any major faction, running a business where magical items sit openly on the shelves. That would be an impossibility in India. Without the support of one of the major parties, you wouldn't last a year."

"Ended up being pretty dangerous here too," I said. "Okay, I get your point. How do you fit in to that?"

"The reason for the relative freedom you mages have here is because of the balance of power," Chalice said. "The Council can't fully enforce their laws against the Dark mages because they don't want to risk starting a war. The Dark mages can't openly attack the Council because they know that if they push the Light mages too far, they risk retaliation. What Morden is doing will change all that. He's trying to bring the Dark mages—or a majority of them at least—into the Council under his command. If he succeeds, he'll turn this country into a one-party state. There'll be no room for independent Dark mages. Or independent mages at all, for that matter. With the Council and the most active Dark mages forming one power bloc, everyone else will be forced to fall in line."

"And you want to avoid that?"

"I rather like the way things are in Britain now," Chalice said. "For the most part, Dark mages like me are left in peace. Morden and Drakh have gathered a group who think that by joining the Council, they'll come to rule the country. What those mages don't seem to understand is that what will *actually* happen is that they'll end up ruled by Drakh. I've had to leave one country. I don't want to have to do the same thing again."

"Huh," I said, leaning back in my chair. I'd ordered tea as well, but like Chalice's, it was sitting untouched in front of me. What Chalice was saying sounded a little odd, but it had the ring of truth to it. The more anti-Dark factions within the Council had been making a lot of noise about the Council being "invaded" by Dark mages. For the most part the debate had been dominated by them and by the Unity Bloc, one side wanting to keep the Dark mages out, the other trying to welcome them in. Neither of them had spent much time considering whether the Dark mages *wanted* to come in. Sure, there are some Dark mages like Morden, who get involved with Council politics and build their empires. But most don't. They don't want any masters, be they Light or Dark.

"So," Chalice said. "Now you know where I stand. Do you wish to maintain our alliance?"

I looked at Chalice thoughtfully. "You want to stop Morden and Richard."

"Say rather that I want to limit them." Chalice looked back at me with her dark eyes. "I don't expect you to share my beliefs. But as I understand it, you have your own disagreements with Morden and with Richard Drakh. They're somewhat more personal than mine, but as I see it, our goals are essentially the same."

I thought about it for a moment. "I suppose they are," I

said after a pause. I might not have the same mind-set as Chalice, but nothing she'd said really put her in opposition to what I wanted, or the people I cared about. And given my position, I needed all the allies I could get. "It's a deal." I held out my hand.

Chalice smiled and reached across the table, her smaller hand disappearing into mine.

⸱⸱⸱⸱⸱⸱⸱⸱⸱

" So with any luck, that should be that," Landis said. ... I was back in Anne's flat, on the phone to Landis. Anne was sitting quietly in the armchair, working away on something in a notebook, while I wandered up and down the living room. Outside, the winter day was grey and cold.

"Have you heard anything about Maradok and Ares?" I asked.

"Ah, yes! I think I've got some good news for you on that front. Did a touch of digging around and the word on the heights is that the contract on you is off. The Crusaders aren't hiring anyone new, and the one member I managed to talk to implied that things are on hold. Looks like you're off their priority list."

"Should bloody well hope so, after what I did for them."

"Yes, well, you know what they say about the gratitude of kings. Could be worse. They don't seem to want you dead badly enough to do it themselves any more."

"It's sad that that's actually an improvement. Have you heard anything about the sponsorship change for Anne and Vari?"

Anne stopped what she was doing and looked up. "No," Landis said. "It's supposed to be going through tomorrow morning."

That would put it around the time of Luna's test. Something about Landis's tone of voice suggested that there was more to the story, though. "But?"

"But I have to confess to feeling a mite uneasy. Fingers to the wind and all that. Tell that charming friend of yours to watch herself, will you? Would hate for something to happen to her right before the sponsorship goes through."

"I'll tell her. Having a good Christmas?"

"Just off to a family event as a matter of fact. Season's greetings and all that. I'll be in touch."

"Talk to you then."

I hung up. "Tell me what?" Anne asked.

"Landis is jumpy," I said. "He seems to think you and Vari might be in danger."

"Why?"

I shrugged. "Not a clue. But Landis isn't the sort to jump at shadows." I looked at Anne. "Your wards up to date?"

"I've still got those ones that you helped with," Anne said. "It should be okay. Though . . . I suppose they could just do what they did to your shop."

I nodded. "I'll stay over tonight. I should be able to see a night raid coming if I look for it. Anyway, we just need to hold out a couple more days. What are you smiling for?"

"Nothing. Oh!" Anne jumped up. "That reminds me. Stay here for a second."

I watched curiously as Anne disappeared out of the door and came back a second later holding something long and black. "Here." She handed it to me. "Happy Christmas."

I took the thing, caught by surprise. It was a long coat with a leather collar, made of some black, slightly rough material with a softer lining. "Is that for me?"

"You were complaining about being cold since all of your warm coats got burnt up in the fire," Anne said. She watched as I tried it on. "Does it fit?"

I stretched my arms through the sleeves. "Pretty much perfectly. How did you match the size?"

Anne shrugged. "Do you like it?"

I smiled at Anne. "Very much. Thank you."

I saw Anne relax. All of a sudden, she looked happy.

॥ ॥ ॥ ॥ ॥

We ended up spending the day together. I checked in with Luna and Variam; the responses were brief but I got the impression things were going well. I called Caldera to learn that she was being forced to stay in the office and work on Christmas Day, cleaning up the aftereffects of yesterday's operation, a duty that she complained about at length. Sonder, like Landis, was off on holiday celebrations, as presumably were most of the mages of Britain. Mages are pretty divorced from mundane society but they do still have families, and even they usually take Christmas off. Tomorrow everyone would be back to work, but for now everything was quiet.

"So you never do anything for Christmas at all?" Anne asked.

"Well, it's not like I do nothing," I said. Outside, the sun was setting; we were in the living room, listening to the quiet sounds of Honor Oak. Anne still had that little notebook in her lap, and she was doing something with it, either writing or drawing. My guess was drawing, but in each future where I moved to get a closer look, she hid it too quickly for me to see. I was curious but didn't press her. "The last couple of years, I've spent it with Luna."

"But you don't see your family or anything like that?"

"Only family I've got in the U.K. is my father. And going to his house for Christmas . . . God. That would set a world record for most uncomfortable dinner conversation ever."

"Why?"

I sighed. "Let's just say that he and I have some major philosophical differences. I find my life's a lot less stressful when we stay as far apart as possible."

"So you don't have any family you see at all?"

"Not by choice."

"That sounds lonely."

"I'm used to it." I looked at Anne. "What about you?"

Anne twisted her mouth. "I suppose I'm not one to talk."

"You have a foster family, don't you?"

"I usually go each Christmas," Anne said. "I don't think any of us enjoy it very much. To be honest, I always used to dread it. It was a relief to be able to tell them this year that I wasn't going to be able to make it."

"Why is it so awkward?"

"Old memories," Anne said. "I remember how things used to be. So do they."

Anne looked down at the carpet. All of a sudden things felt awkward. I cast around for some way to change the subject. "How are things going with that air apprentice?"

Anne looked up in surprise. "Who?"

"Wasn't there some guy who'd asked you out? Carl something?"

"Luna told you, didn't she?"

"It's not like she's trying to pry," I said. "I think she was just happy for you."

"Well, she shouldn't have been."

"Why?"

"Because the same thing happened that always happens. We went out once, he said he'd call back and didn't."

"That's weird."

"No, it's not," Anne said. "The first time he didn't know who I was. He'd just arrived from Germany, he didn't know all the gossip the way the apprentices from here do. Afterwards, he found out."

"Oh." I paused. "Do you mind if I ask you something personal?"

"No, go ahead."

I chose my words carefully, trying to work out how to say this without giving offence. "So I've known you about three years. For most of that time, you've been single, right? There was that guy a couple of years ago, but since then, from what Luna's told me, there hasn't been anything that's lasted."

Anne nodded.

"So . . . why is that? Given what you've got going for you." I didn't come right out and say what I was implying. Anne is beautiful, kind, and nice to pretty much everyone. I'm not that knowledgeable when it comes to the dating world, but I was pretty sure that she ought to have guys hanging off her. "Are you just not interested?"

"It's not that." Anne sighed. "Do you really want to hear about my not-very-important problems?"

I shrugged. "We've got the time."

"It's not that I'm not interested. It just never turns into anything."

I tilted my head.

"I mean, there are the usual things," Anne said. "Guys who just want to sleep with me, and they lose interest when they find out that that's not going to happen quickly enough. But all girls have to deal with that. It's what I am that's the problem."

"You mean being a life mage?" I said curiously. "I don't understand why anyone wouldn't appreciate that. You've saved my life more than once."

"It's not that simple. Forget about magic for a second. Imagine you're holding a woman who's smaller and lighter than you are. If it came down to a fight, who's going to win?"

I shrugged. "Probably me."

"With me it's the other way around. If I can touch someone, it doesn't matter who they are or what they can do. I can do whatever I like to them."

"Sure. You can knock them out or paralyse them or just puppet their nervous system. But you don't."

"It doesn't matter," Anne said. "Men are used to being in control. Especially mages. When they're with me, then all of a sudden they're not. It scares them. They'll say they aren't, but you can see it."

"It's not that hard to find guys who don't want to be in control."

"I know." Anne sighed again. "This is why I don't like complaining about this stuff. It makes me sound incredibly picky. For a while, when I was with guys, I'd try not to overshadow them. Hold myself back, that sort of thing. But it didn't work. It made me feel like I was making myself smaller. So then I tried going out with guys who didn't mind being overshadowed, you know, the ones who'll tell you how much they like strong women. And *that* didn't work either. For one thing I just couldn't take them seriously, and for another . . . I think I've spent too long in danger. What happened back in our school, then Sagash, then Jagadev. I'd be out with those guys, and I'd look across the table at them, and I couldn't help thinking: if something like that happens again—*when* something like that happens again—is this guy going to protect me? And the only answer I could come up with was no."

I managed not to raise my eyebrows. *Anne* wanted someone to protect *her*? "Seems more likely you'd be doing the protecting."

"I don't *want* to do the protecting." The sudden heat in Anne's voice made me draw back. "I already have to take care of everyone else."

I looked at Anne, startled. For a moment I wondered where that had come from, then an uncomfortable thought occurred. "I know we rely on you a lot for healing—"

"Not that. I *like* helping you and Vari and Luna. Because I know I can count on you too. But when I'm with most people . . . It's like being the only grown-up in a crowd of children. I'm the powerful one, so I'm responsible for everyone else."

"I know a lot of girls who'd give a lot to be as powerful as you."

"That's because they've never lived with it," Anne said. "I know the ones you're talking about. Those apprentices all say how awesome it would be to be as strong as me, and they're all so bright-eyed. They think it's like . . . like some pretty necklace. Something they can put on, and everyone will cheer them and clap for them, until they take it off. They don't understand that you *can't* take it off. Once people know what you are, what you can do, then when they look at you, that's what they see. They don't see you as a girl. They don't even really see you as a person." Anne paused. "Luna understands. I think that's why we're friends."

I grimaced. That sounded familiar. "I guess I do know what you mean." Diviners aren't popular either, for reasons that aren't really all that different when you come down to it. Maybe that's why Anne, Luna, and I get on—we know what it's like to be set apart. Still, though . . . "Anne, I know you don't want to hear this, but I'm not sure there *is* anyone out there who's capable of taking care of you. Not in the way you mean, anyway. You are way into the ninety-ninth percentile of personal power. For someone to be a threat to you, they'd have to be a threat to just about everyone else."

"I know," Anne said. "But you see where that leaves me?

Even if I *did* find someone, it'd just be a matter of time until one of my enemies showed up. And then he'd be dead, or worse. And it'd be my fault." Anne looked away, making a face. "And that's why I'm single, I suppose."

I looked at Anne thoughtfully.

"I did tell you that they weren't very important," Anne said. "Not by the standards of all our other stuff."

"Eh," I said. "Dealing with the other stuff just keeps us from dying. Still have to figure out how to live afterwards."

Anne looked out the window. Night had fallen, and the lights of London sparkled in the darkness. "I wonder how Luna and Vari are doing."

I laughed. "I'm not going to call them and ask how things are going."

Anne smiled slightly. "So has it been a good Christmas?"

I thought about it for a second. "You know, it's weird to say it after everything that's gone wrong this week, but . . . yeah, it has. I just hope the worst is over."

"I guess we'll find out tomorrow."

chapter 14

One day left.

When things go wrong—really, badly wrong—you're never really ready for it. The funny thing is that preparing doesn't seem to help that much. Working out contingency plans might help you survive the physical aspect, but it doesn't make the mental part hit any less hard. I think it's the seductiveness of routine. It's so easy to believe that today's going to be the same as yesterday, and most of the time it *is* the same as yesterday, and so it just goes on, one day after another, blending into a comforting sameness. Until it stops.

I paused out on the plaza outside One Canada Square, and looked up at the towering shape of Canary Wharf. From this angle, it seemed to go up forever. I couldn't make out the pyramid at the top, nor the slim, almost-invisible walkways. Even though it was morning on Boxing Day, the place was still busy, bankers and lawyers and businessmen walking across the plaza and into the skyscrapers. The sun was shining but thick clouds were moving across the sky and it looked as though it would be overcast soon.

The phone I was holding had been trilling quietly as it

rang another number; now there was a click as the person on the other end picked up. "Hello?" a voice said.

"Hey, Lyle," I said. "You said to call?"

"Oh, Alex!" Lyle sounded cheerful. "I've been talking with Undaaris. He just left the building a couple of minutes ago."

"Is he happy?"

"Very happy. Michael from the Keeper office was just in to thank us for the help. I haven't seen Undaaris in such a good mood for a month."

"I'm hoping that translates into a favourable vote. Because I'm kind of running out of time here."

"Don't worry, that was exactly where he went. He's off to the War Rooms right now. It'll be done within a couple of hours."

I let myself relax slightly. Not all the way—it wasn't a done deal yet—but it was the best news I'd had in a while. A familiar face caught my eye from across the plaza: Sonder. I waved to him and he waved back, changing course to head towards me. "Well, that's a relief."

"Congratulations on your good work, by the way. This wouldn't have been possible without you."

"Thanks."

"I'd better go. Doing anything special for Christmas?"

"Yeah, I'm watching some journeyman tests. Call me back when you know anything?"

"Of course. Speak to you soon. And good job."

I hung up and nodded to Sonder. He was wearing a long overcoat, but I could see the bottom of a set of mage robes peeking out from underneath. "Hey."

"Hey, Alex." Sonder looked around. "Where's Anne?"

"We asked if she could come," I said as we started walking for the doors. "They said no."

"Really?"

"She's not a Light mage and she's not Luna's master."

Sonder frowned. "That still doesn't seem fair. Maybe if we talked to them . . ."

"Now's probably not the best time to be ruffling any

feathers. Don't worry—if Luna passes, the first thing she's going to do is head for Anne's flat and tell her the whole story. You should come along."

We passed through ground floor security and were directed to the far lifts. Canary Wharf is supposed to be an office block, and for the most part it is. But the top floors are owned by the Council, and they look considerably different from the pictures you'd see if you looked them up on the internet. We got into the far lift and pressed the button for the forty-third floor.

"Whew, warm," Sonder said, taking off his coat. The mage robes he was wearing underneath were blue and white, and very well tailored. "Nice coat, by the way."

"Thanks."

Sonder glanced down at my black jeans and top. "You're not wearing robes?"

"Burnt." Once all this was over, I'd have to get some new ones from Arachne. "I'm not planning to be the centre of attention anyway."

The lift let us out into a corridor where a couple of security men were waiting. The check was thorough, but I was treated more courteously than usual. One of the security men even asked how I was. I couldn't figure it out until I realised that it must be because of the Syria operation. Apparently the Council security had their own grapevine. Once we were done we were escorted down the corridors and into a small anteroom.

Luna was waiting inside, and as she saw me her face lit up. "You came!"

"Of course I came." I looked Luna up and down. "Was that really your choice of clothing?"

Luna rolled her eyes. She was wearing a white robe, belted at the waist. It didn't look bad on her but it wasn't exactly her usual style. "They wouldn't let me wear anything else."

"It's kind of traditional," Sonder said.

"Still looks dorky." Luna looked between us. "No Anne?"

"Same story as your clothes," I said. "What about Vari?"

"He's at the offices for the apprentice program," Luna said. "I told him he ought to sort things out there first." Luna looked disappointed. "He said he'd come straight here afterwards. I thought he'd be done by now."

"He's not going to have much time to make it," I said. The test was due to start in less than twenty minutes. I thought briefly about asking Luna how things had gone yesterday afternoon, then realised I didn't need to. She looked relaxed and alert, ready to go. Challenges tend to bring out the best in Luna.

Luna paced up and down the room, clearly full of energy. "Got your whip?" I asked.

"Not using it."

"Wait, what?" Now I was worried. That focus wand was made for Luna by Arachne, and it extends Luna's range and control significantly. I'd never seen Luna go into a duel without it. "Why?"

"Not allowed."

"You aren't allowed magic items for the journeyman tests," Sonder said. "Otherwise anyone could pass just by gearing up enough."

"Yeah, but . . ."

"It's okay," Luna said. She didn't look worried. "I've known the rules for months."

"You didn't tell me."

"You didn't ask. Don't worry, I've been practising. My curse still has reach without it, the focus just helps. You were the one who told me that, remember?"

"I did?"

"Sure."

I checked the time. Fifteen minutes. "You know, you might not necessarily have to do this anymore."

"Do what?"

"Your journeyman test. I mean, it isn't confirmed yet, but it's looking as though the resolution's not going to be . . ."

"You're really nervous about me doing this, aren't you?"

"No," I said.

Luna grinned.

"Fine. Maybe a little." Journeyman tests aren't deadly—they're run by Light mages, not Dark ones—and the penalties for failure are pretty minor. But still, accidents happen. "I'm just saying you don't have to if you don't want to."

Luna was still grinning at me. "You're so cute when you're like that."

"I am *not* cute."

"Yes, you are. You've got that whole mother-hen thing."

I decided there was no dignified way to answer that one and looked to see that Sonder was trying to hide a smile. "What's so funny?"

Sonder composed himself. "Nothing."

A man opened the door and looked in. "Apprentice Mancuso?"

Luna nodded. "It's time," the man said.

"Okay." Luna got to her feet. "Let's do this."

"Good luck," I said.

"Eh," Luna said. "I'll be fine."

It would have sounded convincing to most people, but I've known Luna a long time and I knew that she was more nervous than she looked. Made two of us, I suppose. "See you soon," Sonder said.

Luna turned and walked out. I had a last glimpse of her curse layered in around her, tightly packed and controlled, before the man closed the door behind her. I found myself staring after her.

"Come on," Sonder said when I didn't move. "We should go up to the viewing gallery."

I tore myself away with difficulty. "Yeah."

⁞⁞⁞⁞⁞⁞⁞⁞⁞

The top floor of the Canary Wharf complex is a ballroom, with a wide-open floor surrounded by balconies and overlooking windows. The room Sonder led me to was long and narrow, with one wall looking down onto the ballroom floor, which didn't look very much like a ballroom at the moment.

Some sort of maze had been set up in the centre, and a pair of what looked like duelling arenas were spaced out to the side. The window giving us a view of the ballroom looked transparent, but I'd been down on that floor before and I knew that it was one-way glass. No one out there would be able to see us.

"I wasn't expecting it to be this crowded," I said under my breath. There were maybe twenty-five people in the gallery, standing and sitting in small groups, talking quietly. Like Sonder, most were wearing mage robes. I recognised a couple of girls that I thought were Luna's classmates, as well as two of her teachers, but there were at least ten people that I was pretty sure I'd never seen before.

"It usually is," Sonder said quietly. We walked towards the windows at the far end where it was quieter. One of Luna's teachers, a tall mage named Saris who I knew was her duelling instructor, gave us a nod as we passed.

"It shouldn't take this many to run a test."

"Actually, the staff are down there," Sonder said, pointing down to the floor. A couple of men were visible below, standing by one of the maze walls. "So they can jump in if anything goes wrong."

"So who are these guys?"

"Just other mages."

"What is this, a spectator sport?"

"They're just here to see what's going on."

I gave Sonder a look. "On Boxing Day morning?"

"There are always people to watch tests," Sonder said. "Especially if it's someone who's been getting a lot of interest. Some of them are probably scouting."

"For what?"

"You know, positions. Like, if a new battle-mage is testing, then you'll get some Keepers watching, a mind or charm mage might bring a Council politician, that sort of thing. If you put on a good show, then you might get approached afterwards. So even if you know you're going to pass, you still have to try."

"Mm," I said. It must be nice to be connected enough that passing the test was only a formality. "Are they going to bring her out?"

Sonder looked at me in surprise. "Not *now*. Don't you know how the tests work?"

"I didn't exactly go up through the Light ranks, remember?"

"Oh, right. Well, the test's already started, just not the public part. She's probably doing the sensing trials."

"Sensing trials?"

"You're supposed to be tested on each part of the curriculum," Sonder said. "So the basic one is magesight. Identifying magic types and items and stuff like that. It's usually pretty easy. Kind of like the warm-up."

"Oh," I said. Suddenly I felt nervous. Luna is very good at what she does, but she's not a mage in the traditional sense and she doesn't have standard magesight. I'd been aware of that from the start, and so over the years in which she'd been my apprentice, I'd gone out of my way to give her a lot of practice. Luna still can't see magic the way I can, but she'd developed workarounds, and she'd become pretty good with them. Still, sensitivity is not one of her talents. What if they gave her some test that only a full chance mage would be able to pass?

Fifteen minutes passed, then half an hour. A few more people had arrived in the viewing gallery, but they were starting to look restless, and I could see a couple of them checking the time. "Is it supposed to take this long?" I said quietly to Sonder.

"Um, it depends."

"Depends on what?"

"There's usually an oral test after the sensing."

"Does it take this long?"

"It could."

I looked at Sonder. "How long did it take you?"

Sonder looked uncomfortable. "About fifteen minutes."

Forty minutes passed. The crowd were definitely getting impatient. I started fidgeting, then stopped as I realised how I must look. I took out my phone and tried calling Variam, hoping to distract myself. It went to voice mail. I tried again with the same result. I wondered where he was.

"Alex," Sonder said. "Look!"

I put my phone away and turned back to the window. All of a sudden, there was activity down on the ballroom floor, with a couple of men wheeling out some sort of metal cabinet. "What's going on?" I asked quietly.

"They're getting ready for the next trial," Sonder said. "She must have cleared the last one."

Which meant she'd passed. There's no waiting to get your results in journeyman tests; either you make it or you don't. "Any idea what it's going to be?"

Down on the floor, the men wheeled the cabinet up to the maze and then started taking it off the trolley to lower it to the floor. It was a good seven or eight feet tall. "Well, the only absolute rule is that they can't ask you to do anything outside your magic type," Sonder said. "So if you're a fire mage they can't ask you to heal, if you're a life mage they can't ask you to scry . . ."

"So anything that's dependent on chance." *Doesn't narrow the field much.*

"Yes, but usually it's negotiated. The examiners will come up with a list of possible tests, and then the master checks them. Then he'll veto some of them and make his own suggestions and the examiners will decide whether they're too easy. That's why it takes so long."

I looked curiously at Sonder. "Doesn't that mean that by the time the apprentice goes into their test, they'll know exactly what they're getting?"

"Well, they don't know all the details . . ."

"Huh." *I guess that explains how Light apprentices can be so confident of passing.*

"That's probably why there are so many people here," Sonder said. "Pretty much no one does an unrestricted test. It's just . . ." Sonder stopped.

"Stupid?" I said with amusement.

"Well, it doesn't make much sense, does it? You need to be able to veto things you can't handle."

"Planning isn't really Luna's thing," I said. "But she's great at adapting on the fly."

"It's still going to be—what *is* that?"

The men down on the floor had opened the cabinet. Inside was a humanoid figure made of some kind of grey-brown material, either metal or stone. It stood about half a head taller than the men on either side of it, with thick limbs and a barrel chest. The hands were disproportionately big and looked as though they were made for punching or crushing rather than any kind of manipulation. It stood still and inert as the men worked on it.

I glanced down at the thing. "What's wrong?"

Sonder was staring. "That's a combat golem."

"Doubt it's a golem." I gave the construct a critical eye. "Looks more like a standard construct to me. As long as you had a high enough energy reserve, you wouldn't need an elemental."

"You know what I mean! They're doing a combat trial."

"So?"

"But everyone vetoes those!"

I shrugged. "Like you said, we don't get any vetoes."

The people in the gallery looked interested now, and I could see several men and women stepping close to the window to get a better view. The two girls from Luna's class were wide-eyed, and one of them had her hand to her mouth. "This is crazy," Sonder said. "No one does combat trials. Well, unless you're looking to show off, or . . ."

I looked to one side. "There she is."

Luna had appeared through one of the side doors, still wearing her white apprentice robe. A man escorted her to the far side of the maze, where the high walls hid her from view. After a moment's pause, the man reappeared around the side of the maze and signalled to the two men by the construct. One of them nodded back, then reached up and did something to the back of the construct's neck.

The construct straightened and began moving. It walked to the maze entrance, its movements slow and deliberate. We were too far up to feel anything, but I could imagine it sending a tremor through the floor with each step. It paused at the entrance to the maze, the man around the other side disappeared to head back to where Luna was, then the construct marched into the maze and out of view.

"This is so nuts," Sonder said.

"Oh," I said. "I get it. It's not necessarily a combat trial."

"What do you mean?"

"Look." I pointed. "Only two exits. The one on this side, and there must be one on the other side where Luna went in. The goal must be for Luna to make her way through. She doesn't need to destroy the construct; she just has to get around it and out the other side. Luck and chance."

"It's still really dangerous," Sonder said. "No one can see her."

Sonder was right about that; the walls of the maze were blocking our view, save for the odd flash of movement. I caught a glimpse of the construct turning a corner, and then the walls hid it again. A moment later, at the other end, Luna was briefly visible as she walked down one of the corridors, heading for the side of the maze where the construct was waiting.

Sonder glanced at me. "I thought you were worried."

"Not about this."

"This is *really* harsh for an apprentice test. You could ask them . . ."

"Look at how that construct was designed," I said. "No ranged weapons, no edged weapons. I don't think it's meant to actually injure her."

"It wouldn't need any."

"Luna's used to dealing with a lot worse than this," I said. I smiled. The unknown's always scariest. Now that I knew what the test was, all of a sudden I wasn't so worried. "Have some faith in her."

Sonder fell silent. I couldn't see anything from the maze. The window was soundproofed so we couldn't hear anything from the ballroom outside; the only noise was the murmur of conversation from the other spectators. They sounded excited. I wondered if some of them were here in the hope that something would go wrong, in the same way that people watch motor sports secretly hoping for a crash. Sure, no one's supposed to be killed, but there's always the odd accident . . .

There was a flash of movement from within the maze, there and gone, and I caught a glimpse of Luna's white robes as she darted around a corner. One of the walls of the maze quivered. There was a pause, the wall quivered again, then one of the adjacent walls buckled and collapsed. I could see the people down on the floor looking towards the maze exit.

"What's going *on* in there?" Sonder said.

"Beats me."

"Do you think we should stop the test?"

"No, I think she'll be fine."

"How are you so sure?"

The side wall of the maze closest to us exploded outwards, shards scattering and sliding across the floor as the construct burst through. It stumbled out into the open, flailing at the empty air. I could see the men down on the floor shouting—one was running towards it, another backing away—but before they could do anything the construct slowed and seized up, its limbs stiffening. It toppled to the floor with a boom that was so loud I heard it through the glass.

"Just a feeling," I said.

Luna came walking out of the hole in the wall, still empty-handed. She glanced down at the disabled construct and then turned to the man approaching her. I couldn't make out her words but I got the general message. *So what's next?*

Excited chatter broke out from the people to our left. Apparently they were feeling they were getting their money's worth. "Is she okay?" Sonder asked.

"Looks fine to me," I said. Luna's curse is pretty good at messing up existing spells. She'd probably just poured it into that construct until it malfunctioned. A couple more men had approached Luna and were saying something to her. Luna responded, and I laughed.

"What?" Sonder said.

I pointed. "They're telling her, 'You were supposed to come out the exit, not smash a hole through the wall.' And she's telling them, 'You didn't put that in the rules.'" I grinned. "Watching her do this stuff is a lot more fun when someone else has to deal with it."

"She's lucky that worked."

The argument down on the floor went on for a few minutes before trailing off. A cleanup crew arrived and spent some time figuring out how to get the disabled construct back in its box: apparently Luna had managed to sabotage it quite thoroughly, because after several failed attempts they just hoisted it onto a platform and wheeled it off. Meanwhile, Luna had been led to one of the arenas I'd noticed before.

"Wait," Sonder said. "Isn't that Celia?"

I followed Sonder's gaze. "Huh," I said. "I think you're right." Crossing the floor, escorted by another mage, was a slightly built girl with short blonde hair. Celia was a water mage apprentice, quiet and shy; I'd spoken to her a few times, usually while waiting for Luna to finish a class. I didn't really know her very well, but I knew that Luna liked her. *What's she doing here?*

"Those are ceremonial robes," Sonder said. He was frowning. "They must want her for the ceremony? But they shouldn't need a witness . . ."

Two of the men down on the floor were talking to Luna. Luna started to answer them, then she saw Celia and she looked back and forth between Celia and the men. She looked confused, and I knew she had to be wondering the same thing as me.

One of the men walked out into the arena. The arena was a circular model, rather than a piste, with no markings apart from the starting lines. Circular arenas are used in some of the more free-for-all types of duels, where the idea is to drive your opponent out of the ring; they're generally less popular among Light mages, who prefer the more structured azimuth contests. The man set an item down at the centre of the arena, then backed off. The object was shaped like a hemisphere and was dark grey in colour. Once he was outside the arena ring, he turned and cast a spell.

The item at the centre of the ring lit up. Strands of light grew out of the hemisphere, each only a few inches thick, glowing blue-white-green. They floated through the air as though it were water, curving and twisting. Where they reached the arena boundary they flattened, trailing along the edge as though it were an invisible wall. When I was much younger, I used to go to the aquarium at the zoo; one of the exhibits was sea anemones, and that was what this reminded me of now.

I heard chatter from the other people in the gallery; this was obviously what they had come to see. "You have any idea what this is?" I asked Sonder quietly.

Sonder nodded. "Anemone focus. You have to touch the focus to shut it down."

I looked at the twisting tendrils. There were only half a dozen of them, and they weren't moving fast, but the closer you got to the focus, the denser they became. I could probably make it in there without being grazed by a tendril, but it wouldn't be easy. "What do those tendrils do?"

"I think it depends on the model. You don't want to get touched by one, though."

I could feel the magic radiating from the tendrils: life, mixed with something else. The amount of power in each was low, but life magic doesn't need a lot of power to be dangerous. One of the men was talking to Luna, presumably giving her instructions. Luna was alternating between listening to him and glancing at the anemone. The basics of the test seemed simple enough: get in through the tendrils and disable the focus. What I couldn't figure out was what Celia was doing there. There had to be some reason . . .

"Huh," Sonder said. "That's weird."

Down on the floor, one of the other men was placing a blindfold around Celia's eyes. Celia looked nervous but submitted without complaint. The other guy was continuing to instruct Luna. Luna nodded—then stopped. She looked sharply at Celia, then back at the man.

"They can't be making Celia do this too," Sonder said. "She's not due to make journeyman for . . ."

I felt a nasty sinking feeling in my gut. "Oh shit," I said quietly.

"What?"

"They *are* making Celia do it," I said. "They're going to make Luna lead her in."

"Why? That doesn't make any—"

"Luna could make it in to that focus on her own. They know that. So they must have made it so that the only way to pass the test is for Celia to touch it. Luna has to protect both of them."

"How do you know?"

"Because that's what I would have done if I wanted to make it as hard as I possibly could."

"But how is she going to—?" Sonder said, then stopped as he figured it out. With Celia blindfolded, the only way Luna could get her in through those tendrils would be to lead Celia by the hand.

The man talking to Luna gave her what looked like a final instruction, then backed off. The other men withdrew a few steps as well, leaving Luna and Celia the only people near the arena. Luna stared at the anemone, then at Celia, then shot a glance up at the gallery. All of a sudden she didn't look so confident.

Luna's curse is powerful—much more powerful than usual for a chance effect, enough to surprise even mages who really should know better. It's also highly focused. It's why Luna's so good at duels—she's working with her curse, rather than against it. All she needs to do is direct her curse into helping her and hurting her opponent, something her curse is more than happy to do. This was why I hadn't been worried when she'd been dealing with that construct. In sending it to fight her in that maze, the mages in charge of the test had made things easy for her. Luna's curse *loves* being sent out to destroy things, especially if it's protecting her in the process.

But protecting someone else . . . that's another story. With enough concentration, Luna can prevent her curse from soaking into whoever she touches. She can even reverse it, taking the same protection and good fortune that her curse brings to her and sharing it with someone else, at least for a little while. But it's swimming upstream, going against what her curse wants to do, and it's very, very hard. She's done it in the past, and with Chalice's training she's slowly grown better at it, but she's never been able to do it reliably. I didn't know if she could do it with Celia and I didn't know if she could do it on command. I looked into the future, trying to find out.

Luna was going to try. She was searching, probing . . . I frowned. Something was disrupting the futures in which I watched Luna. My phone was ringing, and I was drawn towards the futures in which I answered. Annoyed, I pulled out the phone. I'd set it to mute, and it was vibrating silently. The number displayed on the screen was an unknown one; I hit the answer button and put it to my ear, turning slightly away. "Landis?" I said quietly. "This isn't a great time."

"Are you at Canary Wharf?"

"Yes."

"Get out. Now."

"What do you—?"

"Pay very close attention to what I am about to tell you." Sometimes Landis can seem scatterbrained, but there was no trace of that now. His voice was clipped and precise. "An order has come down from the Council for your arrest. Keepers are on their way to bring you in. They're probably already in the building."

"What— Why?"

"The charge is irrelevant. It's a pretext to keep you contained until the proposal goes through."

"What if it doesn't?"

"I've just been told that the voting is closed. There won't be any more votes against. Come tomorrow, the proposal for your execution is going to pass on schedule." Landis paused. "You've been set up, Alex."

Everything was happening too fast. "Where are you?"

"I'm on my way to find Variam and Anne. I'll do what I can. For your part, you need to run, right now. Good luck." There was a click and the line went dead.

I lowered the phone, staring. Off to my left, the other people in the viewing gallery were still talking. Sonder was looking at me curiously; he'd only heard my half of the conversation. "What's going on?"

I didn't answer. In my head, futures forked. There were three exits from the viewing gallery and I looked into the futures in which I left by all three, following each route simultaneously. Nothing, nothing . . . then my future self going back along the route by which I'd entered ran into trouble. Two Keepers. The future broke up into shards of confrontation and violence; they weren't going to let me past. The other two routes were safe. I took one step towards the far end of the gallery . . . and stopped.

Down below, Luna was still on the ballroom floor. As I watched, she took a cautious step out into the arena. The tendrils swept towards her and she moved quickly back, letting them skate past the boundary just in front of her. She shot a glance at Celia next to her, then took a visible breath and set herself, obviously getting ready.

For one brief, dizzying moment, I felt as though I wasn't seeing Luna as she was now, but in all the time I'd known her. The first day she'd walked into my shop. Leaning in to break me free from the fateweaver. Her apprenticeship ceremony, standing in her white and green robes, swearing to serve and follow me. Trying on outfits in Arachne's cave, laughing and joking, arguing with Variam. All of it had brought her here, and I wanted to be there for it. To help her, to watch her, to make sure she'd be okay. The Keepers were a couple of minutes out . . .

"Alex?" Sonder said. "Are you okay?"

I let out a rough, ragged breath, and turned away. It felt like tearing a scab off a wound. I had one last glimpse of Luna reaching out for Celia, then I was away, walking, not daring to look up. "Alex!" Sonder called as I went through the door at the far end.

I strode down the corridors, walking, not running. I knew that Luna was in the ballroom just to my side, and I wanted to get to her before the Keepers could . . . except that if I came charging in trying to rescue her, it'd disrupt the test and start off a brawl we couldn't win. Light mages take these kinds of formal tests seriously; they wouldn't let anyone else in without direct Council orders. But they wouldn't want to let the Keepers in either. If they held the Keepers out for long enough for Luna to finish . . . it was a horrible risk, but it was the only way out I could see, especially if the Keepers were too busy chasing me to go after Luna as well. Lots of things that could go wrong, not many choices, and not enough time to make them. I kept moving.

As I walked I mapped out the future paths in my head, looking for ways out. It didn't look good. There weren't many Keepers in the building, at least not yet, but they had the lifts I'd entered by blocked off. There were more lifts at the other end of the building—

A voice called from behind me. "Alex! Wait!"

I closed my eyes briefly and kept walking. Sonder hurried to catch up with me. "What's going on?"

"Sonder, this is not a good time." *Damn it.* The futures of conflict had just started multiplying, and they were coming from paths that had been clear before. The Keepers had started alerting everyone else. Now I needed to avoid all the security personnel, not just the ones that Keepers had brought with them. I changed course, turning down a side corridor just in time to avoid a patrol heading the other way.

"I just saw a couple of Keepers go past," Sonder said. "They're Order of the Star, I think. Who are they looking for?"

"Who do you think?" Now all the ways out from the floor were blocked. I could double back and hide . . . no, bad idea. Once the Keepers figured out that I was boxed in, they'd track me down in minutes. There was a lift up to the roof with only one person guarding it. It wouldn't get me any closer to ground level, but it would give me options. I changed direction again, going through a pair of fire doors.

The doors opened into a corner room. Ahead and to the right, windows looked out onto the London skyline, and in the corner was a lift made of glass. A security man was standing in front of it, one hand to his ear as he listened to something coming through on the radio. He looked in our direction, did a double take, and said something into a microphone. *Shit.* I walked towards him, not looking in his direction.

"Why?" Sonder said. "The test's still going on."

"I know." We were halfway to the lift. I kept my head turned towards Sonder, ignoring the security guard.

"Look, I think we should go back," Sonder said. "The Keepers—"

The security guard stepped in front of me, blocking our way. I kept walking as though I hadn't seen him, and he held up his hand to block me. "Sir, could you—"

I slid around the man's arm and struck, hands and feet flashing, ending the fight before the other man realised that it had started. He hit the floor with a thud.

Sonder stopped dead. I stepped over the guard as he lay dazed and walked into the lift. "Sorry, Sonder," I said. I gave him a smile without much humour in it. "Looks like you won't be going with me this time."

Sonder stared at me. "What?"

"Just tell the Keepers the truth when they catch you up," I said. I reached for the controls, then paused. "It was good working with you again." I pressed the button for the roof and the lift doors hissed closed. Through the glass, I had one last image of Sonder's face, looking totally bewildered, then he was gone.

The lifts that serve the top floors at Canary Wharf are much slower than the ones that link the office floors below. If you're not in a hurry, it's a relaxing way to enjoy a view of the London skyline. In my current state of mind, the slow pace wasn't relaxing, it was agonising. I pulled out my phone and dialled Variam's number, then waited as it rang, staring out at the London cityscape without seeing a single bit of it.

Variam picked up. "Vari," I said. "You need to—"

"Where are you?" Variam cut in. "Where's Luna?"

"Canary Wharf, she's in the middle of her test."

"You have to get her to finish it. Do whatever it takes. There's no time to explain, there's—"

"I know, I'm doing what I can. Where are you?"

"Never mind where I am. Listen, I just came from the program office. It's a setup, they were never going to follow through on it."

"On what? Wait—the transfer didn't go through? They didn't let Landis take over your—?"

"They transferred mine," Variam said grimly. "Not Anne's. They were going to keep it secret until the last minute. There are Keepers going to arrest her right now."

"Shit." Everything was spinning out of control. "Okay, you have to—"

"I know what I have to do. I'm going to Anne's flat and making sure she gets out safe, and if the Keepers get in my way, I'm going to kick their arse."

"Vari, no! Then *you're* going to be under arrest too!"

"Don't care. Just get out, there are Keepers coming for you too."

"I know about that! You need to—!"

"Got to go. Make sure Luna finishes that test." Vari hung up.

I swore and dialled him back. It rang and kept on ringing. I stared out over the London skyline as the lift reached the roof and the doors hissed quietly open, letting in a gust of cold air.

The pyramid at the top of Canary Wharf doesn't reach all the way to the walls of the building, though you'd have to look closely to notice. Instead there's a ledge that goes all the way around the pyramid's base, creating a balcony-walkway high up in the sky. There's a transparent barrier around the edge, but you can pretty much look over and take in the whole view, which apart from a couple of ledges mostly consists of a seven-hundred-feet-and-change vertical drop to solid concrete. It's just as well I'm not scared of heights.

Unfortunately, right now I had bigger problems. There was someone else on the roof, and from a glance through the futures I already knew who it was. I looked quickly at the possibilities of reaching one of the other lifts and dismissed them; in the time it would take for the lift to reach roof level, they'd catch up with me. Jumping back into the lift I'd arrived on would just leave me in the same position as before. I wasn't visible yet—the Keeper on the rooftop was on the other side of the pyramid—but she'd come into view in seconds.

When you can't run or evade, you might as well let your pursuer come to you. I dialled Anne's number on my phone and put it to my ear just as a figure appeared around the corner of the pyramid in front of me. The phone rang and rang again. Wind tugged at my clothes, trying to pull me off the ledge and send me falling to the streets below. The phone went to voice mail. I hung up, then turned to the figure approaching me. "Be with you in a second." I redialled and tried again.

Caldera came to a stop about twenty feet away. The pyramid of Canary Wharf was to her right, the sheer drop to the street below to her left. She folded her arms, looking at me.

I listened to the phone as it rang, searching through the futures. Nothing, nothing—wait, was she going to pick up? Maybe, but it was gone. No answer. *Shit.* I hung up and turned to Caldera. "This isn't really the best time."

"What happened to the guy guarding the lift?" Caldera asked.

"He'll have a couple of bruises when he wakes up."

Caldera shook her head. "Couldn't do this the easy way, could you?"

"I could say the same to you." I studied Caldera. "You know, when you made that crack about how if the Council ordered my arrest you'd do it, I'd kind of hoped you were kidding."

Caldera didn't react, at least not visibly. The wind blew across the two of us, ruffling Caldera's short brown hair. Her expression was unreadable: a cop's face. Caldera used to wear that expression a lot when she looked at me, but over the past year, I'd gotten used to seeing her relaxed and smiling. She wasn't smiling now.

"The Council want you to come in," Caldera said.

"I'll bet they do. What's the charge?"

"You're not being charged."

"Really?" I said. "So if I try and walk past you to that lift, you're not going to stop me?"

Caldera didn't reply. It didn't matter—I already knew what the answer was. "They want to ask you some questions about the op."

"Oh? That's funny, because they already did that. All of us, actually. At the debriefing. But you were there, weren't you? Including the part where they said that we were free to go."

Caldera sighed. "Don't make this any harder than it has to be, all right? They want to talk to you, and they're not asking. Let's just go down nice and peaceful and work things out."

"You know, it's the strangest thing," I said. "I have the funny feeling that once I'm in Keeper HQ, they're going to want to keep me there. At least until, oh, say, six o'clock tomorrow evening. Don't you get that feeling? Kind of like clairvoyance?"

"I have no clue."

"I do," I said sharply. "You think I didn't see this coming? Levistus wants me dead."

"It doesn't matter what he wants," Caldera said. "Levistus doesn't run the Keepers."

"The Council does!"

"Look, Alex," Caldera said. "Stop with the voice-in-the-wilderness shit, all right? You've got people you know with the Keepers and with the Council. Me, Landis, Rain, a bunch of others. They want to pass an execution order against you? Then we'll fight it. But they're not going to listen to you unless you're working with the system. You run, you're just proving them right."

"You haven't been keeping up," I said. "They don't want to pass an execution order. They've already done it. Tomorrow at six, it goes public. Are you going to carry it out?"

"No."

"But you're fine with arresting me so someone else can?" I shook my head. I was letting myself get distracted. While Caldera kept me talking, other lifts were on their way up with reinforcements. "I'm guessing you're not planning to let me go."

"Not an option, all right?" Caldera said. "Look, Alex,

there's a full Keeper team here already. The building was sealed off twenty minutes ago, and you can't fly. The only way you're leaving this roof is with me."

"Oh, I don't know," I said lightly. I slid my hand into my pocket as I spoke. "Everyone can fly. Just not for very long."

Caldera caught the motion. Her stance shifted, and her voice took on a warning note. "Don't do anything stupid."

"Like what? Go down with you into custody of an organisation that's about to have me killed?"

"You need to—"

Behind Caldera, one of the lifts climbed into view. "Sorry, Caldera," I said. "Got to go."

Caldera lunged, but she wasn't close enough. I got my foot on the railing and leapt into space.

ı ı ı ı ı ı ı ı ı

Being a diviner is all about being prepared.

I hadn't expected to be attacked at the journeyman tests. At least, not specifically. But it had occurred to me a while ago that if Levistus or some other people on the Council wanted to make sure that my execution went through smoothly, then the most logical thing for them to do would be to arrest me before the resolution was due to pass. And given that journeyman tests are a matter of public record, then from their point of view, that was the best place to catch me. So when I'd decided to come here, I'd taken some time to consider avenues of escape. The lifts were the best way out but they were controlled by Council security, and I didn't trust the Council. Which was why I'd brought the life ring.

Interesting thing about falling: it seems to be one of those things that short-circuits the higher brain functions. My life rings are small bands of metal and glass, imbued with an air magic spell that cuts your falling speed down to a comfortable ten feet per second. They're very reliable, and they have to be, given what they're used for. I've used life rings at least a dozen times before, and I know that they work. When I'd picked up this particular life ring yesterday, I'd taken the time to look into the futures in which I used it, to make sure it'd still work. And just to be sure, while I'd been talking to Caldera, I'd checked yet again.

None of that made the drop any bit less terrifying.

Icy wind howled past as I fell, the coat Anne had given me flapping around my legs, the windows of Canary Wharf flashing past, flick-flick-flick. My stomach lurched in that weightless feeling, light and nauseated at the same time, but it had to fight to get my attention over the animal side of my brain, which was screaming *oh God oh God you're going to die you're going to die* over and over again. My right hand clutched the life ring in a death grip; intellectually I knew that if I triggered it too soon the spell would run out while I was still in the air, but it took all my willpower not to. The street below grew closer and closer, cars and road and pavement growing larger with frightening speed. I could see the spot of road I was heading for and my mind was painting a vivid and horrible picture of my body splattering onto it like a watermelon hit by a sledgehammer. It takes a little over six seconds to fall seven hundred feet, and while it doesn't exactly feel longer, I can say for a fact that you get an awful lot of sensory experience packed into that short time.

I hit the future in which I needed to activate the life ring, and my fist spasmed shut, crushing the item to fragments. Air magic leapt out and the impact of the deceleration felt like a powerful blow that didn't stop spread out over all of my body. My vision went red, pressure spiking inside me, then as suddenly as it had come it was receding and I was sinking down just above street level. I hit the centre of the road with both feet and went down to one knee, breathing hard.

There was the sound of brakes, followed by the noise of a car jerking to a stop. I looked up and saw a black cab stopped a little way in front of me. The driver was clearly visible through the windscreen, and he was staring at me with his mouth open. I pulled myself to my feet, my legs shaky, and started to run.

It doesn't look like it from below, but Canary Wharf is close to being an island: the old docks interlace the area with so many channels that it's like a miniature peninsula. I knew that the only ways out of the area were west towards Westferry or east to Blackwall. West was closer. I ran along the edge of the road, girders flying by overhead, mentally checking off the laws I was breaking. Resisting arrest by legitimate agents of the Council: that was the first clause of the Concord. Dropping out of the sky in front of motorists broke the fourth. Hadn't broken the second clause so far, since I hadn't actually attacked any mages yet, but the day was still young—

Contact. Two men appeared ahead, running towards me, one of them raising a hand to his ear. I changed direction instantly, running up the stairs into the Cabot Place shopping centre.

Pedestrians and shoppers jumped out of the way as I dashed through the mall. The men on my tail weren't far behind, and from one future I glimpsed I was pretty sure at least one was a Keeper. I needed a way to lose them, and flicked though the futures ahead of me. Hiding in the shops— no. Outrunning—no. A sign appeared up ahead telling me that I was heading into Canary Wharf DLR station, and that gave me an idea. Just needed a train with the right timing . . . *there.* I changed direction and ran up a flight of stairs.

The station was crowded, men and women and children scattered across the platforms, carrying coats and shopping bags. A DLR train was sitting in the centre of the station, about to leave for Stratford. I ran up the platform, then slowed, deliberately hanging back a little to let my pursuers catch up. Glancing back, I saw them run up the stairs. I waited a couple of seconds to let them see me, then turned left and stepped onto the train.

I'd timed it very carefully. The doors began beeping, signalling that the train was about to leave. The two men pursuing me raced for the train and jumped onto it, but it was crowded and they lost sight of me. It was only for a few seconds, but it was enough. As the doors began to close, I stepped out the train onto the platform on the other side; the doors shut behind me with a *thump* and I fell into step with the crowd, walking down the stairs back into the shopping centre. On the train the two men would be pushing their way through the crowds, searching for me; the next station was less than a minute away and it wouldn't take them long to figure out what I'd done, but by then I'd be gone.

I moved through the shopping centre and left by the west exit, coming out onto a raised square paved with tiles that circled a flat, round fountain carved from grey stone. I kept searching the futures as I walked, looking into the possibilities in which I went back, tracking my pursuers. The Keepers were spreading out from Canary Wharf, trying to find me, but I was outside their radius now and moving faster than they could. As long as there weren't . . . *Shit.*

I looked back over my shoulder to see Caldera, about a hundred feet back. Our eyes met, and she broke into a run.

I ran along the pavement of West India Avenue, tracking futures in my head. *How did she get down to ground level so fast? Oh, right. Elemental mage.* Caldera must have gated nearby, and either she'd been vectored in by those two or she'd guessed which direction I was going in. Now I had a problem. I'm faster than Caldera, but not by much. I could lose her in a foot chase, but as soon as I did she'd just call in more backup. I needed to find a way to shake her, and it would have to be something extreme. Caldera might not be on the level of Landis or Vihaela, but she's still a heavy hitter and more than a match for me. I looked ahead: we were coming up on Westferry Circus, and a plan jumped fully formed into my mind. *That could work.*

I slowed down, conserving my strength. From behind I could sense Caldera getting closer; fifty feet, then forty. Westferry Circus opened up in front of me, a circular green surrounded by a busy road junction. I dodged a couple walking along the pavement to cross the road, then crossed again, heading for a long stone barrier that I knew had a drop on the other side.

Heavy footsteps and my precognition warned me. I jinked and doubled back as Caldera lunged, and she stumbled past and thudded into the stone. As she turned I vaulted up onto the barrier, taking a glance down at the drop on my right. Thirty feet down to paving stones, interrupted by the white light fixtures mounted on the sheer wall. Only a fraction of the last drop, but still enough to break a leg or an ankle. Beside the paving stones, a double-lane road disappeared into the darkness underneath the roundabout, cars passing back and forth.

Caldera glared at me. "Will you stop frigging running and just *talk*?"

"Stop chasing me and you can talk as much as you want."

"Listen, right now I am one of *very* few people trying to help you," Caldera said. "You want to do this the easy way or the hard way?"

"Hmm," I said. "Let me think." I crouched down, then before Caldera could react I hopped backwards off the barrier.

I twisted in midair, catching myself on the barrier edge then dropping down with a clang onto one of the light fixtures. I lowered myself by my hands, smelling dust and car exhaust, feeling the grime under my fingers, then let myself fall again, kicking off from the wall; I hit the pavement, feeling the shock of pain from my feet and shoulder as I rolled.

Caldera hit the pavement behind me with a *wham*, going down to one knee with the impact before getting up. I could see cracks in the pavement under her boots. "Okay," she said. "You are starting to piss me off."

I ran into the tunnel. The road under Westferry Circus is a wide roundabout, roofed and walled in concrete, with pillars running along the ceiling. Cars and lorries zoomed by, but the pavement was empty; this was a place for vehicles, not people.

Caldera caught me up by one of the pillars, and again I dodged just as she lunged. She turned on me, hands by her sides. "All right, Alex," Caldera said. "I didn't want to play it this way, but you aren't going to be the first mage who's made it come to this."

"Come to what? Wanting to stay alive?"

Caldera lunged, and again I slipped aside. "You're getting slow," I said.

I could tell from Caldera's face that she was angry. *Good.* She came in again, slower this time, pacing forward with hands spread. She was going to try to grapple and turn this into a wrestling match, and I knew that if she did, I'd lose. Caldera grabbed at me, first once, then again and again. I blocked some, backed away from the others, giving ground. Caldera tried a charge, head down and arms wide, the same way she'd taken me down in our first duel. I ducked around one of the pillars and Caldera bounced off the stone. "Not this time," I said.

"How long are you going to drag this out?" Caldera said. "You know damn well you're not going to win this."

"Funny," I said. "I don't remember you beating me in any of our matches."

Caldera stared at me. "You actually believe that?"

I shrugged. "You never knocked me out."

"Jesus Christ," Caldera said. "I haven't knocked you out because I don't want to break every bone in your body."

"You can tell yourself that."

Caldera attacked again. I blocked and countered, hitting her in the head and body. It felt like hitting a stone wall. My hands were already aching, while I knew that Caldera was doing just fine. Caldera charged again, and again I sent her crashing into the wall. "FYI, you're losing on points," I told her.

Caldera turned on me, her face set. "You think this is a game, don't you?"

"Yes." I made my voice hard, contemptuous. No room for hesitation now. "It *is* a game. And you're one of the pieces." I looked at her. "Do you even know why this is happening? Who passed this order, and why? You go where the Council tells you to go, kill who they tell you to kill." I paused, shook my head. "You aren't even smart enough to know when you're being used."

Caldera stared at me, her eyes chips of dark stone, then attacked again, harder this time. I blocked and dodged, steadily giving ground. Caldera is stronger and tougher than me, but she's not any faster than me, and by using the pillars as cover to break up her attacks I was able to keep her at a distance.

The exchange ended with us facing each other between

the pillars. A car came around the roundabout and slowed slightly as it went by, a white face peering out at us through the window, then it accelerated away. "You are just putting off the inevitable," Caldera said tightly.

I felt a flash of shame for what I was about to do but pushed it down. Had to be cold. "You don't understand anything about the people you work for," I said. "That's why you've never been promoted, and why you never will be. You'll always be a journeyman, while every other Keeper you've ever known is raised above you."

Caldera stopped dead.

Caldera isn't the share-your-feelings type, and for all the time we'd spent together, she'd never opened up to me. She'd never told me how many times she'd been passed over for promotion, nor how much it affected her. But if there's one thing diviners are good at, it's finding things out. I knew that for Caldera, her job was all she had, and I knew that she was years past the point where Keepers are usually noticed and groomed for the higher ranks. She was afraid that they didn't think she was good enough, and that she'd be sidelined and forgotten. I'd found her weakest point and struck at it, just as I'd been taught.

"Do you have any idea how much shit I've done for you?" Caldera said. Her voice was quiet, but rage was building behind her eyes, and I knew she was right on the edge of losing control. "I've defended you to other Keepers. I've talked you up to Rain. I've bodyguarded your arse through one mission after another. But you can't dial back that fucking ego, can you? You don't give a shit about the law. You think the rules don't apply to you."

"Actually, I—"

Caldera moved in a blur of motion. I jumped back just in time from a blow that would have broken my ribs. *"Shut up."* Caldera's voice was a hiss. She struck at my chest, then moved in, words spilling out. "Always you want to show everyone else how smart you are. How tough you are. Then when it's time to pay the bill, you get someone else to do it." Caldera struck again, sending a shock of pain up my arm as I blocked.

"I could have broken you in half the first time we met. Could have done it every time you stepped in the ring. But I held back." Caldera struck a third time. "But you can't see that, because you're so . . . *fucking* . . . *full* of yourself."

Caldera delivered another punch with each word. I managed to block each one, my guard posture exactly calculated to minimise the amount of damage I took. It still felt like being kicked by a horse. The second-to-last blow staggered me; the third one slammed me back into the wall.

"Now," Caldera said. She was breathing hard, eyes blazing, fury underlining each word. "You are coming back with me. You can choose whether you come walking, or beaten to crap and in handcuffs. But you do not get to choose anything else. Because I am *sick* of your shit. Understand?"

I pulled myself to my feet as another car zoomed by. My body hurt in a dozen places, muscle and bone aching. It had been a long time since I'd been hit that hard. I've seen Caldera's strength in action, but it's another thing to feel it. "I always knew you were holding back," I said. "So was I."

"Bullshit."

"Just not the way you think." I braced myself against the wall. "Want to know how I beat mages who are stronger than me?"

As Caldera started to answer, I lunged, kicking off the stone. She didn't have her guard up, and I hit her with an open-palm strike right in the centre of the face. Against any normal person, it would have broken their nose. It didn't break Caldera's, but I knew it would hurt like hell.

Caldera lost her temper completely.

A swinging punch came at me with enough force to shatter my skull. I ducked underneath and dashed out across the road. Caldera charged after me in a blind rage.

The container lorry was a twelve-wheeler, painted white and orange with the Sainsbury's logo on the side, and it came around the curve of the roundabout moving fast. The driver saw us as soon as we ran out in front of him and stomped on the brake pedal. Tyres met brakes with a horrible scream, but it takes a lot of energy to stop a vehicle that big. The front cab missed me by a few feet and hit Caldera square on.

It was all over very fast. There was a noise somewhere between a thud and a crunch, mixed with the screech of brakes, followed by the sound of a rolling body. I came to a halt and looked around to see Caldera about fifty feet away, rolling over and over before coming to a stop. She stirred, groggy, as the lorry bore down on her; it finally scraped to a halt about ten feet away from running her over. After all the noise, there was a sudden silence.

"I cheat," I said quietly into the vacuum. "Sorry." There was a sign for a garage off to the right, along with a side road that I knew would have stairs leading up. By the time Caldera had recovered enough to lift her head, I was out of sight.

chapter 15

I gated to the park in Camden Town, then pulled out my phone and started walking. I'd visited this place with Caldera enough times for her to know that it was one of my regular staging points, meaning that there was a good chance she'd be following me. I headed down the nearest street, looking through the futures.

Luna wasn't going to answer her phone. I hadn't really expected her to. More worrying was that Anne and Variam weren't answering either. Odds were that at least one of them was in Keeper custody by now. That meant that the Keepers would have their phones, which meant that they could pull off the number of the one I was using now. How long before they traced it? *Probably not long.* Landis wasn't going to answer if I called, but Lyle was.

I dialled Lyle's number. It rang a few times and then there was the click as Lyle picked up. "Oh, hello, Alex. It's you, isn't it?"

"Yes." I kept my voice as calm as I could. "It's me."

"I'm afraid I haven't heard back from Undaaris just yet."

"Don't bother," I said. "I just got his answer."

"Everything work out okay?"

I was silent for a second. "You really don't know, do you?"

"Know what?"

"I can't believe I actually believed that this might work," I said. "I mean, how many times has this happened now? The Council *always* screws me. Every time I think that things might actually work out, something like this happens to make me realise just how dumb I was."

"I . . . don't understand."

"You know the really hilarious part?" I said. "We're in exactly the same place we were back then. Twelve years and not a thing's changed. Me standing out there, banging to be let in, and you on the inside." I laughed slightly. It sounded odd, unbalanced. "Right back where we started."

"Alex?" Lyle sounded worried. "Is something—?"

"Shut up!" I snarled. "Just . . ." I wanted to shout at Lyle, wanted to scream at him, but all of a sudden I couldn't think of anything to say. What was the point? "Just . . ." My energy drained away. "Forget it." I didn't want to talk anymore. "Fuck you, Lyle. You and the Council." I felt weary, and bitter, and very old. "I hope Morden and the rest of the Dark mages tear you apart. You deserve it."

"Alex—"

I hung up, pulled out the phone's SIM card, and snapped it in half. Then I dropped the phone to the paving stones and stamped on it. I took my foot away to see that the screen was cracked. I stamped on it a second time, then again and again, slowly ramping up, putting more and more power into each kick, feeling the jolt of each impact go up into my leg. I realised I was snarling, my lips pulled back from my teeth as the phone broke under the rain of blows.

When I was done, the phone was a pile of shattered metal and plastic. As I looked up I realised I had an audience. I'd been on a residential street, and several people had slowed to watch me. The nearest ones were a young couple, a man and a woman, and I turned my head to stare at them. I don't know what I must have looked like, but they flinched and averted their eyes, the man moving hurriedly to lead the woman away. The ones watching from the other side of the street backed off too.

I scooped up the pieces of the phone, threw them into the nearest bin, then walked away.

׀ ׀ ׀ ׀ ׀ ׀ ׀ ׀ ׀

I did what I could to shake pursuit. I was having a hard time thinking—too much had gone wrong too fast—and instead I lost myself in the work of making sure I wasn't followed. I went through the Underground and did some basic evasion routines, then used an annuller to foul up any tracking spells. Once that was done I gated to a staging point, then gated again to my safe house in Wales, then looked ahead to confirm that the next few hours were clear.

I'd picked up a clean prepaid phone, but I didn't want to use it unless I had to. From now on I had to assume that any calls I made would be logged and traced. I could still look into the futures in which I called everyone without actually doing it, but a quick check confirmed that Anne and Variam's numbers weren't going to get any results. Luna's was . . . specifically, it would be answered by some guy I didn't recognise. It was a safe bet that he wasn't someone I wanted to talk to, and the fact that he was holding Luna's phone was bad news.

In fact, all the news was bad. I couldn't contact Luna, Anne, or Variam without risking making things worse. I could try to call Landis, but I already knew that he was doing what he could to help Anne and Variam. Having me call his mobile wouldn't help.

I paced up and down the farmhouse kitchen, my feet tapping on the tiles. I wanted to run, to fight, but I didn't know how. If I went charging in to help Anne or Luna or Vari, I'd just make things worse. I'd barely managed to escape myself; the last thing I was qualified to do was some sort of insane rescue . . .

I took a deep breath, grabbed a fistful of hair in one hand, and squeezed, trying to let the pain focus me. *Think. I have to think.* What should I do?

Okay, Variam is probably all right. Or maybe more accurate to say that out of the four of us, he was currently in the *least* bad situation. If that transfer had gone through, then he should be under Landis's sponsorship, free and clear. There was still the possibility of him having lost it and attacked some Keepers, but he had a couple of years as a Light apprentice going for him. Even if the worst had happened, with Landis batting for him, he should have a chance.

Luna was on a knife edge. She'd been in the middle of that test, in the heart of Canary Wharf, surrounded by Council mages. There was no way she could have escaped. The one slim hope that I was clinging to was that the Keepers had been too busy chasing me to go after Luna as well. Caldera hadn't said that she was there for Luna, right? Maybe she hadn't been on their list? But they'd gone after Anne . . .

Anne. Had Variam made it in time? I rummaged through my pockets and pulled out my gate stone to Anne's flat, holding on to the little focus and concentrating. I couldn't risk going there, but if I looked through the futures in which I did . . . *Gate failure, gate failure.* I took a breath and concentrated, forcing myself to stay calm. *I'm too agitated.* Once my heartbeat was steady, I tried again.

More failures. I searched through the futures, and . . . *Wait. That can't be right.* In *every* possible future in which I tried that gate stone, the gate failed to open. *That doesn't make sense.* Maybe there was a space mage there, projecting a gate ward? But even then, I should be able to sense something, unless—

Unless Anne's flat had changed enough that the gate stone wasn't keyed to it anymore.

My heart sank. I didn't want to believe it, but it was the most likely explanation. I felt so utterly helpless. I can see dangers ahead of me, but I'm damn near useless when it comes to stopping something in progress. If Anne's flat was burning to the ground right now, there was nothing I could do to stop it. Or worse, if she and Luna were already—

No. Don't think about that. I tried to think constructively. Assuming the worst hadn't happened, and that Luna, Anne, and Variam were still okay, what would they do? Variam would probably meet up with Landis. Luna's first reaction would be to contact me. Anne . . . I didn't know. Okay, so what would Luna do? First she'd try my phone, and when that didn't work . . . then she'd probably look for me here. I'd made sure that she had a gate stone for the place.

Now I had a plan. I looked into the future again, and this time, instead of looking for danger, I looked for friendly arrivals. Almost immediately I saw a future of an opening gate. It was close, less than ten minutes away . . . not guaranteed yet, but it was becoming more likely with each passing minute. I started pacing again, staring at the spot that the gate stone was keyed to, willing the time to pass more quickly.

Nine minutes and thirty seconds later, the air shimmered. An oval of green light, the colour of new leaves, appeared in midair at the spot keyed to the gate stone, becoming opaque. A foot came down on the tiles, then another, and Anne stepped out as the gate winked out, turning to face me.

The two of us looked at each other. Anne looked exhausted and battered. Her T-shirt was singed down one side, and her arm was reddened and burned. But she was alive, and she didn't look seriously hurt. "Are you okay?" I said.

In answer Anne took two steps forward and put her arms around me, resting her head on my shoulder. I hesitated, then awkwardly reached up to her, not sure what to do. Anne sighed and I could feel the tension gradually go out of her as we stood there.

ı ı ı ı ı ı ı ı ı

"So Vari warned you in time?" I asked.

Anne nodded. She was sitting cross-legged on the bed with a blanket wrapped around her, a mug of tea clasped in her long fingers with a wisp of steam rising upwards. "But not in time to get out. By the time I tried to gate they were too close."

"So what did you do?"

"I fought," Anne said. "I didn't want to, but . . . I've had a long time to think about this, and I decided I wasn't going to let myself be executed. Even if it meant fighting Keepers."

"How many of them were there?"

"Keepers? Three or four, I think. The rest were auxiliaries."

I looked at Anne with raised eyebrows. "You got away from three or four Keepers on your own?"

"Vari showed up midway through," Anne said. "By then two of them were down, so they pulled back to try and deal with him. So I gated."

"What happened to Vari?"

Anne looked down at the blanket. "I don't know," she said quietly. "I left him behind." There was a moment's silence, then she looked up again. "After that, I was on my own. I knew they'd be tracing me, and I didn't have any way of getting in touch with you or Luna, so I came here hoping I'd find you."

"About that," I said. Like me, Anne can't use gate magic; she has to rely on gate stones. "How *did* you get here?"

"Luna gave me a copy of the gate stone to here last year. I kept it cached."

"That was good preparation."

Anne gave me a half smile. "You gave me the idea."

There was a beep from the table. I looked over, then got up off the bed and walked over to pick up one of the two phones lying there. "Finally," I said.

"Who is it?"

"I've got an emergency line to Talisid. Looks like he's ready to make the call."

"Is that safe?"

"Not really."

Anne was silent. I sat back down on the bed, sent a text from the phone, and put it down on the bed between us. After a minute's wait the phone rang. I answered and pressed the button to put it on speaker. "Talisid."

"Verus." Talisid's voice was slightly distorted through the phone's tiny speaker system. "Where are you?"

"Somewhere safe."

"This line's secure."

"Given what's just happened, I hope you'll understand if I'm not too keen on broadcasting my location," I said. "All right?"

"All right," Talisid said. "Undaaris voted against you."

It was what I'd expected to hear, but it was still a blow. Four against two. Even if we could get the seventh vote, it wouldn't matter now. "I see." I kept my voice steady. "Why?"

"I haven't been able to confirm the details," Talisid said. "But one can put two and two together. Levistus's faction has been pressuring Undaaris over the Birkstead appointment. I've just heard that Levistus has agreed to support Undaaris's candidate."

"And in exchange, Undaaris gives Levistus his vote," I said. "Favour for favour."

"It seems that way." Talisid paused. "If I'd known—"

"What's happened to Variam and Luna?"

"Variam is currently in custody," Talisid said. "No charges yet. I believe Landis is trying to get him released."

"And Luna?" I could feel my stomach tightening up.

"That's the one piece of good news. The results haven't been officially released as yet, but from what I've been able to learn, your apprentice passed. Luna Mancuso is officially recognised by the Light Council of Britain as their newest journeyman mage."

I stared down at the phone for a second, then closed my eyes and took a deep breath.

"Alex? Are you there?"

"I'm here." The relief was so strong I felt dizzy. "Is she okay? She's in custody too?"

"She hasn't been arrested. The Keepers are currently questioning her, presumably in hopes of her leading them to you, but she's due to be released shortly."

"Wait." Now I was confused. I looked at Anne; she looked puzzled as well. "There wasn't any order to arrest Luna?"

"No," Talisid said. "The order only mentioned you. I'm sure it won't surprise you to know that I've traced it back to Levistus."

"Not so much." That was no shock, at least. But in that case . . . "Wait. If the order was only for my arrest, why were there Keepers going after Anne?"

"That I'm afraid I don't know," Talisid said. "Landis's request to move Variam and Anne to his sponsorship was approved in the case of Variam but rejected in the case of Anne. Immediately after that information was released, an order was issued to bring Anne Walker in for questioning."

"I don't understand," I said. "Are you saying Levistus tried to get me and Anne arrested, but not Luna and Vari?"

"Levistus was certainly the one behind the order for *your* arrest, but I haven't heard anything linking him to the order for Anne's."

Anne and I looked at each other. I couldn't figure out what was going on, and it didn't seem as though Anne had any idea either. Still . . . I shook my head. *Focus.* "Okay. As I understand it, come tomorrow evening, my death sentence is going to be passed. And since Anne's still my dependent, it'll affect her, too. Is there any way to stop that?"

"With the arrest order out?" Talisid said. "Short of direct intervention by the Senior Council, there's no way to stop that sentence going through. You're going to have to get out of the country. And if you're in touch with Anne, I'd pass the same advice to her."

I noted that Talisid didn't ask where Anne was. He'd probably put two and two together. "Just good news all around, huh?"

"I wish I had better news, but I don't." Talisid paused. "I know it's not worth very much to you right now, but I'm sorry. I didn't want things to go this way."

"Any more good news?"

"Not as yet. I'll look into getting the sentence reversed, but it won't be quick or easy. For now, just focus on staying alive. I'll contact you when I know more."

"Great."

"Is there anything you need?"

"A lot of things. I just don't think you can give them."

"I'm sorry to hear that." Talisid paused. "Good luck."

If I had to talk much longer, I was going to snap. I reached down and pressed the button to end the call. The phone went dead.

Anne spoke into the silence. "We're on our own, aren't we?"

"Yeah," I said. I got up and walked out.

"Alex?" Anne called after me. *"Alex!"*

ı ı ı ı ı ı ı ı ı

The next twenty-four hours were preparation.

We stayed in Wales. I didn't dare travel, and Anne didn't argue. I spent my time looking ahead for another attack and getting ready for what we were going to do when it happened. Putting the last steps in place didn't take all that long. I'd had a long time to get ready for this.

Internally, I spent the time on autopilot. I focused all my attention on keeping safe, not letting myself think any further. Anne tried to talk to me a few times; I shrugged her off. I knew she was hurting, but I was too overwhelmed to deal with her problems too. All I could do was shut that part of myself down while I tried to recover.

Nightfall found the two of us sitting in the kitchen. Through the windows, I could see the last traces of light fading from the western sky, and birdsong echoed through the country air. Outside, it was bitterly cold, but the kitchen stove was burning with enough fuel to keep the house warm. The woodpile was well stocked—Anne had gone out to fetch some more, even though we weren't going to use it.

"How long do we have?" Anne asked.

I checked my phone to see that the clock read 5:25. Give or take a couple of hours, it was a week since Talisid's first call. "Thirty-five minutes."

"How did they find us?" Anne asked.

I shrugged.

"I wish we could go to Arachne's."

"They'd track us down sooner or later. And then Arachne would be on the hit list for sheltering us. I can't do that to her."

Anne sighed. "I know."

Silence fell. Time ticked away. "If they know where we are, why are they waiting?" Anne said at last. "Why haven't they just blown up the house?"

"Why bother?" I said. "For the next"—I checked—"twenty-seven minutes, there aren't any official charges against us. We're just supposed to be brought in for questioning. Once it ticks over to six o'clock, they can kill us on sight."

"Do you think that's what they'll do?"

"I'd give it about fifty percent that we'll be killed 'resisting arrest' and fifty percent that they'll try to interrogate us first."

"I think if it's a choice between those two," Anne said, "I'd rather they got it over with quickly."

"I know the feeling."

More silence. "I wish we could have said good-bye," Anne said.

"Yeah." There were a lot of people I wished I could have talked to. Luna, Variam, Landis. Arachne. Caldera, in a different way. Even my father, though I wouldn't have enjoyed that conversation much. "Maybe we can do it later."

"Do you think Luna and Vari will be okay?"

"Vari's got Landis looking out for him," I said. "And I wrote out some sealed envelopes for Luna a while back. Open-in-the-event-of-my-death stuff. This wasn't how I expected them to get used, but they've got bank account details and places she can go to call in favours. I think she'll be all right."

"As long as no one decides to go after her as well."

I sighed. "Yeah."

I felt the futures shift and looked to see what had changed. It was more or less what I'd been expecting. "Well," I said. "Looks like it's about that time."

"When are they going to come?"

"Six o'clock on the dot," I said. "Bastards are punctual, I'll give them that."

Anne got to her feet, folding her coat over one arm. "Anyone we know?"

"Doesn't look like it. I'm not even sure they're Keepers."

"That's not a good sign, is it?"

"No," I said. It implied that they didn't want to have to deal with even a minimal amount of due process. I picked my backpack up from where it had been resting against the wall, then handed Anne a gate stone. "Want to do the honours?"

Anne took it, but didn't use it straight away. "I remember the first time you brought me here," she said. "I didn't think it was going to be the last part of Britain I saw."

"We'll be back," I said. I wasn't sure how true it was, but I tried to make myself sound confident. "Someday."

Anne nodded. She held up the stone, a soft green light radiating from her hand as she began to channel. I switched off the light—no point in being untidy—but left the fire for the Keepers to deal with. Through the futures, I could sense the attacking force preparing their strike, but by the time it landed, we'd be gone.

The gate spell completed, and Anne and I stepped through and into a new chapter of our lives.

⁙   ͟ ͟ ͟ ͟ ͟ ͟ ͟ ͟ ͟

We came out into daylight. We were standing on a steep hillside, trees rising up all around us, the morning sun sending shafts of light through the leaves. The weather was cool but pleasant, just warming up from the long night, and through the trees we could see the bright blue of a beautiful lake, with white-capped mountains rising up over it. Laid out neatly on the shore below were the houses and buildings of a small town, and the air was fresh and clean. Above, puffy white clouds floated in a cerulean sky.

"Well, that's it," I said. "We're officially outlaws."

Anne was looking around, smiling. I wondered how the natural scenery appeared to her lifesight. "You didn't tell me it was this beautiful."

"Enjoy it while you can." I held out my hand. "We're only going to be here long enough to make sure we're not being followed."

Anne passed over the gate stone and I put it in my pocket. I'd find a place to stash it once we were a safe distance away. "Are we going to stay in the country?" Anne asked.

I shrugged. "One place is pretty much as good as another, for now."

"Then let's stay here."

"Eh," I said. "Why not?"

We started walking down the hillside towards the town below. Its name was Queenstown, and there was a hired car waiting there to take us wherever we needed to go. After that I had three or four alternate routes, depending on how things unfolded. "You know, it's been ages since I've had a holiday," Anne said.

"Always finding the bright side."

"Why did you pick New Zealand?"

"Suggestion from an enemy." I looked at the blue lake and the forested hills beyond. Maradok had been right about one thing. It really was nice this time of year.

⁖⁖⁖⁖⁖⁖⁖⁖⁖⁖

Over the next few days, we travelled slowly northeast along New Zealand's South Island. We stayed in a different place each night, switching between hostels and hotels and private arrangements. It really *was* a holiday, or it would have been if we hadn't been spending three quarters of our time checking for pursuit or for traps. But the weather was beautiful, and so was the scenery, and if we had to throw a tail, this was a nice place to do it.

Levistus's men caught up with us north of Christchurch. It wasn't a bad ambush, and if we hadn't been on guard, it might have worked. But it's hard to ambush a diviner, and it's hard to sneak up on a life mage who can spot you through a solid wall. Anne and I slipped away, leaving the men to pick through our empty rooms.

The Christchurch ambush made me decide that we were going to have to find somewhere farther afield. New Zealand is a separate magical nation to Britain, but its Council is on good terms with the British one. Instead of going to another English-speaking country, Anne and I moved to Japan, in the suburbs of Nagoya. The Light Council of Japan (or the nearest equivalent they have—they don't use that name, but it fills the same niche) is famous for its lack of interest in cooperating with outsiders. Technically, as rogue mages, we were breaking their rules by settling down there without clearing it with the authorities, but the Japanese Council are fanatical about preserving their autonomy, and Levistus would have his work cut out for him getting them to authorise any kind of operation in their territory. We settled down in a quiet little apartment down a back street, hoping that Levistus would decide that going after us on another Council's turf was more trouble than it was worth and give up.

He didn't.

They didn't try for an abduction this time. Instead, they just blew up the house. Anne and I watched the fire from a distance, the orange flames a bright glow in the night. "So now where?" Anne asked.

I sighed. "Anywhere but here."

····

More countries, more cities. The new year came and went, and days turned into weeks. The men chasing us didn't manage to get so close again, but they didn't stop, either.

Time passed, and we became practised at spotting the signs of danger, developing a sixth sense for when it was time to move on. We saw towns and villages, empty countryside and cities packed with people, but we could never truly settle down. A couple of times we discussed fighting back, but there was little point. It was too much risk for too little gain; we might remove a few of our pursuers, but there would always be more. Sooner or later our pursuers would have to realise that what they were doing wasn't working.

I hoped.

····

It was the last week of January.

I leant back on my chair, interlacing my hands behind my head, and stared at my laptop screen. From the corner of the room the fan whirred, blowing air across the room in lazy arcs, struggling to lessen the heat. Bright sunlight filtered through lace curtains, the windows giving a view out onto the walls of our small compound. From outside the walls I could hear the noises of the city, yells and shouts and cars, but it was barely audible over the chugging roar of the generator. The power was out again, as happened about five times a day on average. You really don't appreciate just how easy life is with a reliable power grid until you live in a city without one.

Outside, I heard the grating of the gate, and I knew Anne was back. I turned around and listened for the sound of the door opening. "Hey," Anne called out from the corridor.

"Everything go okay?" I called back.

I heard the sound of the fridge door. "Oh, it was fine," Anne called. "They still keep staring at me, though."

"What, did you think the novelty would have worn off?"

We were in Lagos, the Nigerian capital. The percentage of Europeans in Nigeria is basically zero, and with our light skin, both Anne and I stood out on the streets like a pair of flashing neon lights, to the point where we'd collect groups of kids following us around. It was a fairly terrible place to hide, but by this point we'd had so many better hiding places fail on us that I'd decided we might as well change things up. Besides, it cut both ways. From what I'd seen, the men working for Levistus didn't fit in here any better than we did; if and when they came after us, they'd stand out too.

Anne came in. She was wearing a blue sundress that left her arms and shoulders bare; by Nigerian standards the past few days had been cold, which for someone used to the English climate meant "hot" instead of "boiling." "I think I'm getting better with the accent," she said. "I understand what they're saying about half the time now. Do you like yams?"

"Never tried them."

"Neither have I, but I think they'd be fun to cook."

With a sigh, I hit the minimise button on the e-mail in front of me, watching it shrink into the corner of the screen. It was two lines long, including the greeting, and had been two lines long for the past hour. It was supposed to be going to my father—sooner or later he was going to notice that I'd dropped out of contact—but I didn't want to write it. Explaining what had happened would be a nightmare even if I could tell him the truth, which I couldn't. "Have you found a way for us to talk to Luna and Vari?" Anne asked.

"Not safely," I said. "I'm pretty sure that all of our regular mail accounts will have been tapped by now. If Luna and Vari have set up any new ones, then they'll probably be safe, but . . ."

". . . but they're secret from us, too," Anne finished. "And if they tell us what they are, then anyone who's listening in will find out as well."

"I really should have set up some secure way of talking to Luna," I said. "A synchronous focus or something. I prepared for what'd happen if I was killed, but . . ."

"How long do you think they'll keep looking for us?" Anne asked.

"They might be winding down the search already. We never stuck around to confirm whether that guy in Argentina was working for Levistus or not."

"Do you *really* think he wasn't?"

I grimaced. "No."

"But they'll have to give up eventually, won't they?" Anne sat down on the bed, kicking off her shoes and curling her legs up underneath her. "It must be costing them something."

"More importantly, it's not *gaining* them anything," I said. "The way I figured, if they kept on spending resources with nothing to show for it, then eventually they'd have to write the whole thing off. I just didn't expect them to chase us this hard."

"Why do you think they're doing it?"

"Guess I pissed Levistus off more than I thought." I sighed. "It's not like I didn't have warning. Enough people told me that this was going to happen."

"We're going to keep being on the run, then," Anne said. It was a statement, not a question.

I looked at Anne. "I'm sorry for getting you into this."

"You don't have to be sorry for anything."

"But if it weren't for me—"

"If it weren't for you, I'd already be dead. From the

Council, or from Vitus, or from Sagash. Besides . . . even if they couldn't tie me to you, I'm not sure it would have made a difference."

"What do you mean?"

"I've been thinking about that conversation we had with Talisid," Anne said. "I mean, the one you had. I don't think it was Levistus who wanted me brought in."

"Talisid only said that he couldn't find any evidence . . ."

"Then why just go after me?" Anne asked. "He could have blocked the sponsorship order for Vari too. Or sabotaged Luna's test."

I paused. Looked at that way, it *was* odd. Levistus hated me, no argument there. But while he'd made threats towards my allies, it had always been in the context of getting to me. I'd never had the impression that he cared about Anne, Luna, or Variam directly. "You think someone else piggybacked onto what Levistus was doing already?"

Anne lifted her hands helplessly. "I'm out of my depth with this. I just don't think it's all your fault."

"I suppose that makes me feel a little better. Though I don't know if it should."

Anne smiled slightly, but it didn't last. "What's our endgame?"

It was a good question, and not one that Anne would have asked when I'd first known her. Luna isn't the only one who's changed over the past few years. "Levistus's men can't catch us, not the way they've been going," I said. "The only reason they were able to get close before was that we were tied down to one place. Sooner or later, they're going to have to realise that."

"And then?"

"And then Talisid or Landis or someone else we trust can go to the Council and negotiate," I said. "I hope."

Anne looked dubious. "Won't they just try to kill us some other way?"

"Probably. If I were them, what I'd be doing right now would be trying to lull us into a false sense of security. Find us, wait a while, then get us while our guard's down."

"So we don't let our guard down."

I nodded. "Because they'll still be coming after us. I can't believe they'll keep chucking assassination attempts at us forever."

Anne sat quietly for a while. "And until then, we wait," she said.

"We wait."

We sat in the room, listening to the growl of the generator. The e-mail waited on my computer, but I didn't go to finish it. We had nothing but time.

chapter 16

Once dinner was over, I moved to my bedroom, shut the door, found a comfortable spot on the bed, and closed my eyes, looking through the futures to see what would happen if we stayed here in this house and did nothing. Once I'd confirmed that we were safe in the short term, I extended and broadened my search, looking further and further, wider and wider, always on the alert for the patterns that signified danger. Nothing materialised, but I kept looking. You can never be sure that you've caught all the potential dangers with divination, in the same way that you can't prove a negative. All you can do is slice the probability of being wrong as thin as you can, shaving it down until the futures thread away to nothing, at which point you go back to the beginning and start again.

This is what diviners do when they want to keep themselves safe. And it works, more or less. You can't ever reach one hundred percent, but you can get close enough that your chance of dying is so small that writing it down would require scientific notation. Diviners have a reputation for being impossible to kill, and while it's exaggerated, there's some truth to it. As long as I kept doing this, there was no realistic way that Levistus or his men could pin me down. Long before they'd got a fix on either of us, I'd have seen them coming and moved away.

The problem was that I couldn't really do anything *else*. While I was doing this, I couldn't spend too much time interacting with other people, as it would introduce too much unpredictability. I couldn't be near crowds, or get in touch with friends, or do anything that would draw attention to myself. Sure, I was safe . . . as long as I lived like a paranoid hermit. And if that sounds like a good deal, then try it for a few years and see if it doesn't change your mind.

I'd been at it for about half an hour when something caught my eye. There was a swirl of activity revolving around a set of futures close to midnight—it wasn't completely settled, but it was definitely going to happen and it was firming as I watched. No immediate danger, which was why I hadn't noticed it on the earlier scans, but . . . yes, definitely hostile. I spent another ten minutes thoroughly checking it out before walking out into the living room. "Trouble."

Anne had been sitting on one of the chairs, drawing in a notebook. As I spoke she looked up, then nodded and closed her book. "Time to go?"

"Maybe."

"Maybe?"

"They're going to phone us."

"That seems very polite of them."

"Yeah. 'Hello, Mr. Verus, we're just calling to inform you that we'll be killing you later tonight.'"

"So what *are* they going to say?" Anne asked curiously. "It's them, right?"

"Couldn't get a clear look, but I think they're saying they want to make a deal."

Anne's eyebrows went up into her hairline. "You believe that?"

"Hell no."

"Just wanted to make sure."

"There's no way they're willing to talk terms this fast,"

I said. "The number they've got is from one of our burner phones we picked up in Argentina. Best guess is they're hoping to keep us on the line long enough to get a trace."

"So . . ." Anne said. "Leave the phone and move on?"

"By the time they call, we'll have our bags packed and the gate stone spun up. Looks like you don't need to bother washing those dishes."

Anne shrugged. "We might as well leave the place tidy."

· · · · · · · · · · ·

It didn't take long to pack. Most of our possessions had been winnowed away, lost to raids or to necessity, and both of us were down to a single suitcase each. "You're kind of letting down the stereotypes for your gender," I told Anne. "You should have three suitcases worth of clothes and shoes."

Anne smiled, but it faded quickly. She looked at the phone, lying alone on the table. "Is it even worth answering?"

"I did think about ignoring it," I admitted. "But there's always the chance they'll let something slip. We're really starved for information."

"That's probably what they're counting on."

"Just keep the gate stone ready. I can't see any way they could spring anything, but no point taking chances."

Anne nodded, taking out the small river pebble that marked our next destination. We waited. "Where's our next stop?" Anne asked after a little while.

"China."

"Do we have to go back north? I was enjoying the summer."

"It's Yunnan province. Should be one of the warmer ones."

"I'd still prefer Mauritius." Anne glanced at the phone. "They're taking their time."

"Keeps shifting." I could sense the futures in which the call was made jumping around, going from seconds ahead to as far as five or ten minutes. I wondered why there was so much variation. Maybe they were setting up some equipment. I checked again to confirm that they couldn't stop us gating out, and as I did the futures narrowed. "Here we go."

The phone rang, then rang again. I waited. Ten rings, fifteen.

"Are you just deliberately annoying them?" Anne asked when I didn't answer.

"Pretty much."

Anne gave me a look. "Okay, okay," I said. I picked up the phone and thumbed the green button. "Hi."

"Mage Verus." The voice was calm and polite.

"And you must be Barrayar," I said. I'd only met the guy a couple of times, but I had a good mental picture of him. Slim, a little shorter than average, expensive suit, pleasant expression that revealed nothing of what he was thinking. From what I'd seen, he seemed to function as Levistus's primary assistant. "How can I help you?"

"We were hoping you might spare us a few minutes."

"Sure, why not?" I looked ahead to check that Anne and I could escape if need be. "What sort of things were you planning to discuss? Arsenal's chances in the premier league?"

"Something a little more to the point. We'd like to—"

"We, right. Sorry to interrupt, but just to check, do you actually have any authority to make any deals? Or tell me anything? Because if you're going to need to run everything by Levistus, then it's really kind of a waste of time me talking to you."

"I'm afraid the person I'm representing values his privacy," Barrayar said. "However, he has given me full authority to negotiate in his place."

"In other words, Levistus doesn't want his name or voice going out on an open call."

There was a slight pause. "Verus—do you mind if I call you Verus?"

"Go right ahead."

"Having had some time to consider, both I and the people I represent feel that the current situation is . . . unproductive. This chasing you around from one country to another isn't achieving anything."

"I don't know," I said. "Demonstrating that you can't catch me seems pretty useful from my point of view."

"Yes," Barrayar said. "You have demonstrated that. And the message has been received. With this in mind, I'd like to negotiate."

"Really."

"I'd like to believe that we can come to an equitable solution that satisfies all parties."

"Somehow I doubt that."

"Oh, I don't know," Barrayar said. "We can be quite persuasive. I'd like to show you something, if you don't mind. I'm sending you a web address."

The phone buzzed as the text message came through. I studied it. "So you'd like me to load this up?"

"If you don't mind."

"Sure. Just give me a second."

I checked our escape route again, then pulled my laptop out from my bag. Anne gave me a quizzical look, and I made a reassuring gesture. I put the laptop down, opened a browser, and typed the address in, checking to make sure I got each letter right. Once I was done, I looked into the future in which I hit the return key. I could just have path-walked without moving at all, but it was easier to do a few of the physical steps first. "Looks like a video link," I said into the phone.

"It is," Barrayar said. "Shall I give you the encryption code?"

"I wouldn't bother," I said. "Given that there's no way in hell I'm visiting it. Honestly, Barrayar, how stupid do you think I am?"

"I can understand why you would be suspicious," Barrayar said. "But I can assure you there are no traps. No viruses, no tracer programs. Just a simple video feed."

"Sure. I'll just take your word for it, shall I?" I shook my head. *This is going nowhere.* I signalled to Anne, who nodded and took out the gate stone.

"The code is 8YST57," Barrayar said. "Why don't you divine it?"

I paused, my hand on the laptop screen. Examining the content via my divination would be safe . . . entirely safe, and that made me suspicious. Maybe he was hoping to lure me in?

"It's not case-sensitive, if that's what you're wondering."

Curiosity won out. I looked into the future in which I navigated to the website and entered the code. My future self found himself looking at a video feed. The scene was a nighttime city, although you couldn't see much of it—the camera seemed to be focused on a block of flats. Something about them looked familiar. I'd been there before. Now where was—?

I stopped dead. My hand froze on the phone as I stared into the future, my heart speeding up.

Anne looked up. She'd been starting the preparations to open the gate, green light beginning to gather at her hand, but now she focused on me, frowning. *What's wrong?* she mouthed silently.

I reached for the keyboard, hit Return, then typed in the code when I was prompted, only half aware of what I was doing. The video feed paused as it loaded, then came up on the screen. The image it showed was dark, in moderately poor resolution but quite watchable. It showed the rear side of a small block of flats, the bottom corner obscured by a tree. It was nighttime and orange light reflected up from the street below. The block of flats was four stories high. Lights were on in the ground and first floors, but the two above were dark. The camera was focused on the top floor.

The vision wasn't great, but it was enough for me to recognise the location. The block of flats was in Crouch End, in London. The flat the camera was trained upon was Luna's.

"Ah," Barrayar said through the phone. "Apparently we have one viewer. I'm going to assume that's you. Just hold on a moment and I'll get them to zoom in."

I kept staring at the screen. Anne looked at me, then at the display, obviously confused. I felt the moment where she understood: out of the corner of my eye I saw her put her hands to her mouth. My eyes were locked to the computer.

On the screen, the view from the video feed magnified, zooming in. There was something on the wall of Luna's flat, a darkish patch next to and slightly beneath one of the windows. "Hello, Verus?" Barrayar said. "Have you got a good view? Sorry if the quality isn't too good, but our men on the ground aren't exactly professional cameramen."

I didn't answer.

"The packs you can see mounted on that wall are made of black webbing." Barrayar's voice was friendly, conversational. "Inside they contain a quantity of C-4 explosive. The man setting it up gave me the details about the exact effects of the detonation, something about kilojoules and effective blast radius, but I have to admit, it went over my head. I'm not really an expert on the subject." Barrayar paused. "What I do know is that your apprentice, Luna Mancuso—actually, come to think of it, she isn't your apprentice any more, is she? Well, either way, her bedroom is on the other side of that wall. She's sleeping quite peacefully. At least for the moment."

Anne looked at the video, then at me, her eyes wide. I couldn't think of anything to say.

Barrayar was still talking. "There are some additional charges too. Apparently our demolitionist was concerned that that curse of hers might interfere with the detonation process, so he went for the redundant approach. To be perfectly honest, it strikes me as overkill, but I've always believed that there's no point in hiring a professional if you aren't going to listen to his advice."

I found my voice. "What do you want?"

"I want you," Barrayar said. "I'm going to be very clear, so that there is no chance for confusion. It is currently twelve twenty-one A.M. The explosives around that flat are armed, but not detonated. They will remain undetonated until exactly two A.M. GMT. That's one hour, thirty-nine minutes from now. When the second hand ticks over to two o'clock, I will press the button in front of me and Luna Mancuso will go from being the most recently promoted mage in Britain to the most recently deceased. Unless you come here."

"You can't do that." It was a stupid thing to say, but I wasn't thinking clearly. "The Concord."

"An inconvenience."

"Luna isn't part of this. You've got no quarrel with her."

"I agree," Barrayar said. "And though I doubt you will

appreciate it, I really do not take any pleasure in doing this. Quite honestly, your former apprentice is exactly the kind of mage we would like to have more of. But sacrifices must be made, and unfortunately we want you more than we want her."

"I can't make it back to London that—"

"Verus, please don't insult my intelligence. I do not believe for a moment that you can't get yourself from your current location to here in . . . let's see . . . one hour, thirty-seven minutes."

"I need more time."

"You have until two A.M. Make the most of it. Good-bye, Verus. I imagine I'll be seeing you soon."

"Wait—"

There was a click and the line went dead. I lowered the phone, staring at the screen.

I I I I I I I I I

It was a little over a quarter of an hour later.

"Okay, forget the bomb," Anne said. She was pacing up and down the room. "What if we go for the guy with the detonator?"

"That's going to be Barrayar," I said. "And who says there's only one?"

"If I can get close enough—"

"*If* you get close enough, you could stop him pushing that button. But there is no way they are going to let you walk up to touch range."

"How many of them are there?"

"Enough that every future in which I saw that I went there, I was blown up before I got into range."

"But they went for you? They didn't set off that bomb?"

"Why would they?" I said. "It's me they're after. Luna's a Council mage now. If they kill her, it'll start an investigation."

"So maybe they're bluffing?"

I shook my head. "They're not bluffing." I'd looked at the futures of what happened if we stayed.

Anne stopped pacing and put her hand to her forehead.

"Okay," she said. "Okay. What if we use our emergency alarm? Ring Luna's phone. If she wakes up in time . . ."

"I already tried," I said. "The call's not getting through. Either a jammer or they've shut down her number."

"We could—"

"It's not going to work," I said. I was still sitting in the same chair, the computer on the table, my suitcase opened and forgotten on the floor. "They've had too long to set this up."

Anne looked at me. "Then what do we do?"

I stared down at the carpet, then smiled suddenly. "Helikaon was right."

"What?"

"I thought he was just making a point," I said. "He wasn't. He saw this coming." I looked up at Anne. "The only way I can keep hiding and keep running is if I'm willing to let Luna and anyone else they target die."

Anne looked back at me with a strange expression on her face. "Are you going to?"

I stared into space. It's funny how the most important decisions in your life can go so fast. It only took me a few seconds to know what the answer was . . . but really, it was something I'd decided a long time ago. I wasn't going to take Richard's path, and I wasn't going to take Helikaon's either. "No."

Anne relaxed slightly. "So we fight?"

I rose to my feet. "Except for the 'we' part."

"Oh no," Anne said. "You are *not* telling me to stay behind on this one."

"It's me they're after. There's no reason—"

"No reason?" Anne said. There was an edge to her voice. "Are you serious? You know what I can do. If you are going to have *any* chance of winning this, you'll need me."

"I don't want you to get killed because of me."

"And you think I want to sit here and watch?" Anne looked at me, her eyes challenging. "How do you think I'd feel if you don't come back?"

"I can't—"

"No," Anne said. "I'm not letting you leave me behind. And you can't make me."

I hesitated, looking at Anne. Her expression was set, and as I looked at the futures I realised that she wasn't going to be swayed, not on this. "All right."

           ı ı ı ı ı ı ı ı ı

We gated back to England. The park was silent and deserted. I didn't have a gate stone for where we were going, and we had to make do through mundane means.

The building was in Bromley-by-Bow, and it was a wreck. Five stories of shattered windows and defaced walls rose up out of an urban wasteland, scrubby weeds growing through cracked concrete and around two smaller ruined buildings nearby. Above us, traffic rumbled north and south along a raised A-road, but the area below was dark and empty. To the right were the tracks of a tube line.

"You're going to fight them here?" Anne said quietly.

"No bystanders," I said. The stairs leading up into the building were half blocked by a broken door, and I picked my way around it as I climbed them. The last time I'd visited the place, there had been a few homeless people living on the upper floors, but they were gone now.

The inside of the old offices looked like it had been bombed out and left to rot. Debris hung from the ceiling, and rubble and shards of glass were scattered across the floors. The furniture had been stolen or smashed, and the stair rails and wiring had been ripped out and taken away. Graffiti covered the walls; a monstrous head with jagged teeth leered at me, the spray paint just barely visible in the light coming through the broken window frames. The place smelt of decay and old urine. Anne wrinkled her nose as she looked around—to her heightened senses, this place was probably even more unpleasant than it was to me—but she didn't complain.

I set the bag down on the floor and unzipped it. The razor wire glinted faintly in the light. "Okay," I said. "Trip wires in each of the corridors, hidden as well as you can. If you have any left over, use it on the stairs. I'll be up on the third floor."

Anne nodded and took the bag, disappearing into the darkness.

The wrecked building would have been dangerous for most people, but my divination let me know where to step. Up on the third floor was a windowless closet, and half buried in rubble at the back was a metal chest. I felt around in the darkness until I found the combination lock that chained it closed, flipped it to its right setting, then levered open the lid.

Inside was a stack of dark green items, rectangular and slightly curved so as to form a convex shape. Each was about a foot long, with caps on the top. The outer casing was plastic, and embossed on the front were the words *FRONT TOWARDS ENEMY*. Two coils of wire sat beneath them, along with some tools. I stayed there for thirty seconds, staring down at them, then shook my head and checked my phone. Fifty-five minutes left.

ıı ıı ıı ıı

Anne came up to find me just as I was setting the last one. "The entrances are all covered," she said as she walked into the room. "And I put a double set in the main corridor."

I unwound another strip of duct tape, nipping it off before turning to wind it around the pillar. "Stairs?"

"Ground floor and first floor. I don't know how well they'll stay in. There wasn't much to attach them to."

"They only need to work once."

Anne looked around. The green plastic items were mounted at various places around the room, concealed behind debris and joined with wire. "Are those . . . ?"

"Barrayar isn't the only one who can use explosives," I said. I placed a last strip of tape and straightened. "There."

Anne eyed the mines warily. Tucked away in the corners and against the walls, they didn't look like much, but appearances are deceptive. Each of those mines contained hundreds of tiny steel balls, and when detonated, the explosion would hurl the spheres outwards in a sixty-degree spray at thousands of miles per hour. One mine could easily kill every living thing in a room. I'd set eight. "Are they safe?"

"Until I hit the detonator. Then they're very unsafe." I checked my phone. Thirty-one minutes. "Ready?"

"Wait," Anne said. "What's the plan?"

"That's going to depend on whether they play along."

"You're going to try to draw them in and blow them up," Anne asked. "Isn't that going to catch us too?"

I shook my head. "No."

"But how—?"

"Anne, I'm sorry, but we're short on time. I'll explain in a minute."

Anne hesitated, then nodded reluctantly. Her expression said clearly that she hoped I knew what I was doing.

I took out my phone and dialled Barrayar's number. I stood in the darkness of the derelict building, Anne a shadow to my left. Through the empty windows, I could hear the traffic passing by. The phone rang and rang . . . then clicked. "Verus," Barrayar said in greeting. "Good timing. Exactly thirty minutes left."

"Yeah, you can stop your clock. I'm here."

"I don't see you."

"I'm in Trad House, just east of the A12, next to Bromley-by-Bow station. Come get me."

"I want you here. Not—"

"You wanted me. You've got me. But I'm not walking into your trap for you. Now, do I need to tell you the address again, or did you get it the first time?"

Barrayar was silent. I knew what was going through his head. He could kill Luna . . . but that wouldn't get him what he wanted. "All right, Verus," Barrayar said. "We'll play it your way. But your time limit is still running. If we reach the address and you're not there . . ."

"I'll be there," I said. "Get moving." I hung up.

Anne was watching me, her features shadowed in the darkness. "That was—"

"Not as dangerous as you think," I said. "It's me he wants, not Luna." I took out a gate stone and started working on the spell. "Come on. We need one last thing."

The gate opened into bright light, revealing a simply furnished room with a bed, a TV, and a table. The curtains were drawn but the small amount of sunlight leaking through was still enough to make us both shield our eyes, adapted to the darkness. I stepped through, coming down into warm, dry air, then turned and beckoned to Anne. "Come on."

Anne followed me through. "Where are we?"

"Melbourne." I watched Anne as she looked around. Her hair brushed her shoulders as she turned her neck, those odd reddish-brown eyes searching the room. The sunlight filtering through the curtains lit up her skin, banishing most of the shadows from the gate behind. *She really is beautiful.* I tried to fix the image in my memory, standing there and taking it in.

When I didn't speak, Anne looked at me. "Alex?"

I shook my head. "It's a hotel. We need that bag from the other side of the bed."

"Luna is still—"

"I know," I said. On impulse, I reached up and touched Anne's face, drawing a finger down her cheek and along the line of her chin. Her skin felt soft and clean, and I could smell her scent. It made me think of flowers.

Anne stood still, looking back at me. She'd caught her breath when I'd touched her, but she hadn't pulled back. She almost seemed to be waiting for something.

"Hurry," I said. I hadn't let go of the spell, and the gate back into London was still hanging to my left. "I can't hold the gate open for long."

Anne hesitated but obeyed. She walked around the bed and was just reaching down for the bag when I stepped back through the gate. Anne whirled instantly, sudden realisation flashing in her eyes, but before she could move I let the spell go. The gate winked out, and I was in pitch darkness again. The portal was gone, and Anne with it.

I sank down to my knees. All of a sudden I felt very tired; the energy had gone out of my limbs and I didn't want to move. My phone rang, first once, then again and again. I didn't want to answer it. For some reason, I did anyway.

"Alex!" Anne was as furious as I'd ever heard her. "You tricked me, you bastard!"

"Sorry."

"Don't you *dare* leave me behind!" Anne's voice vibrated through the phone. "You're not doing this on your own. Not again!"

"You don't have a choice," I said. "There are gate stones in that bag, but they won't get you here. Not in time."

"And what, you think you're going to win this on your own? All those times you told me that I was more powerful than you—were you lying all that time?"

"I wasn't."

"Then why are you *doing* this?" Anne's voice was pleading.

"Because I'm not going to win."

"What—" Anne said, then stopped.

"It was never on the cards, Anne." Wearily I straightened, looking ahead into the futures. Barrayar's men would be here in a few minutes. "Too many of them, too few of us. From the minute Barrayar made that phone call, there were only three ways this could go. In the first, Luna died. In the second, you and I died. I took the third choice."

"Don't do this," Anne said quietly. "Please. There has to be another way."

"I've always had a feeling this would catch me up sooner or later. Didn't know how many of you would be caught up in it too. Vari's okay. Luna's okay. Sorry I couldn't do more for you. Tell Luna . . ." I took a breath. "Sorry I missed her graduation. Would have liked to see her as a mage."

"Alex—" Anne's voice broke.

"Good-bye, Anne." I hung up, then leant against the wall, sagging. *That was harder than I expected.*

· · · · · · · · · · ·

I stood alone in the dark, waiting. In the distance the sounds of the city ebbed and flowed, but here, in the ruined offices, everything was quiet.

I've thought about my death. I think most people who go in for my sort of lifestyle do. I've read a few writers who claim that no one can ever really believe in their future demise (apparently they think everyone in the world is secretly delusional enough to believe they'll live forever, or something), but frankly, it's bullshit. The truth is that once you make a habit of getting into danger on a regular or semiregular basis, then it doesn't take long for it to sink in that you have a finite life expectancy, and that goes triple when you're a diviner and you can actually *see* yourself die over and over again.

You can never completely rule out an accident. It wouldn't take much—a bullet slipping past my precognition, a fireball when I was just a little off guard. But I'd always had the feeling that it was more likely to be something on purpose. I've made a lot of enemies over the years, too many for any one mage to handle alone. Just as Arachne had said, the problem was my independence. Too many foes, not enough friends.

So I'd had time to think about what I was going to do in this sort of situation. Not *exactly* this situation; I hadn't seen the threat to Luna, though with hindsight I probably should have. Maybe if my preparations had been better, I could have avoided it . . . but then again, maybe not. I'd considered outcomes in which I fought, and others in which I didn't. I'd made plans to run if I had to. But one thing I'd decided for sure: I wouldn't sacrifice Luna or Variam or Anne. In the end, all of this was about paying for old mistakes, and the mistakes were mine, not theirs. What goes around comes around, and I've taken enough lives in my time. Maybe it was my turn.

I felt a flash of gate magic, followed by another. *Finally.* I moved down the hallway, navigating in the pitch darkness, feeling rubble crunch under my feet. Path-walks located Anne's trip wires, and while I was at it I double-checked the weapons I'd hidden. Just because I was going to die here, I didn't see any reason to make things easy for them.

Five minutes passed, then ten. I could feel movement outside. The sky was overcast, showing neither moon nor stars, and the wasteland outside the building was an expanse of darkness. I kept moving, slipping from hall to hall.

My phone rang and I picked it up. "Are you going to sit out there all day?"

"I was about to ask you a similar question." Barrayar's

voice was smooth. "Is there any way I can motivate you to come out?"

"Hmm, nope," I said. I glanced through a window frame, checking the rear quadrant. "I don't think so."

"I've been authorised by Levistus to guarantee your safety, as well as that of your apprentice," Barrayar said. "Should you fully cooperate."

"Gosh, what a great deal," I said dryly. "Sounds a lot like the one he gave me the first time we met. Has he told you that story, by the way? I wonder how long *you'll* stay useful to him?"

"Yes, he didn't think you would take him up on the offer." Barrayar sighed. "You realise I can send enough waves of men into that building to fill it from floor to ceiling."

"Sounds like my kind of odds."

"Come now, Verus. You're just being childish."

"You want me?" I dropped the pretence, letting my feelings show through in my voice. "Then come and get me, you prissy little fuck." I hung up.

Barrayar didn't call back. A tube train went by to the south, the carriages going past one after another, rattle and bang, rattle and bang. The futures shifted and as I looked ahead I saw danger zones opening up on the eastern side of the building. If I showed myself in the open window frames, I would take sniper fire. The shots didn't seem to be lethal; they must still be hoping to take me alive. *Good*.

Minutes ticked by, tense and slow. I kept moving; it was a safe bet that they had a mage or adept from the living family reporting my position, and I didn't want to give them an easy shot. I was expecting the first wave to be unaugmented humans, Council security working as Levistus's hit squad. They wouldn't enjoy the experience. When I'd told Barrayar that I liked the odds, I hadn't been lying. I have a whole set of tricks up my sleeve that I never normally get to use, because they're too extreme or desperate or cause too much collateral damage. It would be fun to cut loose, just once. After they lost enough security men, they'd send in the constructs. Then if those weren't enough, it would be the turn of the mages. Sooner or later, they'd have enough to overwhelm me. I'd let them drive me back, into the room with the mines. And then . . . well. End of the road.

More time passed, and I started to fidget. *They're taking their time.* I found my mind wandering . . . what were my odds of getting one of the mages? I figured I could probably catch one or two. That many mines, with the element of surprise, could overwhelm even the shield of a battle-mage. I wondered what it would feel like. From looking into the futures, I didn't think it would hurt. The speed of the projectiles would outpace my body's nerve conduction velocity; I'd be ripped to pieces before my brain could process the damage. *Suppose if I get bored of waiting, I could just go up and press the button. But I'd really like to take a few of the bastards with me.*

Futures shifted. *There.* A squad was advancing from the building to the south, covered by the snipers. I darted up to the first floor, finding a viewing point where I could see them without exposing myself to fire. Leaning against a wall, looking through a doorway and a window, I could just glimpse movement in the darkness. I looked into the futures in which I moved out for a better look. They'd be in range in only a minute. *Here we go . . .*

Suddenly the futures changed. The lines in which the squad kept advancing vanished. I pulled back, expecting an attack, but nothing came. I took a closer look with my divination and frowned. It was hard to tell in the darkness, but one of the men seemed to be using his radio. As I watched, the squad hunkered down. *A diversion?* I checked, but no one was approaching from any other direction either. Before, I'd only been scanning for movement, but now, as I looked ahead, I realised that I couldn't see any attacks at all. Even the futures in which I was shot for walking in front of a window were gone. They were holding fire. *What the hell?*

A minute dragged by. It became five, then ten. My hands were shaking from adrenaline. Were they going to come, or what? At last the squad of men out in the open began to move . . . in the opposite direction. Staring in disbelief, I watched them withdraw back into the night.

I checked the futures, and checked again. No attacks. I couldn't see any trace of danger, not even if I walked out into the open and waved my arms. The only movement I could see was . . . *phone calls?* "This is getting ridiculous," I muttered under my breath, and pulled out my phone to dial Barrayar's number again.

It rang and kept on ringing. My irritation rose. It was bad enough that the guy was going to murder me; he could at least have the courtesy to be punctual about it. Still Barrayar didn't answer, and I wondered what he was doing. Maybe he'd spotted the mines? *But then why hold back the snipers . . . ?*

Barrayar picked up with a click, and I didn't hide the annoyance in my voice. "Can we hurry this up?"

"I suppose you think you're very clever."

"Apparently not enough. Are we going to get this started?"

"Please don't play stupid."

I paused. There was something wrong with Barrayar's voice. Before he had been calm, relaxed. Now all of a sudden his tone was cold. He was . . . angry? *Angry about what?* "What are you talking about?"

"Do you really expect me to believe that you knew nothing about this?" Barrayar said. "Or that the timing was a coincidence?"

"What is going on with you?"

"I suppose I should have expected it," Barrayar said. "Congratulations, Verus. You have your victory. I wonder how much you'll have to pay for it." There was a click and the line went dead.

I stared at the phone, then looked out into the darkness. The men who had been moving to surround the building were gone. Looking into the futures in which I left the building, I couldn't sense any contact. I was alone.

⋅ ⋅ ⋅ ⋅ ⋅ ⋅ ⋅ ⋅ ⋅ ⋅

I waited there for over an hour, searching the futures. Barrayar didn't come back and neither did the Keepers. Inside me, hope warred with fear: I was alive, but I was afraid to believe I was safe. It had to be some sort of trick. As the minutes crept by, I started to shiver. The January air was icy cold and I was still wearing the thin clothes I'd been using in Nigeria.

It was almost three A.M. when my phone rang. I pulled it out, vaguely recognised the number, and answered. "Landis," I said. "Long time."

"At least you're alive to answer the phone," Landis said. Despite the hour, he sounded alert. "Now perhaps you can explain to me just what on God's green earth is going on here. I'm woken up in the middle of the night by Variam, who tells me that *he's* been woken up in the middle of the night by Anne, who has a garbled story about bombs and blackmail and that you're planning to commit suicide by immolating yourself somewhere down in the East End. Since you're talking to me, I'm going to take a wild leap into the unknown and speculate that you haven't emulated our lord and saviour by returning from the dead."

"Not so much."

"Good. So what the devil is happening?"

"I don't know," I said wearily. To the west, a truck rumbled along the raised A-road, the concrete pillars vibrating in the night.

"Not the best time and place to be under the veil of ignorance and all that. You do know that the Keepers still have an open warrant on you?"

"It's not the Keepers I'm worried about," I said. "Barrayar's men just had me, but then they pulled back. Can you find out what's going on? I'm spinning in the dark."

"You don't ask much, do you?" Landis sighed. "All right, all right. I suppose it can't hurt to check. But don't expect quick answers." He hung up.

I kept waiting, and kept shivering. I wanted to leave this place, but I was afraid of what would happen if I did. My fingers were starting to tremble when Landis rang back.

"Thought you said no quick answers," I said. I had to work to keep my teeth from chattering.

"It seems a few things have changed."

Something about Landis's voice made me sit up and pay attention. "What do you mean?"

"You're now a Council Keeper." Landis's tone was . . . neutral. All of a sudden, somehow, I had the feeling he was studying me. "Of the Order of the Star. There was quite a commotion in the office. It seems the documentation was brought in just a couple of hours ago."

I stood very still, staring into the darkness. "What?"

"You didn't know?"

"I . . . No. How?"

"You've been appointed as Light Council liaison to the Keepers. Turns out the position grants Keeper status. They had to look it up to make sure that was really how it worked."

I looked at the phone. I couldn't think of anything to say.

"Verus? Are you there?"

". . . Yeah." I tried to process what had just happened. "I'm a Keeper?"

"And as such, you're a recognised Light mage. Which also means that you have the right to a full trial before any judgement can be passed upon you. Until that happens, the resolution delivering your death sentence is suspended. So, on the positive side, I'm not obliged to go execute you, which frankly I think is an improvement on the existing state of affairs."

Landis's earlier words caught up with me. *A couple of hours.* That was the call that had stopped Barrayar. "Well then," Landis said. "Since the excitement appears to be over, I think I'll bid you good night."

"Wait," I said. "How did this happen? Was there a resolution?"

"No resolution," Landis said. "Just an appointment. By one specific Council member."

"Who . . . ?" I stopped.

"Yes," Landis said. "Your old friend Councillor Morden. Apparently you're now his personal liaison." Landis paused. "Welcome to the club." He hung up.

I stood very still, the phone still held to my ear. I stayed there a long time, the cold seeping into my body, alone in the ruined building.

chapter 17

'd planned for all the different ways I could die that night. I hadn't planned on staying alive. Now that I'd been left alone, I didn't know what to do. The aftereffects of adrenaline shock had set in, and I was shivering and exhausted. I used the gate stone to travel back to the hotel room in Melbourne, wondering if Anne would be there. She wasn't, but the bed was. I collapsed and was asleep in seconds.

I woke up to find that the sun had set. My body clock was out of sync and I felt disoriented, out of place. I lay awake in the room for more than an hour, listening to the city and feeling the warm breeze through the blinds. Eventually I got up and emptied out my dwindling supply of gate stones onto the bed, then stared down at them for a long time, trying to figure out where to go. In the end I picked out the one for my safe house in Wales. It seemed as good a choice as any other.

I gated back into a cold winter's day. The weather was overcast but dry, and thick masses of cloud drifted overhead, their undersides forming a pattern of light and dark. My house had been damaged, but not seriously—the lock had been broken, and the rooms inside had been searched, clothes and food thrown out of cupboards and left scattered on the floor, but the walls and windows were intact. I spent an hour or so clearing up, then sat down at the kitchen table to wait.

It was about two o'clock when the futures steadied enough for me to be sure when my visitor would arrive. I left by the front entrance, drawing the broken door closed behind me, and stood by the garden wall. The brambles growing around the leafless trees were denser than they had been last year, and were starting to encroach upon the front lawn. From off to the right, the rush of the small river blended with the sound of the wind, and the green hills looked down upon the valley from either side. I waited.

The sun was starting to sink in the western sky when the figure appeared through the trees. My farmhouse is at the end of the valley, and the road doesn't go any farther. I stood waiting as the man came down the road and crossed the broken-down old bridge over the river. He walked up onto the overgrown lawn, formal shoes leaving imprints in the thick grass, and came to a halt twenty feet away. "Verus," Morden said. "It's been a while."

I looked at Morden, studying him. The Dark mage looked the same as ever: dark hair and eyes, smooth good looks, with a smile that always seemed to hover at the corners of his mouth. He wore a long black coat and a scarf, and his hands, clasped in front of him, were covered with a pair of leather gloves. He didn't wear his Council chain of office, but he didn't need to. We both knew what he was.

"Well then," Morden asked when I didn't speak. He nodded to the door behind me. "Shall we go inside?"

"I'd rather not drag this out any more than I have to."

Morden inclined his head slightly. "As you wish."

"I always had the feeling that you gave up on that relic a little too easily," I said. "I knew you weren't going to kill me inside that bubble. I didn't know why." I watched Morden, standing alone in the afternoon light. Dressed in his city clothes, he looked out of place against the green valley. "Did you have this planned all along?"

"Say rather that it was one of a range of acceptable alternatives. It's really quite fortunate for you that it was."

"How did you do it?"

"Ah, yes." Morden smiled. "I'll admit, I was pleased with that. Council members are allowed to appoint a small number of personal assistants as their liaisons. It turns out that any such liaison is for all intents and purposes treated as a member of the organisation they're assigned to. An old law. Originally it was put in place to enable Light mages to appoint independents."

"And they never got around to specifying that it didn't apply when the Council member in question was Dark," I said. "Very neat of you."

"I do try. Oh, incidentally, a similar arrangement is in place with your friend Miss Walker. She's now a Light mage and a member of the Council healer corps. If you could pass that on to her, I'd appreciate it."

"I see," I said. "I'm going to assume you didn't do this out of sudden altruism."

"Nothing in life is free, Verus."

"So. What's the price?"

"Do you remember that conversation we had back in my living room?" Morden said. "No? Well, it was quite some time ago. I was speaking to you about rogues. And how they often end up rejoining the tradition in which they were initially trained." Morden looked at me. "We've given you a long time outside the family. It's time you came home."

"And if I don't?" I said. "No, wait. Let me guess. These appointments of yours are reversible, aren't they? As long as Anne and I are in your employment, that death sentence is suspended. But if you ever decide to let us go . . ."

"I'm glad we're on the same page," Morden said. "You'll be reporting to Richard directly. There's a meeting at his mansion tomorrow at ten o'clock. You're expected at nine. I understand your old master is very keen to catch up."

"No."

Morden paused. "Excuse me?"

"Screw Richard," I said. "And screw you too. I've spent

my whole life getting away from him. You think threatening me is going to make me go back?" I shook my head. "Not in a million years."

Morden studied me for a long moment. "I see."

My precognition warned me, but there wasn't anywhere to go. I was almost at the door when thunder cracked and black lightning blotted out the sun. Death energy filled me with nausea, and the kinetic strike picked me up and threw me into the door with enough force to smash it off its hinges and send me rolling across the kitchen, fetching up against the legs of the table.

My vision was dim, white and grey spots flashing across my eyes. I struggled to pull myself up, retching; I could taste bile and my limbs were weak, barely able to move. A silhouette appeared in the doorway.

"You know, Verus, I think I've allowed you to develop a mistaken impression of me." Morden's voice sounded faint and I could barely hear him over the buzzing in my ears. He stepped into the house, broken splinters of the door crunching beneath his feet, and as he entered he pulled off his gloves and tucked them into his pocket. "I've tolerated your past behaviour out of respect for your former master. I had hoped that you would appreciate this. Instead it appears to have encouraged you to believe that I am some sort of paper tiger, full of empty threats. All you need to do is to stand up to me and I will crumple away." Morden squatted down in front of me. His dark eyes bored into me, and he wasn't smiling any more. "Allow me to correct your misapprehension."

I choked as Morden's hand closed around my throat. Morden straightened, dragging me to my feet, black energy crackling about his arm. I'm taller and heavier than Morden, but the Dark mage's face showed no trace of effort as he lifted me up. I clawed at his fingers, struggling to breathe, then lost my breath in a gasp as Morden slammed me into the wall. My feet dangled six inches above the floor.

"Now that I have your attention," Morden said, "let me make myself quite clear. You will be resuming your position as Richard's assistant. If you choose not to cooperate, I will select someone you care for and I will have them killed. I will not choose your ex-apprentice, at least not at first. Instead I will choose a casual friend, perhaps a distant relation. You will not be informed of whom. The first you will know of it is when you are informed of their disappearance. If that is insufficient to persuade you, I will move on to someone else. And then to someone else. Your mother might make an interesting choice. After that, perhaps your father. Then that giant spider you seem so fond of. If you still do not cooperate, then I will move on to your young friends in the magical world. And if I am somehow able to work my way through every member of your friends and family without motivating you, do you know what I will do?"

I couldn't answer. Morden's hand was like a steel vise around my throat. The spots swimming in front of my eyes were going from grey to black. I clawed uselessly at it, growing lightheaded.

"Nothing," Morden said. "I will leave you alone, and alive, knowing that you have sacrificed everyone and everything you cared for to preserve your own life. At which point I will give up on you and wait for you to come after me in a hopeless attempt at revenge. Because by that point you will no longer be of any use to me. This—and nothing less—is the price for attempting to defy me. Do you understand?"

I couldn't speak. My ears were starting to roar, and I could barely make out Morden's voice.

Morden dropped me. My feet went out from underneath me and I crashed to the floor. I sucked in great gasps of air, my sight slowly returning. My throat felt like steel knives were stabbing into it, but I pulled in the air frantically.

"I said, do you understand?" Morden asked from above me. "Or perhaps you would like a demonstration? I believe there's a Chinese adept in London that I can have brought here on short notice."

It took my pain-dulled thoughts a second to realise who Morden was talking about. *Xiaofan.* Fear stabbed through me. "No," I said hoarsely.

"Are you going to cooperate?"

I had to take another breath before I could answer. It hurt to talk, but my fear was greater than the pain. I knew Morden wasn't bluffing. "Yes."

"The exact words, please, Verus."

I didn't want to say it. But what choice did I have?

None. "I'll do as you say," I said. My voice was raw, but even so, I could hear the hate in it.

But if Morden heard it, he didn't care. "Good." Something fell past my field of vision, bouncing on the tiles with a *tak-tak-tak*. It was a piece of black stone, obsidian maybe. "Your new gate stone," Morden said. His shoes squeaked as he walked to the door. Painfully, I raised my head to see him pulling on his gloves once again. "Oh, and please, no more overly dramatic suicide attempts," Morden said. "Should you die before I release you from your service, I will have your entire family killed. Your life is no longer yours to spend." Morden paused, silhouetted in the doorway against the winter sky, and glanced back at me. "See you tomorrow." He turned and was gone.

chapter 18

I t was the next morning.

The gate formed out of thin air, darkening and becoming opaque before taking the form of a vertical oval. It opened and I stepped through, coming down onto grass.

I was standing on a green hillside, bare branches of leafless trees reaching up into a grey sky. Bushes and creepers grew all around, and below, the hill fell away before rising up again into a long meadow. At the top of the meadow, a few hundred yards away, was a long rectangular mansion with two jutting wings. No roads led to its door, and there were no cars or vehicles parked outside.

"This was where you lived," Anne said from behind me. Her voice was subdued. "Wasn't it?"

I stared at the mansion, wondering whether what I was feeling was hate, fear, or both. An icy wind blew over the hillside, but I didn't shiver. Cold as it was, I'd still rather be exposed to the elements than in there.

Anne stepped up next to me, looking across at the building. Unlike me, there was no recognition in her eyes. "What do you see when you look at it?"

I answered quietly without turning. "All the evil in the world."

We stood side by side in silence. The wind whipped around us, carrying the scent of bark and cold earth. "We could leave," Anne said. It was half a statement, half a question.

I let out a breath, feeling the wind blow it away. "No, we can't."

Anne didn't reply, but she didn't move away. I knew what she was thinking. Morden had spoken to Anne, and he'd given her the same choice he'd given me. She'd found me last night, curled up alone in the house in Wales. We'd stayed up into the early morning, trying to think of a way out. We hadn't found one.

I'd spent my whole life running away from what was inside that mansion. Now I was going back.

"I'm afraid of what'll happen when we go down there," Anne said.

I looked across at the empty windows. "So am I."

Anne was silent. We hadn't talked about what had happened the night before last, and what I'd done. Sometime soon, we'd have to. But right now, none of that seemed to matter. "Are you ready?" I asked.

Anne gazed across the valley. "I don't know."

We stood there a little longer, then I glanced sideways at Anne and took a step forward. Anne followed, catching me up. Side by side, we walked down the hill towards Richard's mansion.

ALSO AVAILABLE FROM
NATIONAL BESTSELLING AUTHOR

Benedict Jacka

Veiled
An Alex Verus Novel

Diviner Alex Verus and the Council that governs the
magical community have never gotten along. But with
his former teacher back in Britain, Alex is in desperate
need of allies, and he'll do whatever it takes to get
them—even if it means accepting a job with the
Keepers, enforcing magical law.

Alex forms an uneasy alliance with his new partner,
Caldera, but his attempt at legitimacy quickly turns
lethal when a mission puts him in possession of an
item that factions both inside and outside of the
Council would kill to get their hands on.

Once again caught in the middle of a deadly conflict,
Alex will need all his abilities to figure out who his
friends are—especially when enemies are hiding
on all sides...

Available wherever books are sold or at
penguin.com

r0220

From national bestselling author

BENEDICT JACKA

ııııııı

h i d d e n

An Alex Verus Novel

ıııııııı

With his talent for divining the future, Alex Verus should have fore-
seen his friends' reactions to the revelations about his previous life.
Anne Walker no longer trusts him. She's also cut ties with the mage
community, and the last time Alex tried to check on her, he was told to
leave her alone.

Then Anne gets kidnapped. Working with the Keepers, Alex dis-
covers that Anne has been taken into the shadow realm of Sagash, her
former Dark mage mentor, and he must find a way to rescue her. But
another shadow from the past has resurfaced—Alex's former master
may be back in London, and Alex has no idea what his agenda is...

"Harry Dresden would like Alex Verus tremendously—
and be a little nervous around him. I just added
Benedict Jacka to my must-read list."

—Jim Butcher, #1 *New York Times* bestselling author

benedictjacka.co.uk
facebook.com/AceRocBooks
penguin.com